GHOUL

The Beginning

Kelvin V.A Allison & Lisa Hutchinson

*This novel is dedicated to Louise, Nathaniel,
Frankie and Rahne.*

*Special thanks to Louise Chapplow
and Jess Collom for proof reading
and keeping us on track, and to
Andy Hardy; our military
and weapons advisor*

Chapter One

Sighing heavily, Lauren raised her cup of coffee to her lips, drinking deeply she turned to look out of the window of the hospital restaurant, eyes widening slightly as she studied the fledgling city of Thames with a critical eye.

It was hard to believe that a year ago this place hadn't even existed, yet now with London, Leeds, Birmingham and Manchester decimated by the virus that had ravaged the entire world for nearly two years, plans had been drawn up, and the survivors from each relocated to one of the four new smaller cities that had been built to house them, spread around the country, Thames being twenty miles south west of Darlington beside the North Pennines, halfway between the small towns of Barnard Castle and Richmond.

The world was back to normal.

No, that wasn't quite true.

It had been six months since the world-wide lockdowns had been lifted and although societies across the globe had gradually taken their tentative steps back towards what had been, things were never going to be back to normal.

Six months.

Lauren shook her head, sighing heavily as she turned her face, staring across the city in the

direction of the small house she had been given,
part of the deal to entice nurses to move to the
new cities and take up positions in the hospitals.
It was home but it was nothing like the home that
she had shared with Juliet back down in Leeds.
Juliet.
She blinked as she pictured her fiancée, a shaky
breath escaping her as the image changed to that
of her at the end, frail and gasping, fighting to
draw breath, and she turned away from the
window, a finger sliding behind each of her
glasses lens in turn, wiping tears from her eyes.
It seemed a lifetime ago now.
Yet as she turned her head, a hand rising to brush
away a lock of her shoulder-length copper hair
that had swung before her face, her gaze drifting
over the occupants of the hospital restaurant, she
knew that everyone had suffered in some way.
She could see it in their eyes, and on their faces.
They were all survivors. Every one of them.
She turned as raised voices suddenly sounded on
the far side of the restaurant, her eyes narrowing
as she studied the security guard that stood in
the queue, his bald head shaking as he slammed
his money down on the counter, muttered
something at the shocked woman behind it then

turned to swagger away, a pack of sandwiches in one hand and a carton of coffee in the other.

As the security guard walked, he turned his gaze slowly about the restaurant, a scowl of superiority upon his bearded features, an overweight lion holding court over a savanna filled with geriatric antelopes and infirm gazelles. As she studied him his eyes flicked upon her, and he arched an eyebrow in challenge, seemingly amused that someone would dare to meet his gaze, and despite her best efforts she looked quickly away, staring down at her coffee.

Lauren glanced back as there was a grunted curse, concern touching her as she found the security guard standing glaring at a woman nearly half his size who was apparently trying to pass him by in the same aisle between tables. Frowning, Lauren allowed her gaze to drift over the woman, noticing that she was not one of the staff and didn't look like a patient. A visitor then. The young nurse chewed the inside of her cheek as she studied the other woman putting her in her mid-twenties, her non-descript shoulder-length brunette hair contrasting the leather jacket that she wore over tight jeans and black Dr Marten boots, then glanced away only to look back quickly as the security guard spoke again.

"Watch where you are bloody going, woman" the large guard shook his head, his voice lowered to a threatening hiss so that only his potential victim could hear, but seated close as she was, Lauren heard it all, anger coursing through her. On instinct she made to speak, her refusal to stand up for herself mocked by her sudden desire to defend a stranger, only to stop as the woman met her gaze and gave her a tight-lipped smile, and a barely perceptible shake of her head.

Lauren winced, smiling sadly back and nodded.

She knew that smile of resignation well.

She had worn it herself growing up and still took it out and brushed it off occasionally to wear.

It was the mask of least resistance.

I will be OK. Just let it go.

I do not want any trouble.

Please don't make it worse.

Her free hand forming a fist beneath the table, Lauren watched as the overweight security guard shook his head once more, grumbled, then noisily pushed two chairs out of the way before walking off, casting the stranger another glare as he went. Sighing heavily, the woman nodded as if to herself and continued onwards to the queue for the food, Lauren watching with interest as she collected a tray and joined those waiting already.

Grimacing as she turned to glance at the security guard as he sat at a table at the rear of the restaurant, Lauren shook her head, a sudden anger coursing through her at his existence. Why couldn't a man like that have caught the Red Banshee and died, instead of her Juliet?

Turning away from the guard, Lauren's eyes settled upon a couple that were seated a couple of tables away from her, a slender black woman with short hair almost to the scalp, and a tall, red faced man with ginger hair and a beak-like nose, she dressed in a tye-dyed strappy dress that left her shoulders and neck bare and he in a white shirt-sleeved shirt and a pair of black trousers.

As she studied them, the man began to shake his head, a long finger jabbing down at the table, features twisted into a sneer as he spoke to the woman opposite him, her features wincing slightly before she nodded, and glanced away.

"Hey, I'm talking" the man's voice was suddenly audible as he reached out, clicking his fingers right in front of the woman's eyes, and Lauren flinched internally as the woman cringed, her shoulders dipping as she turned back to the man.

"I'm sorry, Peter"

The man gave a smug grin, reaching over to take the woman's hands in his own as he kissed them, and as Lauren watched, the black woman smiled back, but the light didn't reach her almond eyes. "No drink"

Lauren flinched and glanced round, forcing a smile as she met the gaze of the young black man that sat on the other side of the table from her, a puzzled look upon his features as he suddenly rattled his cup, the ice within loud in the silence of the restaurant. For a moment, she let her gaze drift over her charge, taking in the black and white tracksuit that he was wearing, and the red chunky earphones that hung about his neck, then met his gaze once more, smiling, "Have you drunk it all, Brandon?"

As if in answer, he gave the cup another rattle and she winced, glancing about as she reached over the table to take the cup from him, and place it back down upon the table surface between them, "Would you like me to get you another?"

"You look like my sister" he frowned, then gave a broad smile, "But she is black like me, not white"

"Oh" Lauren gave a genuine laugh, "OK cool"

"Yeah" Brandon gave a sigh, a look of infinite sadness creeping onto his features as he shook his head, "She doesn't come and see me no more, or mum and dad...I think they don't know where I am...maybe I should write them a letter"

Lauren felt her throat catch at his words, her stomach lurching in dread as she recalled what she had been told about her charge for the day where she was based in the Learning Disabilities Department of Thames Hospital. He was the sole survivor of his family, formerly of London, and lived upon the ward with three other patients, his autism and processing deficits making him unable to care for himself, despite being Laurens senior by six years at twenty five years of age. Once more, she glanced back at the security guard, this time mentally trading the man's life for one of Brandon's parents or even his sister. Hey, maybe throw the ginger Peter into the deal and save a couple of Brandon's family instead.

"Do you mind if I sit here?" Lauren glanced around as a voice spoke, a smile creasing her features as she found an old woman standing several feet away, a tray in her hands as she smiled at the young nurse and nodded to the table beside them, "Could I sit here?"

Blinking, Lauren glanced at the table and then back at the woman, shrugging as she smiled back at her, "Sure, no-one is sitting there"

"Oh, I know" the elderly woman gave a soft chuckle, throwing Lauren a wink as she took a step closer, "But after you know what…some people still don't like others too close to them"

"Oh, I'm fine" Lauren nodded in understanding, then smiled again, glancing at Brandon over the table, "You don't mind if this lady sits near us do you, do you?"

"Does she know my mum?" Brandon frowned at her, then shrugged and went back to staring down at the book that he had bought with him.

Smiling, Lauren nodded at the old lady, "Go on"

"Thank you" the elderly woman nodded as she placed her tray down, and took a seat at the table, her eyes drifting to Brandon, "And thank you young man, I don't know your mum but I am sure she is very proud to have a son like you"

As Lauren raised her coffee cup to her lips once more, Brandon gave a broad smile at the old woman's words then nodded as he pointed down at his book with a finger, "Did you know rabbits have sex three times a day?"

As Lauren spluttered into her coffee, the old woman nodded sagely and gave a chuckle, winking at the nurse, "Thank God someone is"

Chapter Two

As the old lady began to unwrap her sandwiches with shaky hands, Lauren turned away, suddenly feeling as if she were intruding, a hand raising her coffee to her lips once more as she turned to gaze back out of the window at the city beyond. For several minutes she lost herself in the calm, enjoying the warmth of the sun through the floor to ceiling window beside the table where she was seated with Brandon, one of the set which made the Southern wall of the hospitals restaurant. "Where are you from originally, dear?" the voice of the elderly lady made Lauren turn back to meet her gaze, smiling as she found the other watching her, a cup of tea held in both her hands. The young nurse paused as she was about to reply, her brow furrowing as she noticed the woman that the security guard had nearly collided with hurrying away from the counter, her head down, a tissue dabbing at her eyes. Mesmerised by the strangers actions, Lauren watched the woman until she had exited the restaurant and then turned back to the old woman, head shaking in apology, "Sorry, I am from Leeds originally, I moved here after..." Her words trailed off and she winced, not wanting to voice aloud what had happened, to make it real with her words, and on the other table the old woman smiled in understanding. "Who did you lose?"

"Juliet...my fiancé" the nurse nodded, her voice monotone as she held the gaze of the much older woman, stunned that she was being so open.

"Oh" the old woman nodded, head shaking slightly as she sighed, "It took my George too" *Strangers united in a common grief.*

"I'm sorry!" Lauren winced, hating how paper-thin and meaningless her words sounded, nearly two years of commiserating with others on an almost daily basis having given the once heartfelt emotion a depth of the mundane and ordinary. The old woman smiled nevertheless, her head bobbing, "I'm Mary Kent, from London...you can probably tell by the accent...the amount of people who say I sound like I'm off EastEnders!" She finished her sentence with a dramatic roll of her eyes and Lauren chuckled in amusement.

"Hi, I'm Lauren...Lauren Teacher"

Mary took a sip from her tea, and then glanced about before meeting her gaze again, nodding as she suddenly seemed to notice the pale green trouser and tunic uniform that Lauren was wearing, "Work here do you, luv?"

"I do" the young nurse nodded, smiling, "Brandon here is living at the hospital, since moving up from London, and I am his care worker for today" Mary nodded, casting a glance at Brandon as she chuckled, "London eh? Which part, son?"

Lauren turned, watching as the young black man looked up from his book, a finger rising to tap repeatedly at his ear as he frowned, and she reached out, placing a hand upon his other, her voice soft, "Hey its OK, Mary is just being curious"

"B...Bermond...sey" he nodded, eyes downcast as he turned in the direction of the old woman, refusing to meet her gaze, "But I live here now"

"Oh I see, Bermondsey eh, a South of the river boy" Mary gave a chuckle, jerking a thumb at herself, "Northumberland Park for me, North London, I'm a Spurs girl ain't I"

Brandon frowned, "I don't like football"

"Must be an arsenal fan are you" Mary grinned.

"No" the young man shook his head, not understanding the joke, "I said I don't like football. My dad does though...him and my mum and my sister don't come and see me...I am going to write them a letter so they know where I am"

Mary winced at his words, glancing over at Lauren, and the young nurse nodded in answer.

"All of them?" Mary mouthed and once more

Lauren nodded, emotion coursing through her as she saw the sudden grief register upon the old woman's face as she looked back at Brandon, her head shaking, "Oh you poor boy"

But Brandon was already back studying his book intently, and smiling, Lauren met the gaze of Mary and nodded, "Thank you"

The old woman smiled as she placed her cup of tea down, her wrinkled hands sliding onto the surface of the white table either side of it as she gave a sigh, nodding at the nurse, "We've all been through it haven't we...if we are honest"

The young nurse nodded and Mary grimaced suddenly, "How many did we lose in the end?"

"In England?" Lauren winced, "Eight million, three hundred and twenty-one thousand, four hundred and fifty-seven"

Mary studied her for a moment, a sad smile upon her features, "That is very precise my dear"

Lauren nodded, "I know, but Juliet was one of them, so was your George...every single digit of that figure mattered, we can't forget them"

There was a heavy drawn out silence as the old woman held her gaze, nodding silently then glanced at Brandon and then back at her, a sad smile on her features, "We won't forget them"

Lauren nodded, shrugging, "Still, it might have been more if the antidote hadn't been found" Mary made a face at her words, a hand waving dismissively, "Bah, I hold no stock in that" "What?" Lauren blinked, her stomach knotting. "The antidote" Mary continued, her eyes focused upon her sandwich as she broke a tiny piece off and placed it in her mouth, chewing for a moment before she shrugged, "I didn't have it" Lauren flinched internally as the words of the old woman registered with her, the fear of the past two years resurfacing in a rush and it was only with supreme effort that she avoided letting her sudden fear show upon her features, yet the old woman chuckled nevertheless, "Don't worry dear, I have been tested, I don't have it...no-one does now do they...but I didn't take the antidote" "Why?" Lauren's voice was tight with barely controlled anger as an image of Juliet returned to her, a victim of the virus just a month before the antidote had been discovered in America.

The old woman studied her in silence for a moment, her lips twisted tight together and then she gave a shrug, her voice thick with emotion, "I wanted to die...I belong with George, only he's not here is he, dear?"

Lauren winced, recognising the mindset of the old woman as one she herself had experienced. The sudden burning desire to give up and die. But she hadn't and neither had Mary.

Feeling a sudden kindred spirit with the stranger, Lauren shrugged, "Well, we made it through, the first wave and the worst second wave...we lived"

"We did" the old lady nodded, then gestured to the large window, chuckling as she spoke, "And we ended up here...Thames...lovely"

"It comes in threes" the voice of Brandon had both women turning to study the young man as he stared down at his book, not paying attention to them but joining their conversation, "Mum says it always comes in three's...always"

Grimacing, Lauren raised her eyes to meet that of the old lady and then chuckled as Mary threw her a grim smile, "I fucking hope not"

They both flinched suddenly as the sudden squeal of chair legs upon the restaurant floor sounded at the back off the room, and half-turning in her chair, she watched as the security guard rose to his feet, a two-way radio raised to his ear, his voice loud and disgruntled, "Well, I was having my lunch...what is it...down in A&E?"

There was a silence as he scowled at whatever was being said to him, and frowning, Lauren glanced at Mary to find that the old woman was also listening intently as the man began to speak once more, "Can't Barry handle it…typical…you owe me lunch tomorrow…yeah…I'm on my way!" Without another word, he stormed from the restaurant, the door banging shut behind him, and Lauren turned back to find Mary shaking her head, "I don't like that man very much"

"No" the nurse gave a smirk, "Me neither"

For a moment they sat chuckling softly, and then Lauren sighed, turning to Brandon, "Shall we get you back to the ward then?"

He looked up, closing his book, and rose, "Are we going to write a letter to my mum and dad and my sister…they don't know where I am"

"Yes, we are" she smiled softly then turned to nod at the old woman, "It was lovely to meet you Mary…I mean that"

"You too dear" Mary nodded, then turned to wink at Brandon, a hand gesturing to Lauren, "And you young man, look after this one for me will you"

"No, she looks after me" Brandon frowned, glancing between the two women, and smiling at the old lady, Lauren gestured for him to follow her as she moved through the restaurant only to freeze halfway across it as loud shouts sounded beyond the door. Grimacing, she took a step back

that brought her level with the table where the ginger man and the black woman were seated, a hand rising behind her to keep Brandon back as she frowned in confusion, "What on Earth…"
She screamed in shock, as did countless others within the restaurant as the doors suddenly crashed open and two figures surged through, colliding heavily with one of the tables, skittering chairs across the tiled floor. They landed hard, one atop the other and Lauren frowned; realising in shock that the one on the bottom was wearing the white shirt and tie of a security officer, his long hair tied back in a pony-tail, while his assailant appeared to be wearing a hospital gown, its bald head and bare arms and legs looking as though they were covered in hard white calloused skin like the heel of a worn foot. Without warning, the hospital patient suddenly pinned the hands of the security guard to the floor, and sank its teeth into his face, head shaking as it tore away what looked like a lip. With a snarl, it staggered to its feet, chewing upon the stolen morsel, blood running down its features and snatched up one of the broken chair legs, holding it before it like a primitive club.
"Hey!" a stocky man with tattoo's and the uniform of a hospital porter took a quick step

into Lauren's peripheral vision, two of the other men from the restaurant beside him, a hand pointing at the enraged patient, "Drop it!"

With a snarl like a trapped animal, the patient raised its makeshift weapon above its head in both hands, milky beige eyes staring out from the coarse whiteness of its hard-skinned blank features, more of the beige liquid leaving tracks like tears down across its white calloused cheeks. Then it brought the chair leg down, caving in the face of the security guard, the mans hands dropping limp beside his bloodstained body.

"No!" the word escaped Lauren like a gasped breath, her head shaking as she heard the cries of other patrons of the restaurant, the couple at the table beside her, now also standing in disbelief. Then as if in slow motion, the patient raised its head to stare at those gathered watching it, its hard-skinned features, bald head and athletic build beneath the green hospital gown that it wore giving no clue as to its gender at all.

Time seemed to stop as it turned its head, teeth bared in a bloody snarl at the men who were now edging towards it, and then it charged them.

Chapter Three

Alice paused as she stepped out of the elevator, head turning as she glanced ahead, towards the stairwell that sat through the doors opposite her, her brow furrowed slightly, certain that she had just heard screaming from the floor below. Taking a step towards the door, she narrowed her eyes as what sounded like raised voices drifted up the stairwell, the hairs on her arms rising eerily as she considered what might be happening. She knew that the restaurant lay that way, having just left it herself moments before, a sense of embarrassment and anger rising within her as she recalled the large security guard that had nearly knocked her over and then acted as if it had been her fault. More than anything she had wanted to step right up to the guard and tell him to go and fuck himself but that wasn't her way. For a moment she had thought that the young nurse with the glasses and the shoulder-length copper hair was going to intervene on her behalf and she had sent her a pleading look not to do so, a look that the woman seemed to understand. Saved from a potential scene, Alice had tried to stand in line and order herself a drink of tea but had been forced to flee the restaurant in raw grief, overcome with sudden emotion as she recalled her reasons for being at the hospital. Sarah was gone. The one true love of her life. She flinched as what sounded like a scream floated up the stairwell, her head shaking as she forced herself from her thoughts, and without consciously doing so, she stepped back slightly. Alice jerked and spun about as the door to the corridor beside her swung open, and the old man that now stood there raised an eyebrow as he saw her standing staring at him, "Are you OK?" "Yeah" she nodded quickly, then frowned, "I am looking for the chapel of rest"

The mans face had split into a smile as he nodded, turning to point back through the doors that he had just left, "Follow the corridor, its near the far end, at the back end of the second floor" Alice smiled in thanks as the man nodded and stepped towards the lift, then she turned, pushing open the doors to the corridor beyond. Moving quickly through them, allowing them to swing closed behind her, Alice began to make her way down the long corridor, following it as it suddenly angled left, her gaze rising to study the multitude of ward signs hanging overhead. She winced slightly at the smell of bleach and cleaning products that hung in the air, a constant presence in hospitals across the UK since the eradication of the virus that had decimated the world, an improved effort to ensure that it never returned. The Thames hospital, like the city in which it sat, was new, not even six months into use and it still carried that brand new feel to it, the markings on the floor still bright and unchipped and the paint on the walls still crisp and fresh, like a show home for potential owners. For someone that spent a lot of time in the buildings as she did in her job, as an embalmer, collecting bodies from wards to take back to her practice, the Thames was a breath of fresh air. Yet she wasn't here on work business.

If only that was the case.

Alice winced as she considered her reasons for being at the hospital, her stomach knotting in grief as she recalled receiving the phone call from the doctor that morning, telling her about Sarah. Dumbstruck, she had stood beside her desk, her eyes filling with tears as the doctor in charge of her treatment had listed the woman's injuries, until finally, Alice had found the ability to speak, asking why it she who had been contacted. The doctor had grunted at that, and she had almost been able to picture him glancing down at the notes before him before he spoke again, his voice thick with confusion, telling her that she was listed in the patients records as next of kin. "Is that not the case?" the doctor had asked, drawing Alice out of the fugue state in which she had found herself and she had nodded, knowing that he could not see the action but doing it out of instinct as she had lied through her teeth to him. "Yes, sorry, that's right. I will be there as quickly as I possibly can"

And so had begun the unexpected drive down from Newcastle-Upon-Tyne to Thames, a journey of just one hour down the A1M, yet as Alice had sat behind the wheel of her black Nissan Qashqai, it had seemed to take a lifetime, her mind caught up in memories of her relationship with Sarah. Four long years they had been together before they had finally parted ways, the pair unable to deal with each other's mental health issues any longer, their love changing shape into friendship. That had been two years ago, just months before the onset of the virus that had destroyed the world and there had been many times as Alice had worked, snowed under with the amount of deaths, that she had wanted to rush back into the embrace of Sarah but it just wasn't to be so. They hadn't spoken in several months, the last time being a happy birthday inbox that Alice had sent via Facebook, both promising to make more of an effort with the other, and Sarah had mentioned that she was moving away from Sunderland, where she had gone after their split to work in the new city of Thames as a teacher, and Alice had promised to make time to visit her. Well now she was here.

And it had been too late.

Releasing a shaky breath, Alice stopped walking, her eyes fixed to the small sign on the left-hand side of the corridor, that said Chapel of Rest, a sudden uncertainty flooding through her core. She had never been a church goer, yet there had always been a deep-rooted faith system within her, one that stuck to no strict doctrines, but which simply offered her solace in times of need. This was such a time.

Nodding, as if to encourage herself, she stepped forwards, entering the doorless opening, and found herself in a narrow rectangle room set with chairs either side of a walkway which led towards a small altar. She winced as a woman with reddish-brown hair and glasses turned to study her, a sudden urge to flee washing over Alice as she realised that she had disturbed someone's private time only for the stranger to rise to her feet, a handbag in one, a half-eaten sandwich in the other. Dressed in black trousers and a black blouse, bearing a hospital staff card, the stepped towards Alice, her voice thick with a Scottish accent as she smiled pleasantly, "Dinnae mind me lass, ah was just having my lunch, I'll leave ye to it"

"Oh" Alice winced, unsure what to say in reply but the woman was gone out of the door, leaving her alone with her thoughts and her sadness.

Chapter Four

For a moment longer, Alice stood just inside the door to the chapel, her head turning as she studied her surroundings, taking in the rack on the wall beside her that had pamphlets for all types of religion in a large variety of languages. She frowned, studying them all intently for a second, and then made her way down the centre aisle, taking a seat on the left side, halfway down. Sighing heavily, Alice turned her gaze upon the small altar at the front of the chapel and the crucifix which sat atop it, wincing as if the eyes on the small figure of Christ were staring back. Without giving it conscious thought, she bowed her head, hands pressing together in prayer, and with no warning the tears came, her throat swelling with the sudden onset of raw emotion. Keeping her palms pressed together, she turned her face, wiping the tears from her green eyes upon her left forearm, and then gave a shaky sigh, trying to focus past the guilt she was feeling. If only she had tried harder to deal with her own mental health issues, she could have helped Sarah learn to handle her own demons better. If only she had fought to save their relationship. If only she had kept in contact better, she might have seen the danger signs in her former lover.

If only.

The two biggest words in the history of mankind. Despite the guilt which was settling about her shoulders like a blanket, Alice knew that the blame didn't lie at her door, no, not completely. But maybe, just maybe things might have worked out differently if she been more open with Sarah. Maybe then she wouldn't have jumped from the roof of the apartment building she called home. According to the doctor on the telephone, the apartment building had been three stories high, more than enough to kill a person but Sarah's plight had been made worse by the fact that she had crashed through the roof of a greenhouse, adding countless deep lacerations to her blunt trauma injuries, and she had been unconscious upon admittance, and lost a great deal of blood. Heart in her mouth, she had driven as fast as she dare down from Newcastle, and raced inside the hospital only to discover, that despite it all she had been too late by nearly an entire hour, the doctor explaining that he had returned to Sarah's bedside after contacting her to find she had gone, possibly before Alice had even got in her car. Suddenly angry, the embalmer raised her gaze to glare angrily at the figure upon the crucifix as she shook her head, her voice little more than a whisper, "Where were you when she jumped eh? Where have you been for the last two years?" Naturally, there was no answer, and she gave a bitter laugh, leaning back in the seat as she wiped at her eyes with her thumbs, imagining how Sarah would react if she could see her now.

She had always been mildly amused by Alice's dalliances with faith, herself a lifelong atheist, and the pair had gotten in several deep debates about the subject which had always ended with Alice feeling belittled and mocked by her lover. She winced as the thought occurred to her, guilt surfacing once more as she realised she was thinking ill of the dead, and then flinched as she heard movement at the back of the small chapel. Turning, she winced in awkwardness at the man and woman that stood there staring back at her, the former closest to where Alice was sitting, dressed in a long yellow robe set with tiny flowers, a flowing burgundy scarf draped across her chest and shoulders. As Alice stared back awkwardly, their eyes met and the young woman, probably in her mid-twenties gave a nod, her sad smile bright against her soft brown skin, framed by long black hair that seemed to shine. "Jiyaa" the voice of the woman's male companion muttered, the tone deep, and letting her gaze drift from the attractive young woman, Alice studied the man, taking in his trousers, shirt and black turban, the beard that covered his features making him look older than his eyes suggested. Turning towards the man, the young woman gestured to the chairs on the other side of the chapel from where Alice was seated, her voice thick with an accent as she spoke, "Opinder!" The man winced, eyes glancing towards Alice, as he gestured for the woman to join him, "Jiyaa!" Turning quickly away, realising that she was intruding on whatever had brought them to the chapel, Alice was filled with a sudden desire to leave, but standing as they were, she was unable. Glancing down at the floor, Alice listened as a chair squeaked as someone sat down, and turning her head slightly, she saw the young woman now seated in the same row as she, on the other side of the small room, her eyes closed. "Jiyaa" the man was suddenly moving to sit down at the edge of the row behind the woman, his legs half turned so that he was still blocking the aisle, his brow furrowed as he studied his female companion in what looked like exasperation, words that Alice didn't understand leaving his mouth, quick and fluid. Unable to turn away, Alice watched as the woman took a deep breath, her shoulders rising and falling, but she kept her eyes tightly closed, clearly ignoring the man.

"You have my apologies" the man suddenly spoke, his head turning to Alice and she cringed, turning awkwardly in her seat to meet his gaze as he gave a grim chuckle and gestured to the woman, speaking in a perfect London accent, "My sister hasn't been in the country long, she's a pain in the arse...we've just lost our aunt Seemo"

"Oh" Alice nodded, unsure what to say, and began to turn away once more, then glanced back as the man gave a soft grunt of pain to find him leaning forwards, head facing the floor, "Are you OK?"

For a moment he stayed still except for his right hand that had risen to scratch at his forehead, drawing another grunt from him, and then he glanced back up, "I just have a headache"

She nodded at him, glancing at the young woman named Jiyaa but she was still sitting there with her eyes closed, hands clasped tight on her lap, then turned back to stare at the man as he began to scratch at his forehead once more, fingers pushing against the hem of his turban, and Alice cringed as she saw the thick, white, calloused skin that came into view, several pieces flaking away.

Grunting again, the man sat up quickly, muttering in the language he and his sister had previously been speaking, rubbing at his eyes with the balls of his hands before removing them to stare down in shock. Concerned, Alice followed his gaze, cringing as she saw the thick beige yellow liquid that coated them, like chicken soup flecked with blood, then she raised her gaze to his face, rising to her feet as she saw the same liquid leaking from the corners of his eyes, "Oh my God!"

"Opinder?" the man's sister was suddenly there beside the stricken man, a hand touching his face and Alice shook her head in disbelief as she saw that the calloused white skin seemed to have somehow spread beyond the hem of the turban to cover the area above his left eye, pieces of beard dropping from him as he raised a hand to scratch feverishly at his face. Without warning, Opinder began to cough uncontrollably and dropped to his hands and knees in the aisle between the two woman and the door, his body convulsing violently as if he were having a fit, the force of his throes dislodging the turban he wore. "Opinder!" the sister of the stricken man cried out, a hand leaping to grasp at her mouth in shock and without thinking Alice cursed aloud as she saw the calloused white skin covering the top of the man's bald head, his dislodged turban appearing to be full of hair and white skin flakes. "Jiyaa!" the man suddenly glanced up at his sister, drawing a scream from her and another curse from the embalmer as they saw his now beardless features, covered in white hard skin, his deep voice barely recognisable as he gasped, his eyes now covered with that milky beige fluid. Then without another word, Opinder died.

Chapter Five

"How's the knee, Moonshine?" Victor Doggart turned from where he was driving the Forestry Commission, dark-green Land Rover at high speed down the A66, grimacing as he saw the pale, sweaty features of his colleague and best friend staring back at him from the back seat. "It'd be a lot better if you kept your eyes on the fucking road, Dog" the shorter, blonde man tried unsuccessfully to chuckle at him, using his nickname as he tried to smile through the pain and nodding at his words of advice, Victor turned away, focusing back upon the road before them. "So, the knee?"

"Well, I don't think I'll be doing the macarena anytime soon" the forced chuckle came from the man in the back, and reaching up, Victor adjusted his rear view mirror so he could see his friend, his stomach tightening as he saw him grimace each time the Land Rover hit a bump in the road. Shaking his head, Victor pushed down slightly harder upon the accelerator pedal, glancing in his side mirror to make sure no-one was passing him and then pulled out to overtake the slower moving car in front of him and then pull back in, the action drawing a pained laugh from his friend in the back, "If I had known me breaking my leg was all it needed to make you get out of second gear I'd have done it months ago"

"Twat!" Victor sent his friend a smile in the mirror and Moonshine, Spencer Davis to his parents, laughed aloud, nodding in agreement.

"I must be to have tried to have done this!" Victor grimaced, head shaking as he cast his mind back to just over an hour ago when his friend had tried to walk through the water at the top of Spurlswood Beck, directly above the edge of Black Ling Hole Waterfall in Hamsterley Forest where the pair worked for the Forestry Commission, ignoring Victors calls to stop and take the long walk around to the other side.

"I'll be fine!" Moonshine had turned to throw him a grin, a hand gesturing to the twelve-foot fall to his right, "Even if I do go over its not a big drop"

"For fuck sake Moonshine" Victor had shaken his head as he scowled, a hand scratching at his full reddish brown beard, then rising to make sure that his dreadlocks were still secure in his bandana, "Cut it out before you fall over!"

"I told you, I'm f..." and with that he had slipped on a rock and gone over the fall, his gasp and curse of dread, as he had plunged into the cold water replaced by a scream of agony as he bashed his left knee on the rocks on route.

In moments, Victor had been sliding down the grassy bank towards the bottom of the falls, grimacing as he made his way across the dangerously wet rocks and hauled Moonshine from the ice-cold water. Wrapping an arm about his friend, he had tried to help him up, only for the shorter man to cry out in pain and nearly fall, his left leg raised off the ground as he cursed. "You silly bastard" Victor had grimaced, dropping to crouch before his friend, hands reaching out to feel through Moonshines soaking wet trousers to touch his left leg, shaking his head as he had felt the aberration in the surface, "You've broke it" "No" the shorter man had shaken his head, "I have probably just sprained it...I'll walk it off" Without another word, he had tried to do that very thing, then cried out in shock and pain, only the quick hands of Victor stopping him from falling back into the churning waters below. For long moments they had held each other's gaze then Moonshine had winced, "Sorry Dog" "Fucking hospital job then" Victor had grimaced, wrapping an arm about his friend, and together they had painstakingly made their way back up the bank and along the track to where they had parked the dark green Land Rover, emblazoned with a yellow stripe down the side. Reaching it,

Victor had opened the back doors, nodding at his friend as he had moved around to open the back of the vehicle, "Get your clothes off"

Moonshine had given a pained chuckle, "I like you and everything Dog, but you ain't my type"

"Shut up and change your bloody clothes before you freeze" Victor had closed the boot and returned with a set of dry, green trousers, beige shirt and green body warmer, "Put these on"

It had taken the best part of fifteen minutes but eventually Moonshine was in the dry clothes, minus his underwear, the left leg of the trousers cut up the side with Victors work-knife to avoid hurting the broken leg when they slid them up.

"Hey, I really appreciate this" the voice of the injured man sounded from the back seat and glancing in his rear-view mirror, Victor chuckled.

"I don't really have a choice do I?"

"You could have left me there?" Moonshine gave a heavy sigh, "Freezing to death or drowning would be preferable to what Daisy is going to do to me when she finds out I am going to be off work for fuck knows how long"

Victor grimaced and braked hard as the car in front suddenly swerved and swung over to the hard shoulder, his quick reactions saving them from driving into the back of the vehicle, yet his sudden manoeuvre brought a gasp of agony from Moonshine, "What the shit was that about?"

"I don't know" Victor checked his passenger side mirror, watching as the driver appeared to stagger from the car, but then they were lost to the distance, and he grimaced and drove on.

"Maybe we should stop and see if they are OK, Dog?" the voice of Moonshine sounded concerned, "What do you think?"

"I think I should have taken you to Durham or Darlington hospital instead of this new one" he replied, his thoughts having moved on from the dangerous driving of the other car, his brow furrowing as he glanced in his mirror, "I don't understand why you wanted to go to Thames"

"Six and two threes, isn't it" Moonshine gave a shrug, "They were all roughly the same distance away from where we were…I haven't been to Thames yet…I thought it'd be a nice change"

"A nice change?" Victor half-turned watching as a silver BMW sped past, his head shaking as he sent his friend a grimace before turning back to the road, "You've broke your fucking leg, this isn't a day out…we are meant to be at work"

"I know" Moonshine groaned, "I know"

Resisting the urge to moan at his friend again, Victor drove onwards, his brow furrowing as he

saw a car suddenly swerve on the opposite side
of the road, skipping up onto the hard shoulder,
like the vehicle had before them moments ago.
What the Hell was going on with people today.
"Did you see that?" Moonshine's voice was filled
with shock, a hand pointing as he gestured wildly
to the other lane, "Fuck me there's another one!"
Victor swore, head shaking as further along the
A66 on the opposite side of the road from them, a
blue transit van suddenly swerved out of control
and crashed sideways into a family saloon, the
pair of them careening sideways off the road.
"Fuck...dude!" the voice of Moonshine was loud
in Victors ear as his pale face suddenly appeared
between the seats of the Land Rover, right hand
gripping to the back of Victors seat as his left arm
thrust forward, a finger pointing ahead. Cursing,
eyes widening in dread, Victor slammed on the
brakes as he saw the articulated lorry that had
been ahead of them for most of their half hour
drive from the forest, suddenly swerve to the left,
crushing the silver BMW that had been
overtaking it against the centre reservation, then
swerved back the other way, the rear of the lorry
tipping over, flipping the cab off its wheels,
blocking the road ahead of them.

Cursing, Victor braked harder, their vehicle swerving slightly as he fought to keep control, Moonshine cursing in the back seat and then finally they were still, the front of their Land Rover feet from the upturned wheels of the lorry, several of them still turning around with inertia. "What the fuck just happened?" Moonshine groaned from the back seat, "Mate, what…"

"Out, out, out!" Victor snapped off his seatbelt and slid from his side of the car, hands dragging open the door beside a wide-eyed Moonshine. "What are you…" the shorter man winced, a nervous laugh escaping him, then he cursed in shock as Victor reached in, dragging him over his shoulder in a fireman carry, "Dog…fucking hell!"

Legs pumping, cursing the fact that he wasn't as fit as he had been in his youth, Victor hurried away from the Land Rover towards the side of the road, over the hard shoulder and up onto the edge of the field beyond, before dropping to a crouch, Moonshine sliding down to the ground. "What the fuck are you…" the shorter man began then screamed, eyes widening as a green car suddenly slammed hard into the rear of the Land Rover, throwing it heavily forwards against the undercarriage of the overturned lorry, a second vehicle crashing into it hard just moments later.

Kneeling beside a stunned Moonshine, Victor felt
nausea wash over him as he turned his head, his
ears ringing with the noise of the collisions, eyes
widening as he watched the same awful scene
play out repeatedly upon both sides of the A66.
He glanced down as with an almost childlike
voice Moonshine spoke, head shaking as Victor
met his gaze, "Dude...what the fuck is going on?"
"I have no idea" Victor grimaced, "I have no idea"

Chapter Six

Blinking, head shaking at what he was witnessing unfold before him, Victor stared at the section of the A66 before him in total disbelief, then began to hurry forwards, ignoring the warning calls from Moonshine behind him. Their Land Rover was half the size that it had been previously, crushed against the underside of the overturned lorry trailer, the green car that had hit it, so badly damaged by the impact it had also suffered from the second car that Victor couldn't discern the make. In seconds, he was beside it, head shaking as he realised that the vehicle was perhaps a third of its original length, the windows broken and crouching down to stare inside, he saw that there was literally no room between the steering wheel, the driver's seat and the seats behind, nausea washing over him as he saw a broken and twisted bloody mess amid the seating. Turning quickly away, before he recognised any body parts and made the horror of the drivers death even worse, Victor hurried to the second vehicle that was half embedded in the green car, hands resting upon the passenger side door as he stared in at the driver, wincing as he saw a woman with her neck bent at an angle nature hadn't intended, dead eyes staring up through her shattered windscreen, her bloody legs crushed and mangled under the steering column. "Dog?" the voice of Moonshine had him glancing back at his friend and he shook his head slowly. "Two drivers...both gone"

"Fuck!" his friend winced, then his eyes widened as he raised an arm to point past Victor in shock. Turning quickly, the bearded ranger stared past the pile-up directly in front of him and across the central reservation at the roads other two lanes. Just feet from the metal barrier that ran down the centre of the dual carriageway, a dark blue Hyundai Matrix had swerved and crashed into the side of a red estate car, the pair drifting around to collide with a VW Beetle, the impact dislodging the first car and leaving the latter two together. Shaking his head, Victor took a step forwards towards the hard shoulder, his blood running cold as he studied the cars, the elderly female driver of the red estate car trying to open her door while in the VW Beetle, a young, dark-haired woman sat up slowly, a hand rising to touch her forehead. Frowning, Victor turned to study their side of the road, relief hitting him like a bucket of ice cold water as he saw that there were no other vehicles coming at the moment, though the bend back the way they had come left a twisting worry in his gut. If someone came around that bend too fast, they would crash into the lorry and the three cars already piled up.

"I need to get back that way and warn people about this! You try and get hold of the emergency services" Victor grimaced at Moonshine, taking a step in that direction, only to pause as the driver of the Hyundai that had caused the crash in the opposite lane suddenly opened their door and exited the vehicle, their bare arms and bald-headed features white beyond their tee shirt.

"What the fuck?" the barely audible voice of Moonshine muttered, and Victor nodded, watching as the figure took a couple of faltering steps along the side of their vehicle, their head turning about as if unsure where they were.

"He's concussed, dude" Moonshine gave a grunt, an arm gesturing towards the individual, but Victor grimaced, noticing the swell of their chest.

"That's a woman"

"What?" Moonshine was incredulous, "No way"

They both flinched, cursing as a white van suddenly drove into view past the upturned lorry, brakes screeching as it swerved to avoid the white skinned woman and the trio of cars in the road. For a moment, it looked like the person behind the wheel had lost control, the white van swerving wildly but then somehow it stopped on the hard shoulder, the door opening as a black man in painters overalls started to get out, only to vanish as yet another car crashed into his van, crushing him under the force of the impact. Victor was aware of Moonshine shouting in shock, arms waving wildly, and heart in his mouth, the bearded man saw the fire burst into life beneath the newest car, the flames spreading across the road as fluid ran from the vehicle. Grimacing, Victor stared at the driver, eyes narrowing as he saw that like the driver of the Hyundai, they too appeared to be totally bald with white skin, like some ancient undead ghoul. Without warning, the flames sheathed the car, those that had followed the leaking fuel setting fire to the tyres of the Estate and the VW Beetle. "No!" Victor took a step forwards, head shaking as the old woman finally managed to open her door, then staggered back inside as the flames set her legs alight, the interior of her vehicle catching fire as she thrashed about, her screams loud. "Dog!" the voice of Moonshine sounded and with shock Victor realised he was moving towards the VW Beetle, both his hands cupping his mouth as he shouted at the young dark-haired woman. "Get out of the car!"

She turned to him then, though whether she had heard him or not he wasn't sure, a confused frown creasing her features, and he raised his hands again, preparing to shout only to curse in dread as her vehicle burst into flames about her. "Dog!" another panic filled scream from his best friend had Victor turning to look about, legs pumping at the tarmac as he saw the lorry bearing down upon him on their side of the A66, wheels locking as it tried to stop, the two cars on the inside lane doing the same, the sound awful. With a curse, he threw himself back onto the grass verge beside where Moonshine sat with his phone held up before him, and rolled to his back, watching in dread as the cylindrical trailer of the lorry suddenly went over, crushing one of the cars in the inside lane. As the trailer landed hard, the cab twisted violently to the side, and Victor felt nausea wash over him as he saw the driver's door fly open, and the occupant come free, only to be crushed between the central reservation and the lorry as it finally stopped moving, the car that it hadn't crushed stopping right beside it, two of the large wheels against the driver's side door.

"Fuck my life!" Moonshine cursed, following the lorry with his camera as it skidded to a halt on its side, and suddenly aware of what his friend was doing, Victor turned to him, head shaking slowly. "Are you filming this?"

"Its fucking mental!" the reply came, the voice of his friend sounding like he was unsure whether to laugh or cry, "This needs recording!"

"What....are you insane?" Victor grimaced, starting to hurry towards the car that had stopped near them, "I told you to phone the fucking emergency services!"

"I couldn't get through!" Moonshine gave a wounded whine, head shaking as Victor glanced back at him, "There's no signal out here!"

"For fuck sake!" Victor turned to glance at the estate car and the VW Beetle, stomach turning over as he saw no movement within either, both vehicles now fully ablaze and then turned to look through the thick smoke for the white-skinned driver of the Hyundai, but was unable to see her. Forcing himself to focus, trying not to look at the flames, Victor stepped towards the car ahead of him, cursing as he saw the liquid fire seeping under the central barrier in the road, heading towards the cylindrical lorry trailer upon its side. Blinking in shock, as if suddenly seeing the huge overturned vehicle for the very first time, Victor realised that it was a petrol tanker, "Oh God no!"

Without thinking, he was rushing to the car, a blue Renault Scenic, hands pulling at the door handle of the passenger side as he sought to get them out before the tanker exploded in flames, the figure inside staring at him through the glass. "Daddy!" the little red-headed girl screamed, her hands pressing to the window, her features twisted in utter terror, "Daddy, get us out!" "Rebecca" Victor muttered, his penis shrivelling in dread as the face of his daughter stared back at him, small fists beating frantically against the glass, coughing as she held his gaze. Blinking, the bearded man turned his gaze, a sob of grief escaping him as he saw the figure of his son on the back seat, eyes closed, coughing weakly, and then he saw his wife, head turned to one side as she stared back at him through the glass, her short black hair messed, soot upon her features. "Carol!" Victor's voice was a roar, as he fought to open the door, "Carol, wake up…Rory…Rebecca!" "Help us!" the young Asian girl in the front of the car shouted, hands banging upon the window, the younger Asian boy sat upon her lap in tears. Taking a quick step backwards, his head shaking in confusion, Victor stared at the children in shock before finally noticing the elderly Asian man that sat behind the wheel, one hand clasped

to the left side of his chest, eyes locked to that of
the park ranger, his bloody lips moving silently.
"Please" the girl banged the glass once more,
tears on her cheeks, "Please mister...help us!"
Forcing himself to focus, Victor nodded in reply.

Chapter Seven

Gritting his teeth, Victor stepped back up to the passenger side window, a hand pressing against it as he tried the handle unsuccessfully again for a moment before he nodded at the girl, realising now that she was probably around thirteen, "I can't open it from the outside…is the lock on?" She shook her head, arms hugging the boy on her lap tightly, her voice barely audible over the crackle of the flames from the burning cars on the opposite side of the dual carriageway, "No, granddad didn't fix the door…we get in his side"

"Fuck" Victor turned, about to reach for the rear door handle before realising that the car was a hatchback, then headed quickly around the front of the vehicle, fully intent on getting them out of the drivers side until he saw the wheels of the lorry against the door, restricting it from opening more than an inch or two. Casting a quick look, back over the central reservation at the burning vehicles, Victor cursed, eyes dropping to stare at the fire which was licking at the cab of the lorry. He needed to get the kids and the man out before the entire thing exploded and killed them all. Cursing under his breath, he started to walk back around the front of the car, then froze as he saw something white move suddenly on the other side of the dual carriageway, a brief glimpse of something or someone moving amid the smoke. Frowning, he stayed frozen on the spot, eyes narrowing as he scanned the smoke and flames for any sign of what he had seen, but it was gone. Shaking his head, he continued back around to the passenger side door, and cast a quick glance back at where Moonshine was sitting upon the grass verge, his friends features puzzled as he stared off in the direction of the burning vehicles. Had he seen the white figure in the smoke too? Victor frowned as he glanced back over to where he had seen the woman with the white head leaving her vehicle earlier, realising that it had most likely been her that he had just noticed. But what was she doing? Was she hurt?

He flinched at the sound of sudden banging and turning, he met the gaze of the girl and boy, his heart lurching as he remembered their plight.

"Can you open the window?" he asked moving back up to the glass, raising his voice as he addressed the girl, "You are going to have to climb out, I can't open your fathers door!"

"Grandpa" the girl shook her head and he nodded, his stomach lurching as she pointed down at the door on her side, her head shaking again, "It doesn't have a handle!"

Cursing, Victor took a step back, studying the car, and within it the girl turned her head, suddenly shouting at the driver in a language the ranger didn't understand, one hand gesturing angrily to the car door while the other hugged the boy.

"Right, get your heads down!" Victor stepped back to the car, his right hand unfastening his knife from the pouch on his belt, "I am going to smash the rear passenger window, and you are going to get out of that!"

The girl blinked at him, eyes darting to the window before meeting his gaze once more and he grimaced, "Yes? Can you hear me?"

She nodded quickly, fear in her eyes and leaned forwards, arms encircling the young boy, and raising the point of his blade, Victor aimed it at the edge of the window nearest the rear of the car, knowing from experience that it was the easiest way to break it. With a quick, hard jab, he thrust forwards, the glass breaking under the impact and he grimaced, stabbing at it more to dislodge the remaining sections of window.

He flinched, dropping to one knee as a loud metallic crunch sounded from close by, his heart leaping to his mouth, stomach knotting as he heard screams over the now nearly deafening crackle of flames, and he rose once more, arms sliding out of the body warmer he was wearing. Stepping back to the window, he placed the green clothing over the rim, his free hand sliding with the knife, clearing away stray bits of glass still stuck in the frame and then called out to the children, urging them to climb into the backseat. They did as instructed, the girl pushing the boy through first, Victor stepping closer as he reached through the empty window frame, a hand brushing as much glass as he could to the floor, "Come on, we don't have much time!" Cringing, the boy reached the window, suddenly unsure as he saw the bearded, dreadlocked man standing before him, and grimacing, Victor reached in, dragging the boy out to stand beside him on the hard shoulder, his grey eyes turning to watch as the young girl reached the back seat. She cried out, dropping flat to the upholstery as flames suddenly engulfed the cab of the lorry pressed against their vehicle, her head turning to stare at the man behind the wheel, "Granddad!"

"Get out!" Victor grimaced, one hand pushing the boy back away from him towards the grass, the other reaching in to grab the hooded top of the girl, "You need to get out now!"

"We cant leave him!" she spat angrily, turning to glare at him, head shaking, and Victor cursed, reaching through the window with his other arm to grasp her under the armpits, dragging her free. "No!" she was like a wildcat despite her small stature, desperately trying to get back to the car as Victor dragged her away, grimacing as he stared through the passenger window of the car and met the blank staring gaze of the old man. "He's gone" his words were monotone, and empty, "I'm sorry, but he's gone!"

As if on cue, the car suddenly caught light, the flames that had been sliding fluidly over the overturned lorry shrouding the Renault, and grimacing at the sudden heat, Victor stepped away to where the boy was waiting quietly, the struggling girl, still held in his strong arms.

She slapped him suddenly, twisting in his grip and cursing he released her to fall back to the grass, head shaking as he raised his voice, "He's gone...there's nothing you can do!"

"Grandad!" the confused voice of the boy had Victor snapping his head round to stare at him as he stood on the grass, staring blankly at the car, and without a word, the girl was beside him, arms encircling his frame as she hugged him. "I'm so sorry, Eric...it's just us now!"

Stepping away, Victor turned his head towards Moonshine, a curse escaping him as he found his friend gone from where he had left him, his blood running cold as he stepped back onto the road, calling out frantically for his friend in concern. "Dog!" the voice of Moonshine sounded to his left, and spinning he found him standing feet from the central reservation, balanced on his good leg, using what looked like a car bumped as a crutch. "Stay there!" Victor turned, jabbing a finger at the children, grimacing as the girl told him to fuck off, then he began to move towards Moonshine across the road, brow furrowing as he saw figures moving amid the drifting smoke ahead. "Hey!" his best friend nodded at him as he reached the shorter man, the pair of them flinching at the heat from the burning vehicles on both sides of the dual carriageway, "I found some people, look...there, I told them to come here!" Turning his head, Victor watched as a woman moved into view, her attractive features streaked with soot and blood, her blonde hair hanging about her face, as she staggered towards them, her left arm hanging uselessly by her side, an overweight man in a suit appearing behind her. "Come on!" Victor stepped forwards as he addressed the pair, flinching as another collision sounded from somewhere in the maelstrom of fire and smoke about them, "We need to get off the road before…"

His words trailed off as he caught sight of the white figure once more amid the smoke, several feet behind the overweight man, then Victor turned, the hairs rising upon the back of his neck as he spotted two more white figures to their left.

"Dude?" the stunned voice of Moonshine gave a nervous chuckle, taking an awkward hobble backwards with his makeshift crutch, "What…"

Without any warning the white faced figure behind the overweight businessman suddenly surged forwards, hands reaching for him as it emerged clearly from the smoke, and Victor felt his stomach knot as he finally saw them clearly. It was devoid of any hair, its genderless face and head covered in hard, cracked white skin, it's features twisted in anger as it rushed forwards, beige eyes seeming to be streaming tears the same colour as it reached for the man.

At the last moment, he seemed to sense the danger and turned, a squeal of terror escaping him as the figure leaped upon him catlike, the pair falling heavily down to the hard tarmac.

"Run luv!" Moonshine shouted, his free hand gesturing frantically towards the dazed blonde woman but instead of doing as he had bid, she turned on her heels at the scream from the overweight man, staring back at the struggling pair just feet behind her, head shaking in shock. The first of the other two white figures came charging from the smoke to her left like a cheetah pursuing a gazelle, leaping full stretch to crash her from sight, the second figure joining it. Shaking his head, his hand dragging his knife free from his belt pouch once more, Victor stepped closer to the metal barrier, eyes narrowing in dread as he stared over it, a cold place opening up inside him as he saw the two white-skinned figures savaging the screaming woman with their teeth. Eyes wide in terror, she tried to rise, only for one of them to snap her arm at the elbow, turning the limb around and around until with a powerful jerk it tore it free from her body. Her screams of agony no longer recognisable as that of a human, the woman sagged to her back, the mouth of the second figure finding her exposed throat as she tipped her head back and met Victors gaze, her scream soundless as it tore her voice box away with a powerful tear of its teeth. Fighting both nausea and terror, Victor took a step back, pointing at his friend, gesturing for him to start moving, a finger rising to his lips to encourage Moonshine to try and keep quiet.

Nodding, Moonshine took another hobble back, cursed and fell off balance, a scream of agony coursing through him as his left leg hit the ground, his eyes rolling in his head. On instinct, Victor dropped to a crouch beside the central barrier, his head turning to watch as one of the bald, white-skinned figures rose quickly upon the other side, hands grasping the metal as it vaulted up to sit astride it, top lip curling as it stared down at the fallen Moonshine in hatred. Without thinking, Victor rose suddenly, his knife punching out to stab at the figure, only for the blade to turn harmlessly aside on its hard skin. Cursing, Victor took a step back, half-turning as he saw Moonshine struggle to his feet, leaning heavily upon the car bumper once more, then swore in dread as he saw the other two white-skinned figures rising to join the other, their features coated with blood and beige tears. Gritting his teeth, Victor began to slowly back way, making sure that Moonshine kept behind him as he did so, a quick glance to the rear showing that the two children were stood watching upon the grass, fear on their faces. Before him, the figure that he had tried to stab dropped down to the ground, and took several quick steps towards him, fingers flexing, and the other two vaulted the barrier with ease to join it, the white-skinned trio advancing upon them, a pack of lions hunting their prey, snarling loudly. Somehow, they reached the grass verge beyond the hard shoulder, and Victor tensed, head shaking as he saw the foremost of the figures crouch low as if preparing to throw itself at him, the other two starting to spread out, their eyes staring past him to where the children waited. They were fucked. Well and truly.

With a snarl, the foremost figure lunged forwards, some fifteen feet between the trio and Victor, Moonshine and the children, but the bearded ranger knew it would cover it in no time. The petrol tanker exploded with a roar like a demon, and Victor cursed as a wave of heat hit him, the force lifting him from his feet with ease. He had the briefest of moments to see the charging white-skinned figure incinerated by the river of fire that surged across the A66, and then he was flying backwards, legs and arms windmilling about him before he landed heavily in the field beside the road, groaning in shock and pain. Pushing himself to his feet, he raised a hand, rubbing at his tender cheeks, scorched by the heat, and then turned his head, sighing in relief as he saw the children and Moonshine starting to rise about him, the boy sobbing but none of them apparently injured other than his friends leg. Turning back to the road, Victor cursed in shock as he studied the numerous fires and collisions in both directions for as far as he could see, his breath catching as he saw white figures moving amid the accidents.

"Dude" Victor glanced at Moonshine as his friend spoke, following his gesture as he pointed back towards the road, and the bearded ranger swore as he saw the two white-skinned figures that were trying to get past the flames towards them, hands raising before their faces at the heat. Shaking his head, Victor glanced at Moonshine and the children and then began to back away, head shaking, "We need to go now!"

Chapter Eight

"Come on!" Lauren backed slowly away across the restaurant, her right hand now gripped firmly to the sleeve of Brandon as he moved with her, her eyes wide with shock behind her glasses. On the far side of the restaurant before the doors, the white-skinned, bald figure was still struggling with two of the three men that had approached it, the third man lying upon the floor, blood pouring from a hole in the side of his throat. All around her, shouts and screams sounded, some calling for someone to phone security or the police, others offering encouragement to the pair fighting to control the deranged patient. The young nurse flinched as a scream sounded behind her, over near the counter and turning, she watched as a woman crouched down, a hand rubbing at the back of a man on hands and knees, and Lauren cringed as she saw his hair start to fall away to reveal hard white skin beneath. Just like the patient fighting over near the door. "Come on" the male voice close-by made Lauren turn, her eyes settling upon the thin ginger man as he gestured towards the black woman that had been sitting opposite him, "We need to go!" As Lauren watched, he took a quick step away from the table, edging along the wall towards the doors and then paused as he glanced back at the black woman, his top lip curling, "Jennifer!"

"Aren't we going to help them?" she blinked, a hand rising to gesture towards the men fighting to control the patient, the three of them now on the floor, the former cursing, the latter snarling.

"It's nothing to do with us!" he hissed; his thin features twisted with anger, but Lauren could see the fear in his eyes as he snarled at the woman.

"Peter..." she began then fell silent, shoulders seeming to cringe together as he jabbed a finger in her direction, his features etched with anger.

"I am your husband...you will do as I say!"

For a moment, the black woman hesitated, her sad eyes meeting that of Lauren but then she was heading past the nurse, following her husband as the thin man crept out of the restaurant doors.

As if the departure of the couple had signalled an alarm, the majority of the restaurants patrons suddenly began to hurry towards the doors, pushing and jostling each other as they tried to avoid the fight happening nearby, the curses and gasps of anger and fear loud in the restaurant, and grimacing, Lauren took a quick step back, leading Brandon safely over near the far wall.

"Are we still going to write my letter?" Brandon suddenly asked, turning to face Lauren and she blinked, trying to deal with his calm in the face of the madness around them, knowing that the young man didn't understand what was happening. A grim giggle of mania escaped her as she considered her reasoning, realising that she didn't understand what was happening either. The nurse flinched, shoulders dipping, head ducking slightly as a snarl sounded close by, followed by a scream, and turning her head she found the man that had been upon his hands and knees now attacking the woman that had been helping him, his features thick with hard, cracked white skin, his eyes streaming with beige tears. As Lauren watched, the woman fell to her back, a hand rising to ward the man off only for him to bite down on her hand, his fists pummelling powerfully down at her with unhinged fury. Shaking her head, Lauren edged between two high racks, semi-filled with used and clean trays for the restaurant, dragging Brandon in with her as the man continued to punch the woman until she stopped resisting him, and then savaged her face with his teeth, hands holding her by her hair. Fighting the urge to scream, Lauren turned her head towards the door, weighing up their chances of escape but the trio of fighters had risen and careened into the crowd trying to leave, chaos now ensuing as people screamed and fought to get away from the enraged patient. Then Lauren cursed, her eyes widening as she suddenly saw the old woman that she had been speaking with, Mary, still sat at her table, her cup of tea raised in both hands as she sat staring at the crowd, a look of confusion upon her face. "Out of my way!" a roar of anger and fear suddenly sounded from the doors of the restaurant, and snapping her head towards it, Lauren watched in disbelief as the overweight bearded security guard that she had seen earlier burst back into the room, violently shoving at the crowd before him as he tried to pass through. As the nurse watched, he turned his head, casting a look over his shoulder and then turned back, a look of raw terror on his bearded features as he fought his way through the people, his right fist swinging out to catch a woman in his way on the side of her head, throwing her down to the floor. Suddenly those at the front of the fleeing crowd began to scream, turning direction as they tried to fight their way back inside and Lauren gasped as she saw more of the white-skinned figures attacking the crowd, snarling like rabid animals. With a howl of terror, the security guard, charged away from the crowd and edging forwards,

hating herself, Lauren called out, "Help us!"
"Fuck off you dumb cunt" the man snarled, then
gave a yelp of fear as he saw the white-skinned
figure that was now eating the face of its former
female companion, the guard angling his run
towards the counter, his overweight form
clambering up and over it to vanish from sight,
towards what must be the restaurant kitchen
With a roar, the white-skinned figure closest to
them suddenly rose and charged towards those
that were beginning to get back inside the
restaurant, a casual sweep of its left hand
throwing a table and chairs from its path, the
strength of the man seeming somehow increased.
What had happened to him, and the others?
She had seen him earlier in the queue and he had
seemed fine, just another ordinary human being.
Whatever he was now was anything but human.
Snarling, it reached those furthest from the door
and threw itself at them, and heart in her mouth,
Lauren burst from her hiding place, literally
dragging Brandon along behind her as she
headed for the counter, intending to take the
route that the security guard had just taken,
gambling that there was maybe an exit that way.
In seconds she was beside the counter, hands
pushing at Brandon as she urged him up and

over, the young black man muttering irritably that he didn't want to drop his book about animals as he began to crawl up onto the metal surface as if he had all the time in the world. "Come on!" she hated herself for raising her voice, something knotting inside her as he flinched in fear, and she turned away, glancing at the doors, a whimper escaping her as she saw people on the floor being attacked by more of the white-skinned figures, blood pooling about them. "What about our friend?" the innocent voice of Brandon suddenly asked and Lauren turned to find him standing upon the counter, one hand clasping his beloved book to his tracksuit, the other pointing past her, and grimacing she turned, her eyes settling upon the old woman. "Go!" she gestured with a hand, as she began to walk away from the counter, her eyes locked on the frail old woman still seated at her table, "I will catch you up!"

"I am not allowed to wander off!" Brandon's matter of fact statement had her turn to face him, her hands waving wildly at him as she grimaced. "Go…just fucking go!"

He winced, head dipping to stare at his shoes for a moment, a look of infinite sadness upon his face before he began to climb slowly down on the other side of the counter, and grimacing, Lauren began to walk quickly towards where Mary was still sitting, the eyes of the nurse locked to the crowd, head shaking at the violence she saw. Then suddenly the table was before her, and she reached out a hand, placing it upon the right shoulder of the old woman, "Mary!"

"Oh, hello dear" the Londoner turned her head, a smile creasing her features as she looked up into the nurse's eyes, her head turning as she glanced about, "Lauren isn't it? Where's the lad?"

"Mary" the nurse winced, her eyes glancing at the scene of carnage by the doors, before looking back at the old woman, "What are you doing? We have to get out of here!"

Mary blinked, head shaking, "I have lived through a lot girl, if you think I am going to run because some idiots in face paint are having a ruck..."

"A ruck?" Lauren blinked, head shaking slowly.

"A ruck...a fight...a bit of a to-do!" Mary nodded, jerking a thumb towards the door, "My George would have kicked the shit out of this lot!"

"Please, Mary, come on!" Lauren reached down, placing a hand on the old woman's arm, "We have to get out of here!"

The features of the grey-haired old woman were like stone as she gave a soft chuckle, head shaking, "I'm sorry love but I don't run from wankers…I'm not scared of this lot!"

Blinking in disbelief, both impressed and terrified by the old woman's words, the nurse shook her head, an idea suddenly occurring to her, "I know…but Brandon is…can you help me with him…please"

"The boy?" Mary rose to her feet, sudden concern on her features, "Where is he?"

"In the kitchen" Lauren gestured, leading the old woman by the crook of her right arm, "Can you come and see him with me please?"

"Of course love" Mary gave a nod, allowing herself to be led across the restaurant, towards the counter, and forcing a smile, Lauren glanced past her, trying not to cry out as she realised that there seemed to be more of the white-skinned figures than normal amid the crowd by the door.

"Oh" Mary paused as they neared the body of the woman that had been killed by the man, her free hand rising to her mouth and Lauren nodded, fighting the sudden urge to be sick as she saw her nose, lips and cheeks had been fully eaten away.

"This is bad Mary, we need to get out of here"

"Too fucking right" the old woman suddenly seemed to grasp the gravity of the situation, as they reached the counter and she turned to glance at the door and the violent scene there, "What the fuck are they?"

"Ghouls!"

Lauren nearly cried out as the voice spoke from behind the counter, her head snapping about to find Brandon standing there, nodding wisely as he spoke again, "I think they might be ghouls" Stunned, the nurse stared at him in shock for a moment then winced as she stared at the old woman, trying how to work out how she was going to get the old woman over the counter when suddenly, Brandon lifted a section of it high, revealing a small walkway to the other side, nodding as he spoke, "Oh and I found this"

She flinched as a sudden roar sounded and she spun about, a hand rising to brush her copper hair from her features as she stared at the doors, the hairs rising on the back of her neck as she saw two of the white-skinned figures rise from the bodies that they had been savaging and turned towards where she and her two companions stood watching, "Oh fuck me, no!"

"Come on!" the voice of Mary had her turning to find the old woman and Brandon on the other side of the counter, the features of Mary grim as she frantically beckoned the nurse towards her with a hand, "Fucking run!"

Chapter Nine

"Opinder...Opinder!" the black-haired, young woman was seated on the floor before the still form of her brother, one hand clasped to her mouth and the other hovering over the back of his bald scalp, as if afraid to touch his bare skin. Standing behind her, Alice winced, head shaking as she stared down at the man that she had been speaking with just minutes before, his physical appearance changed so dramatically that she was almost unable to believe it was the same person. Whereas before he had been heavily bearded, his skin a rich brown with a dark-blue turban upon his head, concealing the sight of his natural hair from strangers as per the dictates of his faith, now he was bald, and beardless, the cracked white skin that she had spied beneath the hem of his turban having somehow spread across his entire face and head, even the skin of his hands appearing to be suffering the same condition. Yet what had caused it?

In her time as an embalmer she had seen more dead bodies than a normal person could imagine and had seen all manner of causes of death, but nothing like this. How had it spread so fast?

She cringed as the thought occurred to her and took a step back, a hand rising to cover her mouth and nose, the fear of infection coursing through her with the intensity of a wildfire.

As if sensing her movement, the young woman turned to glance up at her, a frown upon her tear stained face, and Alice extended her free hand, beckoning towards her, "Please...come here"

The woman shook her head quickly, finally placing her hand down upon the top of the head of her dead brother, her eyes closing, her lips moving and Alice cringed, wondering what the infection rate was for whatever the man had, her stomach lurching as she considered the deadly pandemic that had lain waste to the world.

Was this the third stage?

Had it returned to finish them all off?

Shaking her head, she took another step back, frowning as the woman stared down at her brother, trying desperately to remember what the dead man had called his sister and then it came to her in a flash, "Jiyaa...please"

The woman raised her head as she heard Alice speak her name, a look of confusion upon her features as she rose to her feet and turned to stare back at the embalmer, lips moving silently as if she wanted to speak but was unsure how.

Hadn't her brother said she had not been in the country long? Did she not speak any English?

Shaking her head, Alice took a shaky breath, wanting more than anything to speak to the young woman and explain her concerns but she was unsure what nationality Jiyaa might even be. It was obvious from the turban that Opinder had worn that he was a practising Sikh but that didn't really help at all. She knew that the majority of Sikh's came from the Punjab province situated in Northern India, but Sikhs lived all over the world. Sighing heavily, she beckoned once more with her hand, her other gesturing for the young woman to cover her mouth and nose with her hand, then she froze, the breath leaving her lungs in a rush as she saw the feet of Opinder twitch. "What?" she shook her head, her features twisting in confusion as she stared down at the man that she had been sure was dead, the man whose pulse she had been unable to find after his collapse. Had the skin about his wrists been too thick and calloused for her to feet his heartbeat? Before her, Jiyaa noticed her stare, and turned, her gasp of elation loud as she had seen her brother's hands struggling to push himself up from the floor, "Opinder!"

"Oh God no" Alice's words had tasted like bitter acid in her mouth, her stomach lurching as she had seen the white, cracked and calloused features of the man stare up at his sister, his milky beige eyes locked to the face of Jiyaa as he had snarled like a wild animal, the sudden noise almost deafening in the confines of the chapel. With mind-numbing speed and athleticism, the man suddenly threw himself forwards, his hands encircling the waist of his sibling, the weight of his body throwing his sister back to the ground in the aisle between the chairs. Jiyaa screamed in terror, and teeth snapping like a wild dog, Opinder crawled along her body, his right hand rising to hammer a punch down into her face. Without thinking, Alice stepped forwards, her right leg sweeping out in a flash, the toe of the Dr Marten boots that she wore constantly striking the snarling Opinder hard underneath the chin. He grunted, beige eyes rolling and fell back from her, falling like a felled tree to the carpet beyond his sisters feet, and Alice hurried forwards, extending a hand to help Jiyaa stand, only to wince as she saw movement beside her.

With a snarl, the white-skinned figure of Opinder, already back upon his feet, grasped her by the arm that was reaching towards a wide-eyed Jiyaa and swung her across the chapel as if she were weightless, his strength terrifying. Heart in her mouth, Alice felt herself leave the floor, her body turning in the air as she sailed over the chairs on the left side of the chapel, arms and legs waving, and then she hit the wall beside the door hard. With a grunt of shock and pain, she fell, crashing down atop the rack containing the leaflets she had been studying earlier, destroying the display, the contents of the rack scattering everywhere. Dizzy, head aching, she somehow made it to her feet, leaning heavily upon the wall as she stared back at the siblings, a cry of shock escaping her as she saw Opinder grasp his sister by the bare right arm and bite down hard, head shaking. With a scream of pain and terror, Jiyaa reached out her hands pushing at her brother's chest, and Alice shouted, "Leave her the fuck alone!"

With a growl, Opinder released his bite upon his sister's forearm, and turned to stare balefully at her, the embalmers blood turning to ice as she saw the hatred and hunger in his milky eyes, his bloodstained lips drawing back as he snarled. Then it screamed in agony as Jiyaa suddenly drew her left arm back from her brother's chest and stabbed him in the right eye with the small curved knife she now held tight in her fingers. With a roar like a bear, Opinder grasped at his sister with both hands, throwing her back against the wall away from him, and screaming she struck it hard and fell down atop the chairs beneath her, legs and arms at all angles as she groaned in shock and pain. Hands balled into fists, Opinder staggered back, body spinning wildly as he roared like the wounded beast he was, blood and more of that milky liquid pouring from the ruin of his eye socket down his face. Off balance, he staggered into the right side of the aisle and nearly tripped, his arms swinging wildly as he lashed out, his powerful blows throwing chairs about as if they weighed nothing. Ducking as a chair crashed into the wall not far from where she stood frozen in shock, Alice watched, hope taking flight within her heart as the maddened man suddenly tripped and fell, his disorientated attempts to rise tangling him in the chairs he had been throwing about like confetti. To her left, Jiyaa was trying to rise, blood running freely from her wounded right forearm, her left hand clasped to the small, curved knife, an expression of confusion upon the woman's face. "Come on!" Alice took a step towards her and raised an arm to beckon to the woman, wincing as pain from her collision with the wall and then the chapel floor surged through her upper back. This time Jiyaa responded to her gesture without any argument, the Sikh clambering past the chairs between them quickly to stand before her, a gasp of genuine surprise escaping Alice as the woman threw her arms about the embalmer, hugging her tight for a moment before stepping back, her eyes locked to those of Alice as she spoke slowly in whatever language she and Opinder hand been speaking in, nodding slowly. "I'm sorry" Alice shook her head, "I don't und..." Her words trailed off as at the back of the chapel, the white-skinned man screeched at them, hands pushing at the carpet as it started to rise once more, and taking the hand of Jiyaa, Alice ran.

Chapter Ten

Victor had never liked running.

As a young boy, he had always been far more comfortable sitting reading books and comics than running around playing games with the other children in the street where he had lived.

Even as an adult he had never liked running. Even after his life had been destroyed and he had been forced to rebuild it from the ground up, changing his entire lifestyle and outlook, growing physically stronger and tougher, he had never been fond of running. It just wasn't his thing. After all, like his gentle and studious father had always told him, a man should only run when he is chasing something or when he is being chased. The latter certainly fit the bill now.

Gritting his teeth, his right hand wrapped about the right thigh of Moonshine, his left gripping his friends right arm as the injured man lay across his broad shoulders in a fireman's lift, Victor ran on through the wheat field, his eyes fixed to the backs of the two Asian children running ahead. Cursing as he nearly stumbled upon the uneven ground, a jolt of pain exploding in his right knee, the bearded ranger ran on, wanting more than anything to turn and look back at their pursuers but he didn't, knowing that if he attempted to do so while carrying his awkward load, he was going to trip and fall, and then they, and the two children that they had somehow found themselves responsible for would be killed.

Yet in truth he didn't need to turn to know how close they were on his tail, the snarls and grunts of the figures loud in the sudden stillness of the countryside, the crash of their path through the wheat almost deafening in its raw intensity, the ragged sound of his breathing filling his ears.

"Oh fuck!" the whimper from Moonshine atop his shoulders put an extra surge of energy into his step, his gut knotting as he pictured the white-skinned figures surging from the wheat behind them, dragging them down to be torn to pieces like they had done with the woman on the A66. That had been just three of the creatures.

Yet as he had urged the children to run and dragged an arguing Moonshine atop his shoulders, Victor had seen three more of the white figures run from further along the dual carriageway to join the two rushing at them past the flames from the exploded petrol transporter. What was wrong with the people?

Because he knew, despite the vast assortment of horror films that he had watched since he had rebuilt his life, that was what they really were.

People.

There were no such thing as monsters.

These were just people, driven mad by whatever was had turned their skin all hard and white.

Could it be another virus outbreak?

It didn't look like any photos that he had seen of those infected with the virus that had besieged the known world for two years but in truth he hadn't really paid it much attention, secreted away as he had been in his new home, turning his back on the world amid his guilt and grief.

Victor grimaced as he studied the girl running ahead through the wheat, her left hand clutched to that of what was obviously her younger brother, she probably about twelve and he six.

The same rough ages as his Rebecca and Rory.

He grimaced at the thought of his children, face twisting in grief as he recalled thinking that it had been them trapped within the car earlier, the sudden memories of that night five years before returning to him in a rush of pain, grief and fire.

"For fuck sake" he gave a growl, head shaking slightly as he ran onwards, wincing as upon his back, Moonshine spoke, raw fear in his voice.

"Are you OK, Dog"

"Don't make me talk" Victor grimaced, head shaking once more, then he cursed, his blood running cold as he saw sudden movement in his peripheral vision, a white figure racing through the field of wheat some distance of to their left. Heart in his mouth, he turned his head, watching the area where he had seen the movement then cursed once more as he saw one of the white-skinned figures running almost parallel to them. Was it one of the five he had seen or another? Grimacing at the thought, he nodded with his head, "Look over there!"

"Oh fuck my life" Moonshine's whine had been loud, "Fucking Hell, what are we going to do?"

"I don't know"

"Where are we going?"

Gritting his teeth, resisting the urge to tell his friend to shut the fuck up, knowing that he had no real answer to the last question, Victor turned back to the children, nausea coursing through him as he realised that they seemed closer now. They were slowing down. The poor fucking kids. Snarling in sudden anger, he raised his gaze, eyes widening as he suddenly noticed that they were nearing the end of the field of wheat, another field of grass and sheep laying directly ahead of them, while to their right beyond some fences sat thick woodland, extending off in both directions.

"Right!" he shouted suddenly, releasing Moonshines right leg to gesture wildly with an arm as the girl glanced back at him, "Go right!" Without hesitating, the girl angled her run, nearly dragging her younger brother from his feet as she changed direction, and ignoring the curses of pain from Moonshine, Victor grasped at his right leg once more and followed the children's lead. They reached it several metres ahead of him, the girl releasing her brothers hand just before it as she slid effortlessly through the centre gap of the thick wooden fence, he scrambling under the bottom beam, and then they were running again. Gritting his teeth, Victor almost ran into the fence, swinging about so that Moonshine could drop down to the other side, grunting in pain, then cursed in dread as he saw the three figures rushing towards them through the wheat, two more charging on towards the field of sheep. Cursing, Victor reached down to withdraw the knife from his belt, then grimaced as he realised he had no idea where it was. He had been holding it back on the A66, his attempt to stab the leading figure turned aside by its hard skin, and then the tanker had exploded, throwing him into the field. Had he dropped the knife then? Damn it! Turning his head, he glanced at Moonshine, seeing his friend gritting his teeth as he stared at the three creatures hurrying towards them, and for a moment their eyes met, the injured man wincing, his voice a whisper, "Go on, run mate"

"Fuck off" Victor grimaced, head shaking slowly.

"Seriously" Moonshine nodded, sweaty features pale, "You run, I'll hold them off!"

Victor shook his head, smiling grimly, "You cant fight without an Xbox controller in your hand"

"Fuck off" Moonshine's reply was a grim chuckle, and grimacing, Victor turned to stare at the three white-skinned figures as they slowed to a stop just metres before the fence, preparing himself to fight for his life, his eyes scanning the ground for something, anything he might use as a weapon. Snarling, one of the figures stepped forwards, and Victor grimaced as he studied the cracked-white skin that covered its face and bald head, ridged uneven flakes that gave it the sudden appearance of cracked earth beneath the sun. Bending at the waist, its movements almost ape-like as it took two steps forward, the figure turned its head quickly from side to side, large breasts swaying within the confines of the red tee-shirt that it wore, and with shock Victor realised that the figure before them was female.

Grimacing, he turned his gaze upon the other two, judging both to be male from their attire, then took a shaky breath as the female took another step towards where he waited before the fence, ready to defend himself from her attack, only for the figure to snort and turn to look past him, her distorted features twisting in confusion. Behind it, one of the other two grunted, and suddenly moved forwards to stand at the fence, just inches separating it from Victor's body as it turned its head, seeming to look straight through the two Rangers, before snarling in apparent anger and stepping up onto one of the wooden beams. Not daring to breathe, Victor stared ahead, his grey eyes narrowing as he studied the features and movements of the female and the other male, realising with shock how primitive their behaviour and body language was, his brow furrowing as he studied their eyes, flicking to and from as if trying to latch onto something moving. Was that why they appeared unable to see him and Moonshine? Because they were stationary? Grimacing as he considered the children that he had just sent running off through the woodland, Victor released a shaky breath and then nearly cried out in shock as a frenzied bleating sounded from the field with the sheep. With a growl, the male that had been upon the fence leaped down and loped back several steps, head turning to stare at its two bestial companions, snarling at them until they began to move towards it, the trio standing in a small group, faces turned towards the distant bleating, grunting excitedly. Then, without warning they began to charge across the field towards the sound, leaving Victor and Moonshine unharmed beside the fence.

"What the fuck?" the voice of the injured man was a harsh whisper, and turning, Victor nodded.

"Yeah"

"How the fuck are we still alive?"

Victor grimaced, head shaking, "I don't know, but we are, now let's go find those kids before those ugly fuckers change their mind and come back"

Chapter Eleven

"Fucking Hell, Dog" Moonshine's coarse whisper had Victor turning back to study the man as he stood against the trunk of a wide oak, head shaking as he leaned heavily upon a large branch that they had found for him to use as a crutch, "I wonder how far they have gone?"

Victor grimaced, turning away from his friend to let his eyes drift over the surrounding woodland, blinking as the sunlight filtering down through the thick green canopy made his eyes water. He wanted more than anything to call out to the children, but he didn't want to make a noise that would bring their pursuers back towards them. The three that had chased them right up to the fence bordering the woodland had seemed unable to find them when they had stopped moving, indicating that their eyesight was in some way movement based, like that of a toad. Yet it was obvious their hearing worked perfectly well, and he didn't want to bring them running, not when it looked like Moonshine was about ready to pass out on the ground at any moment. As soon as Victor had clambered over the fence to join Moonshine beneath the trees on the edge of the woodland, they had begun walking, the shorter man refusing the offer of being carried.

That had seemed like hours ago when in truth, Victor knew that perhaps only ten minutes had passed, ten minutes which the pair had spent searching for the children and glancing back over their shoulders, expecting to see their pursuers. He had so far seen neither groups, and while he was pleased about the absence of the latter, the fact that they had seemingly lost the children was like a large stone in the pit of his stomach, the weight of it growing with each passing minute. Moonshine had suggested after several minutes of unsuccessful searching for the missing pair that perhaps the children had climbed a tree to escape from those that were following, maybe thinking that he and Victor had both been slain, but as they had searched the woodland, they had continuously looked up, searching the branches. Yet they had seen no sign of the children at all. For several minutes, Victor had become certain that they been attacked by more of the strange white-skinned people and torn to pieces, only for that theory to fade as he realised that in the quiet of the woodland they would have heard the screams of the children had they been set upon. So, where were they?

"Are you sure this is the way they ran?" the voice of Moonshine had him glancing back once more.

"Yeah" Victor nodded, glancing at the woodland ahead once more, "The ground rises slightly on our left and drops on our right, this is the only level bit, I think they'd stick with it"

"Hark at Crocodile Dundee" Moonshine gave a sudden smile, "Or is it Daryl Dixon?"

"Abraham Ford" Victor threw him a smile, "Now come on, you son of a dick, let's get moving"

Chuckling at his joke, Moonshine stepped away from the oak, leaning upon the makeshift crutch once more, the pair of them walking on in silence for several minutes, before Moonshine spoke once more, "I wonder where the farm is"

"Farm?" Victor sent him a frown, "What farm?"

"The one that owns the sheep" his friend made a face, then waved his free hand at him, "No, you are right, it could be anywhere couldn't it...it doesn't have to be near here I suppose"

Turning his face, Victor studied the woodland once more, wishing that he could get a bearing on the sun so that he could work out which way they were going. It seemed like they were heading South, parallel to the A66 but he wasn't sure, knowing how easy it was to get turned around in woodland, the uneven ground making it hard to keep one hundred per cent straight in a direction.

Could there be a farm somewhere nearby?

If there was then they would be able to call for assistance in finding the children, although there was every chance that the majority of the local emergency services were busy with the crashes upon the A66 and the white-skinned maniacs.

He grimaced as he suddenly considered the cause of their affliction once more. Could they be infected with some new strain of the old virus? If so then he and Moonshine could be as well.

Swallowing the tightness in his throat, he turned to his friend, "Let's stop for a minute, try and see if you can contact anyone on your mobile"

Leaning back against a tree, Moonshine fished his mobile phone back out of his pocket, "I'll try, I didn't have any reception earlier remember"

Shaking his head at his friend's words, Victor turned his head, studying the land about them. Several feet beyond where they stood to the right, the ground began to slope considerably, what looked like a fast moving stream visible at the bottom through the trees and undergrowth, while to their right, the ground rose sharply.

"Nope…I've still got no signal" Moonshine sighed heavily, and casting a glance down at the stream, Victor turned to throw him an exasperated look.

"You probably fucked it falling in the water at

Black Ling Hole Waterfall"

"I did think that earlier" Moonshine winced.

"Great" Victor grimaced, rolling his eyes only for Moonshine to shake his head, suddenly angry.

"Hey, don't get shitty with me Dog, at least I have a fucking mobile phone...I mean, come on, who doesn't have a fucking mobile...its 2020!"

"Me" Victor grimaced, his back teeth clenching.

"Yes, fucking you, you tit" Moonshine gave a shake of his head, a weary smile creeping onto his features, his anger fading almost at once.

For a moment, the two friends stood grinning wearily at each other and then Victor gestured with a hand, "Still, if you are right about the farm, we might be able to use their phone to call help!"

Moonshine gave a chuckle, "That'll be nice"

Victor nodded, "Yeah, I am thinking all of it, police, ambulance, fire brigade..."

"How about the fucking X-Men" Moonshine grinned but it didn't reach his eyes, "I'm not joking. Those crazy fuckers were biting people!"

"I know"

"People don't just bite people" the injured man shook his head, fear creeping onto his features.

"I know" Victor repeated, nodding at his friend.

There was a moment silence and then suddenly Moonshine winced, "Mate, I am fucking scared"

"Don't be daft" Victor began to walk, turning away from the fear in his friends eyes, recalling the same look in the eyes of his children, the memory sending a sensation like fire sweeping across his back. Gritting his teeth against the heat of the flames that his memory had conjured, telling himself that they weren't really there, he turned back to tell Moonshine that they were going to be OK, then felt his stomach lurch as he saw the white-skinned figure rushing through the trees, what looked like a club in its left hand. "No!" without thinking, Victor was rushing back towards his friend, time seeming to slow as he saw the white-skinned figure suddenly snarl, the club swinging in at the side of Moonshine's head. Unaware of the danger, seeing only his friend suddenly rush at him, Moonshine flinched, and took a quick step back away, and off balance he fell hard against the trunk of the nearest tree. The end of the club swung past his face, the side of it catching him across his right cheek and screaming in sudden shock, Moonshine toppled to his back on the ground. Snarling, his attacker, twisted, the club rising once more, intending to bring it crashing down upon the face of the prone man, only to grunt in shock as Victor reached it, his right fist swinging up to hammer into its face.

Stunned but clearly not hurt, the figure, male by its dirty and blood-stained clothes, swung its club once more towards Victor, snarling as it did so, and with shock he realised it looked like a bone. A human leg bone.

As the club swung in at him, Victor raised his right arm, deflecting the attack from striking him in the head, only for pain to shoot through the limb, his fingers going numb. With a snarl, his attacker raised the club once more and gritting his teeth, Victor rushed forwards, body slamming it backwards towards the steep slope downhill. With a snarl, the figure stumbled under the impact, slipping from the even ground and then Victor cursed in shock as it grasped at him with its free hand, pulling him along with it as it fell. They struck the ground hard, the pair of them rolling down the forest slope together, the white-skinned figure snapping its teeth at the bearded features of Victor as he fought to keep it away. "Fuck off!" he snapped his head forwards as he rolled to his back, wincing as it felt as if he had headbutted wood, then grunted in shock and pain as they suddenly rolled sideways into a tree trunk, stopping their descent. Blinking past the agony that was coursing through him, certain that he had just broken some ribs, Victor stared up as his attacker rose to its feet above him, the club raised once more as it snarled excitedly, the sunlight flickering through the leaves above it. Somehow, driven purely by pain and anger, Victor surged forwards, rugby tackling the white-skinned figure above the waist, and then they were rolling once more, their speed increasing as the ground dropped dramatically and then they came apart, inertia separating the pair of them. Victor cried out in shock as he suddenly felt air beneath him, his arms and legs kicking and then he gasped as cold water wrapped about him, turning his clothes to a second skin, the sudden chill of the water stealing the air from his lungs. For what seemed an eternity, he floundered, turning about as he tried to right himself and then he got his feet underneath him and broke the surface, the water coming up to his chest. Almost at once the attack came, no club this time, but from fists, powerful blows that had Victor staggering back, his grey eyes streaming with tears as he felt his nose break under one of the punches, a second splitting his bottom lip wide. With a roar like a man possessed, Victor swept his arms out before him, managing to turn aside several other clumsy but powerful blows and then he slid behind it, arms fastening about its throat and head as he crouched in the water, dragging the face of his foe under the surface. Head bent so that he was almost staring up at the canopy of leaves above him, mouth clamped tight shut as the surface of the stream lapped at his face, disturbed by the thrashing of the white-skinned figure that he was attempting to drown, the figure that was already threatening to overpower him, Victor closed his eyes and pictured the night that his family had died in detail for the first time in years, picturing the faces of his children as he fought to get them out of the burning house, a raw primal scream escaping him as anger swept through his body. Time lost all meaning to him as he stood there, all but sub-merged in the cold stream, screaming in pain and hate and guilt until he could scream no more, only then realising that the figure in his arms was no longer fighting to be from of him. Blinking, suddenly numb both emotionally and physically, Victor released the white-skinned figure, watching as the stream collected it and took it away from him, meandering out of sight around a bend like an albino alligator. Then with what felt like the last of his strength, he climbed from the river and raised his head, staring up the slope at the worried features of Moonshine, and the stern features of the attractive woman that was now standing beside him in black jeans and a black and white chequered shirt, her silver hair shaven to the skin on both sides while the top stayed long, a shotgun held ready in her hands. *Great. Someone new. The more the merrier.*

Chapter Twelve

Pushing himself to his feet on the bank of the river, Victor straightened, wincing as pain flared in his left side where he had struck the tree, and then began to walk carefully back up the slope. His face was a throbbing car crash of pain, his broken nose and split bottom lip, sending waves of agony washing around his face each time he moved, just as each breath made his side hurt. Yet thankfully, his hand was working again from where the club had struck him, the realisation that if it hadn't been he would have been unable to defend himself and would now be dead settling about his broad shoulders like a shroud. Grimacing, cursing at the pain the expression brought to his bearded features, Victor paused to cast a last glance down at the river and then continued upwards, meeting the gaze of the pair that were stood watching him climb in silence. Moonshine was leaning upon the makeshift crutch once more, features tight with concern as he watched his climb towards them, and forcing a grim smile, Victor threw his friend a nod, then let his gaze settle upon the woman standing beside him, brow furrowing as he studied her. She was tall, perhaps an inch or so bigger than Victors five-foot eight-inch frame, her form athletic and lean, a look of readiness in her brown eyes as she continuously glanced about. But there was something else to those eyes, a haunted look of pain and loss, of having survived while others hadn't, and as she turned to face him, Victor recognised it as the same look that he saw each and every time he looked in the mirror.

"Dog" Moonshine took a hobble forwards as he finally reached the flat area where they waited, a hand reaching out to pat Victor upon the arm, and despite his usual uncomfortableness with tactile displays, the bearded ranger felt moved.

"Hey" he nodded, wincing as he spoke, the fingers of his left hand rising towards his split lip only to frown at the woman as she suddenly spoke.

"Don't touch it…it needs stitches…you'll infect it"

He nodded, a corner of his mouth twitching up as he held her gaze, noting her thick north-eastern accent, "My name's Victor…"

"Call him Dog, I do" Moonshine interrupted, and Victor cringed, head shaking as he sighed heavily. "Ignore him"

The woman nodded, features devoid of emotion, yet her eyes continued to glance about them constantly as she spoke, "Any other injuries?"

Victor grimaced, shrugging, "My nose is broken, I might have broken a couple of ribs too"

She nodded, and Victor tensed as he saw her fingers tighten upon the shotgun, "Anything else? Any itchy white skin...memory problems?"

For a moment, he stood staring back at her in silence, eyes travelling over her features, and then he gave a nod, "You've seen them...not just the one I drowned down there...you've seen some of your own haven't you"

It wasn't a question, and the woman took a step back, the shotgun rising to point at Victors face, "I asked you a question...any white skin patches?"

"No"

"Any memory loss or tiredness at all?"

"No"

"You?" she took another step back, the gun turning to point at Moonshine, "White skin?"

"No, fucking hell!" he shook his head, "Not me"

"Memory loss?"

Moonshine gave a chuckle, "I can't remember!"

With a grimace, the woman clenched her teeth, looking like she was about to open fire and as Moonshine cursed and dipped his head, Victor stepped in front of his friend, hands raised beside his head, "He's fine...he's just a fucking idiot!"

"I am!" Moonshine announced, his free hand raising like Victors, "Just ignore me...fucking hell"

She nodded, her mouth twitching, her shoulders

seeming to loosen slightly and then she lowered the gun to the ground, "You are lucky I found you out here, these albino fuckers are everywhere"

Victor nodded at her, "Where are you from?"

She gestured off along the track with a jerk of her head, "My grandparents farm...you?"

"I told you there would be a farm!" Moonshine interrupted, sounding pleased with himself, only to fall silent as Victor sent him a weary glance.

"The A66" the bearded ranger sighed, "We work for the Forestry Commission in Hamsterley Forest. Moonshine here has broken his leg and I was trying to get him to the hospital at Thames"

The woman raised an eyebrow, "Surely Durham hospital would have been nearer for you?"

"Actually its six and two threes..." Moonshine began to explain, his words trailing off as both Victor and the woman turned to look at him.

Sighing, worried that his friend was about to start gibbering once more, Victor nodded, "So we were on the A66 and the lorry in front of us went over...proper crashed. We got out of our jeep but then that got destroyed in another crash. Another lorry crashed behind us and then we had to rescue some..."

His words trailed off as he grimaced, head turning to stare off through the woodland, stomach lurching as he remembered the two children. Before him, the woman raised an eyebrow, "What is it?"

"Two children…they were with us…we rescued them from the car on the A66 and then we got chased through the wheat…"

"The creatures?" the face of the woman was pale.

"Whoa" Moonshine raised his free hand, a nervous smile on his face, "They are people, lets not start calling them all sorts of silly names"

Ignoring his friend, Victor nodded, "Yeah, three of them chased us to these woods, I sent the kids on to safety…then the others seemed to not be able to see us and headed off towards some sheep. We were trying to find the kids when that bastard attacked us…using a bone as a club"

The woman grimaced, head shaking as she glanced down at the river and then met his gaze once more, "Is that the first one you have killed?"

He nodded, "You?"

She stayed silent for a moment, the muscles of her cheeks tensing, throat tightening as she swallowed, "Two…I killed two…in the early hours of this morning"

Victor grimaced, nodding, "At the farm"

Once more, the woman winced, the effort of trying to keep calm showing upon her features, and the bearded ranger nodded in sudden understanding, "I'm sorry...I really am"

She winced, casting a glance at Moonshine as he frowned, "I don't get it...what's happened?"

"Nothing" her voice was thick with emotion, her head nodding as she met the gaze of Victor once more, "My name is Bella...Bella Atkinson"

He nodded, then frowned as she took a step away, gesturing for them to follow, "Come on"

"We can't" Victor shook his head, sighing as spoke, "I have to find the kids"

"I've found them" Bella Atkinson nodded, taking another step away through the woodland, "They are at the farm"

Blinking, Victor exchanged stunned glances with Moonshine and then took a step towards her, an eyebrow rising, "Seriously? You found them?"

She gave a soft chuckle, "They found me but yeah...what did you think I was doing out in the woods...I was looking for you two"

Chapter Thirteen

"Come on!" pulling Jiyaa's hand, Alice felt like she was dragging the poor girl along behind her. Jiyaa still had not spoken but appeared to have given in, letting the stranger pull her to safety. Safety? Alice thought, was there anywhere safe? Alice had one goal and that was to get herself and Jiyaa as far away from Opinder as possible. Racing out the door of the chapel, Alice quickly scanned the corridor that lay ahead, then the commotion coming from the chapel spurred Alice to take a quick left, hoping that Opinder, or whatever he was, had not seen them head that way. As much as Alice wanted to call for help, she knew that it would attract the girl's brother. Both women proceed to edge down the corridor, then froze upon hearing a snarl from what used to be Opinder, closer than they had expected. Hearing a gasp, Alice turned and saw the fear in Jiyaa's eyes. Putting a finger to her lips to remind Jiyaa to stay silent, Alice gently guided her further from the chapel, her heart hammering in her chest. As they turned another corner, they almost crashed right into a nurse heading around it. "Whoa!" the nurse exclaimed, her wide eyes taking in the blood coming from the wound in Jiyaa's arm, "You need that looking at!"

Before either woman could silence the caring nurse, Opinder was suddenly upon her, drawn by the sound of her voice. She screamed as he sank his teeth into her plump left cheek, his arms and body pinning her to the wall, her eyes wide as she screamed in confusion and fear, blood running freely down onto her uniform. Teeth still clamped to the woman's face, Opinder began to bang her against the wall, over and over, her head making a sickening *thunk* each time it struck the surface. Knowing there was no way that they could save the nurse, Alice took a step away, realising that she and Jiyaa had to get some distance between themselves and Opinder. Yet again, dragging Jiyaa, they ran, Alice realising that they would be better off getting out the corridor. Quickly scanning the doors, not knowing which room to go into then Jiyaa signalled to the female bathroom. Without any thought the two women raced towards the door and barged inside as behind them the nurses agonised screams eventually faded to nothing. Pushing Jiyaa into the restroom ahead of her with force, Alice did not think there could be anyone else in there, till Jiyaa collided straight into the admin woman that she had seen eating in the chapel, before all this madness had begun.

"Fuck, what the hell is going on? " the admin called out as Jiyaa knocked her slender frame backwards into one of the sinks, her eyes then noticing Alice as she shut the door, "You are tha lassie from the chapel aren't ye?"

As Alice nodded, grim faced, the admin noticed the blood on the Sikh girl, "Geez hen, we need to get that seen tae! Was it you tha was screaming?"

Unable to reply, Jiyaa tapped a finger on her lips. "There is someone...something out there" Alice whispered, pointing back away from the rest room door, "It has just murdered a nurse, if we don't get out of this hospital, we will be next!

Confusion washed over the Scottish admin's features, as she glanced between them, "Are ye shitting me?"

"Look at her arm!" anger started to rise through Alice, "Does this look like a joke? Please, you work here, what is the best way to get out?"

Head turning as if she was viewing the whole hospital in her head, the Scots eyes suddenly lit up, and she smiled grimly, "The quickest way we are getting off this floor is the lift near the stairs"

Alice nodded, contemplating the idea when the roar sounded from outside, deafening in its intensity. Jiyaa was instantly cowering in the corner of the bathroom, the small curved knife raised before her, knowing it was her brother.

All three women looked at each other nervously, Geri's eyes widening, "What was tha?"

"The thing...it was her brother" Alice gestured to Jiyaa, and then looked back at the admin, "Look, I'm Alice, this is Jiyaa. We need to make a move now! Do you think you can get us to the lift?"

"Geri...Geri Larkin" the admin nodded, "I will give it ma best shot!"

Gathering Jiyaa to her feet, Alice firmly grabbed the young woman's free hand, pulling her into an embrace, the Sikh woman returning the gesture, then stepping back, she looked into the confused woman's eyes and motioning for her to follow. "Let's do it!"

As Geri opened the bathroom door, the women edged slowly out, their eyes scanning the corridor, relief flooding over Alice as she saw it was clear. Still holding tight to the free hand of Jiyaa, they moved on, the three of them walking single file down the corridor until they hit the corner where they left Opinder. He was still there, down on the floor now squatting in a pool of blood, his broad back to the women, gnawing upon the leg of the now dead nurse, the wet chewing sounds making Alice grow nauseous.

Grimacing, a hand motioning for them to follow, Geri led Alice and Jiya slowly away in the opposite direction, down another corridor. As they moved, Alice swapped places with Jiyaa, gesturing for her to move behind Geri while she followed keeping an eye behind them, still holding tight to the hand of the Sikh woman. Elation coursed through Alice as she spotted their safe haven at the end of the corridor, so near yet so far away, her stomach knotted with the fear that at any moment they could be attacked again. Each step made Alice's heart felt like it would burst from her chest and the closer they got to the lift, the harder Jiyaa squeezed upon her hand. Somehow, some way they reached it unscathed, and the admin, Geri, turned and gave both her new companions a cheesy smile and thumbs up, her other hand gently tapping the button to call the lift. Relaxing slightly, Alice glanced along the corridor they had traversed, seeing that it was still clear, then turned to watch the elevators descent on the screen, right boot tapping in anticipation. She almost cheered as the lift arrived, but then as the doors slid open the bell made its usual ding. *Oh fuck, no. The bell!*

Instinctively Alice turned, heart skipping a beat as she found Opinder at the end of the corridor facing them, the now severed leg of the nurse clasped by the ankle. He let out a menacing roar of anger as he began to charge down the corridor towards the almost free women, snarling in hate. Unable to move, Alice cringed, her head shaking. *This is it. This is how I die.*

Then hands were on each of her shoulders, and she was dragged back into the confines of the lift, though she was still unable to take her eyes off the monster, tearing towards them, howling now. "Shit, Shit, Shit!" Geri's words grew louder each time as she pounded on the buttons, begging for the doors to close, while Jiyaa stood sobbing in the corner, the knife of her brother clasped in her hand still, her back to it all. Grim-faced, Alice still watched as the white-skinned, hairless creature approached, closer and closer, snarling in hatred, one eye a bloody ruin from Jiyaa's attack on it. *Fourteen feet, twelve feet, ten feet.*

Somehow Alice still kept her eyes on the beast's blood covered, snarling face as it drew closer. *Eight feet, six feet, four feet.*

Then with another soft chime of its bell, the doors slid shut, taking the image of the monster away, and groaning, Alice collapsed to the floor.

Chapter Fourteen

"I don't think we are allowed to be here" the voice of Brandon made Lauren flinch as he spoke suddenly, the nurse wincing as she saw him repeatedly tapping a finger against his right temple, the fingers of his left hand fidgeting as he clutched his book, and despite his monotone statement, she could tell that he was agitated. Turning to face him, she reached out a hand, resting it gently upon his left shoulder as she gave a nod, "I have permission from the cook"

"The cook who cooked our food?" he blinked.

"Yes, that cook" Lauren nodded, humouring him as he went with her lie to calm him down, "Now the cook has said we can be here but we have to be quiet, we need to be as quiet as mice, we can't talk too loudly, do you understand?"

"Mice don't talk" he shook his head at her, "They squeak. Its talking to other mice but its not words like we would use"

"OK" she winced as he spoke, gesturing for him to be quiet, her hands waving downwards, "Cool"

"Did you know that there are over thirty species of mice?" Brandon tapped her upon the shoulder as she started to turn back around, only to glance at Mary as the old woman nudged him gently, a finger rising before her lips as she winked at him.

Throwing the elderly woman a nod of gratitude, Lauren turned back to peer around the edge of the wall, grimacing as she saw the three white-skinned figures that were crouched down on the floor of the kitchen some twenty feet away near a bank of ovens, their hands and teeth tearing into the body of what might have once been human but was now little more than just bloody meat. Releasing a shaky breath, Lauren dropped down to a crouch, eyes narrowing as she stared past the metal wash station beside the wall, studying the three white-skinned figures in disgust and confusion, realising that one of them was dressed in nurses scrubs, while the other two wore what looked like kitchen overalls, each of them bald, their skin covered in the same calloused and cracked flesh as the others in the restaurant. They had rushed past the counter from the carnage in the main restaurant to discover that the way to the door leading out was blocked by the trio of figures that were crouched around a struggling figure upon the floor, their hands hammering punches down and tearing at it, and heart in her mouth, she had led her companions behind the large workstation where they were now hiding. The figure they had been attacking had long-since stopped moving, and Lauren had initially been content to wait, hoping that the trio would wander off so that she could get herself, Brandon and Mary out of the hospital to safety. Yet it had only taken a couple of moments for her to realise that as hidden as they were from the murderous trio of what Brandon had named ghouls, if any others from the restaurant came to the counter behind them they were in plain sight. Leaning back slightly, she turned to study her companions, the severely autistic young man, and the elderly lady, neither capable of fighting their way clear of the kitchen if the need arose. No, that was the worst-case scenario.

They needed somewhere better to hide, to wait. Then, and only then, when the coast was clear, would they be able to escape themselves.

A grimace creased her features as she glanced back at the trio, realising that maybe they wouldn't even need to escape. Reports of this would soon reach the emergency services and they would send people to help, most likely armed police or local territorial army reserves. Frowning, she let her gaze drift over the ghouls, wondering just what had happened to them. They had clearly been in good health earlier today, the very fact that they were wearing their work uniforms a clear indication that they had recently had their wits about themselves.

So, what had occurred?

What had turned them from everyday normal human beings into these mindless ghouls?

She shook her head as the white-skinned figure in the nurse's scrubs suddenly snarled at one off those in overalls, snatching the hunk of meat from its hands and Lauren fought the nausea that washed through her as she saw that it was a foot, the remains of a blood soaked sock hanging from the ragged stump. As she watched, the nurse thing shoved the foot into its mouth, crunching down, as it began to chew, and she realised how perfect Brandon's name for the creatures was.

Ghouls.

Creatures that preyed upon the dead.

What better name could there be for them?

She flinched as the ghoul that had lost possession of their victims foot suddenly turned in her direction, its face tilting as if it were sniffing the air, that thick beige liquid still running from its eyes like tears, dripping to its bloody clothes. Lauren winced suddenly, her stomach knotting as she caught the sudden stench of something, recognition touching her almost at once as she recalled growing up in her parents home, and how a cat had got stuck in the closed off chimney. It had been summer, the hottest on record, and the first that they known of the cat's presence was when it had begun to fester and rot away, the stench of its decaying carcass lingering in the home for weeks. Even afterwards, in subsequent summers, whenever it got too hot it was if the faint smell of that rotting cat had returned. Trying not to breathe through her nose, she edged back, her stomach knotting as she turned her gaze, desperately seeking some place that she and her companions could find sanctuary. They had entered the kitchen not that long after the arrogant security guard had fled that way, yet they had not seen him anywhere within it yet. Had he managed to get out of the door before the trio of ghouls had begun attacking their victim? No, surely not. The fact that two of the ghouls appeared to be kitchen staff suggesting that they had been here all the while. So, where was he? She flicked her gaze back to the bloody ruin of the figure between the trio of ghouls, eyebrows rising as she suddenly thought that she had worked out the location of the vile man, then realised her mistake as one of them moved and she saw the long blonde hair sprouting from the skinless bloody skull that one of them was gnawing upon, its teeth crunching on the spinal cord as it held the decapitated head upside down. Gagging, Lauren turned her head quickly away and suddenly saw the security guard watching her through the small round window in a door that she had not noticed until now, across the aisle where she and her companions were hiding. His eyes widened as she raised a hand, his bearded features twisting as she mouthed the word, *help* us, prayer hands forming before her. Yet instead of reacting in a positive manner, the guard took a step back from the window, his features barely visible through the thick glass.

"What is he doing?" the hushed voice of Mary appeared at her shoulder, and Lauren turned to find the elderly woman staring at the door in disbelief, her head shaking, "Is he ignoring us?" Lauren grimaced, knowing that it was exactly what the security guard was doing but not wanting to confirm the old woman's suspicions and steal away the brief chance of salvation.

"Maybe he didn't see us"

"He saw us" Mary grimaced, her voice a hushed whisper, "The cunt...he's left us out here!"

"Are we going back to the ward soon?" the voice of Brandon suddenly asked, speaking at his usual booming volume, no sense of danger in his voice, and feeling like she had been kicked in the gut by a horse, Lauren rose to her feet, and cast him a look of shock, Mary moving alongside him, her winkled left hand rising to cover his open mouth. Not daring to breathe, her heart hammering in her chest, Lauren turned slowly, glancing back around the edge of the workstation, trying not to whimper in dread as she found all three of the ghouls on their feet, heads turned their way. Head shaking in dread, she took a step towards her two companions, one arm slipping about Brandon as he covered his eyes with his free hand, her other grasping to the free hand of Mary as she and the old woman stared at the corner. With a snarl, the ghoul in the nurse's scrubs edged past the workstation, bent forwards slightly if she was suffering back problems, her white features turning back and forth as she stared at Lauren and her companions then glanced away, moving towards the counter. Dumbstruck, the nurse let her gaze drift back to the corner, watching as the other two ghoul's crept into view, the heads turning back and forth as if searching for something they had lost, snarling and jostling at each other as they moved.

Grimacing against the sudden smell that came with the trio, Lauren watched as the two in the kitchen overalls became suddenly embroiled in a shoving match, snarling at each other like a pair of cats fighting, one of them dislodging a large pan that had been boiling on one of the hobs. As the pot tipped, it deposited its contents over the chest and legs of the nearest ghoul, steam rising from the clothes and hard white-skin off the figure yet it seemed unfazed by the boiling liquid, its pus filled eyes following the heavy pan as it struck the floor with a clatter and rolled towards the counter, the trio moving to follow it. For several moments there was chaos as the three ghouls fought each other to pick it up, the nurse finally succeeding only to cast the pot aside with another snarl, leaping effortlessly up onto the counter, and then down the other side, its two brethren following it as it moved out of sight. Time lost all meaning for Lauren as she stood there, staring at Mary in shock, the expression upon the old woman's face showing that she was as stunned as the nurse that they were still alive. "Come on!" she suddenly pushed herself away from where they had been standing, Brandon uncovering his eyes as Lauren led him across the kitchen, and past the remains of the unfortunate victim of the ghouls, Mary close behind them. Gritting her teeth, Lauren reached out a hand, turning the handle on the door, and opened it a crack, her breath leaving her in a shaky sigh as she saw that the corridor beyond seemed empty. She flinched as a snarl came from somewhere out of sight along the corridor, towards where she knew the entrance to the restaurant was, then turning her head right, she saw the elevators. "Come on!" she opened the door wider, leading her two companions out into the corridor, cringing as more snarls sounded from the direction of the restaurant, then cursed as a scream floated down out of the door to the stairwell situated beside the elevator doors. *Was this happening all over the hospital?* Grimacing, she hurried to the elevator, reaching out with her free hand as she punched the call button, Brandon and Mary moving alongside her, then the nurse gasped in dread as the door to a utility cupboard suddenly swung open opposite them, a pair of familiar figures rushing out. "Wait for us!" the red-faced features of the ginger man from the restaurant earlier demanded as he reached them, one hand clutching to the handle of a mop, and Lauren grimaced at him, then turned her face to meet the weary gaze of the short-haired black woman who was with him. For a second, they held each other's gaze in silence and then with a soft chime, the doors to the elevator slid open beside them and Lauren turned, staring into its confines at the three woman that were inside it, one standing, one lying down and the third crouching at her side.

Chapter Fifteen

Almost before the doors had widened enough for him to enter, the ginger man was pushing his way inside, throwing a glare at the thin brown-haired woman with glasses that stood staring back at him, "Is there a problem?"

"Aye ye prick" the woman, clearly Scots gave a sneer, stepping past the ginger man as he moved to stand with his back to the rear of the elevator, her right hand reaching out to help Mary and Brandon inside, "Did ye nae hear of lasses and bairns first?"

He grimaced but stayed silent, and at the back of their small group, Lauren watched as his eyes fell to the two women on the floor near his feet, a brown-haired unconscious woman in a leather jacket, jeans and boots, and the Indian woman that was crouching down beside her, a knife held in one of her hands. For a moment, it looked like he was going to make a comment but then changed his mind, a hand gesturing towards the black woman that waited beside Lauren, "For fuck sake, Jennifer, will you get inside now!"

The woman flinched, eyes half closing and then she was stepping forwards, ignoring the look of the Scots woman as she turned to glare at her husband, her eyes locked to the elevator floor.

"Are ye coming?" the Scots woman turned to throw Lauren a questioning stare, and she blinked, suddenly realising that she was the only one still standing in the corridor, a sudden roar from the restaurant area sending her rushing forwards and inside. Instantly, the Scots woman stepped forwards, fingers reaching out to press the button for the ground floor, nodding as before her the doors began to slide together. Suddenly there was the sound of a door crashing open, and footsteps upon the tiled floor, and then the familiar features of the bearded security guard appeared through the gap in the doors, his hands reaching through to stop them, "Wait for me!"

Grimacing in anger, well aware that he had left her, Mary and Brandon to be killed, Lauren glared at the man as he forced his way inside to stand with his back to the doors as they closed. For a moment, their eyes met and his top lip curled amid his moustache but then he was glancing away, his eyes dropping to the figure of the woman in the leather jacket who was now sitting up, the Indian woman still crouched beside her, knife in hand. Grimacing, the guard pointed with a finger, his tone thick with anger and dread, "What's up with her!"

"She fainted" the Scots woman sent him a glare, undaunted by the large man as she held his gaze confidently, "We were attacked by something on the second floor"

"Did it bite her?" the guard made a face, edging away, "If its bit her she will become like them!" At his words, the ginger man edged away from the two women upon the floor, dragging his wife roughly with him, and frowning in confusion, the Indian woman rose to her feet, her words lost to her own language, and the security guard made a face of disgust, "Fuck sake, what's it saying?"

"She!" the woman in the leather jacket pushed herself to her feet, her tone angry and Lauren recognised her suddenly as the woman that the security guard had shouted at in the restaurant earlier, "She's not an it!"

"Whatever" the bearded man turned away, his eyes drifting towards the control panel, a near sob of terror escaping him as he saw the lit numbers, "No...we cant go to the ground floor, stop the fucking elevator now!"

"We need tae get outta here!" the Scots woman grimaced, stepping in front of the control panel as the man took a step towards it, "Are ye mad?"

"I've been there!" he shook his head, and Lauren felt her stomach knot as she saw the fear in his eyes, "It's chaos...these fucking bastards are everywhere! I got called down there, but I came back up straight away...this whole place is infested with them...stop the fucking elevator!" For the first time, the Scots woman looked unsure, her face turning to glare at the ginger man as he suddenly pointed at her, "For fuck sake woman, do what he says and stop the elevator!"

"Wha did ye call me, prick?" her features were suddenly grim, nose crinkling as she took a step towards him, "Dinnae call me fucking woman!"

"Out of my fucking way you silly bitch!" the security guard suddenly pushed at the Scots woman, sending her stumbling off balance into Lauren and Brandon, the young black man letting out a scream of denial as he dropped his book. "Bastard!" the Scots woman snarled, spinning about to grasp at the security guard as he stood before the control panel, hammering on the buttons, a grunt escaping him as he fought to shrug her away, his voice loud as he shouted. "Get of me you silly cunt! I am trying to save us!" One hand banging against his head, Brandon had dropped to his knees, his free hand clasping to his book, and suddenly angry Lauren dropped to a crouch beside him, hugging the autistic man against her, watching as Mary pointed across the elevator at the guard that was still trying to disengage himself from the Scots woman, "Save us? You left us all to die, you horrible cunt!"

"Fuck off!" the bearded guard turned to snarl at her, one hand still pressing buttons on the control panel, his other trying to get the hand of his assailant from his neck, "Get off me!"

"Please will you all stop shouting!" Lauren glanced up, her head turning as she pleaded with the elevators full of strangers, one hand stroking the back of Brandon's head as he sobbed, "You are making him worse!"

Her eyes met those of the woman in the leather jacket, and without a word, the other dropped down to crouch with her, a hand gently patting Brandon upon the back as she too began to implore the others, "Please, everyone stop!"

"I will when this prick stops trying ta stop us getting outta here!" the Scots woman snarled.

"Leave him alone!" the ginger man suddenly made to move towards her back, his words a snarl as he reached out with his hands only to stagger back against the wall of the elevator as the Indian woman turned towards him, the knife that she was holding pointing against his chest.

"Are you insane!" he demanded, his eyes wide as he glanced from the woman to the knife and then back again, and as Lauren watched, she snapped at him in her language, the words a mystery but her anger evident, and the man raised his hands either side of his face, "OK, OK, calm down!"

Without warning, the elevator suddenly rumbled and stopped, the lights fading briefly, drawing a curse of shock from several of its occupants, and then just as quickly the lights came back on.

"What have you done?" the Scots woman released the guard as if he was on fire, her head shaking as she stepped back to the wall, "Ye have gone and fucked the lift ye stupid bastard!"

"I stopped us getting killed, you dumb bitch" he gave a snarl, glaring at her as he stepped away.

"What's happened?" the voice of the black woman, Jennifer was little more than a whisper, and as Lauren glanced up, she saw her husbands features twist into a sneer as he glared at her.

"Will you stop asking stupid fucking questions!" Resisting the urge to intervene, knowing that her priority lay in calming her charge who was still sat sobbing gently held by both her and the woman in the leather jacket, Lauren turned her gaze among the others, her brow furrowed as she studied them each in turn. The security guard was now standing back against the doors once more, glaring angrily at the Scots woman as she stood before him, unafraid, the frail form of Mary standing nearby, watching with a grimace upon her features. To the left of Mary, the Indian woman had stepped back from the ginger man but the blade was still held ready before her, her attractive features set with a mask of anger, and as Lauren studied them, the Indian reached out with her free hand and gently touched the shoulder of the woman in the leather jacket, the pair exchanging smiles. Were they a couple?

As the woman turned back from the Indian, she nodded at Lauren, and the nurse gave an awkward smile in return, her gaze drifting to study the ginger man and his black wife as they stood silently at the back of the elevator, the features of the former set with anger, and the latter standing staring down at the floor below. Nine strangers. Trapped together in a metal box.

"What do we do now?" the voice of Mary asked suddenly, the eyes of everyone but Brandon and Jennifer turning to study the old woman and she shrugged, "Are we on the ground floor?"

"We are safe" the security guard gave an arrogant sneer, a thumb jerking towards where the Scots woman stood glaring at him, "Despite this idiot trying to get us all killed, I have saved us all…" His words turned to a curse as with a soft chime, the elevator doors suddenly opened and he almost toppled backwards, barely managing to right himself as he spun about, a whimper escaping him. On the floor of the elevator, Lauren stared out past his legs at the scene of carnage that lay beyond in the foyer and the accident and emergency area of the hospital, her hair feeling like it had a thousand spiders in it as she saw the horde of white-skinned ghouls that were there all turn and stare at them in curiosity, then hatred. With a curse, the Scots woman leaned to the side, pressing a number on the control panel and as the ghouls gave an almost unified roar and surged towards them, the doors began to close. They were almost shut, barely a foot remaining open when the closest of the ghouls slid through into the elevator with them, its body clad in what looked like a tracksuit, trainers upon its feet. As it charged in, it tripped over the woman in the leather jacket and fell heavily into the far corner, a hiss escaping it as it pushed itself fluidly to crouch cat-like, teeth baring at the nine figures around it as they fought to get away from it. Then as the elevator began to slowly travel back up through the hospital it snarled and attacked.

Chapter Sixteen

"This is it" Bella stopped as she left the tree-line, a hand gesturing ahead of them, while she turned to meet the gaze of both Victor and Moonshine.

"You live here alone?" the shorter man asked, and beside him Victor winced as he saw the cheek muscles of the woman suddenly tense.

"I do now"

Without another word she turned, heading across the open ground towards another fence that lay ahead and casting his friend a look of disbelief, Victor began to follow her, the voice of Moonshine a whisper, "What? I only asked"

"They are dead" Victor winced, casting a glance at the back of the woman as she climbed over the fence ahead of them, then met Moonshine's eyes once more, "She said she had killed two of these white-skinned creatures...that was them"

As he began to walk once more, Moonshine hobbled after him, still using the large branch as a crutch, "How on earth do you know that?"

"I listened" Victor sighed heavily, pausing as he reached the fence where the woman was waiting, his head turning back to Moonshine, "Come on"

The shorter man nodded, wincing as he reached them, and carefully, Victor helped him negotiate his way up and onto the top bar of the fence.

"Wait here" the woman gave them a nod, clasping the shotgun with both hands as she began to move away from them, and nodding, Victor let his gaze drift over their surroundings in interest. They were at the edge of a farmyard, several large outbuildings and a barn laying over to their left inside the wooden fence, the woman Bella, vanishing down that way, while ahead of them sat the farmhouse itself, a wide two level building constructed of what looked like magnesium limestone, a sense of sadness settling about Victors shoulders as he realised that his church had been made from the same material, the sadness replaced by anger almost immediately.

"Hey, are you alright, Dog?"

Victor blinked as Moonshine spoke, and turning, he raised his gaze to where the man sat atop the fence, one hand resting atop his broken left leg.

"How's the leg?" Victor grimaced, ignoring his friends question as he suppressed his memories.

"Oh, it is just wavering between burning agony and raw agony" Moonshine forced a smile, and gave a shrug, "I'm trying to decide which of the two I prefer"

Victor shook his head, smiling grimly, "I am going to get you to the hospital, I promise you mate"

Moonshine nodded, smiling, then gestured to the

farmhouse with a hand, "So what you reckon happened here then...you really think she had killed her grandparents?"

Victor shrugged, his voice grim, "She implied she did, I think she has, yeah"

"Fucking Hell"

Grimacing, Victor opened his mouth to speak once more then turned his head as he heard a car, his brow furrowing as he watched a marine blue Land Rover drive into view from the direction Bella had walked, the roof a dirty beige.

"Is that her?" Moonshine raised an eyebrow, his own eyes locked to the rapidly approaching vehicle, his voice unsure, "Those fucking things can't drive can they, Dog?"

"It's her" Victor sent his friend a smile, climbing over the fence himself to watch as the old Land Rover drew nearer, the familiar figure of Bella sat behind the wheel as she pulled up next to them.

"Put your friend in the back" the silver-haired woman nodded at Victor as she got out of the Land Rover, the shotgun in her hands once more as she glanced about, "I'll keep watch"

"If you tell anyone about this, I'm going to kill you" Victor stepped to the rear of the vehicle, opening it wide before he moved back to where his friend waited and held out his arms to pick

Moonshine up like a blushing bride. Carrying his friend to the back of the vehicle, he sat him on the rear of it, and nodded, "Can you slide in on your own OK or are you going to need help?"

"Nah, I'm good" Moonshine gently rested his broken leg down, and gritting his teeth, he began to scoot himself back into the open rear of the Land Rover, until he had his back to the wall behind the front seats, and Victor turned to meet the gaze of the woman as she moved to their side.

"You two wait here" she nodded, "I'll go and get the kids and Lexi and Castiel and bring them out...then we can get your friend to the hospital"

The two men exchanged glances at her words, Victor raising an eyebrow, "I thought you said you lived here alone with your grandparents?"

She gave a half-smile, "I said this was my grand-parents farm...Lexi and Castiel are my kids"

Victor nodded, casting Moonshine a glance and then he shrugged, "I'll come with you"

"What?" she seemed unsure, "It's fine"

"What if there are more?" he stated, his features grim, "What if the ones that chased us from the A66 find their way to your farm...what then?"

Before him, Bella grimaced, then nodded, "OK"

"Wait here" Victor turned to look in at a pale-faced Moonshine, "Keep the doors locked OK"

His friend winced, and nodded, "Yeah, sure"
Suddenly regretting his decision to leave his
injured friend alone but not wanting to back out
of his offer to help the woman that had come
looking for them, Victor swung the back door of
the Land Rover shut and turned, "Let's go"
She nodded, turning away as she began to walk
towards the farmhouse, pausing every ten steps
or so, her head turning as she glanced about, the
shogun held ready in her hands, expression grim.
"Army?" he asked, as she stopped for a fourth
time, and before him she tensed, head shaking.
"Ex-army"
He nodded, knowing that she couldn't see the act
but feeling inclined to show acknowledgement.
Before him, Bella began moving once more, then
paused with ten feet separating them from the
house, her eyes scanning the yard beyond them
before meeting his gaze, "How did you know?"
Victor winced, shrugging, "There were a couple
of guys in my therapy group who were ex-army,
you just seem to have that same feel about you"
Bella nodded, her eyes travelling up and down
him, taking in his wet and muddy clothes, before
she raised an eyebrow, "You are a therapist?"

His chuckle was bitter, "No, I was a patient"

She licked at her lips, "What was the issue?"

"PTSD" he held her gaze, "Survivor guilt"

Something seemed to flicker in her eyes at his words, the muscles in her cheeks trembling like a vibrating guitar string and then she was turning away, moving towards the backdoor of the farmhouse, her right hand leaving the shotgun to drag a small black key from her jeans pocket.

As she stuck it in the lock and turned it, Victor shifted his feet, glancing about at the farmyard and the distant treeline, searching for trouble, then turned back as the voice of Bella sounded.

"Come on, get inside"

Glancing about, he saw her standing inside the property and with a nod, he hurried to join her, stepping into the cool of a large kitchen as Bella stepped back to the door, locking it behind them. Without pausing, she turned heading through a door to their left, and into a hallway, the walls clad with wooden panelling, and decorated with a set of embroidered images in picture frames.

"This way" Bella led him onwards, around a corner and towards a closed door at the end, the sound of excited barking coming from behind it.

"Do they bite?" Victor grimaced and she gave a faint smile, her head shaking as she paused.

"Lexi and Castiel? No…not unless I tell them to"

"Your children" he gave a smile, nodding in sudden understanding, then frowned as he caught her suddenly staring at the closed door directly to his left, her cheeks tensing once more. Turning, his back to the wall, he studied the door for a moment and then glanced back at her, his voice barely audible, "What is it?"

She winced, head shaking, "My grandparents"

Victor grimaced, reaching out for the door handle only to pause as she shook her head, her voice a hushed whisper, "Stop…don't"

He grimaced, holding her gaze, "Are they dead?"

She nodded, a haunted look in her eyes and he nodded, his right hand grasping the handle and turning it before she could protest once more.

The door swung open with a creak to reveal what appeared to be a sitting room, a large television sitting upon a stand against the far wall, a sofa and two armchairs spread around the walls.

For a moment, he studied the décor, immersing himself in the homely feel of the room, despite its dated carpet and wallpaper, his grey eyes fixing to a large crucifix which hung upon the wall behind the sofa, his hands forming into fists as he studied the diminutive figure upon the cross.

Then with a grimace, he let his gaze drift down to study the two white-skinned figures that lay on the floor, one slumped on its side against the base of the television stand, the top half of its head missing, the other lying upon its back near the fireplace that dominated a wall of the room, its chest a bloody ruin, the former in trousers, shirt and braces, the latter in a pink dressing gown, a slipper still attached to one of its feet. Without thinking, he moved to crouch beside the figure in the dressing gown, brow furrowing as he studied her features, the same thick white calloused skin on her face as that which had been on the other figures that they had encountered. On instinct, he raised his right hand, making the sign of the cross before him, his lips moving as he closed his eyes, "Eternal rest, grant unto her, O LORD, and let perpetual light shine upon her, may she rest in peace, amen"

He tensed as movement sounded in the doorway, and he opened his eyes, turning to find Bella watching him in a mixture of grief and disbelief, her head shaking, "What are you doing?"

"Praying for their souls" he turned away from her, moving to crouch beside the figure that had obviously been her grandfather, repeating the male version of the prayer before he rose once more, shrugging as he held her gaze, "What?"

She frowned for a moment, her eyes drifting over him in silence and then she gave a shake of her head, "You said that you worked for the Forestry Commission, not that you were a priest"

Victor winced, "I'm not, not anymore, I failed"

She shook her head, "How do you fail at being a priest, I don't understand"

Releasing a shaky sigh, Victor shrugged, a hand rising to rub at his forehead, "I lost my faith"

Bella studied him in silence for what seemed an eternity, then shook her head, "If you lost your faith why are you praying for my grandparents?"

Victor's laugh was bitter as he held her gaze, "I never lost my faith in God...I lost my faith in me"

Chapter Seventeen

Nearly a minute passed by as they stood holding each other's gaze in the sitting room, the barking of the dogs cutting off in the background, and then Victor forced a smile, "The children?"

Bella nodded, stepping back through the door, turning towards the door that they had been approaching before Victor had entered the sitting room, and once again, the dogs began to bark. Reaching out with yet another key, Bella placed it inside the lock and turned it, her hand resting upon the handle for a moment as she turned around and gave Victor a grim smile, "Best to just stand there for a moment and let Lexi and Castiel get to know you first"

He nodded in reply, grimacing, and then with a turn of her hand, Bella pushed the door open wide to reveal a large downstairs bedroom. Victor had the briefest of moments to see the familiar faces of the two children at the back of the room, the girl seated upon the edge of the bed, the young boy beside her, then two furry shapes barged past the legs of Bella towards him, a large German Shepherd and Border Collie. Barking excitedly the black and white collie rushed about the legs of the bearded ranger, his hands shoved firmly into his pockets on the off chance that they did bite, while the German Shepherd squatted before him, growling low in the back of its throat, ears flat against its head.

"Cas!" the voice of Bella took on a stern tone, and as if she had flipped a switch, the tail of the bigger dog began to wag lazily and he moved forward to sniff at the shoes of the ranger.

"Hey guys" Victor lowered his gaze to watch as apparently satisfied, the German Shepherd sat down before him, and the border collie joined it, then he raised his eyes to find Bella watching him curiously, "Are we good?"

They seem to like you...I trust them" she nodded back at him, "More than most people"

"I get that" he found himself smiling grimly, "I do"

For a moment, the woman matched his awkward smile, and then she gave a short whistle, the dogs turning to move back inside the room and sit by her, as she gestured towards the children, "There you go, as promised"

Suddenly awkward, realising with shock that he didn't actually know the children's names, Victor took several steps towards the bed and stopped, unsure exactly what to say, "Hey"

Upon the bed the brother and sister exchanged glances, and then to his surprise raced across the room towards him, the boy wrapping his arms about his legs while the girl threw hers about his waist, their faces pressed against him. Throat tight with emotion, touched by the moment, Victor raised his face to meet that of Bella and she gave a smile, gesturing for him to embrace them, but he shook his head, wincing as he did so. as if on a pre-arranged cue, both children suddenly broke their hold upon him, the girl raising a eyebrow as she met his gaze, her nose wrinkling in disgust, "Why are your clothes soaking wet...oh my God"

"Is it sweat?" the boy asked with interest as he glanced up at Victor, "I sweat a lot"

"Shut up, that's gross!" the girl sent him a glare then turned to stare at Victor, "It's not, right?"

He shook his head, "No, I fell in a river"

"How did you fall in a river?"

Victor winced, glancing at Bella and then looked back at the boy as he spoke again, his voice a hushed whisper, "Were you fighting one of those snow people!"

"Snow people?" Victor frowned for a moment and then nodded in understanding, "Yes"

"Are there more?" the girl asked, fear in her tone.

"Are we going to be eaten?" the boy sounded close to tears, his face screwing up, and forcing a smile, Victor turned from the girl and dropped to a crouch in front of him, "What's your name?"

"Eric...Eric Kim...I'm six"

"OK, Eric" the ranger nodded, forcing a smile, "My name is Victor, but people call me Dog"

"Why?"

"They just do" Victor frowned, "It's a nickname"

"What's a nickname?" Eric made a confused face. Closing his eyes, wishing that Moonshine was there with them, Victor shook his head, and met the gaze of the boy again, "It doesn't matter, what matters is that you are not going to get eaten"

"Promise you'll keep me safe?" Eric held his gaze.

"Sure" Victor blinked, recalling a similar time with his own children many years before, the subject of the moment gone from his memory.

"You have to say promise, or it isn't true" Eric looked suddenly scared, his eyes drifting to the face of his sister before drifting back to Victor.

"I promise I'll keep you safe" he nodded, the words like ash in his mouth, the cries of his children sounding in his memory as they burned. Suddenly dizzy, he rose to his feet, a hand rising to rub at his temple for a moment, then he glanced back at Bella as she spoke, "Are you OK?"

He nodded, knowing that it showed upon his face that he wasn't, but instead of seeing judgement, he saw the look of understanding in her eyes. Oblivious to the tension, the young boy suddenly raised a hand gesturing at the girl, "This is my sister Emily Kim, she's twelve or something old like that"

"I'm thirteen you toad"

"Don't call me a toad!" the boy was indignant.

"Then don't call me old" she sent him a withering glare, rolling her eyes as she turned back to look at Victor, "Are the police here?"

"No" he shook his head at her, eyes drifting to Bella, "Can we phone them?"

Her expression was grim, "I've tried...all morning...I can't get a response from anyone, they all seem to be too busy..."

"Too busy?" Victor swallowed the tightness in his throat as he pictured the pile-up on the A66, suddenly unsure how far spread this event was.

"We should get your friend to the hospital in Thames" Bella held his gaze, "I'll drive, we can contact the police there for these two"

"Sounds like a plan" Victor nodded, "How far?"

"About fifteen minutes if there's no traffic"

No traffic. Christ.

"Come on" the woman began to head back out of the room, the shotgun brandished before her once more, the dogs running beside her, and nodding, Victor and the children followed, he taking up the rear. They turned as they reached the bend in the corridor, and then Bella cursed, turning to throw them a glance, "Wait here" "Problem?" Victor raised an eyebrow and she shook her head as she moved to a door to their right, holding the shotgun with one hand as she opened it wide to reveal what looked like a study. "I only have about three shells in my pocket and two in the gun, I better grab some more from grandads gun cabinet just to be on the safe side" He nodded, watching as the dogs ran off down the hallway towards the back door, and then turned to study Bella as she took three steps into the room then stopped, her eyes turning to stare to the left as she cursed, the sound thick with dread, and on instinct, he stepped to the door. His bearded features twisted in dread as he saw the trio of white-skinned figures that stood outside the rooms wide window, one of them pressing its hands to the glass as it stared in at them, smearing the pane with the sickly beige liquid that had run from its eyes down its face.

"Easy, the ones in the forest couldn't see us when we stopped moving...keep still" Victor let out a shaky breath, as he edged back from the door, his hands gesturing for the children to back away.

"If I keep still, they won't see me?" the voice of the woman was tight, her words barely audible.

"Maybe" Victor whispered back, his brow furrowing as he saw her right hand leave the shotgun and slide down towards her jeans, the movement so slow that the action took almost a minute. Heart in his mouth, he watched as she reached into her pocket, and withdrew the car keys, her whisper sounding again, "I am going to throw you these...get the kids, my dogs and your mate out of here"

"No" his voice was a hiss, his head shaking even though she was facing away, "Don't you do it!"

"Shut up" she gave a soft chuckle, "Not your call"

He grimaced, "Bella!"

She flinched slightly as from beyond the glass, one of the creatures suddenly gave a snarl, and instantly Castiel and Lexie were back, rushing down the hallway and into the room with their mistress, barking and snarling defensively. Almost at once there was a smash of glass and shouting in fear and anger, Bella spun, the shotgun sweeping wide across at chest height, discharging both barrels into the intruders. There was a roar of rage or pain, and then the woman was backing from the room as she broke the shotgun and ejected the shells, her fingers snatching two more from her jeans pocket to fill the barrels, voice loud as she called to her dogs.

"Run!" Victor shouted at Emily as he snatched Eric up into his arms, a gasp of pain shooting through his ribs from his collision with the tree. Instantly she was off, racing for the back door, and following her, Victor glanced back, watching as Bella backed towards him, still calling for her dogs, concern in her voice as frenzied snarling from both the animals and the intruders erupted within the study. Then suddenly they were there, barking like mad as they raced from the room, barging past as they raced into the kitchen. Turning back around, the young boy hanging tightly onto him, Victor saw Emily already at the back door, and he called out, "Get to the car!"

"It's locked!" she cried out, fear in her eyes as she glanced back at him, "I can't open it, Dog!"

"Bella!" Victor spun about as he reached the girl, his voice loud, "We need the fucking key!"

She turned as she reached the kitchen, a hand thrusting deep into a pocket and then she threw the small black key to him, his right hand releasing his hold on Eric to catch it cleanly. Heart in his mouth, trying to focus past the terrified screams of the children, and the barking of the dogs, he passed the girl the key, and turned back to stare down the hallway past Bella, his stomach knotting as he saw the trio of white-skinned figures shambling into view, snarling.

As one, the dogs moved to stand before Bella, growling and barking angrily, the muzzles of both twisting as they vented their anger at the strange intruders into the home of their mistress.

"Shoot them!" Victor shouted, "Shoot them!"

She did, the boom of the discharging barrels loud in the confines of the hallway, and as Eric scream aloud in his ear, Victor watched as the figures were thrown heavily back by the payload, thrown from their feet to collapse into a pile.

"I've got it!" Emily cried out, the door suddenly swung open behind them, and without hesitating, Victor was charging from the kitchen, following the girl as she raced for the Land Rover ahead. As they drew near, the rear of the vehicle opened wide, the voice of Moonshine urging them on. They reached it in no time, Emily clambering up inside, and turning, Victor passed Eric to his friend, then turned back, watching as Bella charged towards them, the dogs at her side. "Are you OK?" he threw her a glance as she let the pair of dogs jump into the back and shut the door, then passed him the shotgun, as she hurried around to the driver's side. Grimacing, he turned, heading around to open the passenger sided door to clamber in beside her, "What is it?" "They aren't dead" her voice was grim, and he blinked, following her gaze as she turned to look at the door that they had just left, his blood turning to ice as he saw the trio of white-skinned figures emerge into the sunlight, crouching low as they screamed in hatred at the Land Rover. As Bella gunned the engine, swinging the vehicle around in a big circle, Victor kept his eyes locked to the creatures, no longer human in his eyes, then they were racing past and away, leaving the primitive white-skinned monstrosities behind.

Chapter Eighteen

As the white-skinned figure surged forwards, teeth snapping at the air, hands reaching wildly, chaos broke loose among the elevator's other occupants. With a curse, the security guard backed hurriedly into the control panel beside the door, the Scots woman named Geri doing the same, their previous confrontation forgotten, and on the floor in the centre of the elevator, Alice pushed herself to her feet, one hand dragging at the arm of the young black man that she had been trying to help the young nurse placate, trying to encourage him to move out of the way. "Come on, Brandon!" the nurse urged as she too rose, grasping the man's other hand, "Get up!" "My book!" he screamed, shrugging both women away from him, his strength surprising as he dropped back to his hands and knees, fingers grasping for the book that he had dropped. With a snarl, the white-skinned figure in the tracksuit rushed for the kneeling man, the screams of both young women loud as they saw its rapid approach, but then there was a flash of yellow as Jiyaa stepped towards it, her left leg stretching out to trip the enraged figure over. With a grunt of shock it fell, crashing to the floor just a foot from the black man, and as if suddenly realising it was there, he screamed in terror and recoiled away, hands clapping his ears, "Ghoul!" Snarling, it started to rise, and young black man scooted back, huddled in tight against the legs of Alice and the nurse, their small group of three pressed against the wall beside where Geri and the guard stood shouting in shock. With a cry of anguish, Jiyaa suddenly lashed out at their assailant with her brother's knife as it tried to rise, yet the blade seemed to simply turn aside on its hard, cracked skin, and she grunted as it lashed out with a forearm, the blow catching her across the head, sending her crashing into the old woman that was stood behind her. As the two women fell to the floor, the knife dropped from the fingers of the Sikh woman, skittering away across the floor of the elevator to be suddenly snatched up by the grinning ginger man, "Got it!" Heart racing, Alice watched as the creature that the man named Brandon had just called a ghoul, suddenly turned at the sound of the ginger mans voice, its milky beige eyes widening as it saw that he was now clasping the weapon that it had just been attacked with. Snarling, it surged to its feet and threw itself at him, the force of the impact crashing the ginger man back into the wall of the elevator and forward once more, the pair crashing heavily to the floor, the ghoul growling like a feral cat, the man screaming in pure terror. "Get it off me...get it off me!"

Without hesitating the black woman with the short hair that had been standing with the arrogant man rushed to the struggling pair, her hands reaching down to grasp at the tracksuit of the enraged ghoul, screaming in horror as she tried to drag it from atop the sobbing ginger man. With a roar, it reared up, turning its head her way as it snarled in hatred and grunting in triumph, the ginger man lashed upwards with the knife, and Alice watched in disbelief as the blade glanced off the exposed throat of the ghoul and continued on its way, slicing into the hands of the black woman, blood splattering them both. Howling in dismay and shock, the black woman raised her hands before her, blinking as she stared at the deep cut that ran across them both, dark blood running from the wounds, and with a snarl of excitement, the ghoul threw itself at her. They landed hard, crashing down onto the floor beside Alice, Brandon and the nurse, and the embalmer cried out in alarm as she saw the latter quickly reach down to drag the ghoul free from the black woman, only to stagger back as it

lashed out with an arm like an iron bar, sending
her crashing over the kneeling figure of Brandon.
She grunted as the back of her head hit the floor
of the elevator, and cursing, Alice dropped down
beside her, wincing as she saw the nurse's bloody
nose, her hands trying to drag her to her feet.
Somehow they made it, the pair of them leaning
back against the door of the elevator, watching in
dread as the ghoul suddenly dipped its head, face
pressing against the shoulder of the black woman
and she screamed in agony, her body thrashing
beneath it as she fought to free herself from it.
"For the love of God, someone help her!" the old
woman that had been knocked to the floor by
Jiyaa cried out, and turning her head, Alice saw
that they were both back on their feet, the Sikh
having helped the older woman rise, yet her
bottom lip was split and the bite on her arm from
her brother's attack was bleeding profusely.
Time seemed to slow as Alice turned her head
about the elevator, taking in the terrified features
of the bearded security guard as he stood beside
the grimacing Geri, and the sobbing face of
Brandon as he sat with his back to the wall
beside the legs of the admin, hugging his book to
his chest, and then she turned her face past Jiyaa
and the old woman to study the pale horror

etched expression upon the face of the ginger man as he sat huddled in the corner where the ghoul had first landed, his knees brought up before him, the knife held limply in his left hand, his eyes watching the ghoul savage his saviour. "Help her!" Alice shouted at him, and his eyes met hers, his head shaking as he stared back. "She's your fucking wife!" the voice of the nurse grunted from beside the sobbing black man, as she shook her head, her left hand rising to try and stop her nose bleeding and Alice glanced back at the man in shock at her words, his refusal to get involved when she had just saved him even more galling now she knew their relationship. With a grunt, Alice rushed forwards and swung her right leg, her steel toe-capped boot sweeping out in an arc to catch the ghoul hard in the side of the head just as she had kicked Opinder in the chapel, the impact throwing it from the black woman to crash against the wall of the elevator. Instantly, the nurse was there beside Alice, the pair of them dragging the black woman to her feet and away towards the door, the embalmer wincing as she saw the ragged bite wound upon her bare left shoulder, blood running from it. The elevator suddenly stopped moving, the sudden lack of motion making Alice giddy slightly, and she turned, staring in dread as with a soft chime the doors behind her opened wide. Yet instead of the view of a dozen of more ghouls that they had been greeted with down in the foyer, there was nothing but an empty corridor. "Out of my fucking way!" the bearded security guard suddenly pushed past Alice and the nurse as they tried to support the semi-conscious black woman, the three of them nearly falling over. "Prick!" the nurse shouted at him, and unsure whether to laugh or cry, Alice met her gaze, the pair of them practically dragging the woman they had rescued out of the elevator into the corridor. "Move!" the ginger man was next, pushing over the figures of Geri and the old woman as the former attempted to help the latter from the elevator, the Scots woman cursing in anger as she landed hard and slid several feet upon the tiled floor, while the old woman lay groaning in pain. At the back of the elevator, the ghoul snarled and began to rise, and both Alice and the nurse cried out as it latched a hand to the right leg of Brandon as he attempted to escape into the corridor, helped by Jiyaa. With a grunt, the autistic man fell to his chest, a scream of terror escaping him as the ghoul began to drag him back inside the elevator, the unintelligible cries of Jiyaa loud as she clasped at his arms, trying to stop him from being taken. Without a word, both Alice and the young nurse were suddenly there beside Jiyaa, the three women, dragging upon the clothes of the autistic man as the fought to save him, their screams of denial loud in the corridor, while the ghoul snarled back at them in hatred. With a soft chime, the doors began to close, Brandon screaming in terror as they touched his waist and began to open once more, only to start to close again, his eyes wide and Alice cried out in dread as she felt them all sliding, the strength of the ghoul staggering as it began to pull them. Then without warning, the old woman was there, her wrinkled hands clasping to the closing doors as she stepped over both them and Brandon, her face etched with a look of raw determination. Without a word, she seemed to throw herself forwards at the ghoul, hands reaching for it, and with a snarl, it released its grip on the autistic man, and grasped excitedly to the old woman. With the opposite force gone from his legs, the three woman suddenly dragged the screaming Brandon out into the corridor, and cringing, Alice watched as the doors closed, her final view being of the old woman her beneath the ghoul, her eyes closed as it raked her with its hands, teeth bared.

As Brandon lay sobbing on the floor, his body curling into the foetal position, Alice rose unsteadily to her feet, joining the nurse and Jiyaa in staring at the closed elevator doors in shock.

Chapter Nineteen

"I can't believe she's gone" Lauren muttered, her throat feeling swollen with emotion, her eyes brimming with tears and as she blinked, several left her orbs and raced each other down her cheeks, dripping from her chin to the floor below. It had all happened so fast, one moment she, the woman in the leather jacket and the Indian woman were desperately trying to drag Brandon from the clutches of the ghoul, and the next the old woman had thrown herself into its grasp.

She had saved them all at the cost off her life.

It seemed unreal, that one moment she could be there and then gone the next, and Lauren had to remind herself that she had actually known the old woman for just an hour, maybe even less. Yet it seemed as if she had known her for years and had not been a stranger. She winced as she considered her words, head shaking slightly.

No, she hadn't been just another stranger.

She had been Mary Kent from North London, wife of George Kent and she had been a hero. Shaking her head, the nurse raised her gaze, studying the brown haired woman in the leather jacket once more, remembering that it was she that had come to her aid when the ghoul had struck her, and it had been she who had helped them drag the bitten black woman from the elevator while her husband did nothing to help. Fighting back the wave of anger that coursed through her unchecked as she considered the cowardice of the two men, she turned her gaze from the brown haired-woman and studied the Indian woman on the floor beside her, wincing as she saw her studying the bite wound in her arm. "Are you OK?" she asked, kneeling up and the woman glanced up at her, wincing as she shook her head, one hand rising to tap against her lips. "She doesn't speak English" the brown-haired woman announced as she crouched back down beside them both, "Her name is Jiyaa...I'm Alice" The nurse nodded, smiling weakly, gesturing first to herself and then the young black man who still lay sobbing upon the floor, "I'm Lauren, this is Brandon, are you two a couple?"

As the woman named Jiyaa frowned, her head shaking as she glanced at the woman in the leather jacket, Alice gave a soft laugh, "Not quite, I have only known her about half hour...we met in the chapel on floor two... her brother...well, he became one of these things...we ran, its where we met up with Geri"

"Geri?" Lauren raised an eyebrow, then turned as Alice gestured past her to where the Scots woman was sitting up staring at the lift doors as if in shock, her head shaking from side to side.

"Are you OK?" the voice of Alice made Lauren turn away from the Scots woman to find her kneeling down beside the black woman that they had saved from the elevator, "Can you hear me?"

Rising, Lauren moved to join the pair, dropping down to crouch beside them, a gently touching the black woman upon the hand but she seemed oblivious to their presence, her wide eyes staring straight ahead of her, one hand clasped to the bite in her shoulder, her lips moving soundlessly.

"She's in shock" Lauren nodded, turning her face to meet the gaze of Alice, nodding as she spoke.

"What can we do for her?"

Lauren winced, her head turning to study the signs hanging from the ceiling, realising that they were on the fifth floor of the hospital, the surgical unit, and then met the gaze of Alice again, "We need to keep her warm, clean her wound and stop the bleeding in her shoulder and her hands, the same with your friend's forearm"

Alice nodded, turning to glance back and Lauren followed her gaze, smiling weakly as she saw Jiyaa sat beside the sobbing figure of Brandon as he still lay curled upon the floor, one hand resting upon his shoulder as she softly hummed, perhaps attempting to soothe the young man. "Ye spineless fucking cunts!" Lauren flinched as she heard the bitter snarl, her head snapping to the side to watch in shock as the Scots woman that Alice had referred to as Geri pushed herself to her feet and turned to look past the women. Grimacing, Lauren rose to her feet, Alice joining her, while Jiyaa stayed where she was with Brandon, still humming but her face troubled as Geri took six quick steps that brought her level with the badly injured black woman, a finger pointing off down the corridor, "Ye killed her!" Releasing a shaky breath, Lauren turned, her nose wrinkling in disgust and anger as she saw the two men for the first time since they had barged from the elevator, the pair standing some distance on down the corridor, on opposite walls. "Geri!" Alice took a step alongside the ginger-haired woman, her voice soft, "Come on, leave it" "Leave it?" Geri was incredulous as she turned to stare back at the woman in the leather jacket, her head shaking as if she couldn't believe what she had just heard, a hand gesturing off down the corridor once more, "Tha old lady just died because these wankers were too busy running!"

"Fuck off!" the taunt came down the corridor and grimacing, Lauren turned her head to see the bearded security guard waving a dismissive hand at the Scots woman, head shaking as he glared. "What did ye just say?" the voice of Geri lowered, her head half turning to stare at him sideways. "You heard me, you mad cunt...fuck off" he took a step towards her, still some thirty feet between them and with a snarl, Geri began to run forward, Lauren and Alice breaking into a run to stop her. Grimacing, the security guard took a step back, but then suddenly the ginger man stepped away from the wall that he had been practically hugging, the knife that he had snatched from the elevator floor pointing towards the woman as he snarled, "Back the fuck off...I'm warning you!" Cursing, Geri stopped her run, Lauren and Alice doing the same, and the ginger man gave a broad smirk, "Yeah, not so tough now are you!"

"Like you, you mean?" Alice turned to glare at him, "Wouldn't do fuck all to help your wife when she was being attacked but you are quite happy to threaten three women with a knife"

"Aye" Geri gave a humourless chuckle, "He's definitely a big man, ain't he lasses"

"Don't you laugh at me...don't! the ginger man waved the knife before him, his features turning

red as he snarled, "I am warning you...!"
Grimacing, Lauren turned her gaze from the man
with the blade, glancing past him to where the
security guard stood with the ghost of a grin
twisting the corners of his mouth amid his beard.
"What are ye grinning about!" Geri suddenly
seemed to notice it too, and she took a quick step
to the side as if intending to try and go around
the ginger man, but he moved to block her path.
"I'm warning you!"
Between Lauren and Alice, Geri bristled but
stayed still, her gaze upon the security guard
instead of the man before her, and grimacing, the
nurse turned to stare back along the corridor at
where they had left Brandon, Jiyaa and the black
woman, relief touching her as she saw that her
charge was now sitting up, cross-legged, his book
on his lap, the Indian woman sitting before him.
She winced as the sound of footsteps sounded,
and she turned, frowning as she saw the security
guard walking away down the corridor, the
ginger man following after him, and shaking her
head, Lauren called out, "Where are you going?"
They paused, the guard sneering as he glanced
back at them, "I'm getting out of here"

"What about us?" the nurse hated the needy tone in her voice, "We should all stick together, there is safety in numbers at the very least!"

"Fuck you" the ginger man sneered as he walked backwards, his steps taking him past the figure of the security guard, "Fuck all of you!"

"What about your wife?" Alice spoke up, drawing Lauren's gaze as the woman gestured back down the corridor towards where the black woman sat. For a moment, the ginger man stared at his wife in silence and then he gave a shake of his head, his top lip curling in disgust, "She's been bitten, her and that Paki!"

"Prick!" Alice grimaced and the man shrugged. "No way am I getting killed because they got too close to me and turned into one of those things!"

"It's not a zombie bite, you cretin!" Lauren snarled, filled with a sudden overwhelming anger as she stared at the ginger man with knife of Opinder, "This isn't a TV show, this is real!"

"I don't fucking care!" the man shook his head, his eyes locked to her, "There's no way you ar…"

"You can come with us" the security guard grunted, interrupting the ginger man, a finger rising to point at Geri, "But no more shit from you…do you understand…we all stick together for now…but any sign of either of the bitten

157

getting weird and you are all on your own!"

As the ginger man stared at the security guard in shock, the bearded man stepped towards him, muttering something and the other gave a smile, head nodding as he turned to study the women. Grimacing, Lauren turned away, heading back down towards the where their three companions waited, her head turning to find Alice was with her, the attractive features of the brown-haired woman twisting in confusion, "What's his game?"

Lauren turned, casting a glance past the figure of Geri as she stood staring at the two smiling men, then met the gaze of Alice once more, "If we are with them and more of the ghouls attack, they can escape while we get left behind...has to be it"

"Wankers" Alice grimaced, drawing a chuckle from Lauren as they reached Brandon and Jiyaa.

"Come on Brandon" Lauren stood before him, a hand gesturing down for him to take, "We have a letter to write remember?"

"We do" he nodded, a smile creasing his features as he rose, the trauma of their escape from the elevator and the death of Mary apparently forgotten as he nodded, "I need to use the toilet"

Groaning, Lauren winced, "We are going to have to get you to hold on for a few minutes OK?"

He nodded, rising slowly to his feet, and beside

him, Jiyaa did the same, smiling at both Alice and Lauren before moving to crouch beside the black woman, trying to help her rise. As Alice moved to assist Jiyaa, the black woman turned her head, her hand moving from her wound to her eyes, widening at the blood she saw on her fingers. Lauren moved before them as they managed to help her rise on shaky legs, the right hand of the nurse holding to one of Brandon's as she nodded at the black woman, "Jennifer isn't it?"

"Yes" her voice was soft, her eyes filled with the promise of tears, "Where's my husband?"

Lauren winced, wanting more than anything to remind the confused woman how her husband had abandoned her in the elevator and had just been about to leave her behind. Instead she smiled, gesturing with her free hand, "He is going on ahead to make sure we are all safe"

"Peter?" the black woman turned her head, her voice pleading, but in the distance the ginger man turned away, and Lauren felt suddenly sick. "I don't think he heard you"

As Jennifer turned her head to look, the two men began to walk away around the corner, and Geri turned to look back at them, gesturing with a hand, "Come on, girls"

Throwing the angry looking Scot's woman a grim smile, Lauren began to walk on with Brandon, while Jiyaa and Alice followed behind, supporting the disorientated Jennifer between them.

Chapter Twenty

One arm wrapped about the waist of Jennifer, Alice helped steer her down the long corridor, Jiyaa upon the other side of the black woman. It was easier now than when they had first helped her to stand, Jennifer finally managing to take steps and support herself much better than before, although she still looked like she had no idea what was going on, her eyes wide and blank. Grimacing, Alice turned her head, glancing down at the bite mark in the woman's shoulder beside her, trying to stop the dread that ran through her. Her husband had seemed convinced that she was now going to turn into one of the white-skinned creatures, Lauren had said that she and her small group had taken to calling them ghouls, but if that was the case, if she was going to turn into one then so was Jiyaa. Wincing, Alice glanced past Jennifer to where the Sikh woman was helping the black woman to walk, the eyes of the embalmer fixing to the bite mark in her forearm. The wound was grim, two bloody sets of teeth marks around a small island of flesh, and Alice imagined what would have happened had the young woman's enraged brother been able to complete the bite and tear that piece away.

Was she a danger? Was Jennifer?

How long had passed since the chapel attack? It seemed like hours ago but couldn't be more than thirty minutes at the most could it?

Thirty minutes and Jiyaa was still normal.

That had to mean something, after all, from Opinder first showing signs that something was wrong he had changed to the new ghoul form in less than five minutes. Surely if bites carried whatever virus it was that was changing people, Jiyaa would already be a slavering insane beast. Alice forced a smile as she caught Lauren glancing back at her from where the young nurse was walking ahead, and despite the dire situation the embalmer felt the flush of attraction course through her, only for guilt to replace it as she recalled her reason for being there in Thames. Sarah was dead. Dead and gone.

She frowned at the thought, realising what a strange turn of events it had been to have put her in this hospital at the very moment that this new outbreak of whatever it was occurred, her stomach tightening as she suddenly wondered if it was happening elsewhere across the country. The first virus had been bad enough, the second wave even worse, but despite the fact that it had killed over eight million people in England alone, the disease had just turned people into frail figures, coughing and gasping for breath.

Not like this, not transforming them into violent murderers. She grimaced as she recalled how Opinder had thrown her and his sister around in the chapel as if they had weighed nothing, and how strong the ghoul in the elevator had been. What sort of virus was this? What was going on? She blinked as she suddenly realised that they had reached the corner, and followed it, watching as ahead of them, Lauren and the young man Brandon walked together, the Scots woman several paces in front of them, while in the distance the security guard and the ginger man, Peter, were walking cautiously, glancing about. Suddenly nervous, Alice turned her head, glancing back at the corner that they had just rounded, her ears straining for any sound.

What if somehow the ghoul managed to open the door to the elevator? It would come for them without question, and there would be deaths. Like that poor old woman who had sacrificed herself to save Brandon. Shaking her head, Alice grimaced, turning to Jennifer, "Are you OK to walk by yourself now?"

"What?" the black woman met her gaze, blinking slowly and then nodded, "Of course, yes"

Wincing, Alice glanced at Jiyaa, a hand pointing to herself and then over to where Lauren and Brandon were walking, and the Sikh woman nodded, smiling weakly, surprising the embalmer as she spoke in broken English, "Please...to do so"

"I will be straight back" Alice nodded, not sure if the young woman understood her words, then she turned, walking quickly to catch up with the nurse and the Scots woman, "Hey"

"Hey" Lauren nodded back, turning to glance at Jiyaa and Jennifer, "Is everything OK?"

"Yeah, yeah" Alice nodded then made a face and shrugged, "Well, considering..."

Lauren nodded, letting out a sigh, "I get that"

For a moment, they walked side by side, Brandon on the nurse's far side and then Alice gestured back to the two women that she had just been walking with, "I think we need to get them out of the corridor and somewhere safe, they have both been bit...their wounds need treating"

"I agree" Lauren nodded at once, "Definitely"

"And so do you" Alice pointed with a finger, studying the blood on the younger woman's features, "That one back in the elevator...I thought it had broken your nose!"

The nurse gave a soft chuckle, "It's stopped bleeding...I'm just glad it didn't break my glasses"

Alice nodded, about to open her mouth when there came a curse from further down the corridor, the hairs rising upon her neck as she suddenly saw the two men backing from a door to their left, Geri taking a step backwards as well. "Oh God, no" Alice stopped walking, while Lauren shook her head, stepping protectively in front of Brandon, and letting out a shaky sigh of dread. "What is it?" the voice of Jennifer was loud as she and Jiyaa reached where the two women waited with Brandon, sudden awareness seeming to come over her as she saw her husband ahead. "Peter!" she took a step forwards, her voice raising in volume as she waved a hand, "Peter!" Near the end of the corridor, the ginger man turned to stare back at them in a mixture of shock and terror, while the guard stood with his back against the wall, his eyes locked to the door. "Peter?" the black woman began to move down the corridor, her steps suddenly quick, and as Jiyaa reached out to help, Jennifer shrugged her hands away, her eyes locked to the ginger man. "Shut up!" his hissed voice was nearly as loud as that of his wife, the irony of his words and his volume not lost on Alice as she gave a grim smile. "Peter!" Jennifer cried out again, her steps taking her past Geri as the Scots woman backed towards where Alice, Lauren, Jiyaa and Brandon waited, watching the scene in shock, "Help me!"

"Shut it up!" the security guard snapped his head towards the women as he took a step back in their direction, a hand gesturing towards the door, "There's something in there...somebody shut her the fuck up befo..."

The door suddenly crashed open, countless objects falling from within and the security guard gave a scream of terror, his feet catching upon each other as he turned to flee, his bulky form crashing down onto the corridor floor, while cursing and ducking, the ginger man rushed forwards, and grasped his wife, spinning her around as he stood behind her, one arm about her waist, the knife pointing out before him at the threat as he used his wife as a human shield. Standing back down the corridor, Alice stared on in disbelief as she saw the figure that had fallen from what had clearly been a cupboard push itself to its hands and knees, its shoulder length brown hair hanging about its features as it rose.

"Don't kill me!" the woman gave a cry that was half-snort, half sob, a hand brushing her hair back to reveal a face that seemed pinched together, the cheeks pale and doughy, eyes that were blank and set too far apart as they sat either side of a turned up nose. For a moment, the woman continued to whimper and sob, and then it suddenly seemed to notice the rising figure of the security guard, "Nick…is that you?"

"Tina?" the bearded guard straightened, brow furrowing as he stepped towards the woman.

"Oh thank fuck" the voice of the woman was coarse as she threw herself at the guard, arms wrapping about his back for a moment before she broke the embrace, her piggy eyes imploring him as she looked up, "Get me out of here Nick, I'll do whatever you like…name it…you know me, I'll make it worth your while!"

Despite the language barrier, Jiyaa muttered under her breath, understanding the woman's intentions, and Alice nodded in agreement.

With a curse, the ginger man suddenly released his hold on his wife, pushing the back of her neck so that she stumbled forwards away from him, a sneer creasing his features as he moved to stand behind the security guard and the woman, his eyes flicking to the small group of women that were watching, "You can have that back"

As Jennifer dropped to her knees, her head shaking in shock as she stared back at her husband, Geri moved to crouch beside her, a hand gently rubbing at the centre of her back.

As if woken from a dream, the woman, Tina, glanced behind them at the ginger man and then suddenly seemed to realise that there were other people in the corridor with them, her eyes widening as she studied the woman, "Who the fuck are *they*, Nick?"

He turned his head, his gaze drifting over the group that stood watching them, a strange look in his eyes as he studied Alice and Lauren, and then he shook his head, "Nobodies, Tina, just a bunch of nobodies"

The woman gave an almost porcine snort and chuckle, sneering as she looped an arm through one of his, "You only need me, doll"

The guard, apparently called Nick, nodded then grimaced as Geri rose and took a step towards the pair of them, "What did ye just call us?"

"Nobodies" he grimaced, nodding as he spoke.

"You heard him luv" Tina took a step away from Nick, a smirk on her features, "Go on, fuck off"

"Let me stop ye right there" the Scots woman gave a humourless chuckle, her head turning to glance at the woman, "If ye talk to me like tha again, ah'm gonna kick ye fucking cunt in!"

Blinking, the woman glanced at the guard and then shook her head at the Scots woman, "Easy, you don't know who you are messing wit..."

"Oh aye, ah know exactly who ye are" Geri gave a grim laugh, "Tina Williams, cleaner, the hospital bike, ye've had more prick than Ker' Plunk"

As the cleaner gave a gasp of anger, a finger rising to point at Geri, Alice shook her head, and glanced at Lauren, "We haven't got time for this"

"Come on!" the nurse glanced up at the signage above the door that they had stopped beside and opened it carefully, making sure that it was empty before gesturing for Brandon, Alice and Jiyaa to join her, closing the door behind them.

Turning, Alice flicked open the blinds on the window that ran the length of the room, sighing heavily as she stared out into the corridor to find that Tina and Geri were face to face, arguing.

"We should get back out there" the embalmer groaned, "Before they gang up on Geri"

On the other side of the room, what looked to be a changing room, Alice was standing beside another door, her hand upon the handle as she glanced back at the embalmer, "Shall I?"

Alice stepped forwards to stand beside Jiyaa and Brandon, the latter staring down at his book, and nodded at the nurse, "Do it"

As she watched, the nurse released a shaky breath, turned the handle and pulled towards her, peering through the crack that she had made for a moment before opening the door wide.

"Wait here" Alice pointed to Jiyaa and then at the floor, and the woman nodded, moving closer to where Brandon stood waiting, oblivious to the tension, and the embalmer turned to follow Lauren as she crept into the room she had found. For a moment, the two women stood side by side, studying the small wash area that they had found themselves in, and then Alice took a step towards another door to their left, listening carefully for a moment before opening it and glancing inside. For a moment, she stared about the operating theatre in disbelief, her throat tightening as she studied the three figures that lay upon the floor in pools of blood, a dismembered arm beside one, then she raised her gaze to the bald white-skinned figure that lay upon the operating table.

"What is it?" Lauren asked, a hand resting gently upon Alice's right shoulder and shaking her head, the embalmer opened the door wide and entered, the nurse following, cursing under her breath.

"Fucking hell"

"Fucking hell for sure" Alice agreed, studying the figures on the floor for a moment in disgust, her stomach knotting as she saw that one of them, a man by the clothes, appeared to have had his face eaten away, while a woman had died clasping her greasy looking intestines to her split abdomen.

"Look at this" the voice of Lauren had Alice turning to find the nurse standing beside the figure upon the operating table, and moving alongside her, the embalmer raised an eyebrow as she stared down, realising it had been in the process of having an operation when the change had taken it, and the doctors had been slain.

The folds of skin that had been cut and folded back to reveal the inner workings of the ghoul were, like the rest of its body covered in the same cracked white-skin as the other ghouls that they had seen, making the flesh seem like old leather, while inside the shell of its body, the organs themselves seemed to be taking on a similar transformation, their outer membrane turning a dirty white, all except for the creatures heart.

"We should kill it" Lauren muttered, and Alice met her gaze, staring deep into her eyes for a moment before wincing, and shaking her head.

"It's asleep...it doesn't even know this has happened to it..."

Lauren nodded, "So we better do it before it wakes and tries to kill us like the others"

Nodding, Alice watched as the nurse moved to where a tray of surgical instrument stood on the other side of the operating table, selecting a scalpel before moving back alongside Alice, "I have no idea how to do this"

"Me neither" Alice grimaced, reaching out to take the scalpel from the nurse, "But I'll do it, I work with dead bodies and peoples insides every day" Stepping closer to the operating table, she raised the scalpel, the point scraping over the hard skin of the ghoul with a rasping sound, and on instinct, she turned it around, gently poking at the stomach, lungs and other internal organs with the blunt end, her head spinning as it sounded as if she were tapping against sea shells.

"What the hell?" Lauren shook her head and Alice nodded, taking a deep breath as she reversed the scalpel once more and slid it in the beating heart, the blade finding no resistance whatsoever.

"At least they have one soft spot!" Lauren gave a humour chuckle, and Alice turned to nod at her. "The eyes too, Jiyaa stabbed her brother in the eye before we managed to escape from him" The nurse nodded, the two of them holding each other's gaze for what seemed an eternity, finding comfort in their shared experience, a bond seeming to forge between the two strangers, and then with a sigh, Lauren turned to glance about the operating theatre, "You keep that scalpel, I will try and find dressings for Jiyaa and Jennifer" Nodding, Alice turned back to the body upon the table, realising for the first time that it was a man, a sigh of relief escaping her as she considered how bad it would have been for her and Lauren if the ghoul hadn't still been sedated from the operation that the doctors had been performing on it then blinked, her eyes widening. "Oh God, we need to get out of here!"

"What is it?" Lauren began to move back towards her, her right hand clasping a small pile of bandages, "What is the matter?"

"It was still anesthetized" Alice pointed at the dead ghoul with the scalpel, "It was unconscious" Lauren nodded, "Yeah, I know"

Wincing, the embalmer gestured to the three dead bodies on the floor, "So what killed them?" The young nurse gave a grunt, blinking in shock, and then together they were running from the operating theatre, calling for their companions.

Chapter Twenty One

"It looks blocked" Victor grimaced, sitting forward slightly in his seat, grey eyes locked to the small road ahead of them where several cars were stopped, one of them nose first in a fence, four others sideways in the road behind it, smoke coming from the engine of one of the vehicles. Beside him, Bella gave a grunt, and opened her door, stepping up onto the edge of the car as she stared ahead of them, "I can't see any of them"

Them. The things. The white-skinned monsters. How had those that she had shot back at the farmhouse not been killed by the two barrels? Victor had realised that their skin was thicker and harder now since their change, but surely a shotgun should have been enough to kill them. After all, hadn't she killed two that way earlier? Grimacing, he turned to glance at her as she got back in, asking her that very question and she winced, head shaking, "I used both barrels on grandad...at nearly point blank range to the head, then just as I reloaded gran ran in, I tried to shoot her in the head but she grabbed the gun and took both shots in the chest from than a foot away" Her words were precise, her voice monotone, as if she were giving a report, and Victor nodded, realising it was her counselling, breaking everything down into logical no-nonsense facts. He had learned the exact same techniques in the long course of his therapy in the aftermath of the fire that had claimed the lives of his entire family.

"What do you think?" Bella turned to look back out of the windscreen, her face screwing up as if deep in thought, "Shall we try and move the cars out of the way?"

"And if we find some of those things out there?" Victor grimaced, glancing down at the shotgun he was holding before looking back as she met his gaze, "How many shells do you have left?"

"Three" she reached into the right breast pocket of the chequered shirt that she was wearing, fishing out the three shells, red jackets with gold tops, and handed them to him, "Here you go"

He took them, breaking the gun as he pushed one into right barrel and then closed it once more, an eyebrow rising as he found her studying him with interest, "What?"

"Why not fill both barrels?"

Victor gave a soft chuckle, "And get scared and fire both together...then only have one left?"

She nodded, "But what if it takes two to take one of these things down? Even at close range?"

Victor shrugged, "Then three shells isn't going to make much difference no matter how we try it"

For a moment they sat staring back at each other in silence and then he closed the shotgun, handing it across to her, "You take it"

"Are you sure?" she eyed him curiously, "Why?"

He shrugged, "Well, for starters its your gun...and you are ex army...you know weapons"

"So do you by the look of it" she nodded and he sighed heavily, shrugging as he held her gaze. "Where I grew up there was a massive forest surrounding a stately home, it had pheasants, grouse and the like, poachers were always trying to take the birds, and the gamekeepers had to stop them and keep the birds safe, so my dad taught me to use a rifle and a shotgun"

Bella nodded, a hand rising to run back through her silver hair, "Ah, your dad was a gamekeeper"

What...oh God no" Victor gave a chuckle, "No, my dad was a poacher...but I learned guns"

A comfortable silence settled over the pair of them and then she reached out, taking the offered shotgun, and Victor smiled grimly, turning his head to look into the rear of the Land Rover behind them, his stomach tight as he found Moonshine lying on the deck of the area, usually red features now pale and bathed in sweat.

He had been that way within minutes of driving away from the farmhouse, the stress and pain of his injury and the exertion of the day finally seeming to have taken their toll upon the man.

"Is he going to be OK?" Emily glanced up from where she was sitting near the rear door, the border collie named Lexie asleep on her lap.

"Yeah" Victor nodded at her, trying to sound positive, "He's just got a broken leg but he's in a lot of pain...he could use the rest"

"I think he's dead" the voice of Eric dragged Victor's attention and he found the boy sitting several feet to the left, a concerned look upon his face as he stared at the unconscious Moonshine, the larger dog Castiel sitting protectively at the side of the boy as if it had known him forever.

"He's not dead" Victor shook his head, "Trust me"

The boy nodded, looking unconvinced and Victor turned back to the front, staring out through the windscreen at the blockage ahead, his head shaking as he glanced at Bella, "Maybe I should go alone...leave my door open...if there is anything there I can run back and we reverse"

"No" Bella shook her head at him, a hand rising to point at several different places, "There's too many hiding places...you could get caught out in the open if you go alone...I'm coming too"

He winced, his voice lowering as he gestured back with his head, "And leave these alone?" Bella grimaced, nodding at his words and then shrugged, "I get that, but its not safe to go alone" "Then maybe we need a new plan" he suggested, head turning as he studied the road ahead of them for a moment then turned to look at the fields either side, his brow furrowing. They had headed west from leaving the farmhouse where Bella had lived, the former soldier throwing the Land Rover around the small country roads with skill, and thus far they had only seen one other car, a red Vauxhall Cavalier which had been embedded in a tree and on fire, the burnt and blackened remains of one of these bald new humanoids hanging through the windscreen on the driver's side, flames rising from its corpse. "We could go through the field" the voice of Bella had him turning his head, studying her intently as she pointed out of her window at the fence that the car ahead of them had driven into, a strange smile on her face as she looked back at him, "The fence has been weakened by the impact up there, if we can knock it down with the front off the Land Rover the four wheel drive on this thing will get us through the field with ease" "Are you sure?" he raised an eyebrow and she nodded, turning to glance back at the old fence. "If we hit it between posts on the old slats, it will break, I am sure of it...here, take the gun back" Victor nodded as she passed him the shotgun, placing it back down between his feet, the barrels pointing at the ceiling, "OK, let's do this"

Smiling grimly, Bella turned to look back at the two children behind them, "This is going to get a bit bumpy but we are going to be alright, OK?" There was a chorus of uncertain agreements, and then throwing Victor a grim look, she turned the wheel, easing down on the accelerator as she angled the Land Rover across the road so it was facing the fence on the left hand side, "Ready?"

"No" Victor shook his head, and she gave a humourless chuckle, her head shaking back.

"Me neither" without another word, she suddenly floored the accelerator, and Victor cursed as the Land Rover lurched forwards. The old wooden fence slats broke under the impact, and then they were through, the Land Rover bouncing as they drove over the uneven ground of the field, and grimacing, Bella slowed down and then stopped. "Everyone OK?" she asked turning her head to the rear once more and again the chorus of confirmations sounded, this time accompanied by one of the dogs barking, and Bella smiled, turning to meet Victor's gaze, "You good?"

He gave a nod, turning his head to study the crash as she began to drive on, brow furrowing as he saw movement amid the smoke, "What...?"

The white-skinned figure burst from the black smoke like a greyhound out of the starting trap, casting aside what looked like a bloody hunk of meat as it leaped effortlessly atop the bonnet of one of the vehicles and cleared the fence, landing cat-like in the field as it gave a roar of hatred.

"Go!" Victor muttered, a strange sense of horror washing through him as he realised that the figure was wearing the white shirt, black trousers and black stab vest of a police officer, the fact that even those who were supposed to keep people safe from harm were changing too seeming to be the final horror. Yet of course they could change as well, why couldn't they do so?

With another roar, it began to charge at the Land Rover and cursing, Bella put her foot down on the accelerator, clearly intending to get them quickly away from it, only for the back wheels to suddenly slide sideways, edging themselves into the soft earth of the field, the curses of the former soldier growing louder as she snarled, "Fuck it!"

"What...fuck it what?" Victor turned to throw her a look of dread, "Speak to me...what?"

"We're stuck at the back" Bella's voice was grim, her features looking like she was going to be sick, and cursing Victor snapped his face back to watch as the thing that had once been a police officer charged at their vehicle, snarling in rage. Gritting his teeth, Victor turned the handle on the window beside him, his other hand swinging the shotgun back up over his lap just as the figure reached the Land Rover, the end of the barrels butting it in the forehead as it reached for him. The retort of the shotgun was loud as the former priest pulled the trigger, drawing screams from both children and sending the dogs into a barking frenzy as the shotgun discharge, and wincing, Victor watched as the force threw the white-skinned figure back to the field beyond. Instantly regretting only loading one barrel, he passed the now empty weapon to the silver-haired woman beside him, his other hand slipping her the two remaining shells, "Here!"

"Where are you going?" she grimaced, loading the gun as she held his gaze, clearly so adept at the task that she didn't need to look, "Dog?"

Without replying, he closed his window and opened the door, stepping down into the field, his heart hammering in his chest as he began to approach the body that now lay sprawled in the grass, arms and legs bent at obtuse angles. He stopped by its left side, fighting the wave of nausea that washed over him as he saw the top half of the figure's head was missing from the left eye upwards, a nervous chuckle escaping him as his mind conjured up a sudden image of a hard-boiled egg with the top cleanly sliced off.

"Is it dead?" the voice of Bella had him glancing back through the door that he had left open, nodding as he saw the grim look upon her face.

"Slightly, yeah" he grimaced, his gaze drifting from his new friend down to the belt that was fastened about the waist of the dead police officer, and he crouched, his hands searching through the various pouches and clips.

"What are you doing?" Bella called out once more, and he turned, holding up his finds.

"Handcuffs, baton, taser and a torch"

"Wonderful" she grimaced, "Come on"

Victor nodded, rising to his feet then turned towards the cars as he heard something move upon the road, his pulse quickening in dread. The second creature came scrambling over the wooden fence somewhere between where they had crashed through it and where Victor stood, roaring as it landed in the field and saw him. Instantly he was running, clutching his finds to his chest as he did so, cursing as he almost slipped but then he was back inside the car, slamming the door behind him. Once more, Bella put her foot down on the accelerator, the engine roaring but still the back of the Land Rover swung back and forth as it slid in the wet mud, the wheels refusing to find purchase on anything. Victor cursed in dread as the white-skinned figure was suddenly there beside his window, snarling in hatred and excitement, and as the children began to scream again and the dogs went crazy, he tried to bring the shotgun up. Beyond the window, the figure snarled once more, its right fist rising to hammer a punch into the glass only for the sliding Land Rover to strike it side on, throwing it back to the ground behind. Victor cursed, Bella following suit as something slammed into the rear of the Land Rover, and turning his head, the bearded ranger watched in dread as he saw yet another of the figures there, brutish cracked-skinned features pressed up against the rear window as it snarled loudly. With a scream, Emily threw herself away from the rear door, arms encircling Eric as he sobbed

183

hysterically, both dogs moving to stand before the window, snarling and snapping angrily, and cursing, Victor glanced down at his friend, shouting angrily, "Moonshine...wake up!"

Yet the shorter man stayed unconscious, his face awash with sweat, oblivious to the creature that was trying to get into the rear of the vehicle. Without warning, the Land Rover lifted slightly at the rear, and gritting his teeth, Victor glanced in the side mirrors, his mind reeling in disbelief as he realised that the newcomer had lifted the rear of the vehicle from the earth with ease.

How strong had these things become?

"Look!" the voice of Bella was grim as she motioned past Victor, and turning his head he saw three more of the white-skinned figures creeping into sight beyond the fence, snarling aloud as they saw two of their brethren below. Without warning, the figure that had chased Victor was back beside the window, one hand swinging back, the white skinned fist smashing through the glass with ease, showering Victor in sharp fragments, and cursing, he turned to scream at Bella, "Throw it in reverse!"

With a grimace, she did as instructed, her left hand slamming the gear stick back into the reverse gear, and with the wheels suddenly free of the clogging earth, held aloft as they were by the enraged figure behind, the Land Rover lurched quickly back with a sickening crunch, the figure that had just been trying to gain access through the broken window beside Victor falling sideways as the vehicle moved. Without having to be told, Bella switched gear once more, shoving it back into first as she gunned the engine, the Land Rover surging forward across the field, Victor grimacing as he turned to look back out of his broken window as the figure that had smashed the glass began to rise, joined by the others from the road, while the one at the rear lay still, crushed by the reversing vehicle. Without even telling the children to prepare, Bella smashed back through the fence, having cleared the small obstruction and the Land Rover sped along the road, leaving the horror behind.

Chapter Twenty Two

Several minutes passed by as they drove on in silence, the children finally calming in the rear of the Land Rover, and the dogs settling back down. Yet Moonshine was still unconscious, his body having slid slightly about upon the floor in the rear of the vehicle, yet still he hadn't woken up.

"I'm worried about your friend" Bella finally muttered as she steered the vehicle along a ridge of ground that crossed between two large sections of open countryside, the Northern Pennines in the distance showing that they were heading west. Victor grimaced at her words, his head turning as he glanced into the back of the Land Rover, shaking his head as he saw his friend was still unconscious, his features even paler.

"I think the pain has gotten to him, he's in shock"

"Maybe" Bella nodded, casting him a quick glance, her mouth a tight line, and he frowned.

"What?"

"Nothing" she lied, the act obvious, and Victor nodded, turning to look out of the windscreen as they drove on for several more minutes, then frowned as the former soldier suddenly pulled the car over at the side of the long narrow road. For nearly a minute the pair of them sat there in silence, she gripping tight to the steering wheel as she stared ahead and he turning to study their surroundings, refusing to ask what she meant. If she wanted to tell him the problem she would.

"Why have we stopped?" there was panic in the voice of Emily as she moved to look between the seats, and turning his head, Victor forced a smile.

"We are just checking the route to the hospital"

"Yeah?" she raised an eyebrow, her head jerking towards where Bella was still sat staring ahead like a statue, "What's wrong with her?"

"I'm fine" the former soldier muttered, and Victor nodded at the girl in the rear of the Land Rover.

"See, she's fine, why don't you check on your brother for a moment…me and Bella have to talk"

"Ugh" she grimaced, moving back away from their chairs, her head shaking, "You better not be about to do it"

Despite his best efforts Victor laughed, "What?"

"You heard me" Emily looked disgusted, "That's the excuse adults use when they want time alone to do stuff…its sick…especially at your age…"

He raised an eyebrow, "I'm forty"

"Exactly" she shook her head, "I'm appalled"

"Me too" he threw her a grin, then opened his door and got out to stand on the side of the road, hands gently brushing the broken glass from his Forestry Commission uniform, grimacing as he found that sections of it were still wet from his unexpected tumble into the river in the woods. Satisfied it was all clear, he turned his head, studying the road about him in both directions and then the fields either side of them, a sense of calm opening up deep inside him as he saw no sign of any more of the white-skinned creatures. Shifting his position, he glanced to the south, watching the sunlight glint of a city at the bottom of the rise upon which they were parked, sighing as the wind suddenly swirled about him, caressing his long beard, and he reached up, unfastening the bandana about his head to let his dark brown dreadlocks fall about his features.

He turned as he heard the drivers door opening, nodding at Bella as she moved over to stand beside him, the pair of them staring out over the scenery for a moment in silence and then Victor spoke, "Is that Thames?"

"Yeah" she raised an arm, pointing, "The hospital is at the west end of it, if we follow this road we come in at the rear, so we don't actually touch the city roads that much"

"Like Durham hospital?" he raised an eyebrow. Once more, the silver-haired woman nodded at him, "Yeah, they are quite similar"

Another silence settled over them for a moment, the wind whipping up slightly and Victor gave a shiver, drawing a wince from Bella, "I should have let you change into some of my grandads clothes...I didn't think"

"It's fine" he forced a smile, lifting his chin against the breeze, letting it caress his beard once more as he closed his eyes, smiling as somewhere above a bird cried out on the wing.

"My Grandad was like your friend"

"What?" he opened his eyes, turning to look at the former soldier, "I don't understand"

She sighed, the escape of air seeming to take the fight from her as her shoulders slumped, a hand rising to rub at her eyes, "I am so fucking tired"

Victor nodded, not daring to speak, as she stood staring down at the grass beneath their feet for a moment and then met his gaze again, "Last night my grandad took sick...well, not sick as such but really tired, he got really sweaty, and just crashed out on the sofa in the living room. We tried to wake him, but nothing worked. I suggested calling the local doctor, but gran said to just let him sleep it off. He hated doctors, did grandad"

Victor smiled as she spoke the last part, seeing the same expression upon her features for a moment before she winced, head shaking as she looked away to stare off at the vast expanse of the North Pennines to the west, her voice grim as she continued, "Then I woke up today and he was in the living room…one of them…I didn't recognise him at first with no hair…and that white, cracked skin…he tried to kill us both, he broke my grans left arm and she ran off…the dogs were biting him but he didn't seem to care…he was just so angry…so angry"

Victor nodded, knowing what had come next but she continued anyway, her words cascading from her now as if the gate had been opened and there was no stopping them, "I grabbed his gun…I tried to stop him…to warn him off but…I shot him…I managed to reload the gun and then gran…she came running in…the same…bald…white skin"

She gave a shaky sigh and looked down at the ground, her hands grasping to her knees as she bent and vomited, and stepping closer, Victor began to gently rub her back, "It's ok, get it all up"

Several minutes passed by, the two of them locked in that act of companionship, strangers an hour ago, now bonded by survival and madness. With a sigh, she rose, the back of her left-hand wiping across her mouth, and Victor winced, his eyes searching hers, "Are you OK, now?"

Bella gave a weary grin, nodding, "Sorry, not

usually one for puking"

He shook his head, forcing a smile, "I think considering the day we are having its allowed"

They stood studying each other for a moment, and then Bella turned her face towards, the Land Rover, "I reckon we let the dogs out for piss and then get to the hospital"

Victor nodded, picturing Emily and Eric, "Yeah, we need to find these kids some relatives"

"They haven't got any" she turned back to him.

"What?"

She nodded, her expression grim, "Before I came to find you in the woods, after they had come running into our farmyard, I asked where their parents were...the little one, Eric, told me that their grandad had just died"

Victor grimaced, "Yeah, heart attack, I was there"

"Damn"

"Parents?" he raised an eyebrow and she shook her head, her voice grim, as she replied to him.

"Dead, traffic accident"

Letting out a shaky sigh, Victor turned to study the Land Rover, "The poor little bastards"

"Yeah"

He winced at her reply, seeing how she was staring at the vehicle, "Listen, I am sure that Moonshine is going to be OK, he isn't going to turn into one of those things"

She nodded, her eyes meeting his, "If he does?"

Victor turned away from her, studying the marine blue Land Rover for a moment, an image of his friend entering his mind, then he sighed, nodding as he spoke, "I'll take care of him"

Chapter Twenty Three

"Where the fuck are you going?" the sneered voice of the overweight cleaner made Lauren turn her head to stare back along the corridor at the woman as she stood beside the security guard and the ginger man with the curved knife. Catching the inside of her right cheek between her back teeth she held the gaze of the woman for a moment, resisting the urge to tell her to fuck off. She, Alice, Jiyaa and Brandon had emerged back out into the corridor just moments before to find the trio standing on one side while Geri had been further down upon the other side, crouching beside Jennifer as she sat on the floor sobbing uncontrollably into her cupped hands. Without pausing, Lauren had walked straight past, leading Brandon by the hand, her face turning to the Scots woman, "We need to go now"

"What is it?" the woman had risen from where she had been crouching beside Jennifer, her head shaking as she had glanced at Alice, "Tell me"

"There are people in there, in an operating theatre, that have been killed by one of these ghouls" the brown-haired woman had stated as she reached Geri, Jiyaa beside her, "Maybe by more than one, we need to get off this floor before it or they find us!"

"Ah fuck" the Scots woman had grimaced, turning to glance back at Jennifer, "Come on, hen"

"No" the black woman had met her gaze, staring through tear filled eyes, "I am with my husband"

"Are you fuck!" the ginger man had grimaced, drawing the gaze of everyone in the corridor, and another pained sob from the black woman. Yet instead of appearing concerned, the ginger man, Peter, had grimaced, the knife rising to point at her, "You stay the fuck away from me...you've been bitten...I'm not getting infected by you!"

"Peter!" the woman had made it to her hands and knees, shrugging the comforting hand of Geri from her shoulder as she stared over at her husband, "Please, I love you!"

"Do you...do you really?" his voice had been filled with acid, his features turning crimson as he stared back at her, the veins in his forehead seeming to pulse, "Is that why we are here today...because you love me so very much!"

"Peter!" she had sobbed again, and he had given a bitter laugh, his head shaking as he had turned to glance at everyone else in the corridor, sneering. "We are only here today because my darling fucking wife is a slut...she has been fucking my brother haven't you...and now she is pregnant by him...my own fucking brother...tell them, dear"

The black woman had given a sob, one hand clasped to her eyes, the other reaching out towards her husband, "Please…you forgave me…you said that we could make it work…"

"Forgave you?" his laugh had been bitter, his head shaking slowly as he stared at her, "As if I ever could…you disgust me…"

With a piteous howl, the woman had collapsed to the floor of the corridor, arms wrapping about her face as she had sobbed, the sound more animal than human as it had echoed down the corridor, and wincing, Lauren had begun leading Brandon away; Alice, Jiyaa and a reluctant looking Geri following behind until the cleaner had spoken and Lauren had stopped to answer.

Sighing heavily, she held the gaze of the pig-faced woman, voice even, "We are getting out of here"

Much to her surprise, as she had begun to walk once more, the cleaner had turned to the security guard, "We should go with them Nick, if they are getting out of here we should go with them"

He grunted, head shaking slightly as Lauren turned to stare back at the pair, a look of hatred shooting her way and then he nodded, "Sure, I was about to suggest we do that anyway"

"Course ye were" the voice of Geri sounded, literally dripping with sarcasm, and as the guard

flicked a glare in the direction of the Scots
woman, Lauren sighed and continued walking,
vaguely aware of the others following behind.
Reaching the end of the long corridor that they
had been on, she peered around its end, ears
straining as she listened for any possible sign of
trouble and then edged out, her heart pounding
as she began to move past the various doors,
fully expecting a ghoul to burst out from within.
Yet somehow, despite her concerns the group
reached the other end of the corridor unharmed,
and taking another steadying breath, she glanced
around the edge of the next corner, relaxing
again as she found that the corridor was clear,
eyes widening as she saw the sign for the stairs.
Turning back, she met the gaze of the others as
they gathered behind her, brow furrowing as she
saw that the security guard was now carrying
what looked like a wooden mop handle, perhaps
from the cupboard where Tina had been hiding.
She frowned suddenly as the absence of one of
their number registered with her, "Where's the
woman, Jennifer?"
"Who cares" the reply came from the ginger man
and Lauren grimaced, her head shaking slowly.
"She is your wife"
"Was" he grimaced, then gave a smirk, his hungry

gaze drifting up and down her athletic form, "I am taking auditions for a replacement if you are interested in applying"

The young nurse winced at his words, feeling physically sick as his gaze began to roam her form once more, then Geri snapped, drawing his attention, "What tha fuck is wrong with ye, eh?"

"Fuck off" he wiggled the knife at her, "I've had enough of women telling me what to do"

"One of us needs to go back for her" Alice sighed, meeting the gaze of Lauren, "We can't leave her"

"Well, its not going to be me, or Nick" the nasal voice of Tina stated, surprising no-one with her words, and sighing, Geri gave a shrug, nodding. "Ah'll go"

"See you then" Peter gave a sneer, chuckling as if to himself and Lauren felt her stomach knot as she saw the mania in the ginger man's wide eyes. *He had snapped. One hundred per cent snapped.*

"We'll wait for you" Alice told Geri, glancing at Lauren for confirmation, "Right?"

The nurse nodded, a strange feeling washing over her as she suddenly realised that she was the youngest one present and yet everyone was looking to her as if she was some kind of leader.

"Ah won't be long!" Geri took a step in the direction that they had just come then gave a grunt of surprise as in the distance, Jennifer suddenly came staggering into view, "Oh look, here she is..."

The words of the admin trailed off to a curse, as the four white-skinned figures came charging around the corner behind the wide-eyed black woman, snarling and grunting in excitement.

"Go, go, go!" Lauren shouted, turning to charge around the corner, dragging a whimpering Brandon behind her, the cries of her companions loud as they saw the threat and followed suit. Heart pounding hard in her chest, Lauren reached the double door to the stairwell, and charged through, leading her charge behind her and paused, unsure for a moment which way to run before choosing the stairs leading down, the door clattering behind her as the others began to charge through. Reaching the halfway landing to the floor below, she paused, turning to glance back behind her, relief touching her as she saw that Alice and Jiyaa were just behind them upon the stairs, the brown-haired woman leading the Indian by the hand, the screaming figure of Tina charging down behind them, hands in the air, the security guard trying to pass her on the stairs, his mop handle still clasped in his hands. The doors crashed once more, and in charged Geri, closely followed by Peter and then the sobbing, hysterical figure of Jennifer, the black woman collapsing at the top of the stairwell on her hands and knees, vomiting violently, one hand reaching for the legs of her husband. As the Scots woman began to charge down the stairs behind Nick and Tina, urging the others on in her thick accent, the black woman suddenly rose beside her husband, her hands balling into fists as she finally lost her temper with him, her lips drawn back as she snarled, "You fucking bastard…you fucking bastard, I hate you so…"

"Get the fuck off me!" he snarled, and Lauren cried out as she saw him thrust out with the blade that he was holding, the weapon sinking deep into the black woman's chest, once, twice, three times, and she grunted, her body jerking. With a snarl, he spun, heaving her form over the railing, the black woman's arms and legs flailing as she fell, her scream of sudden terror loud in the stairwell. There was a sickening crack as some part of her body bounced heavily off the stairs beside where Nick, Tina and Geri were descending and her scream as cut short, her body seeming to go limp as she fell through the centre of the stairs before landing with a thud far below.

For a moment, Peter met the gaze of Lauren over the railing, a cold smile upon his lips, and then he was charging down the stairs, knife in hand. Almost at once the doors crashed open again to reveal the four ghouls that had been pursuing Jennifer, their guttural snarls and screeches of excitement loud, sending Brandon into a fit of screams, and it was all Lauren could do to keep him moving and not drop to the floor in fear. They reached the landing of the third floor and charged on, Lauren not daring to look back, and in just moments they were on the midway landing to the second floor and past it, nearing the second-floor landing. She flinched as a woman cried out, and heart in her mouth, suddenly overcome with concern that it might be Alice or Jiyaa, Lauren turned, watching in shock as she saw the pair right behind her and Brandon, while on the mid-way landing, Tina and Nick lay in a heap upon the floor, the cleaner face down on the floor, the security guard atop her, one hand still clasping to the mop handle.

As Lauren watched, Geri reached the pair, picking her way past them and then glanced back, urging them on despite their former arguments, "Will ye fucking move it!"

With a grunt, Nick pushed himself up, and staggered down towards the Scots woman, blinking in shock, blood running from a cut above his right eyebrow where his head had struck the floor, and behind him Tina made it to her feet, only to cry out in shock and pain as Peter charged past, body checking her into the wall. Off balance and stunned, she toppled sideways and fell to one knee, her eyes wide as she reached out a hand towards where the guard stood staring back up at her, "Nick...babe..."

"Fuck off!" he muttered, his voice grim, as he turned and ran, charging past Lauren, Brandon, Alice, Jiyaa and Geri, the ginger man close on his heels, leering at Lauren as he raced past her.

The ghouls suddenly reached the midway landing where Tina was crouched with a storm of snarls and grunts, their white-skinned forms grasping at her in excitement, tearing the clothes from her form as they bit and tore with their teeth, arterial blood spraying high up the walls. With a soft curse, Lauren began to run once more, charging headlong down the stairs and the other four went with her, trying to ignore the screams or terror and agony that followed them.

Chapter Twenty Four

"What the fuck" the words slipped from the lips of Victor before he had even realised that he had spoken, his head shaking as he stared out of the windscreen of the Land Rover, his throat tight. As they had driven closer to the fledgling city of Thames, both he and Bella had taken turns cursing, hands raising to point our various smoke plumes that were rising in the distance, and the former soldier had slowed the Land Rover as they began to encounter cars abandoned at strange angles in the road ahead and in the other lane, some crashed into others, some embedded in fences, thick smoke rising from their engines. Now they were parked on the entrance to the hospital that it seemed like they had travelled one hundred miles to reach, having spent what felt an eternity weaving the Land Rover in and out of the abandoned and crashed vehicles. Ahead of them two bloody bodies lay in the road, a blonde woman lying face down, naked except for the skirt rucked up around her thighs, and an overweight black man lying on his back; his face and naked chest a bloody ruin, both cavities filled with blood and gore, their contents long gone. Letting out a shaky breath, Victor half-turned his head, calling to Emily and Eric, "Don't look out of the vehicle, do you understand me?"

There was a grunt of confirmation and he winced, his grey eyes rising to study the hospital that towered over them, the six floor structure clean and well kept were it not for numerous broken windows that lined each of the levels, smoke coming from several on the fourth floor.

"What do you think?" Bella's voice was tight as she turned to glance at him, "Shall we go?"

"Where to?" his voice was grim, his head shaking as he met her gaze, "Where else is there?"

She winced at his words, nodding, and began to drive onwards, following the curving road then stopped at the entrance to the car park as they found a car angled to the side, embedded in the mechanism that raised the gate to allow access.

"Fuck this" she turned the wheel, bumping up over the kerb in the middle of the small road and down into the opposite lane, then began to drive the wrong way down the street, past the exit from the car park, and down a side street beside the hospital, the words 'No Entry' painted upon the floor before them in large yellow letters.

Grimacing, suddenly picturing an ambulance hurtling around the side of the building and crashing into them, Victor brought the shotgun up to rest across his lap and glanced nervously about, the smashed window at his side making him feel suddenly vulnerable and exposed.

"Oh look" the surprised voice of Eric in the rear of the Land Rover had Victor turning to glance over the seats into the rear, relief coursing through him as he saw that Moonshine was stirring, his face to the floor, one hand scratching at the back of his right leg. For a moment, Victor studied his friend in silence and then turned to wink at Emily and Eric, the children sat huddled together, the pair of dogs lying down before them, "See, I told you he was going to be OK"

"Are we good?" Bella asked as he turned back around, concern in her voice and Victor nodded. "Golden"

"Hey" the nervous voice of Emily had Victor's stomach suddenly turning over, "What's up with his skin...Dog?"

Grimacing, he started to turn, just as Bella steered them around the bend in the narrow road, down alongside a row of steam venting heating systems, then glanced back as he heard the former soldier curse in dread. Victor winced, one hand leaping forward to steady himself as a silver-haired man suddenly ran in front of them from a side door of hospital, the white coat that he wore, giving him the appearance of a doctor.

At the last moment, the man saw them and screamed, hands raising before him as if hoping he could turn the vehicle aside with telekinesis, and grimacing, Bella swung the wheel, cursing once more as a large white-skinned figure ran in front of them, reaching for the screaming doctor as it snarled. The force of the speeding Land Rover smashed the figure hard against one of the large metal compressors, the impact almost lifting the front of the vehicle from the floor, and cursing, Victor had to stop himself from hitting the windscreen. Grimacing, the front view of the vehicle obscured by rushing steam, Victor opened his door and staggered out, raising the shotgun before him as he stepped around to the front of the vehicle and stared at the figure they had just hit, grimacing as he saw that it was dead, its rib cage and chest crushed by the impact, its hands hanging down to rest upon the bonnet. "Dog!" the sudden voice of Bella had him tensing, and turning, he pushed past the open door of the Land Rover, shutting it then hurried around the back of the vehicle to find Bella standing beside the grey haired man that they had nearly hit as he stood bent at the waist, hands on his knees. "Are you hurt?" Victor asked as he approached, and the doctor glanced up, then flinched, hands

raising before him as he saw the shotgun.
"Don't hurt me!"
"Easy" Bella told him, a hand resting upon his left
shoulder, "We are here looking for help...we
aren't going to hurt you"
At her words, the man gave a bitter chuckle, his
head shaking as he glanced up at the building and
then over at the figure they had crushed, "You
came here for help...that place is a place of the
dead...there's no safety in there...none..."
Blinking, Victor turned his head to meet the gaze
of Bella, his mouth opening only to snap his head
around as the children began to scream in terror
in the back of the Land Rover, the dogs barking
and growling only for something to snarl back.
Heart in his mouth, Victor was running, Bella at
his side, and in seconds he was at the back of the
vehicle, the shotgun raised before him as the
former soldier cast him a grim look and then
opened the door wide. Within the rear of the
Land Rover a white-skinned hairless figure was
crouching above the gasping form of Emily, one
hand fastened to her throat as it roared into her
features, her younger brother lying nearby with a
bloody nose, blinking in confusion, while the pair
of dogs snapped and bit at their attacker, jerking
and twisting away each time it turned to swing

its free arm at them. As if time seemed to slow, Victor stared at the figure, eyes taking in the Forestry Commission uniform that it was wearing, and then he was shouting in denial, his heart breaking within him, "Moonshine!"

The figure turned in his direction, blinking for a moment, that awful, foul-smelling gunk running from his beige eyes and then it roared in hatred, no sign of recognition upon its pale features. "Shoot it!" Bella yelled as she darted in to snatch Eric in her arms, her voice loud in his ear and Victor stepped forwards to the back of the Land Rover, the gun aiming for the face of his friend and then he suddenly reversed it, leaning in as he struck it hard in the face with the butt. With a grunt, the figure swayed backwards, rising slightly, its hand releasing its grip upon the throat of the teenage girl, and cursing in anger, Victor struck it once more, this time bringing the butt of the shotgun down on the figures left leg. With a howl of agony, it tried to rise, banging its head off the interior roof of the Land Rover, and toppled backwards, and gripping the shotgun one handed, Victor grasped at Emily's right arm, dragging her out from the back of the vehicle, the dogs, Lexie and Castiel leaping out with them.

"Dog!" the warning cry from Bella had the former priest flinching, then crying out in shock and pain as something grasped at his dreadlocks, dragging him back inside the rear of the Land Rover, the shotgun falling from his hand. He cried out in pain as the white-skinned figure of Moonshine scrambled atop him, both hands reaching down to hammer into Victor's chest, drawing an agonized scream from him as one struck where he had collided with the tree back in the woodland. Blinking past the pain that was coursing through him, Victor swung his arms, blocking several of the punches but then grunted as a powerful blow struck him in the forehead, sending his vision hazy. Arms feeling as if they were as heavy as lead, Victor stared up at the hate filled features of the figure atop him, somehow finding the familiar features of his friend Moonshine amid the cracked and calloused skin, and then watched as the fists began to swing quickly down towards his face. There was a sudden scream of anger from beside him, and then the shotgun sounded, loud in the rear of the vehicle, the force of the weapons discharge throwing Moonshine half over the front seats, the creature screeching in agony.

"Dog!" Bella was suddenly there as she reached in to drag him out, and blinking hard to clear his vision, forcing himself to stand, Victor swung his legs to the ground and stepped away from the Land Rover to stand unsteadily beside Bella, surprised to find the doctor with them, a dazed looking Eric in his arms, Emily standing nearby, a hand on her throat, a haunted look in her eyes. "We need to go!" Bella stated, taking a step away from the vehicle, and grimacing, Victor turned his head, watching in disbelief as the thing that had been Moonshine suddenly dragged itself from where it had been half-sprawled over the front seats, snarling in hatred as it rushed at them. Cursing, Bella raised the shotgun and fired, the hammers coming down on dead shells and Victor grimaced, raising his fists then cursed as the dogs surged past him, teeth snapping. The sudden impact of the pair threw the white-skinned Moonshine back inside the vehicle, the Land Rover lurching as the dogs fought savagely with it, and cursing, Bella called out to them, the voice of Emily joining in with her, both of them frantic. With a roar, Moonshine suddenly grasped at the smaller black and white shape of Lexi as she sank her teeth into his broken leg, and raised her before him, a quick twist of his arms breaking her front leg, the dog howling in agony. With a roar of triumph, it cast her aside, the whimpering canine sliding from the rear of the vehicle to land on the ground outside and snarling, Moonshine made to follow only to stagger back as the larger Castiel hammered against its chest, teeth fastening about his throat. Screeching, the white-skinned figure grasped at the dog, strong hands squeezing at its ribs, drawing a yelp from the German Shepherd but still it clung to the throat of its victim, head shaking in a terrible fury. With a crash, they slammed back against the interior of the vehicle, and fell apart, the white-skinned figure reaching for the rear of the Land Rover only to snarl as the badly wounded dog grasped at its broken leg, dragging him back inside, the enraged thrashing of Moonshine causing the rear of the Land Rover to slam shut. Screaming in denial, Bella was suddenly beside the whimpering form of Lexi, passing Victor the empty shotgun as she scooped the border collie up into her arms, her head shaking, and gritting his teeth, Victor grimaced, "We have to go!" "Castiel!" she shook her head in denial, "No!" An agonized whimper suddenly sounded from within the rear of the vehicle, taken up by the wounded Lexi in the former soldiers arms, and then the white features of Moonshine were against the rear window, snarling in hatred.

"We should go" the voice of the doctor sounded, drawing the gaze of Victor, the man's features filled with fear as he shook his head, "There are more inside…so many more…we need to go now"

Gritting her teeth, Bella nodded, "Which way?"

The doctor winced, "I was going to take an ambulance and get out of here, taking anyone I could with me"

"Which way?" Victor took a step towards the doctor, one hand holding out the shotgun as he took the semi-conscious Eric into his arms. Wincing, the doctor took the gun, then shook his head, "I cant use this…my Hippocratic oath"

"Its not loaded" Bella grimaced, stepping alongside Victor, one hand stroking the dog that she held in her arms, "Now, show us the way to the ambulances"

Chapter Twenty Five

"Keep going!" Alice urged those about her as they charged down the stairs, their small group reaching the mid-way landing towards the first floor as one, Lauren and Brandon in front, followed by she and Jiyaa with Geri bringing up the rear, cursing like a sailor. Gritting her teeth, casting a glance at the Sikh woman that she was still leading by the hand, the woman holding her yellow robe up as she ran, Alice nodded and then turned forwards once more, grimacing as she saw the backs of the ginger man Peter, and the security guard Nick as they ran on ahead, half a level in front of them, the pair on the first floor. Just feet ahead of the pair, the door suddenly swung open to reveal a tall young man with dark hair, and high-cheek boned features etched with fear as he raced from the corridor beyond, his white porter uniform stained with fresh blood. The young man let out a grunt as Peter struck him hard in the stomach as he charged past, dropping him to his knees, and then the security guard, Nick, brought the mop handle down hard across the back of the porters head, sending him crashing to the floor of the landing, groaning. "Leave him alone, you animals!" the cry of Lauren was loud in the stairwell, as the women and

Brandon reached the landing, but the pair were gone, charging ahead down the stairs once more. In seconds, they were at the side of the young man who was already struggling to rise, a hand moving to the back of his head, and cursing, Alice released her grip on Jiyaa and helped him stand, then gently began to coax him, "Dude, come on, we need to get out of here!"

The young man blinked, his eyes a bright blue filled with tears, as he gestured back through the closed door beside them, "These things…"

"Aye, we know!" Geri shouted, pushing at their backs, as she glanced over her shoulder, "There are more of tha fuckers back there…go, go, go!"

As Lauren began to lead Brandon down the next flight of stairs towards the ground floor, Jiyaa moved to the other side of the porter, helping him to walk, just as Alice and the nurse had helped the woman Jennifer leave the elevator, while Geri followed behind, urging them all on.

"Oh no" Lauren paused, head turning back to look up at the others, her features filled with terror, "A&E was filled with them earlier!"

"Well, we cannae go back up!" Geri snapped, looking past Alice, Jiyaa and the porter in shock.

"Where are those pricks?" Alice grunted, releasing her grip on the young man as she moved down to step past Lauren, her heart hammering in her chest as she found that Nick and Peter were nowhere to be seen at all. Releasing a shaky sigh, she turned her head, staring back up in to the five sets of eyes that were focused upon her, and she winced, "Come on, if we can get through A&E we can make it to the car park...do you have cars?"

"Ah came on tha fucking bus" the Scots woman shook her head, a finger pushing her glasses back up her nose, and Alice nodded back up at her. "You come with me...Jiyaa you too, anyone else?"

"I have a moped" the porter winced, head shaking, and Alice grimaced, glancing at Lauren. "Tell me you have a car"

The nurse nodded, and the embalmer forced a smile, "Right, we'll split between the cars"

Without another word, she turned, edging down the remaining stairs to the ground floor, grimacing as the sounds of shouting suddenly rose up from beyond the doors that stood ahead. Heart in her mouth, Alice stepped closer, glanced back to discover the others were close behind her, and then slowly she opened the door a fraction, peering out into the open area beyond. For a moment, she frowned, angling her head as she stared out through the crack, trying not to focus upon the countless bloody bodies that littered the floor of the accident and emergency waiting room that lay beyond the doors. Turning her head, she let her gaze drift over the elevator that they had tried to escape in earlier, then flicked to the side as she saw sudden movement, her stomach lurching in dread as she saw a large cluster of the ghouls fighting desperately to get inside the door of the hospital shop, shock coursing through her as she saw the faces of Nick and Peter staring back out through the window. They were trapped and surrounded by ghouls. Smiling grimly, unashamed to feel pleasure at their potential face considering all they had done, Alice turned her head, frowning as she saw her five companions all standing back beside the bottom of the stairs, their eyes staring down. Shaking her head, she moved back to them, edging past Lauren, and following the nurse's gaze, a gasp escaping her as she saw Jennifer. Somehow as she had moved down the last section of stairway, her eyes glued to the door, Alice had failed to notice the mangled body of the unfortunate woman, bent as it was in the gap beside the railings, her arms and legs bent at sickening angles, her features mashed flat as she lay in a growing pool of her escaping body fluids.

Fighting the shout of anger that threatened to escape her, Alice raised her gaze from Jennifer and turned to each of her companions in turn, her voice a whisper, "We can get out...but we have to be quiet"

"What?" Geri shook her head, matching the volume of Alice's voice, "Are there nae of tha bastards out thare, hen?"

"Dozens of them" Alice nodded, raising her hands to stop anyone else from speaking, "But they are distracted, for the time being at least"

"How?" the soft voice of Lauren had Alice turning to meet her gaze, emotion catching in her throat as she saw that the nurse was holding Brandon to her, a hand stroking his head as if to calm him.

"Nick and Peter...they've got themselves trapped in the hospital shop" Alice nodded, turning to look at the Scots woman as Geri gave a chuckle.

"Serves tha wankers right"

She nodded, then glanced at the porter as he spoke, his voice thick with dread, "Can we get past them without being seen?"

"I think so...I hope so" the embalmer nodded, then shrugged, "We have to try...but we have to be quiet...if they hear us...if they see us..."

She let her words trail off but the message was clear, even Jiyaa seeming to understand and taking a deep breath, Alice moved back to the door, glancing at her companions once more, smiling sadly, "If it goes wrong...run"

"Where to?" the porter asked, sounding as if he was on the verge of a panic attack and Alice shook her head, shrugging as she replied to him.

"I don't know...just run...try and keep someone with you...good luck"

Reaching out, she placed her hand on the door handle once more, then froze as she felt a hand on her forearm, head turning to find the nurse, Lauren, smiling weakly at her, "Thank you"

"What for?"

"Back in the elevator, you saved me"

Alice nodded, smiling, "I'll see you outside"

Without another word, she opened the door a crack and peered through, grimacing as she watched the group of ghouls trying to get inside the shop, the shouts and jeers of the two men inside loud over the snarls of the enraged beasts. Nodding, Alice opened the door and stepped back, holding it wide as she gestured for the others to go through; Lauren and Brandon first, then Jiyaa and the porter, then Geri, the Scots woman pausing to gesture for her to follow, and wincing, Alice closed the door quietly behind her.

As it closed with a barely audible click, Alice turned her head, feeling suddenly dizzy with dread as she surveyed the scene before her. Almost halfway across the foyer towards the exit, Lauren was leading Brandon by the hand, the young black man holding his book across his eyes, while five feet behind them, Jiyaa and the porter were walking with slow, deliberate steps, the Sikh holding her robe about her calves with both hands, the young man with his hands on his head as if he was about to pull his own hair out. Wincing, Alice turned her head meeting the gaze of Geri as the admin gestured for her to follow, and then the pair of them slowly made their way through the foyer of the hospital, picking their way among the mutilated bodies upon the floor. Flinching as a chorus of snarling arose from over to their left, Alice paused mid-step and turned her head, watching as a cluster of ghouls began to move away from the door along the hospital shop window, snarling at the figure of Nick as he in turn stared past them at the escaping woman, his bearded features twisted into an angry grimace. Unable to resist the urge, Alice raised her right hand, her middle finger rising skyward, as she mouthed across at the man, "Fuck you!"

His eyes widened at the gesture, his voice loud

behind the glass as he shouted angrily, although his words were unintelligible, his right fist banging hard upon the window before his face. As Alice began to walk once more, a glance ahead showing that Lauren and Brandon were now outside the hospital, the nurse gesturing for Jiyaa and the porter to join them, and feeling freedom within sight, the embalmer began to speed up. She flinched as a sudden snarl erupted from beside the shop, and turning her head she stared back in shock as one of the ghouls took a step towards her, its crusted calloused features twisting in shock as if it wasn't sure what it was seeing and then it roared once more, a half dozen of its brethren turning towards her, their furious, excited howls and grunts loud in the foyer. "Run!" the voice of Lauren was loud as Alice spun on the spot, arms pumping at her sides as she charged towards the doorway, Geri dashing through it ahead of her to join their companions. "Go!" Alice shouted, arms waving as she raced towards them, "Don't wait for me...fucking run!" They did as she had instructed, Jiyaa joining Lauren in taking the wrist of Brandon's hand that was clasping his book, the trio running in a line, while Geri and the porter ran alongside them all.

Heart pounding away in her chest like a jackhammer, Alice surged through the door and out into the fresh air, following her companions as they charged right along a narrow curving road, and she went with them, the grunts and snarls of the ghouls behind loud in her ears. "Where are we fucking going?" the porter shouted, hands gesticulating like a windmill as he ran ahead of Alice, his voice almost hysterical, and several feet behind him, Geri grunted softly. "Will ye shut up and run!"

Suddenly, the roar of an engine sounded loud, and the group ahead of Alice all cursed and gasped as an ambulance suddenly skidded around a corner, tyres and brakes squealing as it swerved to avoid them then stopped twenty feet ahead in the road. As the group began to run towards it, shouting and calling for help, the passenger door of the vehicle swung open and a bearded man with dreadlocks scrambled out, his body dressed in beige combat trousers and shirt with a dark green body warmer over the top. With a jerk of his hand, the man swung open the rear door of the ambulance, directly behind the cab on the passenger side, a hand gesturing frantically for their group, his voice grim, "Run!"

The porter reached it first, racing on ahead, and the stranger almost pushed him inside the open door, then hurried forwards to help Lauren, Jiyaa and Brandon as the latter stumbled, and fell, dragging the women to the ground with him. In seconds, Alice was beside them, a glance back sending her into a panic as she saw the almost endless wave of ghouls charging towards them from the hospital, grunting in excitement.

"Come on!" the voice of the man was insistent and blinking, Alice turned, watching as Lauren and Jiyaa practically pushed a screaming Brandon inside the ambulance, Geri joining them. With a grimace, the man slammed the door shut, and gestured towards the cab as he glanced at Alice, "Come on, there's a spare seat up here!" As he wrenched open the door, she glanced inside, seeing a woman with silver hair shaven at the sides behind the wheel, then glanced back, a curse escaping her as she noticed something upon the ground, an equal distance between the horde of ghouls and the ambulance. Without thinking, she raced for it, rushing back to snatch it up, almost falling as she turned, then she was running once more, her heart skipping a beat as the ambulance began to drive away, the bearded man hanging from the open doorway, extending a hand in her direction, his features twisted into a grimace as he shouted at her, "Fucking run!" Alice screamed as she felt the fingers of a grasping hand brush against her back, the sudden realisation of how close the ghouls were urging her on and with a curse she jumped for the open door, terror washing through her as she realised she had timed her leap wrong entirely. Then the hands of the bearded man were grasping at her leather jacket, his voice cursing as he dragged her up and into the cab of the ambulance, slamming the door shut behind them. Almost sobbing in relief, her body shaking, the embalmer leaned heavily back against the seat beneath her, her eyes fixed to the wave of white-skinned figures fading back into the distance in the side mirror on the door, as the silver-haired woman behind the wheel put her foot down, steering them out of the hospital grounds. Suddenly weary beyond belief, Alice turned as the bearded man spoke, his voice thick with confusion, "What the Hell was so important you nearly got yourself killed back there?"

Unable to stop chuckling as adrenaline kicked in, Alice raised the prize that she had snatched up from the road, nodding as she met the man's surprised gaze, "Brandon's book"

Chapter Twenty Six

Sitting beside the door of the ambulance, Victor stared out through the windscreen as Bella drove them quickly away from the hospital, his hands bracing himself as she was forced to bump up kerbs to cross lanes to avoid abandoned cars. Beside him, the brown-haired woman in the leather jacket and the Dr Martens was quiet, her hands clasping to the book that she had risked her life to save, his stomach knotting as he considered how close she had come to dying.

For a book.

She had said that it belonged to Brandon, but he had no idea who the mysterious Brandon was. Could it be the young black man that the nurse and the woman in the sari, had helped into the back of the ambulance? Were they his carers? Realising that guessing was going to get him no answers, Victor turned to ask her and then thought better of it, his gaze meeting that of Bella as the former soldier turned her face from the road ahead towards him, and he sent her what he hoped was a reassuring smile, only for her to wince and turn back away from him once more. She was angry with him, he knew that, even if she wasn't going to speak the words and admit it.

He had failed to shoot the creature that Moonshine had become, and because of that hesitation, one of her dogs had been killed. Grimacing, he turned to look back out of the windscreen, brow furrowing as he saw rain begin to spatter down upon it, the sky turning grey.

"As if the day couldn't get any worse, now its raining" the woman seated between he and Bella suddenly gave a bitter chuckle, and he turned to meet her gaze, wondering what atrocities she and the others had seen within the hospital. Smiling grimly, the former priest chuckled as she turned to meet his gaze, "I'm Victor Doggart...but most people just call me Dog"

"Alice...Alice Stone" the woman nodded, then turned to glance sideways at Bella as the silver-haired woman spoke, eyes not leaving the road.

"Bella Atkinson"

The woman, Alice, nodded once more, smiling awkwardly, then she glanced at them both in turn, "I really appreciate what you did back there, I know the others will too"

"What we did?" Bella cast her a confused look.

"Yeah, you stopped for us...waited...helped us"

"What else would we do?" Victor gave a confused laugh, head shaking, "Who wouldn't help?"

Alice grimaced at his words, her head shaking as

she met his gaze, "I can think of two people"
Victor raised an eyebrow, glancing to meet the
questioning gaze of Bella before he looked back
at Alice once more, "Who?"
She shrugged at his question, a faint smile
creasing her features, "Oh, just two men that we
ran into back in the hospital…it doesn't matter
now…they don't matter now"
Victor nodded, studying her for a moment, then
winced, "How bad was it in there?"
"Bad" she met his gaze, the pain of what she had
seen evident in her brown eyes, and he stayed
silent as she continued, "There were three of us
at first, then we joined another group…those
things…they were killing everyone they could"
"Did you lose anyone?" the voice of Bella had
them glancing at her, and Alice shook her head.
"No, well, I came to the hospital for my friend
Sarah but I was too late…then all Hell broke
loose, a couple of the group I was in got
killed…an old woman, I didn't get her name, then
Jennifer was killed by her husband…and a
cleaner…oh, and at the start Jiyaa's brother
became one of these things and killed a nurse"
Exchanging glances with Victor, Bella gave a
grunt, "Someone got killed by their husband?"

Alice nodded, "Stabbed and then thrown over the stairs from the fourth floor"

"Fuck" the former soldier grimaced, and Victor did the math, nodding in sudden understanding. "He was one of the two men you mentioned"

The brown-haired woman nodded at his words, then frowned, "Have you had it rough out here?"

He winced, a sudden image of Moonshine filling his mind, "Yeah, its been pretty fucking grim"

She nodded at his words, her voice soft as she studied his face, "Did you lose anyone?"

His throat was suddenly tight, and he nodded at her, "My friend...Spencer...Moonshine...Bella lost her grandparents...there are two kids in the back of the ambulance who lost their grandfather too"

"I'm sorry" she made an awkward face, and Victor forced a smile, shrugging as he replied. "It's no-one's fault"

Alice sighed at his words, turning to look back out of the windscreen and he did the same, watching as the wiper blades swept back and forth, cleaning the glass only for it to be covered again almost immediately by the heavy rain.

"This storm is getting worse" Bella grunted from behind the wheel and nodding, Victor leaned forwards, looking up at the darkening sky overhead, suddenly curious what the time was.

"What time is it?"

"Quarter past one" Alice replied, dragging her mobile phone from her pocket and glancing at the screen, "It looks a lot later"

Victor nodded, "Have you got signal?"

"Yeah"

"Try and get hold of the police or someone"

"Sure" she typed at the buttons and raised it to her ear, holding it there for what seemed an eternity before she lowered it, her features grim as she met his gaze, "There's no answer"

"This is happening everywhere" Bella glanced at them, nodding grimly, and Alice shook her head. "Don't say that...that's a terrifying thought"

"Why aren't they answering?" Bella raised an eyebrow, eyes narrowing as she glanced back out of the window then cursed aloud, the ambulance slowing down to stop, "Fucking Hell"

"What is it?" Victor leaned forwards, grey eyes straining to see through the rain, their vehicle's lack of movement suddenly making him feel exposed and vulnerable, "What's wrong?"

"The road is blocked by cars this way" Bella grimaced, pointing to the abandoned vehicles ahead of them in the road, "This is the way we came...damn it, how is it blocked now?"

"What's that?" Alice suddenly leaned forwards, a

hand rising to point towards a red car that was on its side, "I thought I saw something move"

"Where..." Bella began then cursed as a white figure suddenly charged out of the rain towards them from behind the upturned vehicle, what looked like a metal bar in its hands. With a snarl of her own, the former soldier floored the accelerator, swerving around the charging figure, the ambulance lurching as she bumped up onto a grass verge and steered it among the small trees that grew there, her features set in a grim mask. In moments they were level with the pile-up, Victors blood running cold as he glanced at it and saw the half dozen white figures that waited there as if trying to trap them, his head shaking in disbelief, and then Bella steered their ride right once more, dropping back down to the hard road surface. Gritting his teeth amid his beard, Victor stared out of his side window, studying the area that they were now speeding through, recognising it from their journey to the hospital not so long ago, and then he cursed as Bella suddenly slammed on the brakes once more.

"Fucking Hell!" he turned to the silver-haired woman, head shaking, "What now?"

She grimaced, pointing with a finger to their right, "That's the way we came in...there are cars everywhere now…we have to go left!"

"What's left?" Alice turned to her, suddenly seeming to realise the situation, "Where are we going exactly? I have a car back at the hospital!"

"Fuck the hospital" Bella grunted, throwing her a look of sadness, "That place is a death trap, we need to get out of here and get everyone safe until we can figure out where to go for help!"

"This is madness" Alice shook her head, glancing at Victor as he studied the two women and he winced, turning his gaze forward to study the road sign that stood ahead of them in the driving rain, reading the name of what lay to their left, the only safe direction open for them to travel in.

"The North Pennines"

Chapter Twenty Seven

"I didn't think we were going to make it...I thought that was game over" the porter stated from where he was standing at the far end of the middle aisle of the ambulance, his head shaking as he spoke almost to himself, and nodding at his words, Lauren turned from where she was standing beside the door, glancing at Brandon. The young black man was seated upon the pillow end of the stretcher against the wall beside her, his knees drawn up to his chest as he sobbed and moaned, rocking back and forth slightly, the palms of his hands pressing against his eyes. Concerned, she reached out to place a hand upon his knee nearest her in a bid to console him but he let out a high pitched whine and jerked away, and wincing, she moved her hand back away. For several seconds, she stood staring down at the floor, hands reaching out to support herself against the wall as the ambulance suddenly jerked and swerved, then straightened once more, her mind reeling as she imagined the reasons for their erratic driving. Were there ghouls in the road? Were they on the ambulance? Taking what she hoped was a steadying breath, she turned her face, her eyes meeting those of the Indian woman as she glanced up from the seat that she had taken beside the door, and reaching out, Lauren placed a hand on her shoulder, aware that they spoke different languages but feeling the need to support the woman who had helped them all so much, "Are you OK?"

Jiyaa nodded, her own right hand rising to clasp the hand of Lauren's upon her shoulder, then her eyes drifted to Brandon and she winced, lips moving as if she wanted to speak but didn't know the words. Smiling, guessing her meaning, the nurse gave a nod, "I think he'll be OK"

Jiyaa smiled, squeezing her hand gently once more and removing it from her shoulder, Lauren turned her head, letting her gaze drift over the other occupants of the ambulance, smiling as she found two Asian children watching her from where they were seated at the other end of the stretcher from Brandon, the boy about five and the girl looking like she was almost in her teens. "I'm Lauren" she told them, feeling a sudden need to put them at ease as they stared back, realising for the first time that there was a border collie lying upon the stretcher between them. The boy nodded at her words, smiling nervously but the girl stayed silent, eyeing her with suspicion, yet Lauren wasn't offended by her behaviour, realising that they had probably been through similar situations to her and her companions. Glancing away from the children, she studied the Scots woman as she sat on the floor of the ambulance before Lauren, one hand on her heart, the other holding her glasses as she breathed heavily, her eyes closed, then the nurse was glancing at the porter as he moved to stand at the back of the ambulance, leaning against the doors. Their eyes met and he nodded, smiling, and she returned the expression then shifted her gaze to the tired looking man in the doctors coat that was seated upon a fold-out chair beside the porter, his expression blank, a hand rubbing back through his silver hair as he stared into space. The ambulance suddenly swerved once more, worse than before then lurched as it bounced up something, drawing curses and gasps from everyone in the rear of the ambulance, the dog barking once, its tail wagging weakly as it licked tenderly at one of its front legs, the nurse winced as she realised that the limb was at an odd angle. "Is that leg broken?" she asked the girl, getting a nod in reply, and the young nurse made a pained expression, "How did it happen?"

The girl grimaced, and the boy gave a sigh, his little shoulders slumping, "It was one of the monsters that did it...it broke his leg"

"Her leg" the girl sent him an irritated look, her right hand reaching out to gently stroke the dogs back, "She's a girl...Castiel was the boy"

At her words, the boy nodded, his head lowering as if he was about to start crying, and Lauren shook her head, "Where is Castiel?"

"Dead" the girl replied, her tone cold, "He's dead, just like Moonshine...the monsters killed them"

"Ghouls" the voice of Brandon suddenly stated, and turning, Lauren saw him sitting back against the wall of the ambulance behind him, hands upon his knees as he nodded wisely at the two children, "They aren't monster, they are ghouls"

The girl grimaced, but stayed silent and the young boy smiled, nodding up at Brandon, "I'm Eric, she's Emily"

"I'm Brandon" the black man replied, nodding as he spoke, "I live at the hospital"

"Not now you don't mate" the porter gave a bitter chuckle, an effeminate twang to his voice, and as Brandon snapped his face towards Lauren in sudden concern, she forced a smile back at him.

"Don't worry, I am sure everything will be fine"

"Fine?" the porter gave a sneer from the other end of the ambulance, his head shaking, "You were just out there, weren't you, darling?"

"Yeah" Lauren fought to keep calm, "We saved you in the stairwell, if you remember"

The porter winced at her words and fell silent, and sighing heavily, Lauren turned her face back towards the children, "So...Eric and Emily?"

The boy nodded and she raised an eyebrow, "Is that your dad that helped us out...is your mum here too...maybe in the cab?"

"Our parents are dead" Emily's voice was bitter, her head shaking, "That's Dog and Bella"

"Dog?" Lauren blinked, embarrassed that she had asked about their parents considering the answer, still not troubled by the girl's responses.

"Dog saved us" Eric nodded, a sad look on his face, "Him and Moonshine saved us...our grandad is dead now too"

"Do you have to tell people everything?" the girl was suddenly angry, "They're strangers, stupid!"

"She seems nice" the boy argued, jerking a thumb towards Lauren, "And stop calling me stupid!"

The girl scowled at him, and turned away, her hand leaving the dog to join her other forming fists upon her lap, and Lauren turned to watch as Geri rose to her feet before her, "Are you OK?"

"Not really" the admin shook her head, smiling grimly, "But I have to be aye?"

Lauren nodded at her, watching as the Scots woman placed her glasses back on her face, the nurse's index finger rising to push her own back up her nose as she turned her head, addressing all of those present, "Right, as I just told Eric and Emily, I am Lauren, Lauren Teacher, I am a nurse at the hospital, this is my patient Brandon Milton, beside me, and the lady here on the seat is Jiyaa" At the mention of her name, Jiyaa turned her head, nodding at each of those that she hadn't met in turn, and Lauren continued, "I guess we should at least learn each other's name, right?" "Geri, Geri Larkin...I am an admin back at the hospital" the Scots woman gestured with a hand towards the back of the ambulance, voice grim. "Marcus Wilson" the young man didn't turn to meet their gazes, his eyes closed as he leaned against the rear doors of the ambulance, "Porter" Frowning at the young man, Lauren fought not to snap back at his attitude, reminding herself that she had forgiven the teenage girl for her manner because of the awful experiences that she had endured, and that this situation was no different. "I am Doctor Alan Green" the silver-haired man seated at the right hand side at the back of the ambulance suddenly announced, his features softening as he smiled wearily, giving him an

235

almost grandfatherly appearance, "I too work at the hospital...I am a general practitioner"

"Doctor" Lauren nodded at him, smiling softly.

"So we know each other's name" Marcus gave a weary sigh as he straightened at the back of the ambulance, shrugging as he spoke, "What now?"

"We get to safety I assume" Lauren stated, holding his gaze as he stared back at her, his top lip curling as he gave a sarcastic smile, nodding.

"Oh, and where's that?"

"What?" she shook her head, stunned by his sudden confidence and attitude, and as the young boy upon the bed winced, the Doctor Green turned to look up at the porter, forcing a smile.

"Why don't you calm down, son, you are scaring young Eric"

"Son?" Marcus gave a bitter chuckle, top lip curling as he stared down at the doctor, "I ain't your son, *dad*"

"Hey now" the silver-haired man rose to his feet, one hand steadying himself on the wall of the ambulance as it moved beneath their feet, "Why are you so tense, let's just all be calm"

"Why can't we be calm?" the voice of the porter was literally dripping with attitude as he turned to face the much older man, his body language hostile, "I'll tell you why...I have a brand new

Kismee 50 4T back in the car park...I haven't even finished paying for it yet...and I need to get home to my boyfriend...so no, I wont calm down"

"How about if ah knock some teeth down your neck" Geri took a quick step towards the porter, nodding as she spoke, "Do ye think that might convince ye to watch ye fucking manners!"

The porter winced, hands raising before him, and Lauren sighed heavily, then swayed slightly as the ambulance stopped moving. For long moments they all turned to look at each other, then as one their eyes seemed to drift to the door beside Lauren, fully expecting it to slide open, only for the voice of Brandon to drag the nurse's attention back to him as he spoke, "Where is the lady with the brown hair and the leather coat"

Feeling suddenly sick, Lauren raised a hand to her face, staring in horror at Brandon as he began to speak again, sadness in his voice, "She seemed nice...has she gone home?"

"Alice!" Lauren muttered, drawing the gaze of Geri and Jiyaa, each of them appearing as shocked as she was feeling coursing through her. How could she have forgotten about Alice?

In their brief acquaintance the woman had been a constant support. How could she forget her?

Gritting her teeth, she tried to remember when she had last seen the woman in the leather jacket. They had been running from the hospital entrance, pursued by dozens of what Brandon called ghouls, and Alice had been at the back urging them all to keep running. Then the ambulance had arrived and they had all clambered inside the vehicle, aided by the bearded man with the dreadlocks, presumably the *Dog* that the children had referred to earlier. So just what *had* happened to Alice?

Had the chasing horde of ghouls caught up to her? She winced at the sudden thought, trying unsuccessfully not to picture the woman's death. Fighting the wave of nausea that was assailed her, Lauren leaned upon the edge of the stretcher with one hand, blinking away the tears for a woman she had barely known, another woman that had bravely lost their life in the last hour.

Just like poor old Mary back in the elevator.

Just like Jennifer, murdered by her husband.

Heaving a shaky sigh, Lauren closed her eyes, giving herself over to the jerking motion of the ambulance as it suddenly began to move once more, turning left and then speeding away.

But to where?

Chapter Twenty Eight

"We need to stop" Bella announced after they had been driving for what seemed an eternity, gesturing to what looked like a parking area ahead of them on the windy road that they were traversing through the Northern Pennines, heading west. The heavy rain had stopped for the moment, finally fading away but leaving behind a grey hazy sky which the sun seemed unable to penetrate properly, the foul weather adding to the already gloomy atmosphere of the moorland. They had been driving for over an hour, Bella estimating that they had put around thirty miles under the tyres as they had tried to find safety, yet each time that they had considered stopping the ambulance so far they had been forced to drive on by the sudden appearance of more of the white-skinned people, or by abandoned or crashed vehicles, indicating that some may be lurking nearby. Over the last few miles though, Bella had begun to voice her dislike that they were just driving away from the danger, and not doing anything pro-active, and Dog and Alice had agreed with her. It stood to reason that before long they would run out of petrol and then they would be stranded. Far better to stop and come up with a plan of action before that happened.

Watching as the former soldier drove their stolen ride down off the main road that cut through the moorland and down onto the gravel based parking area, Dog sighed heavily, hoping that Emily and Eric were OK in the back of the vehicle, suddenly wishing that he had gone in with them.

"Right, let's have a quick scout about before we let the others out to make sure it's safe" Bella turned to nod at Dog then her eyes drifted to Alice, "Do you want to wait here?"

"No" the brown-haired woman shook her head, forcing a smile, "We are in this together"

"I like your attitude" Bella smiled back, then opened her door and stepped out, her right hand reaching back in to drag the shotgun from beside her seat, before she closed the door behind her.

"Oh that's a relief" Alice glanced at Dog, smiling broadly, "You have a shotgun!"

"We have an empty shotgun" he shook his head, opening his door and climbing out, gesturing for her to follow him. As she stepped down onto the gravel, Dog reached into the pockets of the body warmer that he was wearing and produced two items, holding them out before him, "You better take one of these"

"What?" she glanced down at the taser and the baton that he was holding, items that he had taken from the police officer that he had killed back beside the road blockage, "I don't know"

"Do you know how to use a taser?" he asked, and she shook her head, wincing as he opened out the extendable baton and passed it to her, "Here, you take this then, I'll take the taser"

The woman raised an eyebrow, "Do you know how to use one of them?"

"No" he shrugged, forcing a grim smile, "If need be I'll just throw it at them"

The crunch of footsteps on gravel made Dog suddenly tense and he turned towards the noise, relaxing as he saw Bella walking around the perimeter of the parking area, holding the shotgun as if she was ready to use it, and sighing heavily, Dog moved over to stand beside her. Nearly a minute dragged past as the two stood side by side, Dog's eyes drifting over their surroundings as they stood side by side in the parking area, the main road cutting along behind them, and a massive drop lying ahead of them. Grimacing as he took a step forward and looked down at the moorland below the steep incline, Dog shook his head, letting his gaze drift over the remote land, frowning as he spotted a farmhouse on a hill directly opposite them, then turned his gaze to study what looked like a village in the distance, the weak sunlight glinting off a window. "Looks like a village or something over there" Bella nodded at his words, her smile forced and he gave another sigh, "Look, I know you are pissed at me...and I get that...I really do, I am sorry about what happened to your dog, Castiel" The muscles clenched in her cheeks at his words and he sighed again, shrugging, "You know what, you are right, I should have just shot my friend in the head...but I couldn't...call it weakness, call it what you want but I couldn't let someone else die because of me"

She turned at his words, her voice a whisper on the wind, "Because of you?"

"Forget it" the reality of his words hit him in the face like a splash of ice cold water and he started to turn away then paused as she reached out, a hand touching his forearm, her eyes meeting his. "Tell me"

He grimaced, a shaky breath escaping him as he once more felt the heat of the flames upon his body, prickling his skin, and the screams of his family, his voice barely audible, "I can't"

"Dog" her fingers tightened and he gave a soft snarl of anger, his head shaking but she was defiant, her eyes boring into his and just like that his resolve broke, his head shaking as he turned to stare out over the drop, his voice pained.

"I was the vicar of Westergate, a small Hampshire village…I lived with my wife, Carol, and Rebecca and Rory, our kids, in the vicarage"

He let out a shaky sigh as he pictured his children as he had last seen them, then shrugged, his shoulders seeming to slump, "The vicarage was old, the lights and the wiring was awful…Carol kept telling me to contact the appropriate people to get it fixed…it wouldn't have cost us anything as it was a church property, but no, me in my divine wisdom, I kept putting it off, then one night I was leading late night worship…it was a Thursday…17th November, five years ago…one of the villagers came running in, you see the old vicarage had caught fire…it was the wiring I found out later…my family couldn't get out…I had locked the doors when I went to the church and taken the keys with me, I had forgotten that Carol had misplaced hers…"

"Oh" the soft word from Bella was filled with so much emotion that it nearly crushed Victor where he stood, and for a moment his knees threatened to buckle beneath him, yet somehow he managed to stay upright, his voice filled with self-loathing now, "I tried to get them out but the heat…it was too much, still, I got the door open, and almost held Rebecca, but then the house…I don't know, they say the gas oven blew…it went up…they all died…I should have died…my back is burned, beneath this beard I am burned…"

His words trailed off and he turned to meet the gaze of Bella, his stomach knotting at the haunted look on her features as she studied him silently, her cheeks clenched, and he gave a shrug, "That's why I couldn't just give up on Moonshine"

Bella nodded, wincing slightly, and he sighed, a hand rising to wipe the tears from his eyes, his head turning to look over at where Alice was studying the pair of them intently, obviously not wanting to intrude, and he sighed, "We best let the others out of the ambulance"

"It was Afghanistan, August 24th, 2013" the voice of Bella stopped him in his tracks and he turned to meet her gaze, realising that this was a big moment for her, and he nodded, staying silent lest she change her mind and clam up once more. Before him, Bella turned to gaze out over the drop, a heavy sigh seeming to shake her, and then she was talking once more, "I was a Sergeant, out there serving with the 1st Regiment Royal Horse Artillery during Operation Herrick as an FAC with a fire support team…"

"FAC?" he shook his head, wincing as he spoke, fearing that he might have ruined her confidence. She turned back to face him, and once more he saw the haunted look upon her features, the look that he saw in himself each time that he looked in the mirror, "A Forward Air Controller, part of a six man team. The infantry go in and we would go with them, and call in artillery or air strikes if and when it was needed"

Dog nodded once more, watching as the muscles in Bella's cheeks seemed to spasm as she fought to control herself, and he shook his head, "You don't need to do this…"

"You did" she countered, taking a step towards him until they were almost face to face, her body language as if she was standing to attention and giving a report, "We were driving down towards Maraj in Helmand Province when an IED went off under the lead Mastiff. It was chaos, smoke and flames, then Terry started shooting at us…

"Terry?"

She winced, "Its what we called the Taliban…this group appeared on our flank, another Mastiff got it…it was chaos…the commander gave me the nod and I called in air support…"

Nodding, Dog watched her, somehow guessing what it was she was about to say, wanting more than anything to stop her having to speak it aloud but his throat was tight as he saw the raw pain in her brown eyes, "It was mental...I had done it a dozen times before...but...the enemy were everywhere like ants...I called the fire in danger close...when Fast Air came flying in they blew up our boys that had survived the IED in the first Mastiff...I got cleared of any negligence because I had followed procedure...but...then we shipped out of that shithole a year later, and then I was discharged in May 2017"

"I'm sorry" Dog nodded, knowing from his own personal demons and guilt that telling her that it wasn't her fault was an exercise in futility, that she wanted him to hate her for her mistake just as he hated himself for his, the pain almost being cathartic and so he stood there, holding her gaze. Raising a forearm to her eyes, she dragged it sideways, clearing her vision and forcing a grim smile, Dog nodded at her, "So, we are both a pair of fuck-ups...what can we do...we have to keep going...we owe it to them to not give in, right?" Bella studied him in silence for a moment, and Dog realised with shock that although the pair of them had been strangers just two hours before she was the only person that he had been so open with about his family, even in therapy, and he suspected he was the first that she had spoken about the war with such open honesty.

Suddenly, she stepped forward, one arm releasing the shotgun to wrap about his neck as she hugged him, not the soft, awkward embrace of the strangers that they were but that of friends, bonded together, unified in their guilt. Without thinking, Dog hugged her back, their cheeks pressing against each other, and then he gave a soft chuckle, "Normally, I get someone to buy me a drink before we get physical"

"Dickhead" Bella released him and stepped back, the pair matching smiles, then he turned and nodded at the ambulance, gesturing for her to walk with him as they made their way to Alice.

Chapter Twenty Nine

Smiling awkwardly as the pair approached her, Alice stepped aside, watching as the bearded man, dreadlocked man reached out and slid open the door to the back of the ambulance, forcing a smile as he peered inside, "Come on out, guys" Stepping back to the side of the vehicle, Alice loaned against its side, watching as Lauren exited the ambulance, nodding in thanks at Dog, and turned to help the familiar figure of Brandon out. As the nurse led the young black man to the side, out of the way of Jiyaa as she began to climb out, Brandon turned his head to study her, frowning in surprise, "There she is, she didn't go home" "What?" Lauren turned her head, her eyes widening behind her glasses as she saw Alice standing there, and without hesitating she rushed forwards, throwing her arms about her neck, "Oh my God, I thought you'd been killed" "Not yet" Alice gave a chuckle, hugging the nurse back, surprised at how emotional she was feeling, then turned to throw a smile at Jiyaa as she moved alongside them, the Sikh woman touching her heart and then placing that hand upon Alice's left cheek, her eyes wet with tears.

"Now tha's a face ah recognise!" they all broke apart as Geri stepped from the ambulance, nodding at Alice as she joined them, "Hen" Alice nodded at her, watching as the thin porter that they had saved from the stairwell got out of the vehicle and strode off alone across the parking area, his phone in his hand, and the embalmer noticed the grim look that Lauren sent him, then turned to study the two Asian children that came next, obviously the pair that the man named Dog had said he had rescued on the A66. As the young boy moved over to stand beside Brandon, the pair wandering away across the parking area, the girl who looked to be near her teens shot their small group a look of suspicion and moved over to stand beside Dog and Bella, the pair speaking to her quietly and being answered with a nod. Beside Alice, Lauren turned, telling Brandon not to go near the edge of the parking area and to stay close by, and then Alice was turning her head studying the silver-haired man in the doctors coat that was exiting the ambulance, a border collie held in his arms. "I took the liberty of making a splint for her broken leg from supplies in the ambulance" the doctor nodded as he passed the dog to Bella, the woman handing the empty shotgun to Dog first.

As the silver-haired woman kissed what was obviously her pet, hugging it to her face, the doctor spoke again, "I think with rest, she is going to be perfectly fine...but I'm no vet"

"Thank you" the silver-haired woman nodded, glancing up at the physician and beside her, Dog raised a hand, gently patting her upon the back, earning a smile for himself from the woman.

As the doctor moved to stand beside the teenage girl, and turned to face them, Alice let her gaze drift over them all, counting them one by one, and then nodded. They were eleven in number. Eleven people and an injured dog.

"We've not met" she glanced up at the voice of the silver-haired man, smiling as she found him nodding at her, "I'm Doctor Alan Green"

"Alice" she told him, and he smiled, turning to glance at everyone else, raising his voice slightly. "Are we all acquainted?"

"I'm Bella" the silver-haired woman moved her gaze among them, "I was driving the ambulance, I only know Dog, Doctor Green and the kids"

There was a mutter of greetings, and then the Scots woman stepped forwards, pointing to first herself then each of the others from the hospital with a finger, "Geri, Jiyaa, Alice, Lauren, Brandon, and that lanky string o' piss over there is Marcus"

As Bella nodded at each of them in turn, Alice shot Lauren a glance, "What went on in there?" "He's a bit of a prick" the nurse muttered, nodding towards where the young porter was storming around the parking area with his phone held aloft, his face fixed with a mask of irritation. "Where the fuck are we exactly?" he turned as they were studying him, a hand gesturing out over the drop, his head shaking, "What is this?" "The North Pennines" Bella replied, watching the man carefully, her tone tight, and Alice felt her stomach knot as she saw Dog tense beside her. Across the gravel parking area from them, the young man blinked, a lopsided smile creeping on to his features and then he gave a soft chuckle, his head shaking, "Well that tells me fuck all" "She's just told you that we are on the North Pennines" Dog's head tilted to one side as he regarded the taller, younger man with a smile, but the light of it didn't reach his sad grey eyes. The young porter gave another soft chuckle, his head shaking as he held the gaze of Dog, "I wasn't talking to you sweetheart" "No, but I was answering" the broad-shoulder man passed the shotgun that he was holding to the doctor as he stepped past him towards the porter, his voice like ice, "Is there a problem"

The younger man seemed suddenly unsure in the face of the bearded mans presence, and he took a shuffling step back, the smile on his features not as confident as before, his right hand raising his mobile phone aloft, "I need to know exactly where we are so I can get someone to come and pick me up"

"Pick you up?" Dog shook his head, "Have you just been through the same morning we have?"

"Don't you talk to me like I'm a bitch" the porter found a reserve of arrogance from somewhere.

"Then don't act like one" Dog took another step forward, fists forming at his sides, and wincing, the doctor stepped alongside him, his free hand resting on the left shoulder of the bearded man. "Come on, let's not do this, please"

Dog nodded, his eyes holding to the porters for a moment and then he stepped back, glancing first at the doctor and then everyone else, "I'm sorry"

"Dinnae be" Geri snorted, "Ah'd have hit him"

Muttering under his breath, the porter cast them all a scowl and turned to walk away once more, staring at his phone angrily, and sighing, the Scots woman gave a sigh, "As much as ah hate to agree with tha prick, he does have a point...wha are we doing out here?"

As the majority of eyes moved back to rest on Bella, she gave a shrug, her tone defensive, "We had to on to the Pennines, there were abandoned cars everywhere, roads were blocked...every time we have considered stopping we have seen more of those things...they are everywhere"

"Ghouls" the voice of Brandon made everyone turn to face where he was standing kicking at the gravel with Eric, the young black man nodding wisely, "We are calling them ghouls now"

"OK" Bella nodded, smiling awkwardly, "There were...ghouls...everywhere...we couldn't stop"

"It's true" Alice felt the need to support Bella, turning to stare at those that she had known longer, her companions from at the hospital.

"Ach no, I wasn't complaining like some" Geri shook her head, "Ah was just curious"

"How far do you think we have driven from Thames?" Lauren asked, Alice watching as the young nurse removed her glasses, cleaning them on her sleeve as she waited for an answer.

Before them, Bella glanced at Dog and he gave a shrug, meeting the gaze of Lauren, "Thirty miles"

"Oh" she seemed stunned, wincing as she pushed her glasses back onto her face and fell silent.

"So, what do we do out here?" Doctor Green handed the shotgun back to Dog and turned to look at Bella, his hands raising defensively before him, "Genuine question"

"I don't know" she admitted, shaking her head slightly, and on the other side of the parking area, the porter gave a bitter laugh, having returned to the conversation, "Well, that's great isn't it…you drag us into the middle of nowhere and then have no idea what we are going to do next"

"Maybe we should have left you" Bella grimaced, her features twisting in sudden anger, "This isn't a fucking game…people have been dying…my grandparents….these kids grandfather…Dog's friend…if we hadn't stopped to pick you up, you'd be dead too!"

"And we appreciate it!" without giving it conscious thought, Alice stepped into the middle of the argument, nodding at Bella, her tone sincere, "We really do…despite what he says"

Behind her the porter muttered something under his breath, and Alice grimaced, head shaking as she turned to look at him, "Mate, just shut up!"

"Fuck off" the reply came, and grimacing Dog took a step towards the porter, Geri doing the same, and the young man took another step back, shaking his head as he changed the subject, "Can anyone else get a fucking signal or a reply on their mobiles? Mine got through to my boyfriend

but there was no reply…now there's no signal"
At his words, everyone else but Jiyaa, Brandon, Eric and Doctor Green checked their phones, a chorus of negative replies answering the porter.
"Fuck this!" he span away, kicking at the gravel then turned to glare back at the group, "I need to get home, I cant be out here"
"We all need to get home" Alice replied, holding his gaze, "I have a business to run in Newcastle!"
Geri nodded, "Ah need to get back to my dogs"
Everyone else stayed silent, exchanging glances, and finally Dog broke the silence, his eyes drifting to meet those of Alice, "Driving here was a nightmare…the roads were utter chaos…I don't want to begin to imagine how bad it would be trying to get to Newcastle"
"Maybe its not happening there" Alice stated, hating how uncertain her voice sounded, and beside her Lauren shook her head, wincing.
"This is madness…Brandon hasn't got any family…I cant look after him indefinitely"
At her words, Dog winced, glancing sideways at the Asian girl but she seemed not to notice, and Alice realised that the brother and sister must be in exactly the same situation as Lauren's charge. Sighing, she turned to glance at Jiyaa, realising that the woman had wandered silently away to

stand staring over the drop, her yellow sari blowing about her legs in the slight breeze. Back at the hospital her brother had claimed that she had not been in the country long. Did she have anyone that was going to miss her? Jiyaa turned as Alice studied her, their eyes meeting, and the woman smiled sadly, and turned away once more. Feeling sick with concern for both her, and everyone else, Alice turned back to face the others, "What do we do?"

"It's going to get dark before too long" Bella stated, glancing about them at the moorland, then shook her head, "We don't want to be outside on the moors at night, we need to find shelter"

"Could we sleep in there?" Geri asked, glancing at the ambulance, "Would we fit do ye think?"

"No" Lauren shook her head, smiling sadly, "We could barely all fit in there standing up on the way here...I don't think that's an option"

"Lauren is it?" Dog asked, waiting till the nurse nodded before he continued, "Lauren is right, we need to find somewhere much larger"

"Preferably something we can defend" the voice of Bella had them all exchanging concerned looks and she shrugged, "These things are everywhere"

"She's right" Dog nodded, turning to point with an arm across the valley, "I saw a farmhouse over there, if we can find a road around there, maybe the owners will put us up for the evening"

"What if the owners have gone like everyone else has?" the voice of the porter was almost a whine. Dog shrugged, his bearded features grim as he met the gaze of the young man that had tried to bait him earlier, "Then we don't need to ask them for their permission"

"Fucking Hell" the porter gave a snort that was part sob and part anger, "This is mad"

"What's that" Brandon turned, head tilting to one side as he stared off out of the parking area towards the long winding road that they had just traversed in the ambulance, "Do you hear that?"

"What is it?" Lauren asked, moving to stand beside him as he stood with Eric, staring off at the rise of the road as it wound through the moorland, and the autistic man shook his head. "It sounds like dogs...or maybe bears"

"Oh God" the gasp of terror slipped from the lips of Lauren as she took a step back, leading Brandon with her, and stepping forward, Alice grimaced as she stared off down the road, the grim voice of Dog sounding from behind her. "Everyone back in the ambulance, quick as you

can, quiet as you can...come on, go, go"
Grim-faced, everyone did as he had instructed,
Bella passing her dog back to the doctor, the
Asian girl grasping her younger brother by the
hand and dragging him to safety, Jiyaa sensing
the meaning of Dog's words as Geri grasped at
her arm and led her back onto the vehicle.
Closing the side door behind them, Dog opened
the passenger door and gestured to Alice, "In you
go, lets get out of here while we can, eh"
She nodded, slipping back inside the ambulance
cab, and he followed her, shutting the door
behind them, Bella clambering behind the wheel.
In seconds, the silver-haired woman had the
engine running once more, and was turning the
wheel as she took off the handbrake and put her
foot on the accelerator, moving as far towards
the drop as she dared before putting the vehicle
in reverse and moving backwards several feet.
"What are you waiting for?" Alice muttered as
they stayed in the same space, lined up ready to
drive out of the parking area, her eyes peering
through a light rain as it began to fall, then Dog
was pointing, his finger shaking and she cursed
as she saw the small group of ghouls come
climbing up over the side of the drop, maybe fifty
metres down the road from the parking area,

shambling like large white spiders onto the road before rising to stand, their forms hunched over like some form of primitive cavemen, many of them hardly wearing any form of clothing now. "What the fuck" her words escaped in a gasp, her head shaking, "God help us all"

Behind the wheel, Bella gave a shake of her head, her voice thick with emotion, as she began to drive away, leaving the parking area and heading in the opposite direction, "I don't think he's listening anymore"

Chapter Thirty

It took over an hour of driving around the moorland, circling back upon themselves each time that they thought they had gone too far in the wrong direction, always keeping the distant village in sight before they finally found the small dirt track that led to the farmhouse Victor had seen from the parking area. Grimacing, Bella stopped the ambulance as Alice pointed, shouting as they drove past it, and then began to reverse down the narrow road, turning the wheel as she steered their vehicle onto the muddy track.

"Are we too wide?" Victor leaned closer to his window, peering out at the moorland beside his side of the ambulance, unable to see the road, and Bella gave a grunt of amusement, nodding. "Almost"

"Oh Christ" Alice winced, reaching out to hold on to the dashboard before her as the ambulance rocked and wobbled as it drove over the uneven ground, and beside her, Victor grimaced as he considered how it must be for those huddled in the back of the vehicle who couldn't see what was going on. Ahead of them, the track began to wind to the left, angling as it did so, and beside Victor the ground seemed to drop quickly away, the moorland sloping downwards as they

climbed the steep hill, Bella's curse causing him to turn his head to her, wincing as he saw the land beyond her window had risen sharply so that she was just inches from rock and peat.
He flinched as the wing mirror on Bella's side struck the wall, and came off with a crunch, dropping out of sight between the ambulance, and the slope, a grunt of shock escaping Bella while beside him, the woman Alice was pale.
He understood her fear entirely.
If Bella was to steer too close to the wall they would come back off it and plunge over the steep slope on his side of the vehicle to crash below.
Turning his head, he stared west out of his window, refusing to let his gaze drift to see how high they were, his brow furrowing as he saw that the sun was beginning to set in the distance. Despite it being only about four O' clock in the afternoon, night was only just around the corner. They needed to be off the dangerous track and settled in the farmhouse before the sun set.
If they weren't then they were screwed.
"So what's the plan" the voice of Alice, had him twisting in the seat slightly, meeting her gaze as she glanced between him and Bella, "Up here at the farmhouse, I mean, what are we going to do, just knock on the door and ask if we can stay?"

He winced, nodding, "When you word it like that it sounds bad...I'm not sure...Bella?"

The silver-haired woman turned from where she was steering the ambulance for a second, just that fraction of time making Victor wince in dread, but then she was studying the twisting track once more, shrugging, "I don't think they are going to be in a fit state for us to discuss it with them"

"You think they will have turned into these ghoul things?" Alice winced, her voice strained and Bella gave a chuckle, her head shaking slowly.

"Is that really what we are calling them?"

Victor shrugged, "The lad Brandon seems convinced that is what they should be called, bless him, why not...it does kind of suit them"

"OK" Bella gave a nod, slowly turning the wheel right as the track turned and then began to level out, ground appearing again beside Victor's window, "Ghouls it is...but yeah, it seems that everywhere we have been everyone is changing into these ghouls...why not here too?"

"We haven't" Alice pointed out, forcing a smile.

"Not yet" Victor sighed heavily, and Alice sent him a worried look, face pale as she held his gaze.

"Go on"

He shrugged, his throat tight, "Remember the

friend that I told you about earlier, Moonshine?"
Alice nodded, and he winced, turning to glance
out of the window, "I was bringing him to the
hospital, he'd broken his left leg...we ran into
some ghouls on the A66 where we rescued Emily
and Eric, but Moonshine seemed OK. Even after
we'd met up with Bella and been to her farm and
driven to the hospital he seemed OK except he
was sleeping a lot...then within minutes he had
turned into one of them...it was so quick"
Alice nodded, her voice tense, "That's how it was
with Jiyaa's brother back in the hospital chapel,
one moment he was OK, the next he sort of went
unconscious, then he was one of these ghouls"
"She was there?" Bella asked, clearly disturbed
by Alice's tale and the young woman nodded.
"Yeah, she saw it all"
There was a moments silence then Victor gave a
sigh, "So, that's what I mean when I say none of
us have turned yet...I guess any of us could"
"That's a terrifying thought" Alice winced.
Victor nodded at her words, then turned to
glance back at the metal wall of the cab behind
them, suddenly imagining how bad it would be if
one of those in the back had turned while they
had been driving, and butchered all of the others.
No, surely, they would have heard the screams.

Wouldn't they?

Feeling sick, he turned his head around as Bella stopped the ambulance and switched the engine off, "There she is, our home for tonight"

Almost five minutes slipped past as the trio in the cab of the ambulance stared out through the windscreen at the large farmhouse which sat about thirty metres from where they were parked, then Victor turned his gaze, staring out across the open moorland which it overlooked, knowing that if the situation were not so dire he would be mesmerised by the beauty of the view.

"Right" Bella turned to look at the pair of them as he glanced back, her features grim, "I propose we let the others know what we are doing then we approach the farmhouse with as many of us that feel up to it and see what the score is...we can spread out and have a look around"

Alice winced at her words, "Is that safe?"

"She's right" Victor nodded, earning a look of irritation from Bella, "What? I'm just thinking, if they haven't turned and they have had trouble up here, the sudden sight of a group of strangers wandering around their house is going to make them think we are either ghouls or looters...we stand a chance of getting shot for trespassing"

Sighing heavily, Bella held his gaze, staring past Alice as she raised an eyebrow, "So what, you want us to go and knock on the door…and if they are ghouls we are going to let them know we are here and where to find us"

He groaned, head shaking, "For fuck sake, well, I don't know then…you decide"

Bella turned away staring back out of the window at the farmhouse, her voice grim as she shook her head, "We need to do something, its getting dark real quick"

She was right. In no time at all the setting sun seemed to have turned to a sliver on the horizon, and the farmhouse was less visible than it had been amid the darkness of the open moorland.

"For fuck sake, we'll try the door" Bella gave a sigh, one hand about to open her door, only to freeze as beside her Alice shook her head quickly.

"Wait…wait a minute"

"What?" Bella glanced back, then turned to stare out through the windscreen, "What is it?"

"The farmhouse" Alice nodded, a hand rising to point at its bulky shape amid the rapidly growing darkness, "Why are there no lights on in there"

As one Bella and Victor followed her gesture, a curse escaping the bearded man as he realised that she was right, "Fuck…you're right"

"Does that mean they are dead?" the voice of Alice was tense, her eyes shifting as she glanced at the darkness around the farmhouse, and he grimaced, shaking his head as he met her gaze. "Maybe they weren't home"

"No" Bella pointed with a hand, "There's a jeep down there beyond the house, I saw it there when we pulled up...someone was home"

Dog nodded, grimacing in dread as he studied the building before them, then turned to look at his companions , "So, what do we do...assume that they have turned?"

"We have to" Bella nodded, "Right?"

Alice grimaced, "Better to be safe than sorry"

"Shit" Victor grimaced, picking the shotgun up out of the footwell and frowning, "We have this with no shells, Alice has the baton and I have the taser I don't know how to use...we're fucked"

"I bet there are more shells in the house, more than likely more guns too" Bella turned from him to study the building, "I've never known a farmer not have guns...we just need to get to them"

"Ah" Victor gave a chuckle, "That's all, good"

For a moment the three of them sat in silence, and then Bella gave a grim chuckle, "I suppose at least we'll be able to see them OK in the dark what with them being white...small mercies eh"

"So, we have a plan?" Alice raised an eyebrow.

"Sure" Bella nodded at her, "We get to the house, get inside, find the shells for the shotgun, then we secure the farmhouse and get the others"

"You make it sound so easy Victor sent her a grim smile, "What if we encounter any ghouls?"

"Run" Bella shrugged, "We've learnt that they seem pretty impervious to harm, shit, even bullets don't seem to have any effect on their thick skin"

As Victor grunted in acknowledgement, Alice shrugged, "Back at the hospital, Jiyaa hurt the one that had been her brother by stabbing it in the eye...could you shoot them there?"

Bella nodded, "We can try...it's softer than their skin for sure...Dog drowned one too didn't you?"

He chuckled, "Yeah, but I don't think there is any chance of me doing that on this hill though"

"There's something else" Alice stated, drawing their gaze once more, "Back at the hospital, me and Lauren found one on an operating table, unconscious, looking like it had changed mid-operation...it was open wide at the stomach and we saw inside it...the organs seemed to have a tougher skin upon them, like their outer skin...only the heart seemed vulnerable to harm"

As Bella let out a curse, her features grim, Victor clicked his fingers, "We don't need to run!"

"What?" the two women eyed him in confusion and he nodded, "When me and Moonshine were chased near some woodland, we got trapped near a fence and we stopped moving...the ghouls couldn't see us...it was as if we had vanished"

"I remember you mentioning that" Bella nodded.

"Why?" Alice raised an eyebrow, "I don't get it"

"Me neither" Victor gave a shrug, "But it's another option for us...we need to test it again"

Again they lapsed in silence, the tension high, and then Bella nodded, "Are we all ready?"

Nodding his head, Victor threw her a grim smile and opened his door, "Come on, let's get this over with before I change my mind"

Without another word, he slid from the vehicle, holding the door open for Alice as he stepped to the door on the side of the rear of the ambulance, opening it a crack so that he could see inside it. Instantly, a horde of faces stared back at him, a myriad of emotions passing over them as they saw him staring in, and Victor released a shaky sigh as he realised none of them had changed.

"What's wrong?" the nurse standing closest to the door, Lauren, asked him, "Is everything OK?"

He nodded, his voice low, "We have finally made it to that farmhouse that I saw from the parking area. Me, Bella and Alice are going to check it out...it might not be safe, you guys stay here, see is there a lock on the inside of this door?"

Leaning around it, the nurse frowned, then nodded, meeting his gaze once more, "Yeah"

He nodded, "Lock it when I shut the door, don't open it until you hear me knock three times"

Lauren winced, "Be safe"

"Sure" he forced a smile, throwing a wink at Emily as she sat watching him, his stomach knotting as he saw the fear on her face, and then he stepped quickly back and shut the door tight, forcing away the memory of his daughter as she had given him the same look moments before the house had exploded in flames, killing his family.

"Are we all good to go?" the voice of Bella was a whisper in his left ear, and he cursed, turning to face her in the darkness, head shaking in shock.

"For fuck sake, I nearly died"

Winking at him, Bella began to move away around the front of the ambulance, the empty shot gun clasped ready in her hands, Alice close behind her with the police baton extended. Grimacing, Victor fished the taser from his pocket, and stared down at it as he walked through the darkness behind them, wishing that he had taken the time to work out how to use it when there had still been some light to see by. It was shaped like a gun, made of hard yellow plastic, and grimacing, he slid his fingers around the handle, nervously touching the trigger.

Ahead of him, Bella was almost halfway to the front door of the farmhouse, her movement slow and measured, her army training evident, and behind her Alice was twisting her head back and forth, her face pale in the moonlight from above. Raising his head, Victor studied the moon for a moment as it stared down at them from amid the dark storm clouds, and then it was gone, plunging them back into virtual darkness again.

"For fuck sake" he muttered, then froze, head turning as he caught a patch of something lighter in the darkness of to his right, "What the fuck..."

The moon emerged just as the ghoul was almost upon him, its powerfully built body garbed in a dirty pair of blue overalls, a body warmer like the one that Victor was himself wearing over the top of them. Snarling in excitement, the bald-headed, callous-skinned figure struck him like a battering ram, throwing him backwards to lie on the mud. Pain from the injury in his side instantly coursed through him, and for a second, he almost passed out, only the shock that he was just feet away from the steep drop to the moorlands below keeping him conscious. Above him, the ghoul gave a roar, the sound taken up by another of its kind somewhere off to their right, and cursing Victor brought the taser up to point at its face, dragging back on the trigger. Instantly two red beams of light shot out from the end of the taser, settling on its cracked features and with a curse of anger, Victor shifted his aim so that the red dots were on the eyes of the beige ghoul and then fired. There was a crack as the taser discharged, followed by a scream of complete agony from the ghoul as two small metal darts shot into both its eyes, the wire connecting each of them to the weapon sending electricity shooting into its face. With a grunt, it toppled and fell back to the ground, and grimacing, one hand clasped to his side, Victor made it to his knees, watching as suddenly Bella and Alice were beside the fallen ghoul, each hammering hard blows down upon its features with their respective weapons. Another snarl suddenly split the night and the trio turned towards it, Victor cursing as he saw another ghoul come charging from the far end of the house in the moonlight towards where they stood, larger than the one they had just killed.

It was just clearing the threshold of the property when suddenly the front door of the farmhouse swung open and a light came on, a voice calling out suddenly, "Roger!"

The ghoul turned towards the newcomer, snarling in hatred as a woman surged into view from the house, then it was staggering back as she swung what looked like a saucepan up towards it, water splashing it right in the face. From where they stood, the trio watched in disbelief as the woman rushed back inside the relative safety of the doorway, watching in terror as the ghoul thrashed and twisted, hands dragging at its features, what looked like steam rising from its face. Off balance, and blinded, the ghoul continued to stagger away from the house, and gritting his teeth, Victor began to slowly run towards it, head down as he changed his angle, charging at it from the direction of the house.

He struck it hard with his left shoulder, the pain of the impact dropping him to his knees, his vision swimming as he clasped at his side in agony, watching as the ghoul staggered back and fell from the slope, its animal screech rising back to reach them before it was suddenly cut short.

Blinking, Victor turned to watch as Bella and Alice began to run towards him, and then he fell to his face in the mud, the darkness claiming him.

Chapter Thirty One

"What a fucking day" Lauren exclaimed nearly two hours later, her hands wrapped about a mug of steaming coffee, head shaking as she sighed. Seated at the table with her, Alice, the silver-haired Bella, and the kindly Doctor Green smiled. A comfortable silence settled over them all for a moment and then the young nurse shook her head once more, her voice thick with emotion as she glanced at each of them, "I didn't know any of you this morning...now look at what we have been through...I cant believe this is happening" At her words, Alice who was seated beside her, reached out and placed a hand upon her forearm, squeezing gently as she nodded, "We will be OK" "Will we?" Lauren sent her a worried look, trying to smile but failing miserably, "This time last night I was sat in my flat, worrying like mad about meeting Brandon today for the first time and taking him to lunch...now I am all he has" The others at the table winced at her words, the doctor raising his cup to his lips as he sipped and then nodded, "I was at my home too, reading a book, drinking tea...quite boring really" "What book?" Alice asked, smiling at the doctor and he gave a chuckle, shaking his head slowly. "A horror book, about a large house in Durham that is inhabited by the ghosts of twelve serial killers...it really is quite disturbingly fun"

There was a soft murmur of amusement at his words and Alice nodded, "I was at my place of work, preparing the last body for the night"

"Body?" Lauren sent her a curious look and on the other side of the large wooden kitchen table, Doctor Green raised an eyebrow in curiosity. "Are you, yourself a serial killer, Alice?"

"Not quite" she shook her head, smiling, "I am an embalmer, I have my own business in Newcastle"

The doctor gave a nod of admiration, and smiling awkwardly, Alice turned to the silver-haired woman sitting on her other side, "What about you Bella...what were you doing last night?"

The woman winced at her words, a sad smile creasing her features as she closed her eyes for a moment and then shrugged, "Watching television with my gran...my grandad had taken ill"

At her words, the other three exchanged glances and Lauren winced, "Did he turn into..."

"One of them?" Bella glanced up to hold her gaze, nodding as she spoke, "Yeah...this morning...then my gran turned as well..."

"Oh, you poor thing" Doctor Green shook his head at her, "You have my condolences"

Bella nodded, forcing a weak smile, "Thanks Doc, we have all lost people close to us though"

He winced, head shaking, "Not me, I have no-one"

The three women exchanged glances at his words, and Lauren nodded in what she thought was understanding, "Did you lose them in the first two waves of the virus?"

"What?" he raised an eyebrow, then gave a soft chuckle, his head shaking, "No, nothing so tragic, I have just never met the right person...I think that perhaps I have left things a little too late"

Again the three women exchanged glances, Alice and Bella raising their cups to their mouths, and Lauren cast her gaze about the large kitchen in which the four of them were sitting comfortably, as if the world hadn't just turned to shit outside. She had unlocked the ambulance rear from the inside as she had heard the three knocks from outside, just as the man named Dog had told her, only to find a pale faced Alice standing there instead. As Bella had appeared beside the woman in the leather jacket, the group had begun to disembark, following the silver-haired woman's insistence that they hurry to the farmhouse.

And so leading a nervous Brandon by the hand, they had hurried through the dark to the building, the nurse smiling awkwardly at the rotund blonde woman that had stood beside the open doorway, beckoning them inside her home. she had gasped in concern as she had entered the living room of the property to find the familiar figure of Victor laid upon the floor, a blanket over him, and a broad-shouldered, red-faced man sat on an armchair nearby, urging them to enter and find somewhere to sit or stand.

She had found out moments later, once everyone was safe inside the building, and the door had been locked, that the couple were indeed the owners of the property, Robert and Valerie Naughton, sheep farmers and local landowners. They had awoken early that morning as usual, and Robert had been heading out to check their sheep with their two local farmhands, Roger and Terry, only for the latter to suddenly fall ill, his hair falling from his body and head, and his skin appearing to thicken and crack, becoming hard. Lauren, like some of the others, had seen the process happen first hand but hearing someone else describe it sent her stomach knotting and she felt a heady wave of nausea wash over her. Somehow, she had managed to hold it together, listening intently as the couple had explained how Robert, already suffering from a badly dislocated right knee cap in an accident several weeks before, had been attacked by the newly transformed Terry, and managed to escape back inside the house, only for Roger to also change. They had spent the rest of the day in hiding, their blackout curtains drawn across the windows, the lights off and only candles giving illumination, and Robert had loaded the farms two shotguns ready to defend themselves while his wife had tried unsuccessfully to contact the local police. Finally, as the thing that had been Roger had begun to hammer upon the front door, Robert had pushed one of the shotguns through the letterbox and given him one barrel, the force throwing the enraged former farmhand away from the door but apparently doing no harm.

"Guns don't work on them?" Marcus had shaken his head at that point, glancing at everyone in the room, his voice almost hysterical, "What do we do if guns don't work...we're screwed!"

"They do work" Bella had grimaced from where she had been seated upon a long sofa beside Alice and the two children, the border collie held protectively in her arms as she had fixed the porter with an angry stare, "They throw them back...they might not kill them but you can still protect yourself to some degree with them"

"Oh great" the young man had given her a look of mock gratitude, clapping slowly, "Awesome"

"There are other ways to hurt them" Alice had spoken up, wincing as everyone had turned to look at her, "Their eyes can be hurt, if you can blind them it stands to reason you have a chance to escape...Jiyaa used a knife to do that back at the hospital, and Valerie here just blinded another with a pan of boiling water...also I believe Dog drowned one...and he's also just electrocuted one through the eyes outside...they can be killed...it's just not easy to do"

Bella had clicked her fingers, then as if suddenly remembering something, "Dog seems to think that if you stand completely still they cant see you for some reason...he and his friend did it to escape some in some woods near my home"

"Stand still?" Marcus had given a sneer, "OK"

"It's true" Lauren had confirmed, the eyes of everyone shifting to study her as she had given a nod, "Back at the hospital, myself, Brandon and a very brave old lady named Mary had been trapped in the kitchen by a group of ghouls, we froze on the spot...I thought that they were going to kill us but then they seemed to look through us as if we weren't there, and walked away"

time had seemed to stand still as everyone had

stared at her, looks of surprise upon the faces of them all except for a cynical Marcus and an unconscious Dog, and then Valerie had risen to her feet from where she had been perched upon the arm of her husbands armchair, "Right, I will sort out somewhere for you all to sleep…there are plenty of blankets to go round, I might need some help though"

"Ah'll help ye, hen" Geri had risen to her feet, Jiyaa joining the Scots woman, and together, the trio had left the room, chatting as they went.

"Thank you for this, Mr Naughton" Doctor Green had nodded at the farmer from where he was standing just inside the door, and the man had waved a hand, dismissing his thanks with a smile. "If me and Val can't help out our fellow man, we don't deserve saving ourselves. And that's a fact"

"You are a good man" Lauren had told him, and he had shrugged, his head shaking once more.

"No, I'm just a man, its how everyone should act"

Now sat in the kitchen of the man's home, Lauren couldn't shake those words, her mind conjuring up images of the brave sacrifice of Mary in the elevator earlier to save Brandon, compared to the foul, cowardice of the men Nick and Peter. It seemed while some people had become the best that they could be, others had devolved.

Now, with darkness having fallen completely, and their small party having all been fed a meal of hot soup and bread, cooked by Valerie and handed out by Geri and Jiyaa, they had spread about the farmhouse with the owners blessing. Eric and Emily were both upstairs in a small bedroom, a recent check by Alice confirming that both had fallen asleep, and Lauren had managed to get Brandon asleep in the small room beside it, the young man hugging tight to the book that Alice had finally returned to him earlier. Shortly after eating, Valerie and Robert had made their excuses and retired to their own bedroom at the back of the farmhouse on the ground floor, leaving a pile of blankets for the others. As they had left, the porter, Marcus, had snatched a blanket in a hand and stormed off upstairs alone. During all of this, Dog had stayed asleep upon the living room floor, a pillow beneath his head, and those still remaining had watched as Doctor Green and Bella had carefully removed his upper garments, and Lauren had winced as she had seen the bruising upon the left side of his ribcage, and then the shiny burns that covered his shoulders, and extended down onto his broad back. Shaking her head, wondering what had happened to the bearded man in his past, she had glanced up, watching the face of the woman, Bella, as she stared down at the naked chest of the man, a strange expression upon her face, then they had both turned to listen to the doctor as he had stated that he believed Dog had broken his nose and at least one of his ribs on his left side. Carefully, the doctor had wrapped the man's torso in bandages that he had taken from the ambulance earlier, and strapped a cold pack against the bruising, then sat back on a chair. For a long while, they had all sat in the living room, lost in their thoughts, and then Jiyaa had fallen asleep in an armchair, her soft moans and sobs drawing the gaze of everyone as she began to call out in her own language, muttering the name Opinder, and Alice had explained in detail what had happened to her brother in the chapel. As the Indian woman had sobbed aloud, Geri had nodded at the others, telling them to go and have a brew in the kitchen and that she would stay and watch over Dog and Jiyaa while they slept. "I am going to try and get back to Newcastle tomorrow" the voice of Alice dragged Lauren from her thoughts, and she winced, turning to glance at the woman that was seated beside her. "Are you sure its going to be safe?" "No" Alice shook her head, "But I cant stay here"

Across the table, Doctor Green cleared his throat as he spoke, "I am sure Robert and Valerie are in no rush for any of us to leave...we don't know how wide this is spread...there's safety together!"

"I know" Alice winced, turning to glance at Bella beside her, "What do you think?"

"I wouldn't risk it" she shook her head, then gave a shrug, "But I can't tell you what to do"

"Maybe give it another day" Lauren suggested, nodding as she spoke as if that would convince the woman, suddenly, inexplicably afraid to lose this new friend, "Let's just make sure its safe"

"How?" Alice sighed, smiling sadly, "We tried watching the news earlier but its not on...there is nothing on the radio...no-one is answering a phone, how are we supposed to find out how bad this is?"

"I think you have answered your question" Bella gave a shrug, "I think this is everywhere"

Alice winced, "I can't think that...I can't...I have a business...I have things to get back too..."

Her words trailed off as she stared at Bella, recalling that the woman had told them she had lost her grandparents, "Oh Bella, I'm sorry"

"Its cool" the silver-haired woman gave a sad smile, "Right, I am going to go and make sure Dog is OK, I'll see you all when you come in"

As one, Alice, Lauren and Doctor Green had bid her goodnight, the physician rising politely as she had left the table before seating himself once more, and Lauren had nodded towards the living room, "I think she likes him"

"Who?" Alice had glanced at her, "Bella and Dog?"

The nurse nodded, and beside her Alice gave a soft chuckle, "They do seem quite close"

"They saved me" Doctor Green announced from the other side of the table, a haunted look in his eyes, "I was being chased but they saved me"

"And then you all saved us" Lauren nodded, chuckling softly as she raised her half empty cup of coffee in the air, "A toast...to new friends"

Smiling, Alice and the doctor did the same.

"To new friends"

Chapter Thirty Two

"Are you still awake?" the soft voice of Eric asked from across the other side of the bedroom, his voice a hushed whisper, and sighing heavily, Emily closed her eyes tight, trying not to bite.

"No, I'm asleep"

"Oh" her brother muttered, a heavy silence filling the darkness before his voice returned, thick with confusion, "You can't be...you answered!"

"What do you want, you little turd" she groaned, staring up at the lighter shade of darkness that was the ceiling above her, "Go to sleep"

"I can't" his reply came, "Can I get in with you?"

"What?" she cringed, raising her head off the pillow to stare through the dark room towards where he lay, "No way, you wet the bed"

"I do not" his reply was angry, "Not anymore"

"Whatever" she muttered, head shaking though she knew he couldn't see her, "You're not getting in here with me...that's just weird"

"I don't want to be on my own" he insisted, and she pictured his face screwing up, "Emily!"

"Ugh" the teenage girl gave a grunt, "Why don't you go and find your new friend and talk to him"

Across the room, her brother gave a soft grunt of surprise, and she heard the bed creak as if he had sat up, "Brandon? Do you think he'll be awake!"

She groaned, "I was joking you idiot"

"I'm not an idiot!"

"No?" she gave a bitter chuckle, "Go to sleep"

There was a moment silence and then his voice came once more, "Emily, I'm scared"

For a moment, she lay in the darkness of the bedroom, wanting more than anything to ignore the pleas of her younger brother but then the realisation hit her that he was all she had left. The death of their granddad during the madness upon the road that morning had seen to that.

Had it really been that day?

It seemed so long ago now.

Closing her eyes, she pictured the man that she and Eric had lived with since their parent's fatal car crash two years before when she had been eleven and Eric had just turned four years old, trying to feel some emotion other than shock at their granddads death but there was nothing.

In truth they had barely seen him since he had taken them in, spending the vast majority of his time slaving away in the small restaurant that he owned in Darlington, while she had become mother to Eric, feeding, cleaning and caring for him, while her friends had done teenage things. And now it was just them once more.

"Emily" the voice of Eric sounded once more, thick with the promise of tears, and sighing, she flipped back the duvet atop her and groaned aloud, "For God sake, come and get in"

As she heard the soft chuckle and the pad of bare feet rushing across the bedroom floor she realised that she had been played but she went with it, cursing as he crawled across her, a knee catching her in the side and then he was laying upon his side next to her, "Thanks Emily"

"Move over" she moaned, pushing at him as she rolled onto her side away from him, "You stink"

"I don't stink" he argued, and she cringed as she heard him suddenly sniffing as he lay beside her. "What are you doing now?"

"Seeing if I do stink, my armpits do…you're right"

"Ugh" she grimaced, sliding further away from him, her head shaking, "You are disgusting"

Her brother chuckled, and she sighed, "Sleep"

For what felt like an eternity, he began to twist and move behind her, patting at his pillow, and talking to himself and Emily groaned inwardly, knowing from her daily experiences of putting him to bed that this was going to take hours. Closing her eyes, she listened to the house about them, blocking out the voice of her brother as she listened to the creaks of the floor downstairs as people walked about, and the ticking of a clock somewhere off in the distance, then raised her eyes to glance at the folded-up blanket beside the bed where the border collie, Lexie lay sleeping. Emily winced as she recalled the moment the poor dog had received the injury, her stomach twisting in dread as she pictured Bella's bigger dog, Castiel, as it had fought to stop Moonshine. Moonshine.

She and Eric had only known him for a couple of hours, maybe less, but in that time, he had seemed like a nice man, and had helped Dog save them from what they were now calling ghouls. Then he had become one and tried to kill her. Her left hand rose to touch her throat as she cast her mind back to the ghoul crawling atop her, choking the life from her body but then Dog and Bella had been there, saving her once more. Where were they now? Downstairs?

The last she had seen of Dog, he had been lying unconscious upon the floor of the farmhouse living room covered in blankets, Bella at his side and she frowned, realising with surprise that she was more concerned with the well-being of the bearded man than she had been her grandad.

"Emily" the soft voice of Eric whispered behind her and she sighed, opening her eyes as she rolled onto her back, her brother doing the same beside her. For a moment, he was silent and then he sighed, "Do you remember what mum and dad looked like?"

She winced, not having expected the question, her eyes suddenly brimming with tears, "Yes"

"Tell me"

She winced, "Mum was beautiful, she had long black hair, and the most amazing smile"

"What about dad?"

"He was the most handsome man ever"

"Like me?" Eric asked, and she laughed aloud.

"Yeah, totally like you"

"Good" his voice was soft, "I miss them"

She frowned, "Do you remember them?"

She saw him shake his head in her peripheral vision, his voice sad, "Not their faces, but I can remember their hugs…I liked their hugs

"Me too" Emily's throat was suddenly tight with emotion and for several minutes they lay side by side in the darkness before Eric spoke again.

"Did they love me?"

"Yeah" Emily had to fight to keep her voice from shaking, a hand rising to wipe a tear from her left eye, "Stop asking stupid questions"

He gave a grunt, "Do you think they like me?"

"I just told you, mum and dad loved you"

"Eh?" he sounded confused, "No, Dog and Bella"
She rolled her eyes, smiling, "Yeah, I guess"
"Do we like them?"
The teenage girl gave a chuckle as she rolled on to her side, staring into her brothers face as he did the same, realising just how young and scared he looked, "I don't know, do you?"
The boy frowned, "You are in charge of me"
She nodded, "But I can't tell you who to like"
"Oh" he frowned, his features thoughtful for a moment before he nodded, "Then yeah, I do"
"Good" she rolled onto her back once more.
"Do you?"
"Like you?" she sent him a look of amusement, "I have to like you, you are all I have left"
Eric grinned at her words, "No, Dog and Bella"
She nodded in understanding, "I think so, they have kept us safe haven't they"
"Yeah" he smiled, "They have...do you like the others yet...I think Brandon is my best friend"
Emily smiled, "You've just met him"
"Yeah, I know"
Turning to look at her brother once more, she shook her head and leaned quickly over, kissing him upon the forehead before rolling away, "Now go to sleep before I smother you"
"OK" he sounded happy, "Night Emily, I love you"

"Night" she smiled as she closed her eyes, her throat tightening once more as she realised for what felt like the first time how much she meant the words she was about to say, "I love you too"

Chapter Thirty Three

It was early when Alice awoke the next morning, stretching as she sat up in the armchair where she had fallen asleep, then blinked, momentarily confused as to where she was as she stared about the large living room, and those asleep around her, eyes straining in the darkness.

Then the reality of her situation, and the events of the previous day returned in a rush and she closed her eyes and lay back, her breathing shallow as she considered what had happened. Sarah was dead. Society was in utter turmoil. Feeling suddenly nauseous, she sat up quickly, pushing the blanket from her body, and then rose to her feet. Beside her on another armchair, Geri was asleep under a blanket, legs curled up, and on the sofa on the other side of the room, Lauren and Jiyaa lay at separate ends, sharing a duvet. As she took a step towards the kitchen, she spied the empty armchair near the door, and frowned, realising that Doctor Green was not in the room, then turned to stare down at the pile of blankets that lay in the centre of the floor where Dog had been, though the figure of Bella still lay beside it on a rough bed made of blankets and pillows. Frowning, Alice turned her head, listening for any sound from upstairs, but there was none, and had it not been for the absence of the men she might have thought she was the only one awake. But they were gone from where they should be. Panic surged through her like wildfire as she considered the possibility that ghouls had somehow managed to get into the farmhouse, only to dismiss it at once, her head shaking. If ghouls had gained entry while they had been sleeping the chances were they'd all be dead.

So where were Dog and Doctor Green?

Stepping out of the living room into the dark corridor beyond, Alice began to creep along it in the direction of the kitchen where she had been sat with Lauren, Bella and the doctor the night before, hands rising to rub at her arms below her tee shirt, shuddering at the early morning chill. She paused as she saw the flickering light of a candle upon the walls ahead and picking up her pace, turning as she reached the kitchen door only to gasp in terror as strong arms grasped her and held her still, a hand covering her mouth. For a moment, she began to resist then stopped as she heard the familiar voice of Dog whisper in her ear, "Don't...fucking...move"

Eyes wide, she started to nod then froze, staring over his hand into the large kitchen beyond at Doctor Green, and Valerie and Robert Naughton.

The kindly physician and the red-faced farmer were both seated at the table, their faces grim as they tried to keep still, a small candle upon a plate in its centre casting strange patterns upon the walls as it danced and flickered, while the farmer's wife stood halfway across the room as if frozen in place, a porcelain cup held in each of her hands, steam rising from their rims.

For a moment, Alice let her gaze stay upon the woman, studying her features intently, her eyes clamped shut and her lips pressed tight together. Then the embalmer let her eyes drift a fraction to the right to stare past the farmer's wife at the kitchen window, the blackout curtains drawn back less than a foot, but enough to reveal the calloused and cracked white-skinned features of a ghoul as it stared in at them, the thick mucus of its eyes appearing more like off milk than the chicken soup coloured orbs of those that they had seen yesterday. Heart hammering in her chest like a pneumatic drill, Alice watched in grim fascination as the ghoul suddenly moved its face closer to the window, its breath fogging up the glass as it peered inside, perhaps attracted to the farmhouse by the faint light from the candle.

Then it was gone, shambling off to their left, and releasing Alice, Dog moved quickly inside the kitchen, past Valerie and shut the curtains tight. As the men at the table visibly relaxed, Alice leaned heavily against the door frame and shook her head, a hand rising to clasp at her chest while in the centre of the room, Valerie slowly opened her eyes, "Oh God, is it gone?"

"It is" Dog muttered, stepping away from the window to sit down at the table, a hand rising to clasp at his side over the bandages that the doctor had applied to him the night before, a frown creasing his features as he met the gaze of the physician, "I take it you fixed me up?"

"I did" Doctor Green nodded, smiling at the bearded man, "Or I did my best, you have a broken rib and a broken nose, you need rest"

Dog nodded at his words, smiling softly, and as Valerie placed the two cups that she was holding down upon the table in front of her husband and the doctor, she turned to Dog, "Cup of tea?"

"Please" he nodded, wincing as he moved his seat further towards the table, and still standing beside the doorframe, Alice let her gaze drift over the tight shiny skin of his broad shoulders, wincing as she recalled from the night before that his upper back was burned exactly the same.

"Are you joining us?" she winced as Dog suddenly addressed her, and stepping away from the door, she moved to sit down at the table beside him.

"I'm sorry"

"What for?" he gave a soft chuckle, and she winced once more, her eyes drifting to his skin.

"Oh" he gave a nod of understanding, then shrugged, "You didn't do it to me...its fine"

Alice shook her head, "I meant for staring"

"I know" he gave another chuckle as he met her gaze, "I'm joking, seriously its fine...I'm fine"

"Apart from the broken rib and nose" Doctor Green nodded from the other side of Dog, a stern look creeping onto his features, "And as I have advised, you need to rest or you'll make it worse"

"The doc is right" Robert Naughton nodded, head shaking as he made a face, "Val's brother, Jack, broke a rib back in the nineties when we all went on holiday to Scarborough and..."

"Whitby love" his wife chuckled from over beside the counter where she was making Dog his drink.

The farmer groaned, eyes rolling, "Whatever, my point is he didn't rest and he made it worse, he ended up with pneumonia didn't he Val?"

"He did" she nodded, head shaking once more.

"I appreciate your concern" Dog nodded at both the doctor and the farmer, then smiled up at

Valerie as she placed a cup of tea before him, and another before Alice, the farmers wife joining them all as they sat around the wooden table.

"I forgot to ask if you wanted a tea dear, sorry, if you don't want it that's fine, just leave it"

"Oh no, I appreciate it, thank you" Alice wrapped the cup with her hands, enjoying the warmth, and then the farmer's wife sighed, head shaking.

"That was my fault...the curtain"

"No point blaming yourself, Val" her husband reached out, bumping her shoulder gently with a large fist, "Nothing happened...everything's fine" Yet despite the support of her husband, Valerie shook her head, her features grim, "I do it every single morning, I come in here...I open the curtains so I can see the sun coming up, and then I make a drink for myself, Robert and the lads, ready for when they arrive...oh God, they are really dead aren't they"

As she gave a stifled sob, her husband reached out and placed a hand atop hers, squeezing gently, surprising Alice with his tender nature considering his size, and looking suddenly uncomfortable, Doctor Green glanced at her and Dog, "So, what does today bring do you think?"

Alice and the bearded man beside her exchanged glances and then he shrugged, "Well, once everyone is awake I think we need to make sure that ghoul is dealt with and that there are no more lurking about"

Alice nodded, noticing Doctor Green's eyes drift down to the bandages about Dog's chest, his lips parting as if he were going to remind him that he needed to rest then chose to stay silent instead.

"Well, as I told the others last night, I think you were out for the count at the time, we have two shotguns here, you have your own, and I have a lot of shells. We can head out and have a scout round when the sun comes up"

"You will do no such thing, Robert Naughton" his wife sent him an angry glare, dragging her hand from under his to point at him, "Your leg isn't working well yet, the last thing we need is you falling over and getting hurt"

Her eyes were brimming with tears by the time she had finished and wincing, feeling awkward, Alice leaned forwards, "I am sure we can find three people to do it...Dog is clearly going to ignore orders to rest, and I am sure Bella will want to help...I can go with them...if you trust us with your guns that is"

The burly farmer gave a chuckle, "Trust you? We let you all stay here, of course we trust you"

"Robert is right...we trust you, and you are all welcome to stay here as long as you need"

At her words, Alice winced, and beside her Dog gave a chuckle, "What's that look for?"

Turning her head, she held his gaze for a moment and then sighed heavily, glancing back at the Naughtons, "I really appreciate the offer, and I know that it might be safer here, but I need to try and get back to Newcastle...I have a business"

The bearded man grimaced at her words, glancing at the others present and she nodded, guessing the arguments he was about to push her way, "I understand that its going to be difficult, I saw the roads when I was sat in the ambulance cab with you and Bella yesterday...but I think I can make it, I have to at least try, right?"

"Are you sure?" the soft voice of Doctor Green dragged her attention, and she shook her head.

"No, not really...but I don't have a choice, I dropped everything to drive down to Thames to visit a friend in hospital" she stated, wincing as she pictured Sarah once more, then sighed, "I have to get back to work...maybe order has been restored by now...have you tried the radios and television again?"

The Naughton's exchanged glances at her words, and beside Alice, Dog gave a frown, "What is it?"

"There's nothing now" the voice of the farmer was grim, "We turned the telly on this morning and there's nothing...the radio is the same"

A heavy silence descended upon the table as the five of them sat exchanging glances and then Robert gave a sigh, shrugging, "As said, you are more than welcome to stay but if you need to go you can take the car Roger and Terry use to come here each morning, sadly they don't need it now"

At his words, Valerie rubbed at his hand beside her, smiling sadly, and Alice shook her head, "Oh, I don't think I'd feel right taking their car...what if the police and everything is back in order...I'd get done for theft"

The farmer blinked, lips moving as if confused and then he gave a sad chuckle, "No lass, the car is mine, I lent it to Roger so they could get to work up the hill. They would never have walked from the village to come to work, the sods"

As she nodded in understanding, Dog leaned forwards, "How far is the village?"

"Ten minutes in the car, but to walk it'd take you about an hour and a half" Valerie answered him, raising her cup and sipping at it for a moment before arching an eyebrow, "Why?"

As Alice watched him, he gave a shrug, "If we are going to be staying here then it is only fair that we try and find supplies and stuff to help…if this is going to drag out then it makes sense to do"

"Drag out?" Valerie sent Dog a shocked glance, and then stared at her husband, "Robert?"

For a moment, the large farmer held her gaze in silence and then he nodded, "He's right Val, we don't know how long this will drag on for"

As she winced, her head shaking, the farmer turned to Alice, "I'll take a look at that car for you once the sun is up and we know this place is safe, and make sure that its road worthy enough to get you to Newcastle"

Taking a deep breath, Alice nodded at him, her stomach tight as she forced a smile, trying not to think of the long and dangerous journey she had committed herself to, "Thank you"

Chapter Thirty Four

"Maybe we should have waited until the morning before doing this" Alice turned to glance at Geri, just under twelve hours later, as they drove away from the Naughton's farm in the car that Robert had provided them with, Marcus sat in the back.

"Nah, this is the right choice" the porter leaned forward between the seats before the Scots woman could answer, the young man stifling a yawn with a hand as he sat back, "The sooner we are in Thames the better"

"Ah hate ta admit it, but he's right" Geri shook her head, gesturing to the porter, "We couldna stay at tha farm forever, hen

"Yeah, I guess" Alice nodded, casting Geri a weak smile, "It just feels weird leaving them all behind"

"I don't see why" Marcus gave a sneer, and she glanced at him in the rear view mirror, "You don't know them, not really, they are strangers"

"So are you" Alice answered quickly, her tone defensive and in the back of the car, the porter gave a grunt and lay down across the seat.

"What tha fuck are ye doing?" Geri turned from the passenger seat to throw him a glare, "You cannae lay down, put ye fucking seat belt on"

"Oh fuck off and let me sleep" he grumbled, his tone irritable as he rolled to face the back of the

seat, "You wake me up when we get to Thames"
Grimacing, Geri turned back to stare at Alice as
she drove, her voice loud, uncaring that the man
in the back could hear her, "I swear tha lazy prick
has done nowt but fucking sleep today!"
Turning to throw her new friend a smile, Alice
nodded, steering the car along the road that they
were driving on, realising that Geri was correct.
Shortly after Robert had offered her the use of
the car earlier that morning, Lauren, Bella, Jiyaa
and Geri had stumbled into the kitchen, half
asleep and Valerie had begun making drinks for
everyone before starting on cooking everyone
some food. The children and Brandon had
awoken just over an hour later, Emily carrying
the border collie downstairs to give to Bella.
Yet of Marcus there had been no sign until just
before half eleven when he had sloped
downstairs, moaning he was cold and hungry.
By that time, Alice had been out on a scout
around the farmhouse with Dog and Bella, each
of them holding a loaded shotgun, although she
had told them both that she had never fired one.
For almost an hour they had searched the area
without success, and Alice had realised that as
places to hide went, the Naughton farm was in a
perfect location. To the south facing front of the

303

farmhouse, thirty feet from the front door was a drop that fell away a good hundred feet to the valley below, a glance over the edge revealing the twisted body of the ghoul named Roger that Dog had pushed over the previous night, the sheer face of the drop appearing unscalable without equipment. Beyond the west of the farmhouse, the land ran on for a hundred feet, housing a couple of large barns filled with a variety of old machines, and a couple of cars, before it too dropped away to the valley, while behind the farmhouse, and its large garden area in the north, the land rose sharply, rising to about sixty feet in a wedge of land that edged around the building to the east and bordered the climb to the farm, that road being the only access point available. For nearly ten minutes, the trio had stood in a group discussing the topography of the farm, Bella stating that it was in defensive terms a dream. It was highly unlikely that anything, even a ghoul, was going to be able to climb up from the valley below, while the rise at the rear looked equally difficult to scale, meaning that anything that fell down from above was going to be in no condition to cause them much of a problem.
If they managed to block the road, the only access point then they should be able to keep the

building secure, especially when taken into account that the creatures seemed only able to see moving targets with any real skill, rendering them useless at night. With three shotguns, a load of shells, their wits about them and the hospitality of the Naughtons, they were safe as anyone could possibly be given the situation. Feeling positive about the safety of the group, the trio had continued scouting about the land, then turned as one as a rasping snarl had come from one of the large barns, all three shotguns rising. Slowly, casting each other grim looks, the trio had approached the barn in question, their steps cautious, deliberate, and before long they were standing before its wide opening, staring in at the ghoul, naked from the waist up, dirty jeans on its legs as it was lying upon its stomach, hands reaching under an old red Cortina Mk2 that was parked there on flat tyres, and covered in rust. Grimacing, the three of them had watched in disgust as the ghoul had suddenly slid back out, one crusted white hand curled around the body of the largest rat that Alice had ever seen, the rodent screeching in a mixture of terror and pain. Without hesitating, the ghoul had sat down with its back to the drivers door of the car and raised its arm, shoving the head of the rat inside its open mouth. Fighting the sudden urge to vomit, Alice had stood beside her two companions, watching in horror as the ghoul had suddenly clamped its teeth down, head shaking as it bit off the head of the rat, blood pouring from its mouth. Grimacing, Dog had moved towards the ghoul, the shotgun pointing at its face, and with a snarl it had seen him and tried to stand, snarling around the bloody gobbets of meat in its mouth The retort of his shotgun had been loud as he had discharged it at almost point-blank range, throwing it back hard against the car behind it, to then bounce off and fall to its face on the ground. "Fucking hell!" Alice had grimaced, spinning about, fully expecting the noise to bring others out of hiding, then turned back to stare in utter disbelief at the ghoul as it had tried to rise. Without a word, Dog had stepped forwards and brought the stock of the shotgun down hard upon the back of the ghoul's head, dropping it back down to the floor, and then tossed Bella his weapon. She had caught it with her left hand, her right clasping to the stock of her own weapon, and Alice had moved alongside her, the pair of them watching as Dog had dragged something from a pocket and crouched quickly down beside the ghoul. Dumbstruck, Alice had watched as he had dragged the ghoul's arms behind it and then fastened them together with a set of handcuffs, before rising to his feet and stepping back away. Nearly a minute had dragged by as the trio had stood studying the ghoul as it seemed to rouse itself, body tensing as it tried to bring its arms around before it but with no success, and then Dog had move back beside it, hands dragging at its body as he rolled it over to lay upon its back. Instantly, the ghoul had sat up, hands cuffed behind it, teeth snapping at the air, and grimacing, Victor had taken his shotgun back from Bella and hit in the face again, throwing it back to lay squirming upon the ground. Shaking his head as he studied it with a grimace, he had held the shotgun in his left hand, while his right dragged a pair of shells free from a pocket. Grimacing, Alice had stood watching as he had emptied the old shell casings, and placed the new ones in their place, snapping the shotgun shut as he took aim at the ghouls face, then froze, his brow furrowing as he stood staring down at it. "What is it, Dog?" Bella had asked, moving closer. He had turned at her voice, holding her gaze for a moment before looking at Alice, "You said that when you were in the hospital you saw one of these that was open for an operation, right?"

She had nodded, moving closer to the ghoul as it lay on its back, snarling up at them, and Dog had frowned, "You said the internal organs were tough like their skin but the heart was still soft?"

"Yeah" she had grimaced, nodding at him, "Why?"

The bearded man had turned his gaze back down to the ghoul, the barrel of his gun moving down to poke gently against the left side of its chest, the voice of Dog intrigued, "Look at that"

Stepping closer, Alice had stared down at the ghoul, her eyes drifting from the crusted and calloused white skin of its features, down over its neck and shoulders and across its chest, the skin there the same as upon its altered features, and then she had given a soft gasp as she had seen the circular patch of clear skin, no bigger than a two pound coin, situated over the ghoul's heart.

"What the fuck is that?" Bella had grimaced, her head shaking as she had crouched down to study it, "Is it a wound or something?"

"I don't think so" Dog had stood staring down at it with a grimace, "It looks like a weak spot in its armour if you ask me...like the soft spot on top of a baby's head"

As the women had both turned to stare at him in surprise, the bearded man had shaken his head and glanced about the barn, before grunting and moving to one of the two workbenches within it, returning with what looked like a rusty old kitchen knife. Moving back to them, he had passed Bella his shotgun, and then as she had risen and stepped aside he had crouched beside the ghoul, one hand resting upon its forehead, holding it down while he placed the point of the rusty blade against the smooth patch of skin. For a moment, Dog had stared down into its milky eyes and then he had sighed, his head shaking slowly, "I'm sorry"

Without another word, he had driven the blade downwards, the rusty knife sliding down into the body of the ghoul like a hot knife in warm butter. Instantly the ghoul had sagged, resistance gone from it, legs and body going limp like a puppet whose strings had been unceremoniously cut. The rest of the day had been a whirlwind of activity as they had returned to the farmhouse to inform the rest of their companions of the new weakness that they had found in the ghouls, followed by Robert heading from the building to check over the Land Rover that she, Geri and Marcus were now driving through the night in. "So, what do you think we will find" the voice of the Scots woman dragged Alice from her thoughts, and turning her head, she cast Geri a curious glance, then glanced back at the road before her, wincing as she steered the Land Rover around a bend that was tighter than she had expected. Beside her, Geri gripped at the dashboard before her, staying silent, and then as Alice straightened the vehicle up on the next stretch of straight road, she gave a shrug, "Do you think that this really is everywhere?"

"If it is we've made a really bad decision leaving the farm" Alice tried to chuckle but the sound came out awkward and off key and she winced. "Aye, ah was thinking that myself" Geri nodded, then turned to throw a glare into the back of the vehicle as Marcus gave a sudden grunt, "Shut up" This time, Alice's chuckle was real, and she shook her head, then cursed as raindrops began to spatter down upon the windscreen, "Oh great" "Wonderful" Geri clapped her hands together, and turning quickly, Alice saw her shake her head, "Rain...what else can go fucking wrong?" With a roar like a lion, the white skinned figure in the porters uniform suddenly slammed up hard behind the seat of the Scots woman, strong arms reaching around to grasp at her head, fingers dragging at her face. Screaming in dread and horror, Alice slammed on the brakes, the road forgotten as she watched the ghoul that had been

Marcus push its fingers against the Scots woman's face, fingers smashing through the lens of her glasses deep into the eyes sockets beneath. Moaning in pain and terror, Geri raised her hands to weakly try and drag off her assailant, choking on a scream as one hand hooked fingers into the left side of her mouth, tearing her open to the cheek, blood cascading down over her body. "Leave her alone!" Alice screamed, realising the futility of her words, Geri was all but dead, and with a roar of excitement, the ghoul turned to stare at the embalmer, a hand reaching for her. Heart skipping a beat, Alice shifted in her seat, desperately trying to ward off its attack, then screamed as the Land Rover skidded and slid. It turned sideways in the road and toppled over, smashing down onto its driver's side as it slid, glass shattering and flying up against Alice. With an almost sober and calm part of her mind, she suddenly recalled the winding roads that she had been negotiating in the dark, and the drop to their right, then screamed as they struck the low wall that bordered it. The vehicle lurched with the impact, flipping back the other way, the bloodied and broken body of Geri lurching like a ragdoll, and then the Land Rover was flying through the dark night towards the valley below.

Chapter Thirty Five

"So, where do you fancy going?" Victor turned to meet the gaze of Bella as the pair of them shut the doors of the dark silver Toyota Landcruiser that Robert Naughton had leant them for their foray to the nearby village of Hanward, and began fastening their seatbelts, "Asda?"

The former soldier chuckled at his words, her head shaking as she pushed the keys into the ignition and began to drive the vehicle forwards, past the front of the farmhouse, the pair of them nodding at the Naughtons as the couple stood outside the building with Doctor Green, the trio waving as they passed. Ahead of them, the ambulance had been moved by Lauren, the young nurse sat behind the wheel ready to reverse it back into the entrance at the top of the winding track and block it again when they had passed. She raised a hand at them as they drove by, and once more, Victor and Bella returned the gesture. Then they were off, driving slowly down the winding dirt track towards the distant main road. They had spent an uneventful second night under the roof of the Naughtons, the couple feeding them all the previous evening and again that morning when they had awoken, neither of them seeming bothered that without any warning their home had been overtaken by eleven strangers. No, that was incorrect, with the departure the previous evening of Alice, Geri and the whining porter Marcus, they were only eight in number. He smiled sadly at the thought of the brown-haired Alice, a part of him missing her despite having only known her for a little over twenty-four hours. She had been with him and Bella during their drive through the moorland two days before, and she had been with them then they had found the ghoul the previous morning and discovered their weakness, be it minor.

And now she was gone, as quickly as shed come.

"I hope she gets back to Newcastle OK" he stated, turning to glance at Bella and the silver-haired woman nodded, smiling at him as she replied.

"I hope so too…nice lass"

He nodded, "Yeah she was, and the Scots woman"

"Geri" Bella chuckled and Victor followed suit.

"That's her…tough one wasn't she"

"Yeah" Bella grinned, slowing the vehicle as they reached the main road that cut across the barren moorland, "She was for sure"

Victor smiled, the pair of them falling into a comfortable silence for a minute and then he glanced back at Bella, "Do you think we will see them all again when this is over?"

Bella grimaced at his words, "If its ever over"

"Yeah" he nodded, sighing, "Alice, she left her phone number back at the farmhouse, I think we should check up on her once we get back"

Again the former solder gave a nod, her head turning to smile at him, "Missing her are you?"

"Oh, jealous are you?" he teased, then regretted it as she winced, her eyes locking to the road, and feeling suddenly awkward he did the same, the silence no longer as comfortable as it had been, not helped by the fact that they had fallen asleep on the living room floor side by side talking the night before, only to wake up spooned into each other that morning, the embarrassed smiles on the faces of Lauren and Doctor Green, and Jiyaa showing they too had witnessed the scene.

They drove on in silence for a moment and then he gave a sigh, "Look, about this morning..."

"It's fine" she shook her head, blushing, "Really, we were asleep...its not like we slept together"

"Exactly" he gave a laugh, surprised by her words, and then he grinned, "Lucky I guess"

"Oh?" she sent him a look, trying not to smile.

"Well" he gave a shrug, shaking his head in mock irritation, "All we did was spoon and you still managed to take all of the duvet"

She laughed at his words, head shaking and he grinned as he glanced at the side of her features, throat tightening as if he was seeing her for the first time, "You look different when you smile"
"Less of a grumpy bitch, you mean?" she glanced at him, trying not to laugh and he nodded back.
"Yeah, of course…but seriously, you should smile more, it suits you"
She blushed, head shaking as if she was going to deny his words, then she sighed as she steered the vehicle around a tight bend in the road and straightened up once more, "Shut up, Dog"
Victor nodded, stunned that he had been so open but then he frowned in confusion as his eyes fixed on something in the distance ahead through the windscreen, "Stop the car, Bella"
"What?"
"Stop the fucking car, now"
Grimacing, she did as he had instructed, turning to glare at him, but he raised an arm, pointing ahead of them, "Someone has gone off the road"
"What?" she frowned, following his gesture, the muscles in her cheeks tightening as she noticed the damaged section of wall he was pointing to.
"Dog!" Victor heard her voice call out to him as he opened the door and climbed out, one hand rising to adjust the straps of the empty backpack

that he was wearing over his shoulders, then he gripped the shotgun that Robert had given him with both hands as he began to cross the road. "Dog!" the voice of Bella called out to him once more, hushed slightly now, and he paused and turned, watching as she moved swiftly over the road to stand beside him, her own weapon ready. As he took another step along the road, Bella gave a grunt and turning, he found her staring down at the road surface and he did the same, his stomach tightening as he saw the skid marks. "They seem new" Bella's voice was grim, and Victor shook his head, voice tight with emotion. "Do you think it was them?"

"I don't know" she answered simply as she began to walk once more and he fell in beside her, the pair stopping once again as they saw scrapes on the road, and a path of broken glass and blood. Taking a steadying breath, he watched as Bella scuffed at the blood with the toe of her left boot, then met his gaze, "It doesn't seem that old" Grimacing, Victor nodded and strode away from her towards the broken section of the low wall, stepping over the loose stones on the road, to stand staring down at the valley below, "Fuck"

"Is it them?" Bella was at his side instantly, her features grim as he gave a nod, the pair of them staring down the steeply sloping ground to the Land Rover that lay upon its passenger side.

"No-one could survive that" she grimaced, and he nodded at her words, his eyes drifting over the glassless window frames of the vehicle, the Land Rover looking like it had been in a fight with a wrecking ball as it lay some seventy feet below. Gritting his teeth, Victor turned to meet her gaze, nodding as he spoke, "We have to check, you know that right?"

Bella nodded back, forcing a grim smile, and sighing, Victor turned back to study the slope, trying to work out a safe way for them to get down to the Land Rover without falling themselves and making things even worse.

"There" as if reading his mind, Bella pointed with a finger, holding onto her shotgun with her left hand, "See where the ground has more rocks showing through the peat...it looks to me like sheep use that route to get up and down...I will try that way down"

"Sure, no problem" Victor grimaced, only to frown as Bella shook her head at him, eyes grim.

"What are you doing?"

"We are going down to see if anyone is still alive"

"No" Bella shook her head, grimacing, "You have a broken rib...you shouldn't even be out here on the run to the village…I only agreed you could come on the promise that you behaved"

"I am behaving" he sent her a tight smile, "Right"

For a moment, she held his gaze in silence and then she shook her head, "No dice Dog, you are waiting here…its not up for discussion"

For a moment, he considered arguing but then he sighed, seeing the determined look in her and he shook his head, "OK, fine, but be careful

Bella chuckled, "Aw, worried about me?"

Victor gave a grim smile, "I'm worried I'll end up spooning Doctor Green if you don't come back"

Chapter Thirty Six

Holding her shotgun before her, Bella watched as Dog made his way back over to their vehicle, and started the engine, driving it to where she stood. "Right listen" she fixed him with an almost motherly stare as she stepped alongside his open window, "You stay here, keep an eye out to make sure no more of those things are coming"

He nodded and she turned to glance both ways along the road as she continued, "If you see any, give the horn one blast and I will hide, you do the same OK...don't let them see you"

"Are you sure you don't want me to come?" he stared back at her, an eyebrow lifting and she shook her head, stepping away from the window.

"Don't start Dog, you aren't fit enough to climb"

"But I'm fit enough to spoon?" he risked a smile and she turned away from him, feeling her cheeks warming as she blushed unexpectedly.

"For fuck sake, just keep your eyes open"

"Sure" he replied, but she was already moving before he could say something else, trying to keep the smile from her face as she forced herself to concentrate on the task facing her, guilt at her smile touching her as she considered the facts. Three of their number were most likely dead, killed in the crash at the bottom of the slope.

Sadness touched her as she pictured the woman Alice, realising that she had grown to like her in their brief acquaintance, and had trusted her. Likewise she had liked the Scottish woman, Geri and had been impressed by her strength and manner, yet she had not liked the porter, Marcus. Still, any death was sad, especially given the dire circumstances that they had found themselves in. Grimacing, she began to edge down the slope, taking the sheep track that she had pointed out to Dog just a few minutes before descending, her heart skipping a beat each time her boots almost slid on the grass, still wet from last night's rain.

For several minutes she moved on slowly, pausing every few steps to cast her eyes about at the wide open moorland stretching away from her in three directions, suddenly aware of how visible she must be out on the open hillside. Grimacing, she turned her head slowly, eyes squinting as she studied the landscape, searching for any sign of white figures, certain that they would be in the open and unafraid of being seen. Yet when they had been driving away from Thames, they had seen a large group hiding behind overturned cars while one of their number had stood in the open, taunting them. Had they really been trying to set a trap?

Did their intelligence stretch that far?

Releasing a shaky sigh, certain that there was nothing out on the moorland watching her, Bella began to descend once more, her thoughts straying to the bearded man back in the jeep, her cheeks colouring once more as she recalled waking with his strong arms wrapped about her body, holding her to him as he lay close behind. For several minutes she had stayed there, her breathing shallow, her heart hammering in her chest as she tried to stay calm, unsure how to react. She had known instinctively that he hadn't been trying anything funny with her, that fact alone settling her stomach and so she had stayed where she was, shamelessly enjoying the warmth and close proximity of him underneath the duvet. It hadn't been sexual, far from it.

It had been companionship that she had felt, a deep-rooted affection forming for the man who was without question the most trusted and important member to her of the fledgling community that she had found herself a part of. Closing her eyes, she had leaned back slightly against him, casting her mind back to the conversation that they had shared the night before, and the way they had opened up to each other in the parking area the day before that.

They were kindred spirits, survivors.

Theirs was a friendship unmarred by attraction.

Then Dog had shifted beneath the duvet, pressing against her in his sleep and she had felt *him*.

As she had stiffened, her throat going tight with shock, he had grunted softly and came awake behind her, his voice thick with embarrassment as he had rolled away, "Oh my fucking God"

"It's fine" she was instantly up, avoiding his eyes as she had stepped towards the kitchen, noticing for the first time that the living room was empty.

As she reached the door, she turned back, unsure whether to laugh or blush as she had seen him sat up with his pillow upon his lap atop the duvet, and she had winced, "Do you want a tea?"

he had nodded, wincing himself and groaning, Bella had made her way through to the kitchen to discover the Naughtons, Jiyaa, Lauren and Doctor Green all seated about the large wooden table, chatting amiably, tea and toast before them all.

As she had stepped into the kitchen, they had all fallen silent and looked up at her, and the nurse Lauren had smiled, "Hey"

Shaking her head, Bella had chuckled and rolled her eyes, "Don't start"

"My lips are sealed" the nurse had chuckled, a fingertip pushing her glasses back up her nose as she had thrown Bella a wink, and then Valerie had risen, fussing about the former soldier.

"A cup of tea for you and your fella?"

Bella had shaken her head, "He's not my fella"

"Not yet he's not" Lauren had teased, taking a bite of toast, and groaning, Bella had flicked the nurse the middle finger of her right hand, chuckled, and joined the small group at the table. Pausing once more on the slope, Bella smiled at the memory, then turned her face to stare at the uneven moorland to her right, realising that it was where the Land Rover had crashed down the slope, pieces of the vehicle strewn about, leaving a trail like Hansel and Gretel's breadcrumbs. Grimacing, her good mood slipping away once more, she changed her direction, picking over towards the trail of debris, her right boot turning various bits over, a wing mirror here, an aerial there, then she paused as she saw something several metres down the slope from where she had stopped, half hidden among some flattened gorse bushes. Nearly a minute passed by as she stood staring at what she had seen, and then she began to approach it, her shotgun raised ready, stomach knotting in dread as she heard its snarls. She stopped once more, just two metres short of the figure in the blood caked uniform of a hospital porter, shaking her head slowly as he turned its hairless, white features towards her, right hand reaching out to grasp at the air between them as it snarled in excitement.

For nearly a minute, Bella stood with the shotgun pointing at the ghoul that had been Marcus, waiting for it to make a move towards her from where it was lying, not wanting to ruin her one chance of getting away from it by shooting early and missing. The moment it rushed for her she was going to give it both barrels and as it fell down the hill she would try and make her way back up towards the top where Dog was waiting. Yet as she stood there, weapon pointing at the face of the ghoul, it did nothing more than reach for her with that one arm, and grimacing, she took several steps to the right, watching it intently as it tried to follow her movement. Snarling like a rabid dog, the ghoul twisted, its right hand grasping at a rock on the floor between them, and with a supreme effort it managed to drag itself from within the bushes. "Fucking Hell" Bella took a step back, the slope behind her now, her eyes wide as she studied the ghoul which was trying to crawl towards her, one hand grasping at the uneven ground as it dragged itself forwards, its left arm hanging beside it, bent the wrong way at the elbow, and his lower back bent at an off angle, its legs dragging limply along behind it as it crawled. The cause of the accident seemed clear.

Marcus had changed into a ghoul, just as Dog's friend Moonshine had done two days before, and the shock of it had no doubt made the driver, Alice, go careening off the road in the darkness. But what had happened to the ghoul?

Had it been thrown from the vehicle as it rolled downhill and broken its back during the crash? She frowned, her eyes drifting over the ghoul as it once more dragged at the ground, edging closer, its teeth snapping at the air, and Bella took another step away from it, realising that it seemed to be suffering from no external wounds. That meant the blood upon its uniform belonged to either Geri or Alice, perhaps both women. Wincing, she turned her head to stare down at the wreckage of the Land Rover, realising that she was now only about thirty feet away from it, then cursed and gasped in dread as the ghoul suddenly grasped at her right leg with its hand. Instinctively she jerked her foot away from it, then cursed as it came down on air as she took a step back, her arms jerking as she fell backwards.

On impulse, she released her grip on the shotgun, not wanting to pull the trigger by accident and then she was rolling quickly, bumping over the sloping peat and stones until with a thud she collided with the roof of the Land Rover, the force off the impact knocking the air from her. Blinking against the pain in her back and shoulders, she forced herself to rise to her knees, eyes scanning the way she had just fallen for any sign as to where the shotgun had ended up, a curse escaping her as she saw it halfway between her and the ghoul which seemed oblivious to her new location, head turning as it looked for her. Keeping her head low, willing her body to work after her tumble down the hill and the collision with the upturned Land Rover, Bella rose slowly, leaning back against the vehicle behind as she studied the shotgun that she had dropped. She flinched as she heard a soft moan come from within the Land Rover and dropping back down to a crouch, she moved to stare in through the broken windscreen which with the vehicle on its side rose like a narrow doorway before her. She flinched almost at once as she saw the mutilated, blood-covered figure of Geri strapped in her car seat, her arms hanging limply down, empty eye sockets staring blankly back at Bella.

The former soldier winced as she studied the dead woman then screamed like a child as the figure suddenly lurched like a marionette, head flopping from side to side, arms flapping wildly, and pushing herself backwards, Bella lay on the damp peat behind her, her eyes wide in terror. Then there was a click, and the body dropped forward, appearing to drop to all fours in the broken windscreen, and shaking her head, Bella pushed herself away on the ground, then froze as a figure appeared between the gap in the seats, its blood-stained features covered in cuts and bruises, as it stared out at her from the back seat. "Alice?" the former soldier pushed herself to her hands and knees, her eyes wide, "Oh my God!" For a moment, the young woman held her gaze in silence, the haunted look in her eyes hinting at the nightmare that she had somehow survived and then she chuckled, "You took your time"

Chapter Thirty Seven

"Eric!" Emily gritted her teeth as she stared at her younger brother, her head shaking, "I swear to God, stop being so annoying!"

"I'm not" the boy sent her a look which proved her point, his tongue poking from his mouth and the teenage girl sighed heavily, raising a fist.

"Keep on and I'll kill you!"

"I'll phone Childline" he taunted her, "I will!"

"Not if you are dead you won't" she grimaced, then turned as a deep laugh sounded behind her. Frowning, Emily held the gaze of the large man that owned the farmhouse with his wife, Robert or Raymond or something, his frame dwarfing her as he stood beside the front door of his property, a shotgun held in his large hands.

For a moment, she was silent, brow furrowed as she lowered her gaze from the mans face to the weapon, then met his gaze again, "Is it loaded?"

"It is" he gave a nod and she smiled broadly.

"Can I shoot my brother?"

Again he laughed and she sighed heavily, casting a look at the young boy as he stood throwing sticks over the edge of the drop beyond the front of the farmhouse, "Eric, get away from the edge!"

Snarling in frustration, she cast a glance back at the farmer, "Are you sure you can't shoot him"

"Sorry" he winked, then turned to glance about the open ground, "I need to save these shells in case one of those things comes mooching round" Emily nodded at his words, then sighed once more, "Bullets don't work on them"

"Then I'll have to kill it with my bare hands" the big man gave a chuckle and she nodded at him.

"You look big enough…they are strong though" He shrugged, "So am I lass, any of those things tries hurting anyone with me about and they'll get thunder and lightning"

"What?" she crinkled her nose up, "Weather?"

Laughing softly, the big man rested the shotgun against the frame of the front door and raised both his ham sized hands before him one at a time, "Thunder and Lightning!"

The teenage girl raised an eyebrow, "What, are you a boxer or something?"

"I was" the man nodded, turning to look over the moorland that stretched away to the South, a sad look in his eyes, "I was good too…I could have been a big name…lucky me though, my dad needed me to help him run his farm"

Emily nodded, eyes glancing about, "It's not much of a farm is it…you don't have any crops or cows" His deep laugh had her frowning as he rubbed a tear of amusement from an eye, "There's more to

farms than cows and crops lass, I got sheep"
"Sheep?"
He nodded, "Six hundred of the buggers"
She turned at his words, glancing about, "So where are they?"
"All over the place" he sighed, picking the shotgun back up, "I have a large number down in the field below the rear barns and the rest scattered on the moorland, I have no idea how I am going to keep an eye on them now my two lads are....well...you know"
"Dead" Emily stated, her tone matter of fact, and the large farmer nodded, smiling sadly at her.
"Aye, they are that"
Nearly a minute dragged by as the two stood in an uncomfortable silence and then she turned once more, groaning as she saw her brother standing closer to the edge than before, "Eric!"
At her shout, he groaned aloud, arms flapping up dramatically in the air but he stepped back and turned away, kicking idly at some loose stones.
"That lad is bored" the farmer gave another chuckle and nodding, Emily met his gaze again.
"He's always bored"
"Why don't you go for a walk?"
"What?" she eyed him suspiciously, "Dog and Bella told me that we weren't to wander off!"

"You aren't wandering off" he gave a chuckle, waving a hand dismissively at her words, "You are on my land, besides, your mam and dad checked it for these thing's didn't they?"

Emily winced at his words, "They aren't my mam and dad...they are just taking care of us for now"

The big man winced, "Sorry luv..."

"Its fine" she looked down at the floor, turned to cast a glance at Eric and then looked back at the farmer, "Are you sure we won't get in trouble?"

He laughed at her words, "From who? I told you, this is my farm, I am in charge here, go have fun"

She smiled, nodding at the large man and then turned, calling to Eric as she approached him.

"Where are we going?" he muttered as he fell in step beside her, "Am I trouble again?"

"No" she rolled her eyes, nudging him with an elbow, "Just shut up, we are going for a walk"

"Why?

"Because we are"

Eric frowned, head shaking, "That is the dumbest reason for a walk I have heard off...are we on an errand for someone?"

"Nope" she sighed, "We are just walking"

He blinked, head shaking, "I don't get it"

"Oh shut up" Emily nudged him again, "We used to go for walks all the time with mam and dad"

"Did we?" he frowned, glancing at her, "Really?"
She nodded then threw him a smile, "Now shut up and stop ruining the moment...every time you speak, I remember you are here"
"Hey, why are you so mean to me, Emily"
"I'm your big sister...it's the law"
Trying to keep the smile from her face as he stared up at her in shock, Emily strode onward, pausing as they reached the two barns that the farmer had mentioned, then gestured with a hand towards a small track leading down beside one, "Come on, I think it's down here"
"What?" he cast her a look of surprise, "We are going to do something aren't we? Tell me!"
Sighing, knowing that for the time being she had her younger brother completely under her control and behaving, Emily paused, nodding as she spoke, "You saw me talking to the farmer?"
Her brother nodded, and she continued, "We are on a secret mission for him, we can't tell anyone"
"Anyone?" he seemed suddenly unsure, "What about Brandon?"
"No"
"What about Dog and Bella?"
"Definitely not Dog and Bella!" she snapped, her head shaking, "Swear to keep it secret or we are going to turn back now!"

"OK" he groaned, nodding, "I swear"

Chuckling, Emily began to walk once more, heading down past the barns, "Right, down here is the field where the farmer keeps all his special sheep, he wants us to make sure they look OK"

"Sheep?" Eric groaned, stopping dead in his tracks, "I don't want to go see sheep!"

Shaking her head, Emily threw him a wink, "But these are special sheep"

"What?"

"No, if you don't want to know"

"No, no, wait" he stepped in front of her, blocking her path as she turned back, "Special how?"

Emily smiled, "How do you think?"

Her younger brother blinked, brow furrowing and then he raised an eyebrow, "Because they are robots?"

She faked a gasp, frowning, "Who told you"

"No-one" his voice was a whisper as he glanced quickly about, "It was a guess!"

Emily frowned, trying not to smile as he stared up at her, "So, can we go see them?"

"Oh, you want to now?"

"Duh" he rolled his eyes, "Of course I do"

"I thought you said they were robot sheep?" the voice of Eric was confused as he stood in front of her several minutes later, their bodies obscured by a large cluster of gorse bushes that bordered the drop to the valley below, the walls of the rise at their backs, the two large barns to their left. She winced at his words, her hands fastened to his shoulders as she stared over his head at the stretch of moorland which sat at the bottom of the slope, not really a field at all by normal terms. The sheep that they had come to see lay strewn across the area, torn asunder, almost every one of them a bloody ruin where their stomachs had once been, blood caking the peat they lay upon. For several moments, she let her eyes drift over the poor unfortunate animals, fighting to stop herself from being sick, and then she let her eyes gaze settle upon the group of ghouls that were clustered in a pile at the base of the steep rise like sleeping new born kittens sharing body warmth, the majority of them naked, their white bodies bright in the cold November sunlight.

"We should go" her voice was a whisper, and before her Eric nodded, tilting his head to her.

"Because of the ghouls?"

She resisted the urge to answer sarcastically, knowing that now was not the time to start another argument, instead pulling gently on his left shoulder, "Yes, let's go"

"No" he shook his head, "I wanna watch them"

"What?" Emily blinked, her head shaking, "No!"

"You're not my mam!" he snapped, taking a step away from her, his voice rising, and she winced.

"Eric, we have to keep quiet"

"No!" he shook his head, turning to thrust an arm down towards where the ghouls lay in a huddle, a sneer on his features, "I'm not scared of them!"

"Well you should be!" she snapped, suddenly angry, a finger pointing at him, "Because of them Moonshine is dead...Castiel is dead...lots of people are dead, stop acting like a child!"

"I am a child!" he argued weakly, and she snarled.

"Yeah, but you don't need to be a dickhead!"

"Fuck off"

"What?" Emily blinked, head tilting slightly as she stared back at her younger brother and he winced, hands raising defensively before him.

"Oh...I....I didn't mean..." Eric began, head shaking as he edged away from her, "Jack at school says it...I didn't mean you...I meant..."

"You little bastard!" Emily shouted, a rage coursing through her as she stared at him, "Do you even have any idea what I have given up to look after you...no...you don't..."

"I'm sorry!"

"Don't you ever swear at me again!" she jabbed a

finger towards him, then snapped her face to the side, her stomach lurching as she looked over the edge of the slope towards the valley below them. "Emily!" Eric stepped towards her, "I am sorry!" She nodded, hardly hearing his words as she stared down at the group of ghouls that were slowly rousing themselves from their pile, several already loping to the side, heads angling as they stared up at the brother and sister, snarling excitedly, hands reaching towards them. "We need to go!" she reached out, snatching at Eric and he followed her gaze, his earlier bravado gone as he whimpered and stepped back to her. "They can't get up here can they?"

She shook her head at his question, then winced as several of them ran quickly at the slope, hands grasping at the soft peat as they tried to drag themselves up, all of them falling back down except for one which clung on, snarling angrily. "No" she shook her head, stepping back towards the barns, dragging Eric with her, but keeping close enough to the edge to watch the climbing ghoul as it somehow moved up another metre. It snapped its face towards her, teeth bared as it gave another excited snarl, and Emily raised her eyes studying the distance it still had to climb. "Emily, its halfway up!" Eric whimpered and she grimaced, head shaking as she watched the ghoul extend a hand, grasping at a bush and then fall as it's handhold suddenly came loose from the peat. Snarling, it fell back to the ground forty feet below, its head striking a small cluster of rocks as it landed, its skull cracking. Instantly, the others were upon it, hands reaching down as they began to gibber and screech in a feeding frenzy, all but one which stood back, the remnants of a black robe hanging from its white-skinned form as it stared up at the pair, its features twisted in what looked like a smile. Grimacing, Emily stepped out of sight, Eric moving with her, and she shook her head, "We better tell the others"

"What?" he looked like he was about to begin crying, "Please don't…they will think it is my fault for shouting and waking them!"

"Don't be daft!" she winced, "We have to tell!"

"No, Dog and Bella will be angry!" Eric looked mortified, "Please…they won't like me anymore!"

For a moment she stood in silence, holding his gaze and then she nodded her head, "Fine, but you don't come back here ever again!"

He nodded and she grimaced, "Promise me"

Smiling, Eric crossed his chest, "I promise"

Chapter Thirty Eight

"Are you sure you are OK?" Dog turned from the front passenger seat to stare back at Alice as she sat in the back of their vehicle, his bearded features fixed with concern as he asked the question for the fifth time in as many minutes. Nodding, touched by his evident concern, Alice forced a weary smile, "I told you I'm fine, just cold and shaken up...I'm so glad to see you guys" He winced, nodding, and turned away, his head shaking, "Jesus fucking Christ...I can't believe I didn't realise Marcus was going to turn weird"

"It's not your fault" Alice shook her head, leaning forward to place a hand on his shoulder and he gave a heavy sigh, his features twisting in grief.

"Isn't it?" his voice was tight, strained, and sitting in the back of the vehicle, Alice saw the grief in his eyes as he turned to look back at her again, "I should have known...Marcus did nothing but sleep for most of the day yesterday before you left...the same as...my friend, Moonshine...damn!"

"Dog" the voice of Bella was concerned as she cast a glance at him and then turned back to the road ahead, "Seriously, I know the guilt game as well as you, this isn't your fault...Alice is alive!"

He nodded, then sighed heavily, "He killed Geri, if I had realised what was up that might have been avoided…damn it…fucking Hell!"

"Hey, if you could have noticed it then so could I have, if you are going to take the blame then so am I!" Bella argued, head shaking, and for a it looked like Dog was going to argue only to change his mind and fall silent, sighing heavily. As Bella drove the vehicle through the open moorland, Alice leaned back against the seat, her head turning to stare out of the window beside her, eyes staring up at the blue November sky as she cast her mind back over the night before.

She had passed out at some point in the Land Rovers headlong crash down the steep slope, but not before it had flipped wildly and the ghoul that had been Marcus had been sucked through the smashed windscreen by gravity as it had leaned between the seats, reaching for her.

Then she had struck her head, and the darkness had taken her for god knows how long until she had awoken with a start in the wreckage, panic coursing through her for a moment as she had tried to recall what had happened, and then she had seen the grisly remains of Geri beside her.

Shaking her head, feeling as if she was all but out of tears, Alice had sat in the overturned vehicle, studying the body of the courageous Scots woman in sadness, casting her mind back to the brutal and unexpected attack, wondering if there had been any way that she could have saved her, then she had felt her blood run cold as she had heard the feral snarls of a ghoul out in the night. Fearing the sudden return of Marcus and having no weapons with which to defend herself, Alice had snatched up a shard of glass and clambered past the dead body of the woman she had shared a brief but strong friendship with, apologising each time she bumped it and sent the corpse lurching as it hung suspended by its seat belt. Finally, she had been within the rear of the car, lying hidden as best as she could, shivering against the cold, her ears straining to hear the snarling of the ghoul over the heavy rain. At some point during the night it had got so cold that she had cut open the seats with the piece of glass she was holding and pulled out pieces of the cushion within, stuffing pieces inside her clothing in a bid to ward of the biting cold, the idea coming to her after she recalled Sarah once telling her that tramps often stuff their clothes with newspaper to keep warm in the winter. Once more, battered and bruised, shivering badly, she had fallen asleep once more, only to awake to the sound of Sarah talking to her, and she had blinked, staring at the figure of her former best friend and lover as it had sat in the darkness of the upturned Land Rover with her. For several moments she had let it talk, listening to it tell her in detail about how the failure of their relationship had been her fault, and that ultimately her suicide was on Alice's conscience, until finally, the embalmer had shaken her head and given a sad chuckle, her voice soft, "You're not here, you are dead"

"So will you be soon" Sarah had replied and Alice had fallen asleep once more for an unknown period of time before awaking to find Geri turning to stare back at her from the front seat, her eyeless sockets fixing to Alice as she nodded. "Ye hang on in there, hen, d' ya hear me! Help will come for ye...ye just have ta hang on!"

Once more, the darkness had taken her and then she had awoken once more, her heart skipping a beat as something heavy crashed against her hiding place, her blood running cold as she had heard the ghoul snarling loudly, its movements loud as it crawled around outside the vehicle.

Except it hadn't been Marcus after all.

It had been Bella.

Sat in the back of the car behind Dog and Bella, she suddenly felt overcome with emotion as she recalled the intensity of the embraces each had given her upon finding that she was alive, Bella beside the upturned Land Rover and Dog at the top of the slope when she had finally reached it, and instantly the tears came, a wave of high emotions coursing through her body, grief at the loss of Geri, and even Marcus, relief at having been rescued, and overcome with the love and care that she had been shown by Dog and Bella Her smile slipped as she recalled how she and the silver-haired woman had stopped on their climb back to the road, Bella collecting her shotgun and Alice standing staring at the thing that had been Marcus, wanting to hate it but not having the energy. After all, he was a victim too. "What do you want to do with him?" Bella had moved alongside her, offering her the gun and Alice had winced, watching as the broken-backed ghoul had tried in vain to crawl towards her. "Leave it" her voice had been little more than a whisper, "If we shoot it we might attract more" Bella had nodded, then gestured to a large rock that had lain nearby, "We could crush it's skull?" Again, Alice had shaken her head, feeling suddenly nauseous as she had stared into the milky white eyes of the ghoul, "Let's just go" And so they had, slowly making their way back up the steep slope, picking their way from the debris site back over to the sheep track as they climbed towards the road and the waiting Dog. "We'll soon have you back at the farmhouse" Dog turned suddenly, forcing a smile and forcing herself to concentrate on the present, she cringed as she saw the look of concern in his eyes still. "I look a mess right" she raised her hands, thumbs trying to clear the tears from her eyes, her palms brushing them away from her cheeks. He chuckled, "I'm just glad you are safe, I wish I'd argued harder against you all leaving last night" Alice winced, "And then Marcus would have turned into a ghoul back inside the farmhouse, who knows how many would have been killed" Dog nodded at her words, smiling sadly and Alice raised an eyebrow, "How did you guys know we had the accident?"

"We didn't" Bella stated, meeting her gaze in the rear view mirror and Alice shook her head.

"So where were you going?"

"The village that we skirted past the other day, I cant remember its name" Dog explained, then turned to glance at Bella as she gave a chuckle.

"Hanward"

"Yeah, whatever" the bearded man smiled, turning to look back at Alice, "We were headed there to try and get some supplies to tide us over at the farmhouse, but we'll get you back first"

"No" she sat forward, her head shaking, "No, we can go to the village still, I'll come with you"

Grimacing, Dog glanced at Bella and she met the gaze of Alice in the rear view mirror once more, her head shaking, "After the night you have had I think you need to get back to the farmhouse and rest...you deserve it"

"How can I?" Alice shook her head, smiling sadly as she gave a shrug, "I wouldn't be able to rest knowing that you two were out there on your own when I could be helping you!"

"Alice..." Dog began then fell silent as she fixed him with a meaningful stare, hands raising, "OK"

Behind the wheel, Bella turned her head quickly, glancing at Dog before looking at Alice through the mirror once more, "Are you sure, really sure"

"I am" Alice fought to control the fresh wave of emotion that was threatening to wash her away, nodding as she met the gaze of each of her new friends, "We make a good team right?"

As Dog chuckled, nodded at her, Bella winked in the mirror, the vehicle speeding up as she put her foot down, "Right then, Hanward here we come"

Chapter Thirty Nine

"Well, it looks quiet" Victor muttered as he and his two companions stood in front of the Toyota Landcruiser, his features grim as he stared at the village of Hanward, hands clasped to his shotgun. Several feet away, Bella stepped forwards, her weapon held ready before her, while Alice stood between the pair of them, glancing about slowly. They had arrived at the small village some ten minutes before and had sat in the car with the engine running, and the windows done up, while Bella had held down the car horn several times, their plan being to see how many ghouls there were in the small village. Yet as the minutes had dragged by, there had been no sign of any of the white-skinned creatures at all and casting each other hopeful smiles the trio had climbed out. Yet now, as he stood beside his two female companions, Victor began to feel exposed and at risk, his previous encounters with the ghouls having set him on edge. They now knew for certain that there was a weak spot upon the chests of the creatures which was great, but unless there were only one or two ghouls that information was next to useless. If they were attacked by a crowd of ghouls they were screwed, even armed with the two shotguns.

"So, what's the plan?" Alice asked, and as he glanced at her she gave a nervous laugh, "You have a plan, right guys?"

As Bella turned to look at Victor, he gestured towards her with a hand, "Well...you are the former soldier...what's the plan?"

She grimaced at his words, then turned to glance at Bella as she raised an eyebrow, nodding as if in approval, "Former soldier...that's cool"

Victor watched as Bella tried to smile, flinching slightly at the compliment then Alice turned to meet his gaze, "Well, Dog...what do you do?"

He winced, shrugging slightly, "I work for the Forestry Commission...just general stuff"

"Oh cool" Alice nodded, smiling then turned to look at Bella as she gestured towards Victor.

"He *was* a priest"

"A priest?" Alice shot him a look of surprise.

"It was a long time ago" he winced, throwing Bella a look of mild irritation, then turned to look back at the village ahead of them, changing the subject, "So, what are we doing? Any ideas?"

She moved alongside him, a worried look upon her features as if sensing that he might be annoyed with her, "Are you good?"

"Yeah" he nodded, forcing a smile, "I'm sorry, I just don't like to talk about myself too much"

Bella nodded, a hand leaving her gun to give his arm a gentle pat, and he lowered his gaze staring at where she had touched him, embarrassed by the fact that she had become so important to him when she was effectively still just a stranger.

So why had a touch on his arm made him smile? He winced as an image of his wife entered his head, a wave of guilt washing through him and he turned away from his companions, stepping further into the village as he stared slowly about.

Behind him, Bella was talking, suggesting that they leave the car at the entrance to the village and carefully scout around, before returning.

Alice grunted, "Wouldn't it be easier to drive?"

"It would" Bella agreed, and casting a quick glance back at the pair, Victor found her nodding at Alice, "It'd be quicker too, but I'm concerned in case we run into a big group of ghouls. If we are in the car we make more noise than the three of us sneaking around on foot"

"But if we do run into a group wouldn't we be safer inside the car?" Alice seemed unsure.

"Again, I agree" Bella replied, "I just don't want us to commit out only way of getting quickly back to the farmhouse into an unknown situation"

"Good point" Alice chuckled, "I can tell you have done this sort of thing before"

As the two women chuckled softly, Victor began to walk slowly forwards, his head turning to stare off up a long driveway to their left, his brow furrowing as he studied a house about thirty metres down it, and then another large structure further back, beside what looked like a hay barn. "Dog?" he turned as Bella and Alice moved up to join him, the voice of the silver-haired woman tense as they both joined him in staring up the driveway, "Everything OK?"

He nodded, forcing a grin, "Just me being nosy" Sending him a smile, Bella stepped past him, to stare off down the main street and he and Alice joined her in doing so, his brow furrowing as he studied the houses on the left and right of the street, the latter appearing to have several small roads leading off, and then he frowned as he stared at a larger building in the distance at the road's end, what looked like railings around it.

"Right" Bella began walking, "Let's do this, we keep quiet and stay together, I'll take point, Alice in the centre and Dog, you bring up the rear"

For some reason he chuckled at her words and she sent him an embarrassed look, her cheeks flushing with colour, "Behave will you"

Between the pair of them, Alice cast each a

glance, a curious smile on her features, "I feel like I'm playing gooseberry"

Victor gave an awkward chuckle, while at the front, Bella shook her head but stayed silent, the trio moving off down the old village street as one. For several minutes they walked in silence, stopping every few metres as they glanced about, not wanting to take any chances whatsoever. They paused as they reached a road entrance on their right, what appeared to be a cul-de-sac, and for several minutes they stood staring down it in silence, waiting for something to move, then moved onwards before stopping three houses down as yet another road opened up on the right. "It looks like this one turns towards the centre of the village" Alice muttered as the three of them stood shoulder to shoulder, staring off down the street, and Victor nodded, his eyes then flicking to settle upon the two cars that appeared to have been abandoned in the street, a red Nissan Sunny which appeared to have driven into a garden wall and a white transit van which sat in the middle of the road with the driver's door open.

Grimacing, Victor swallowed against the sudden tightness in his throat, the hairs rising on the back of his neck as he glanced about, "See that"

"The cars?" Bella muttered, moving into sight in his peripheral vision, "Aye, it looks like the occupants either turned or they were attacked and fled from the scene"

"Why would you leave your car?" Victor winced.

"We did" the voice of Alice had Victor looking at her and then turning to glance back off down the road at the distant shape of the Landcruiser, suddenly wondering if they had made a mistake.

"There's a shop" the voice of Bella had both Victor and Alice turning to watch as she began to walk away from the entrance to the road, their eyes fixing upon the building that she was gesturing to with the end of her shotgun, "There"

Stretched in a small procession, the trio slowly made their way up the empty street, pausing as they reached what appeared to be the centre of the village, the three of them stood looking about. Grimacing, Victor adjusted his grip on the shotgun, and turned to glance across the centre of the village, his brow furrowing as he studied their surroundings. Directly to their left sat a small convenience store, the door closed, and the window dotted with small multi-coloured carboard stars with the special offers written upon them in black marker pen, and blank postcards offering items for sale or services.

"Dog" the hissed whisper of Bella had him turning his body quickly towards her, wincing as the sudden motion sent a stab of pain lancing through his injured side, and a stern look creeping onto the faces of the former soldier, "I told you that you should have stayed back!"

"I'm fine!" he stated, words tinged with pain and she shook her head, seeing his lie for what it was. "Give Alice your rucksack...you wait here and keep an eye out for any trouble...if you see anything come inside and we'll all hide there!"

"Bella!" he grimaced but she was having none of it, her features defiant as she moved to stand in front of him, her brown eyes boring into his own. "Dog, listen to me...I need you safe OK, and so do Eric and Emily...I'm not going back to the farm and telling them you didn't make it because you got hurt due to your stubbornness...don't make me do that!"

He winced at the depth of emotion in her voice, and embarrassed he looked away, one hand releasing the shotgun as he slid his arm from the straps of his rucksack and then repeated the process with the other arm, before handing it to Alice, who took it with a grim smile. Only then did he meet the gaze of Bella once more, "Do me a favour, be careful in there OK"

She blushed at his words, looking unsure whether to smile or not and he felt his cheeks flush with colour beneath his beard, and he gestured to Alice as she stood watching, "That goes for both of you...go on...I'll wait here!" Bella nodded, looking like she wanted to say something else but then turned and stepped towards the shop, Alice nodding at Victor as she moved to join her, "We'll see you in a minute!" "You better" he gave a grim chuckle, then watched as Bella pushed open the door of the shop with the muzzle of her shotgun, and froze as a small bell jingled above it. Wincing, she cast a look back at them, and then continued into the shop, the embalmer following quietly behind her. Turning away from the shop as the door closed behind them, Victor took a breath then winced as it sent another jolt of pain through his side, one hand leaving his shotgun to press against it. For several moments he stood there grimacing, trying to focus past the pain and then shaking his head, he grasped his weapon again then turned to stare about the village centre once more. Directly opposite where he was standing was the building with the railings that he had spotted from near their car, and he raised an eyebrow, realising it was a nursery and primary school.

For a moment, he let his gaze drift over the building, and the small play area behind the railings, and then he let his gaze drift onwards to settle upon the building to the right of the school. Taking a step away from the shop, Victor studied the village hall for a moment in silence, then turned his head again, his breath catching in his throat as he saw the small church and graveyard nestled on the far side of the village centre, partially hidden by a cluster of large Oak trees. Wincing, he took another couple of steps towards it, his eyes drifting over the architecture of the old building, a sadness entering his heart as he recalled the church that had been so dear to him, and the congregation that had been like family. Yet the sadness became replaced with guilt as he recalled once more standing outside the home beside the church, desperately trying to get inside his home while his beloved children had banged upon the glass – *knock, knock, knock.* Fighting the urge to vomit, trying to ignore the phantom touch of fire that always seemed to lick at his back and shoulders when his episodes began, Victor bent slightly, trying to force himself to focus on the present, cursing as the sound came once more – knock, knock, knock, the tapping of his children upon the glass growing in intensity as they fought to be free of the house. "Leave me alone" he snarled, rising to stand, a hand leaving the shotgun to clasp at his forehead in a bid to stop the sea of sweat that was forming there only to stare back in shock at the two figures that stood within the school building, their clenched fists rapping hard upon the glass. *Knock, knock, knock*

Chapter Forty

"Why?"

Lauren winced as Brandon raised his voice, one hand tapping repeatedly against the side of his head, his other clasped tightly to the envelope that he had just shown her. For a moment, she held his gaze in silence as she stood facing him in the kitchen of the Naughton's farmhouse, aware that the eyes of everyone else were watching her, and then she sighed and forced a sad smile, "I just told you Brandon, it's not safe for us to go out"

"But why?" the young black man asked again, his features twisted in confusion, "Tell me why?"

"I just did" she sighed, shaking her head, "You know the trouble we have had...the ghouls..."

"But why aren't I allowed to post my letter"

Lauren winced, unsure what else to say, a hand rising to rub at her temples as she turned her face to meet the gaze of Jiyaa as the woman sat at the dinner table beside Dr Green and the farmer, Robert, all three of them looking uncomfortable. Sighing, trying to come up with a good reason for him to not post his letter, the nurse turned to look the other way, watching as Valerie stood beside the oven talking to the teenage girl, Emily. Turning her gaze back upon Brandon, Lauren shook her head once more, "Because the ghouls might be lurking about...we need to stay safe"

"She's right lad" Robert gave a chuckle, trying to help "Best to be inside instead of out there, eh? No-one is allowed off the farm"

"Not true" Brandon half-turned his head as he addressed the doctor, "The nice lady Alice, and the lady with the funny voice and the thin man all went off the farm and they haven't come back!"

Wincing, Lauren shook her head, "I explained this to you, Brandon, do you remember, they have gone back to their own homes"

He blinked at her words, and she could almost hear him thinking, trying to come up with a new reason, then he nodded, "What about the man with the beard and the silver-haired lady who keep smiling at each other when they think no-one else is looking? They went off the farm too"

Trying not to laugh at his description of Dog and Bella, Lauren turned her head, seeing the smiles upon the faces of Dr Green and Jiyaa, and then she shook her head once more, "They are adults"

"I'm an adult" he argued and she sighed heavily.

"You are, but I have to take care of you"

For long moments he stared back at Lauren in silence and then he spoke once more, his words, slow and deliberate, "I want to post my letter"

Catching the inside of her cheek between her

back teeth, Lauren held his gaze for a moment and then gave another shake of her head, "No, it is not happening, only adults can go out"

"Not true" Brandon's voice was almost a shout, his free hand starting to pat the side of his head repeatedly once more as he began to work himself up, "Not true…stop lying"

"I am not lying!" she stated, trying not to get angry, knowing full well that it wasn't his fault but knowing she had to be assertive with him.

"Lies!" Brandon shook his head, "Stop lying!"

"She isn't lying lad" Robert spoke once more, his deep voice drawing the gaze of the black man.

"Lies" Brandon shouted, head shaking, "Eric and Emily went out…he told me…they saw ghouls"

"What?" Lauren turned her head, staring at the Asian teenager as she gave a curse and turned to look back at both her and Brandon in a mixture of shock and disbelief. Then she stormed to the kitchen doorway, her voice angry as she shouted.

"Eric you little shit!"

"Whoa!" Valerie stepped away from the sink, hands waving in a calming manner, but Lauren was too far gone, her head shaking as she stared at the teenage girl in complete astonishment.

"You left the farm?"

For a moment, the girl held her gaze in silence

and then she grimaced, her head shaking, "We went to the land beyond the barns...that's it!"

"Why!" Lauren was incredulous, her eyes wide behind her glasses, "We all told you guys and Brandon how dangerous it is out there!"

"You're not my mum!" Emily's features suddenly darkened, her voice dropping to barely more than a whisper and as if sensing a storm about to start, Valerie moved across the kitchen and stood beside the teenage girl, forcing a smile as she met Laurens gaze, an arm encircling Emily's shoulder. "Look there's no harm done, I'm sure she didn't mean to cause any bother, right love?"

"Right" Emily shrugged, clearly still angry with being questioned, her eyes locked to those of the young nurse, "Besides, me and Eric didn't just go wandering...we were advised to go for a walk by an adult...the owner of this farm!"

"Oh shit" the deep voice of Robert sounded and beside Emily, his wife snapped her head about.

"Robert, what have you gone and bloody done?"

"Hey now hold on!" the farmer raised his hands, head shaking as he winced, "Don't you start bawling at me woman, the kids are bloody bored, you cant expect them to stay cooped up!"

"We can!" Lauren sighed, glancing at the farmer,

one hand gesturing to Brandon, "Because now he thinks he can go and post a letter to his parents!"

"Ah its just a letter" Robert waved a hand, picking up his cup of tea with the other, "Let him send it, what harm can it do, right Doc?"

As Lauren turned her head, Doctor Green winced, hands raising defensively, "I really don't want to get involved in an argument, but I do feel it might be best if we stayed on the farm"

"See Robert" Valerie pointed at the doctor as she shook her head, "That's medical advice that!"

"But its not a medical issue!" the farmer rolled his eyes, "No offence Doc"

As Doctor Green winced, Lauren turned her head to look at Brandon as he raised his voice, "I want to post a letter to my mum and dad"

"You can't" she shook her head, "I am sorry"

"I want to post my letter" he repeated, and she gave a shaky sigh, hands rubbing at her temples. "Brandon please"

"It is not fair!" he raised his voice, and Lauren grimaced, then turned to look as Eric suddenly entered the kitchen, his siter launching into a tirade at him, one hand pointing in his face.

"You made me promise not to tell anyone then you go and tell, Brandon!"

"What?" the young boy blinked, head shaking.

"About going out!" Emily was beside herself with anger, "You have made me look a right prick!"

"Language!" Valerie shook her head, trying to step between the siblings, and as Brandon began to tug at Lauren's sleeve, demanding loudly for the right to go and post his letter, Robert rose to his feet, clearly concerned for the nurses safety.

"Come on son, stop pulling at her"

"Let me post my letter" Brandon suddenly shouted, his voice loud, and Lauren felt herself get swept away in the storm of noise that was suddenly sweeping through the kitchen like a tsunami, her head turning to stare about her. Emily was now screaming at her younger brother, who was shouting back, while Valerie tried to keep them apart, her own voice rising in anger as she shouted at her husband, the farmer grimacing as he replied to her and also told Brandon to stop pulling on Lauren's clothes, Doctor Green also now on his feet trying to calm the young man, while her charge shouted over and over that he wanted to post his letter. Suddenly, Lauren met the gaze of Jiyaa as the Indian woman sat at the table, her brown eyes fixed with sadness, that depth of emotion for some reason mixing with the cacophony of noise.

"For the love of God, can't you just let him post

the letter!" Valerie suddenly turned, meeting the gaze of Lauren as she glanced at the farmer's wife, the woman's words sending Brandon into more of a meltdown, one hand grasping roughly at Laurens right forearm as he spun her about, his features almost in hers as he screamed aloud. "Let me post my letter to my mum and dad!" "They're dead!" Lauren was unable to stop the words leaving her lips, her voice matching his in volume, and before her, the young black man shrunk back as if she had struck him across the face, his eyes wide, his lips moving soundlessly. As if a switch had been thrown, everyone in the kitchen fell silent, their eyes fixing upon the young nurse and she winced, her head shaking as she met the pained gaze of Brandon, "I'm so sorry, I shouldn't have let you know like that!" "Oh the poor flower" the voice of Valerie had Lauren turning her face towards the wife of the farmer, her stomach knotting as she saw the look of shock upon the woman's face, and she sighed. "I tried to keep this calm...but everyone...I couldn't think...I didn't mean to tell him like that" "It's not your fault, Lauren" Doctor Green moved alongside her, sending her a reassuring smile. "No, its his!" Valerie turned to jerk a thumb at her husband, her head shaking, "If you hadn't let the kids wander off this wouldn't have happened!"

"I'm not a kid!" Eric snapped angrily, only to wince as Emily took a quick step towards him.

"Hey, have some respect for these people, they have put us up and fed us!"

"Fuck off!" he shouted, turning and running out of the kitchen and with a roar of rage, Emily made to follow him, only for Valerie to grab her,

"No love, don't...just calm down!"

"Bloody Hell!" Robert grimaced, then winced as his wife sent him a scathing look, "What?"

"Don't you what me, Robert Naughton!"

"Fucking Hell!" he groaned, dropping back on to his chair, picking up his cup of tea once more.

"Don't you ignore me!" the farmers wife released her grip on Emily, the roar of the teenage girl loud as she raced off in pursuit of her brother, and then Doctor Green was moving to stand between the married couple, pleading for calm. Amid it all, Lauren placed her hands beside her head, closing her eyes as she considered what she had just told Brandon; guilt assailing her.

"He's gone!" the shouted voice suddenly rang through the new wave of noise, and as one everyone in the kitchen turned their heads, the eyes of Lauren widening as she saw Jiyaa now standing at the table, her features twisted in concern as she gestured towards the back door. "Bloody Hell" Robert gave a soft chuckle, "I thought you couldn't speak a word of English!" "Jiyaa?" Lauren shook her head in confusion. For a moment, the Indian woman stared back into the nurse's eyes and then she spoke once more, her heavily accented voice thick with dread, "Brandon has run away!"

Chapter Forty One

"Where on Earth could he have gone?" Dr Green stepped through the heavy rain that they had found when he, Lauren and Jiyaa had stepped from the farmhouse to search for the missing Brandon, all three dressed in heavy rain jackets that Valerie had given them before leaving, their hoods pulled up against the appalling weather
The young nurse, stood between her two new friends, turned to glance at the doctor as he spoke, wincing as she considered his words, her eyes dropping to study the shotgun that he was reluctantly carrying, then shook her head, "I have no idea...the day this all kicked off at the hospital was the first day I had met him...I don't really know Brandon at all"
The doctor nodded as he met her gaze, then forced a smile, "None of this is your fault, Lauren, you have to believe that, many people would have abandoned him already"
"Doctor is right" the voice of Jiyaa had both Lauren and the silver-haired doctor turning to face her as she stood alongside them, the nurse shaking her head as she held her gaze, "Why didn't you tell anyone that you spoke English?"
The Indian woman winced, eyes lowering as if she were ashamed, "I learned to speak English

from a doctor friend of mine in my homeland, a young white Englishman...my brother, Opinder, he would not have approved...better for me to play the doting and meek sister"

Lauren cringed, imagining how hard it must have been for Jiyaa as the woman shook her head, "I loved my brother but he was old ways...er...old fashion...fashioned...it would not do for me to be so new...modern. When I meet Alice...I keep it a secret I speak English...then I worry too much time have passed by...so I stay silent"

"Well, you don't have to anymore" Doctor Green sent her a smile, nodding as he spoke, "We are all in this together now"

"Doctor Green is right" Lauren reached out a hand to gently squeeze the right hand of Jiyaa, drawing a smile from the woman, then she turned, staring around the farmyard for any sign of her charge, "Damn it Brandon, where are you?"

"The ambulance hasn't moved" the doctor stated and the trio all turned to study the vehicle as it sat blocking the entrance to the track to the main road, "Could he be hiding within it perhaps?"

"No" Lauren shook her head, "I locked it all up after parking it back there when Dog and Bella went out this morning"

"I hope they OK" the voice of Jiyaa had the nurse turning to study her, the Indian woman wincing as she met her gaze, "They gone long time, yes?"

"They have" Lauren nodded grimly, turning her face up to study the thick black clouds overhead for a moment, cursing as the rain covered her glasses, and lowering her face, she wiped them with a forearm, "They should be back by now"

"Please" Doctor Green shook his head, chuckling softly, "Let's find Brandon before we start on another problem, one at a time eh?"

Lauren nodded, smiling grimly, then without a conscious decision to do so, the three began to walk through the heavy rain towards the ambulance, pausing as they reached the bonnet.

"Well, he's not here" Lauren muttered turning her head about, then grimacing, she stepped to the side to study the gap between the side of the ambulance and the steep drop to the valley below, realising it was too narrow to move past. Taking a deep breath as her companions watched her, her stomach tight with dread, she turned and peered over the drop, relief touching her as she saw that Brandon wasn't lying hurt below.

"Are we OK?" the doctor asked, and she nodded.

"He hasn't fallen there, but we still have no idea where on Earth he might have gone"

The doctor and Jiyaa studied her in silence for a moment, then the Indian woman turned her head, looking up at the steep rise that reared up behind and to the East side of the farmhouse, grunting softly and Lauren frowned, "What is it?"
"I do not think he climb there" Jiyaa replied in her broken English, "I think it too difficult, yes?"
"I agree" Doctor Green moved alongside her, his head turning towards the two old barns, "We should check that area, didn't Brandon say that Eric and Emily had been out over that way?"
"Oh God" Lauren nodded, almost breaking into a run as she hurried across the farmyard, splashing through mud and puddles, her two companions hurrying to keep pace with her as she called out frantically, "Brandon, I'm sorry...where are you?"
As she glanced about, she saw Jiyaa and the doctor wincing, perhaps worried her calls would attract ghouls, and she shook her head, "We should be safe, Dog and Bella did a sweep of the farm yesterday and today and didn't see any of them...but remember, if we do...keep still"
Doctor Green nodded at her words, eyes glancing to the heavens, "If their eyesight is as bad as it seems this rain will only make it worse, there is always a bright side"
Lauren smiled at his words, and continued

367

walking towards the barns, hearing the splashes
as they both began to follow her once more.
She was touched by their support, and had
grown to like them both in the short time they
had known each other, the revelation that Jiyaa
could speak English both shocking and pleasing
her, knowing that now they could talk properly.
Yet despite the optimistic words of the doctor,
Lauren was struggling to find a bright side in the
fact that she had blurted out that Brandon's
parents were dead, sending him into a meltdown.
It had grown apparent during their two days at
the farmhouse that what had happened in
Thames was not restricted to just that city and
was no doubt happening all over the country,
perhaps the world, and it stood to reason that
with no hospital to return to she was jobless, and
therefore had no real responsibility to look after
Brandon any longer. Yet she knew she couldn't
abandon him. Not now. He had lost his parents
and his sister. Now he had lost his home at the
hospital and everything he had come to know.
For a young man whose entire life was built
around structure and routine this must be even
more terrifying for him than for anyone else.
And now she had sent him running and scared.

Feeling sick with concern, she stepped up to the first of the barns, staring in through the open door at the old pieces of machinery and piles of tools, able to see at once that Brandon was not inside and then moved on to the second barn. For a moment she stood there staring in at the old car, and the small patch of blood upon the floor beside it, grimacing as she recalled Alice telling her about the ghoul that she, Dog and Bella had found eating a rat beside the vehicle. She sighed heavily at the memory, suddenly missing the brown-haired woman with an intensity that surprised her, then gave a smile as she reached down to the trousers of the nurse uniform she was still wearing, her fingers feeling the folded piece of paper that sat in a pocket with Alice's phone number written upon it. They would meet again; she would make sure they did. "He not in there I think" Jiyaa stated peering through the open entrance as she stood between Lauren and Doctor Green, and the nurse nodded, grimacing as she cast her gaze about, then stepped back, heading for the side of the barns. Hadn't Brandon claimed that the brother and sister had gone behind the barns and seen some ghouls? She winced at the thought, pushing away the fear that had already begun twisting her gut as she pictured a mass of ghouls gathering back there, realising that if there were any there they would have seen them appear long before now. Taking a deep breath, Lauren paused, glancing back long enough to reassure herself that Doctor Green and Jiyaa were with her and then she continued down the side of the two barns, stepping through the thick mud and puddles. She turned as she reached the end, her eyes widening in shock as she saw the familiar figure of Brandon standing ahead of them, barely visible amid the rain, his black and white tracksuit soaked through, his red chunky earphones fastened about his ears. For a moment, she stood staring at the man, older than she by six years but made younger by his neurological disorder, in a mixture of relief and anger, both emotions vying for control, and shaking her head, she took a step towards him only to realise that he was facing away from her, "Brandon..."

"Wait" the hiss of concern from Doctor Green stopped her dead in her tracks and turning she saw him gesture towards her charge, "Look!" Grimacing, she turned back, Jiyaa gasping beside her in realisation, the Indian woman noticing the danger at the same time that Lauren realised that Brandon was standing at the edge of the drop.

He turned suddenly as if sensing them, a look of hurt creeping onto his features as he saw Lauren standing watching him, his head shaking, "I don't want you…I want my mum"

"Brandon!" she shook her head slowly, "Please"

"No!" he shouted loudly, taking a step towards them, one hand rising to point at her, his other clasped to the envelope, "No, you are a liar!"

It was Lauren's turn to look hurt, her head shaking as she winced, "Brandon please come away from the edge, let us get you back inside!"

"Brandon…please come" the velvet tones of Jiyaa urged, her head nodding as she took a step towards him, a hand reaching out, "Come now"

He blinked, his shoulders starting to slump as he relaxed, his voice sad as he spoke, "I'm cold"

Turning her head, Lauren watched as the Indian woman nodded, her smile rich, "Come with Jiyaa…we get you hot drink, yes"

He nodded, a lop-sided smile starting to show on his face, and he took another step towards them.

"Ah you found him then" the large figure of Robert Naughton suddenly appeared through the heavy rain from behind them, and as if woken from a spell, Brandon blinked and backed away.

"Son, be careful!" the fatherly Doctor Green called out, and snapping her head from Robert to Brandon, Lauren cried out in concern as she saw him wobble suddenly, both hands wind-milling at his sides as he stood on the very edge of the drop, desperately trying to keep his balance. For a moment, it seemed as though he had been successful but then the envelope which had become the focal point for his grief slipped from his hands, thrown high and to the side by the wind, and blinking, Brandon reached for it, only to be swallowed by the rain as he fell from sight. Instantly the four of them were at the edge of the drop, staring down at the figure of Brandon as he tumbled sideways down the steep slope, rolling like a log, Lauren and Jiyaa crying out in concern, as the farmer and Doctor Green cursed in dread. Somehow, against the odds, he came to a stop upon an open patch of peat, avoiding the rocks and gorse bushes, his tracksuit wearing form barely visible amid the heavy rain as they stared down at him, watching as he pushed himself to his feet and raised his head to stare back at them for a moment, then snapped his head to the side. Atop the slope, Lauren felt her stomach drop away from her as the young man screamed in terror, then turned and ran, charging across the moorland, "What is he doing?"

"Oh good Lord, no" the mutter of shock from Doctor Green had Lauren turning her face, her head shaking in disbelief as she watched the horde of white-skinned, naked bodies that seemed to appear through the rain, shambling quickly along, their snarls and grunts of excitement loud even over the sound of the rain as they chased the departing figure of Brandon.

Chapter Forty Two

Grim faced, Victor stood at the door, his bearded features almost pressed against the window as he stared in at the man and woman. They had backed hurriedly away from the window as he had approached them, shotgun in hand, as if suddenly regretting their decision to inform him of their presence, and the pair now stood at the far side of what appeared to be a classroom for younger children, the brightly painted walls covered in posters displaying the alphabet and the time. For a moment, Victor let his gaze drift over the room, and then he turned his gaze back on the pair, studying them intently. The man, who appeared to be in his early twenties, stood at the front of the pair against the wall, his brown curly hair short, a section seeming to flop over the left side of his face, and the glasses which he wore on his features were black and rectangular, giving him the appearance of the actor Rick Moranis in the movie Little Shop of Horrors. As Victor met his gaze, the man winced, his hands clasping to his chest as if he feared he was about to get shot, the man's lean body clad in a pair of black trousers, pastel blue shirt and a yellow tie. It was as Victor studied the man's attire, that he saw the hands of the woman reaching from behind to grasp at his shirt, as if holding him in place before her rather than it being his decision. Frowning curiously, Victor studied what he could see of the woman, her black hair hanging down to her waist, while her Betty Bangs, a term his wife had used, gave her a stern almost harsh appearance as she stared at him over the shoulder of her bookish and terrified protector. Victor grimaced as above him the sky suddenly rumbled, and rain began to fall upon him, gentle at first but then harder, each drop that touched upon his skin feeling like an ice-cold fingertip. Shuddering, he released his grip upon the shotgun with one hand, raising it beside his head, his free hand raising palm open to face them, as he raised his voice, "I am not going to hurt you!" Within the room, the young man muttered something to his female companion, his head turning slightly as if he were listening to a reply, then as one they began to approach the glass, picking their way carefully across the room as if trying to be quiet, the woman glancing behind her several times at a closed door, and then they were before Victor, but separated by the window. Bending his head against the heavy rain that was now falling upon him, Victor glanced down at the door handle and then back up at the couple, gesturing towards it with his free hand, "Are you going to come outside?"

Behind the window the man frowned, muttered something that Victor couldn't hear and then turned to the side, allowing the former priest his first proper view of the woman that had been hiding as she stepped closer to the window. She stopped short by two feet, her features twisted into a grimace as she studied him through the window, her angular and bony form seeming lost amid the tye-dye dungarees she was wearing, her bony wrists heavy with bangles. Trying his best not to judge someone on their first appearances, Victor met the gaze of the woman, realising that her high-cheek boned features and narrow nose gave her an almost Egyptian appearance, a look that he might have found attractive were it not for the blank brown eyes that held his gaze, devoid of any emotion. For a moment she stared at him in silence, an unspoken challenge on her features as she lifted her chin slightly, her eyes narrowing, and Victor frowned as he turned his attention to the nerdy man, noticing how submissive and nervous he was in comparison to the haughty young woman. Forcing himself to stay calm, realising how the pair might be extremely stressed after becoming trapped inside the school for whatever reason, Victor pointed down at the door handle once more, "Can you open it?"

The woman blinked, an eyebrow rising a fraction of an inch, her top lip curling as she spoke, her voice barely audible through the window, "Do you think we would be here if we could"

Letting out a heavy sigh as he considered the rhetorical question, disliking the attitude of the woman, Victor reached down himself and began trying the door handle, rattling it hard as he tried to turn it around, then paused, raising his eyes as he realised that within the classroom both the man and the woman had frozen, heads turned to stare back at the closed door far behind them.

"Stop!" the young man stepped up to the window, the palms of his hands pressing together as if he was praying, "Please, stop!"

Grimacing, Victor did as requested, his own eyes turning to stare at the distant door, frowning as he saw movement along the bottom edge of the small window that sat high on its surface, as if something had just tried to reach up towards it.

"Help us!" the man pleaded through the window, his head turning to glance at the door before he met Victor's gaze again, the fact that the former priest had not heard his voice at all indicating that the young man had just mouthed the words. Which meant that there was something beyond the door that they didn't want to hear them. Something.

Grimacing, Victor stepped back, trying to see if he could work out a way to open the door without making any noise, then turned as a voice called out from behind him, "Dog, what are you doing?" On the other side of the village centre, Bella and Alice stood staring back at him from outside the shop they had entered, each of the women now carrying full backpacks, their faces concerned as they studied him in the pouring rain. He nodded at them, his free hand raising as he gestured for them to join him inside the school, then stood watching as they made their way quickly across the road towards the open gate in the fence. "What are you doing?" Bella was incredulous, her head shaking as she reached the gate head of Alice, a touch of anger in her voice, "When I saw you weren't outside I thought something had happened to you...why are you in the school?" Her words trailed off as he stepped to the side, and she stopped walking, eyes widening as she stared through the classroom window at the couple within, Alice following suit as she drew level with the former soldier, "Who are they?"

"Teachers I suppose" Victor gave a weary smile, turning his face back towards the man and woman, irritation coursing through him as he saw the former nod and smile at his friends while the latter stared back with complete apathy, then pointed to the door handle, an eyebrow rising.

"She seems nice" Alice gave a humourless chuckle and Victor met her gaze, nodding back.

"Oh yeah, she's a fucking delight"

As the brown-haired woman chuckled grimly, Bella stepped up to the window, a hand reaching for the handle only to freeze as Victor shook his head at her, "No, I wouldn't...they are scared of something behind that door...has to be a ghoul"

Bella winced, head shaking, "So how do we get them out without trying the door handle?"

"Oh, I've tried it already" he shook his head grimly, "Its locked...I have no idea how these two got in there but we cant leave them...especially if there is one of these ghouls behind that door"

"Are there no other ways in?" Alice asked, taking a step back, her head turning as she studied the one storey building, and Victor shook his head.

"I guess there must be but I don't think we have time to go scouting around the school...we need to get them out, the sooner the better"

Turning her head, Bella studied him intently, her lips twisted together as if trying to decide upon a course of action, then she nodded, "We are going to have to break the window to get them out"
Grimacing, Victor nodded back at her, realising that she was right, "What are you thinking, break the window, get them out and then all run like fuck for the car?"
She shrugged, "I can't think of another way"
"Oh fuck" Alice grimaced beside him, "Shit"
"Yeah" he nodded at her then glanced back at Bella, "Are we really going to do this?"
"Do we have a choice?" she countered, "Really?"
Victor shook his head, and stepped back to watch as Bella turned towards the window where the man was now closer as if trying to listen, while the black-haired woman was standing with her arms folded across her chest, chewing the inside of her cheek as if trying not to lose her temper.
Grimacing, Bella turned to throw Victor a grim smile, "What's this bitch's problem? Have you been using your charm on her?"
"No" he shook his head, "I only use that on you"
Much to his surprise, she blushed, her head shaking and as she stepped closer to the window, Alice gave him a slight nudge with an elbow, grinning at him as he met her gaze, "What?"

She shook her head, still smiling, and suddenly embarrassed, Victor turned back to watch as Bella stepped closer to the window and began to address the occupants of the classroom, her voice raising, "We are going to get you out, OK"

Victor tensed as he saw the lips of the woman in the classroom move in an unintelligible sentence, the man beside her wincing in embarrassment as he glanced at the trio beyond the window then turned to glance back at the door behind them for a moment before turning back to them once more, a finger rising to his lips as he winced.

"We need to break the window" Bella stated, and beyond the glass the woman muttered something in confusion then glanced at the man, listening as he spoke, perhaps explaining what Bella had said. Almost instantly she stepped closer to the window, her head shaking frantically, her lips moving in a silent, "No!"

With a grimaced, Bella turned to face Victor and Alice, glancing between them, "What else does she expect us to do?"

"I have no idea" Alice grimaced, glancing up at the sky before raising a hand to her head and Victor grimaced, his head shaking in concern.

"We should have taken you back to the bloody

farmhouse, you have been out in the cold all night and now you are in the pouring rain!"

"I'll be fine" she forced a weary smile and he grimaced, shaking his head at her once more.

"No, you need to get somewhere warm" turning his head, he nodded at Bella, "We need to get Alice back to the farm...let's get this done"

"I'm fine" the brow-haired woman sent him a weak smile, "Seriously, stop worrying about me"

Victor chuckled, "Like you lot keep going on about my bloody ribs you mean"

As Alice gave a soft laugh, Victor turned and met the gaze of Bella again, "Come on, break the glass and let's get out of here while we can"

Nodding, she turned and stepped back towards the window beside the door, spinning the shotgun over in her hands as she raised the butt of the weapon, ready to smash it into the glass. Within the classroom the reaction from the pair was instantaneous, the woman clasping her hands to her ears as she shook her head while the man went pale, a hand covering his mouth.

"Get back!" Bella shouted through the window, the couple reluctantly following her instructions, and Victor took a step back, Alice joining him as the former soldier struck the large window in the bottom left hand corner, beneath a cluster of hand painted rainbows. The glass gave at once under the pressure, smashing through into the classroom and as a crack spiderwebbed its way up the remaining window, Bella struck it again. With a crash that seemed deafening in the silence of the seemingly abandoned village, the entire window crashed through into the classroom, broken glass scattering across the floor, and as Victor stood beside Alice in the heavy rain, he saw the two within move quickly away from it. "Come on!" Bella called to them, sweeping the shotgun from side to side along the bottom of the window frame, removing the few remaining shards of glass that rose like crystal stalagmites. Grimacing, Dog stepped towards the window, beckoning with a hand, "Come on, we have a vehicle parked at the entrance to the village..." His words trailed off as the door at the back of the class suddenly shook as if something had struck it hard, his features twisting into a grimace as he saw the effect it had on the two within the room, "What's back there!"

Without a word, the woman hurried forwards, clambering atop the table beside the window as she began to climb out, and as the visibly shaking man followed her, Victor met his gaze, repeating his question, "What the fuck is back there?"

As the woman slid from inside the room, stepping boldly past Bella and Alice to stand furthest away from the classroom, the man began to clamber up onto the table, his voice almost breaking in fear as the door was struck again, his words thick with dread, "It's the children..." Victor exchanged a glance with Bella, both of them reaching forward with a free hand to help the man then they were snapping their faces up as the door suddenly crashed open and a horde of children surged into the classroom, snarling excitedly, their uniforms caked with dried blood, their young white faces cracked and calloused. "Fuck my life!" Victor fastened both hands to his shotgun, raising it before him to point at the miniature ghouls, their height suggesting that none of them were older than six, Bella doing the same, and within the room, the man screamed in terror as he pushed himself through the window.

Chapter Forty Three

"Go, go, go!" Bella shouted at the top of her lungs as she stepped closer to the window, one hand leaving her weapon once more to snake out and grasp the struggling man by his collar, dragging him forwards and out of the smashed window. He landed on his face, legs kicking high as he flipped over on the rain-soaked ground, his glasses breaking with the impact, and he cried out in pain and confusion. Instantly Alice and Dog were there at his side, dragging him to his feet, the embalmer bending to snatch up the remains of the man's broken glasses, "Here you go!"

"Get back to the car!" Bella shouted at them, turning to the others, then the woman cursed as the wave of white-skinned children scrambled effortlessly onto the table, hands grasping her backpack through the broken window, snarling loudly in excitement, as they tried to drag her in. "Fuck!" she tottered backwards, off balance, but suddenly Dog was there beside her, shouting in anger as he cracked the butt of his shotgun hard into the face of the closest of the young ghouls, throwing it from the table and then reversed the weapon, discharging both barrels into the crowd at close range. Wincing at the sudden retort of the shotgun, Alice watched in astonishment as all

385

of the young ghouls upon the table were thrown back, blood spraying, their forms not seeming as tough as the adults ghouls they had encountered. "Come on!" Dog released his shotgun with a hand to grasp at Bella, urging her away from the window, and she went with him, the pair backing towards where Alice and the young man waited in the heavy rain beside the schoolyard gate.
"Go on!" Dog turned to glance back at them as he accepted a fresh couple of shells from Bella, frantically shoving them into his weapon as he and the silver-haired woman reached them, "Go!"
"Wait" the voice of the man that they had rescued was filled with hysteria as the four of them rushed out onto the village centre, Bella closing the metal gate behind them, and wiping the rain from her features, Alice turned to meet his gaze. "What?"
"Where's Bethany?" he blinked, head turning. Realising his point, Alice spun on the spot, staring off through the heavy rain in search of the woman and then pointed, head shaking as she saw her running off down the street that they had entered by earlier, "There she is!"
"Nice of her to fucking wait" the growl from Bella was ominous as she stepped past Alice and the man, motioning with a nod, "Come on, let's go!"

386

As Bella began to slowly jog off down the street in the direction of their vehicle, Alice began to run behind her, a hand grasping at the arm of the man in the now wet blue shirt, "Come on, we have a car up there, my name is Alice, this is Dog and Bella!"

"Freddy" the man stated, blinking repeatedly, a hand rubbing at his eyes as he ran, "I can't really see...I'm quite dependent on my glasses"

"Just keep running Freddy" the voice of Dog sounded behind them, and glancing back, Alice winced as she saw him half-running at the rear, his freshly loaded shotgun held in his hands, but there was raw pain showing in his grey eyes.

"Dog, your ribs" she began, starting to slow.

"Just keep going" he grunted, forcing a smile. Feeling suddenly nauseous, the fatigue, pains and cold that she had endured the night before suddenly seeming to erupt within her, Alice nodded back at him, and ran on, her eyes focused on the back of the woman ahead, a sudden sense of anger washing through her in a violent wave. They had risked themselves to save her and her friend, Freddy, and she had abandoned them the first chance that she got without saying a word. Where the Hell was she going in such a hurry?

She blinked suddenly, one hand adjusting the straps of the heavy backpack that she was carrying, her other wiping rain from her face again, as she called out to Bella, "Where are the keys to our vehicle?"

The woman glanced back, her silver hair plastered to her face from the rain, "I left them in the ignition ready for us to make a getaway"

"Oh fuck!" Alice grimaced, head shaking, "You don't think she is going for our car, do you?"

"Bitch!" Bella's roar was loud amid the rain and the sounds of their feet slapping down on the wet road, "I swear to God if she is..."

Alice cringed in dread as there was a sudden smashing sound of glass breaking from behind them, the curse of Dog following it, and glancing back, she saw a white figure lying on the street in front of the house beside the shop they had been inside, the front window of the house broken. Shaking her head, she watched for a moment as the figure rose to its feet, turned its head in their direction and then gave chase, snarling excitedly.

"Fuck!" she turned forwards once more, arms pumping at her sides as she charged onwards, the thin man running beside her, his breathing haggard as if he was about to have an asthma attack at any moment, then she cursed aloud as another window smashed loudly behind them. "They are coming from everywhere!" Dog shouted, fear in his voice, "Fucking run, run!" Wincing as she pictured what must be happening behind them, Alice kept running, hands grasping the straps of the backpack that was swaying ungainly upon her back, her leg muscles starting to burn, and then they were running past the first of the side roads, the embalmer turning her head to stare down it at the abandoned vehicles they had seen earlier before facing forward again.

"What the fuck is she doing?" the confused voice of Bella grunted, her run slowing and Alice blinked in shock as she realised that the woman with the black hair in the dungarees was running back towards them through the rain, screaming. "Bitch!" Bella snarled as the woman reached them and she stepped away, hands raising defensively before her as she shook her head. "There's more...up there...near a jeep!"

"Oh shit!" Alice winced, feeling sick, "That's ours"

"You were going to fucking leave us?" the voice of Bella was thick with anger as she snarled at the woman, the young man, Freddy, moving to stand between them, his hands raised defensively. "Please, don't hurt her!"

"What are we doing people?" the voice of Dog was grim, and fighting the urge to vomit, Alice turned her gaze to stare back down towards the school, her heart skipping a beat as she saw a crowd of ghouls rounding the distant corner, no doubt drawn by the breaking glass and the gunshot, then fixed her attention to the two that were just over twenty feet away from them.

"Come on!" Bella turned to run towards the entrance to the side street, "Come on, we'll take the white van!"

Without hesitating, Alice followed her, Dog and the others joining them, the snarls of the ghouls as they pursued them loud over the heavy rain. Ahead of them, Alice was just feet from the van when a ghoul staggered out from behind the open door, its stocky body dressed in paint stained work overalls, its white head turning in their direction. With a roar of anger, the former soldier raised her shotgun, the barrels pushing against the chest of the ghoul over its heart as she ran into it and fired, throwing it back to slide across the wet road as if yanked upon a rope.

"Get in!" she turned, shouting at the others, and Alice charged towards the van as Bella leaned into the vehicle, grunting in excitement, "The keys are in it...come on go, go!"

Gritting her teeth, Alice reached the side door of the vehicle and dragged it open, a curse of horror escaping her as she found the body of a man inside, one hand clasped to the bloody ruin of his throat, bite marks upon his arms, and beside her the man, Freddy gave an almost childlike scream. "Just get in!" Alice shouted at him, then grimaced as she saw the black-haired woman beside the door, clearly assuming that she was coming with them despite leaving them behind moments ago. For a moment they held each other's gaze in silence, Alice's anger growing as she saw no sign of humility of regret on the face of the woman, Gritting her teeth, Alice studied her a moment longer, fighting the urge to close the door on her, but then Dog was beside the passenger side door of the cab, shouting angrily, "Everyone get in!" Without hesitating, the woman clambered inside the vehicle, nudging against the embalmer as she did so and cursing beneath her breath, Alice slid the door shut, and turned to stare over the back of the front seats at her friends in concern. Bella was behind the wheel, throwing her backpack into the rear and then turning the key as she shouted in anger, the battery sounding like it was dead, and then Alice cringed as Dog fired his shotgun at the closest of the two ghouls that

had thrown themselves out of windows, the force
of the blast throwing it back to the ground.

"Dog!" Alice screamed as she saw the second of
the ghoul's charge at her friend, nausea coursing
through her as she saw the wave of ghoul's surge
around the corner and rush into the side street.

"Shit!" Dog was halfway into the open door of the
van when the ghoul reached him, hands grasping
his head, snarling at it tried to bite him, and
roaring in anger and fear, the bearded man
brought his shotgun up between them, trying to
use it as a bar to push the snapping teeth away.
Beyond the front of the van the ghouls were less
than twenty feet away now, and with a curse,
Bella turned in her seat, snapping her shotgun
shut, and thrusting it at Alice, "Kill it now!"
Running purely on adrenaline, she leaned over
the seat, thrusting the barrels of the weapon past
Dog, and into the open mouth of the ghoul, her
stomach turning over as she heard its teeth bite
down on the metal, its hands releasing Dog to
grasp at it. As the bearded man pushed himself
back, cursing as he tried to scramble into the van,
Alice fired the weapon, the sound deafening.

The back of the ghoul's head blew out, blood
spraying everywhere as it was thrown back to
the road, and casting the shotgun to the floor of

the cab, she reached forwards, grasping at Dog's clothes, pulling him inside as Bella gave a cry of triumph, the engine suddenly roaring into life. The wave of ghouls struck the front of the van, rocking it as Dog finally made it inside, the rushing crowd inadvertently slammed his door. "Hold on!" Bella shouted, turning her head back to glance over the seats into the rear of the van and out of the two door windows, the besieged vehicle lurching as she slammed the gearstick hard into reverse and floored the accelerator. With a roar, they flew backwards, Freddy and the woman falling over in the back of the vehicle, the body of the dead man sliding upon the floor, and cursing, Alice clung to the seats for her life while in front of the van, the foremost of the crowd of ghouls toppled forwards in a heap, the others fighting to get past them, in pursuit of them. They turned in a small arc to face sideways in the road, the brakes skidding as they stopped, Alice staring out of the window beside Dog in dread as the ghouls began to give chase again. Then Bella was turning the wheel again, straightening the vehicle up before flooring the accelerator again. Grimacing, Alice turned her gaze upon Dog as he pushed the lock down on his door and leaned heavily against it, his right hand rising to rest against his ribs as he closed his eyes, and then she turned to face to watch out of the windscreen through the furiously moving wipers, as Bella steered the van around the side street and back out into the centre of the village, and past the small school. Only slightly slowing, the former soldier spun the wheel, sending them sliding around the corner beside the shop and onto the road out of the village, completing their circle. The engine roared once more, as Bella worked her way through the gears, speeding past the entrance to the side street that they had just been in, watching as the wave of ghouls charged off in the distance, not realising that they had escaped and were now behind them. Then they were speeding towards the edge of the village, past the small group of ghouls that were standing around their former vehicle, and back out onto the moorland, vanishing into the mist and rain.

Chapter Forty Four

They drove for several minutes in silence, leaving the village behind them as they drove out through the moorland, Bella slowing the vehicle as the mist grew thicker and the rain got heavier.

"Thank you" the voice of the young man they had saved back in the village had Alice turning her head to face him, a weary smile on her features.

"You're welcome...Freddy wasn't it?"

He nodded up at her from where he was sitting back against a wooden tool rack that had been built into the van, a hand gesturing to the glum faced woman that was seated beside him, "This is Bethany...I don't think you had a chance to meet"

Alice nodded, "No, it was a bit difficult what with her running off and leaving us all like that"

The black-haired woman bristled at her words but forced a weak smile, "Hey, look, I'm sorry"

"No need to apologise, this is a situation all of us are getting used to" the pained voice of Dog sounded from the front and turning her face towards him, Alice winced as she met his gaze.

"Are you OK?"

"Yeah" he forced a smile, though it didn't reach his grey eyes, "I'm fine, stop worrying"

"He's not fine" the angry voice of Bella stated, her head shaking as she glanced back at Alice, "He

pushed himself too much when I told him to rest"
"Stop please" he raised a hand, head shaking, "I
am in too much pain to argue with you"
The silver-haired woman nodded, "Yeah, because
you don't listen to me...I told you to take it easy!"
From behind Dog's seat, Alice watched as he
sighed then sent Bella a weak smile, "I'm sorry"
"You should be" she snapped in reply but there
was less anger now, her head shaking as she cast
the bearded Dog a faint smile, "Stubborn bastard"
He gave a grim chuckle, nodding, and then turned
to look back over the seats, grimacing as he saw
the man lying upon the floor and Alice followed
his gaze, realising for the first time that the man
was wearing overalls covered in spots of paint,
just like the ghoul that Bella had shot beside it.
Was he the van's owner? Had they been friends?
She winced as she studied what she now realised
was a bit mark in his throat, his dead eyes staring
at the roof of the van above them as they drove.
Had the two men been on their way to work only
for one of them to change and bite the other,
forcing the unfortunate victim to hide in the back
of the van? She cringed as she considered how
scared the dead man must have been as he had
lain there bleeding out. He must have known he
was dying, yet not realised what was going on.

Or had the ghoul managed to get into the van with him? The driver's door *had* been open. Realising that she was asking herself questions she would never know the answer to, she glanced up as Bella spoke, "We need to drop him off at the side of the road"

Dog gave a grunt, "It seems a bit shit"

Sighing heavily, Bella slowed the van and then stopped, her head turning to meet first his gaze and then that of Alice, clearly uninterested in the opinion of the two people they had rescued, "We don't want to be taking a dead body back to the farmhouse…I know its grim but he's dead…we cant help him, can we?"

"We should bury him" Dog grimaced, meeting her gaze, "We owe him that as a person"

Bella raised an eyebrow at his words, "Who is going to do that? You…no, not happening, you have already done way too much…you are in pain…I wont let you do it"

"I'll do it" Alice spoke up, shrugging as Bella glanced her way, "There are a ton of tools in the back of this van, there must be something I can dig with…the peat will be soft with this rain"

"No" Bella shook her head, smiling sadly, "After the night you have had followed by this you need to rest too…what good are we to the children and the others if we all get ill?"

Alice nodded, sighing, then glanced to the rear of the van as Freddy spoke, rising slowly to his feet to face them, squinting as he tried to focus upon them, "I'd like to help...please...I...we, owe you our lives for what you did back there"

"You can barely see" Alice pointed out and he nodded in reply, looking suddenly embarrassed.

"I know...I just want to help"

"Thank you but it's fine" Bella held his gaze for a moment, looking like she wanted to smile at his words, but then her gaze drifted to the side to settle upon the woman, Bethany, and Alice felt her stomach tighten as the former soldier grimaced, "What the fuck were you doing back there, eh?"

"I was getting away...you did tell us to run" the woman in the dungarees held her gaze unafraid, an eyebrow rising in a challenge, "Why?"

"Why?" Bella's voice was low, her eyes narrowing as if she couldn't believe the audacity of the woman, "Are you taking the fucking piss?"

The woman suddenly seemed to realise the situation that she was in, and she winced, her hands rising beside her defensively, "I am sorry OK, I panicked, like your bearded friend there said, we are all getting to terms with this!"

Bella released a shaky breath, her eyes still locked to those of the woman, and Alice shook her head, "What were you guys doing back there in the school…how long had you been there?" Freddy swallowed at her words, his eyes drifting to settle upon the woman he had been with, perhaps hoping she might explain but then when it became clear she wouldn't, he turned back to meet the gaze of Alice, a haunted look upon his features, "We work there…Bethany teaches Class 1A and my lot are…were…2B"

"Village kids?" Dog asked, and Alice cast him a glance, seeing his bearded face twisted in dread.

"Mostly" Freddy confirmed with a sad smile, "But we have about thirty per cent of our intake from other villages in the area…we are like a melting pot of education"

He chuckled for a moment at his own joke and then shook his head, "It was Monday…two days ago…we were in the middle of the whole school assembly when several of the children took ill"

"Go on" Bella grimaced, though it was obvious what had happened, both, she Dog and Alice studying the thin man in horror as he tried to compose himself, a shaking hand rising as if to push his glasses back up his nose before realising that he was no longer wearing them, "We…we tried to get them to the school nurse but then there were more...they changed into...those things...white skin...those beige eyes..."

"Ghouls" Dog muttered, wincing as the young man met his gaze, "Its what we are calling them" For a moment, Freddy stared back at Dog in silence, as if comprehending what he had said, and then he shook his head once more, his eyes wet as if he were on the verge of tears, "The children that had changed...they...they began to attack the others...they were so strong...our headmaster Mr Chamberlain...he tried to stop them but a group attacked him...they...they..."

"They pulled him to pieces" the voice of Bethany finished, her cold deadpan description making Alice throw her a look of disgust, but the woman was either oblivious or didn't care, "I got Freddy to hide with me in his classroom"

"The screams" Freddy shook his head, his voice breaking, "We should have tried to help..."

"There was nothing we could do" Bethany stated, not even bothering to meet his gaze, "Stop it"

"But..."

"I told you to shut up about those kids" she snapped her face to stare at him, "Two days of listening to you going on about them is enough"

As the man cringed, his head nodding, Alice grimaced, her dislike of the woman growing, then she turned to watch as Dog spoke, "You were there for two days? What have you been eating?"

Freddy turned to squint at him, shrugging, "The kids packed lunches...yoghurts, sandwiches and crisps mainly...and juice...we drank juice"

Dog let out a soft curse, head shaking and as Freddy opened his mouth to speak, Bethany interrupted, a finger pointing at the dead man on the floor, "What are doing about him...he stinks"

"Charming" Alice grimaced, turning to glance at Bella, "We need to bury him...I'll do it"

"We haven't got time for this, I think we should leave him beside the road" the silver-haired woman winced, then turned to look at Dog, "You can say some words for him if you want, like you did for my grandparents"

He sighed, "It just feels wrong"

"OK then, let's put it to a majority vote" Bella grimaced, turning to look at the others, "Do we take time out to bury this poor bastard or just get back to safety? I vote safety"

"Well, I think he deserves a burial" Dog shrugged.

"What about you Frankie?" Bella turned to the young man in the back and he laughed nervously.

"Freddy...er...I'm happy to help bury him but if I

was given the choice...honestly...I'd go safety"

Bella nodded, "Alice?"

She winced, "I agree with Dog"

"OK" Bella smiled then turned her face to look at the woman beside Freddy, What about y..."

"Dump him" Bethany shrugged before Bella had even finished asking the question, her head shaking, "It seems like a weird question right...he is dead...he isn't coming back and he isn't getting any deader...just throw him out!"

"Bethany?" Freddy sounded shocked, "Really?"

"We aren't just dumping anyone out!" Dog was suddenly angry, wincing as he turned to glare at the woman and then with a curse, he opened the door beside him and climbed out into the rain. Throwing a grim look back at the black-haired woman, Alice fought the urge to swear at her as she got a raised eyebrow in response, and then she turned as the door slid open beside her to reveal a grim-faced Dog. Without a word, he reached in, hands grasping to the overalls of the dead man as he slid the corpse towards him, and wincing, Alice stepped out of the way, watching as Dog scooped the unfortunate man up in his arms and then turned to step off the road onto the moorland. Stepping to the edge of the open back door, Alice watched as Dog knelt, carefully laying the body down as if it were a sleeping baby, then turned her head to watch as Bella moved around the front of the van to stand beside him, a hand gently resting on his shoulder, the fingers squeezing gently and Alice smiled. The pair were growing closer, that much was obvious, and she was pleased for them both. She had realised early on in her acquaintance with them that there was something magical happening between them, although she wasn't sure if they had even realised it themselves yet. As she stood studying them, Dog began to speak, his words lost to the heavy rain and she saw him raise a hand as if crossing himself, that strange but comforting relationship that she had with her faith resurfacing in a rush and without giving it conscious thought, she too began to say a prayer, then turned as she heard movement behind her., grunting in surprise as she found the black-haired woman standing there studying her. "What are you do...?" she gasped as without warning the woman shoved her backwards, and her view shifted, the interior of the van being replaced by the grey sky as she fell to her back on the roadside, the soft peat beneath her and the full backpack that she still wore stopping her from hurting herself. Blinking against the rain that was falling upon her face, she stared up, watching in confusion as the black-haired woman rushed forwards and slammed the side door shut, the voice of Freddy loud as he shouted at his friend, "Bethany, no...what are you doing!"

"Bitch!" the roar of Bella sounded loud over the rain, and struggling to her feet, helped by a rising Dug, Alice stumbled forwards to draw level with the cab of the van, staring in shock through the window as Bethany scrambled over the back of the seats and slid behind the steering wheel, quickly leaning out to lock both of the doors. Cursing, her features twisted in a rage, Bella moved to stand in front of the van, a fist banging down on the bonnet, "You fucking bitch!"

Behind the wheel, a triumphant smile upon her features, Bethany raised her middle finger, reached down and then cursed in disbelief, the smile slipping from her features, her eyes wide. "Looking for these?" Bella dragged the keys out of a pocket of her jeans, her features a mash of anger, "Get out of the fucking van, now!"

For a moment, the teacher sat behind the wheel, eyes locked with those of the former soldier, and then she gave a smile, and bent once more, a hand rising with a shotgun in it, only for Bella to laugh bitterly, "Both empty bitch...and I've got the shells...now get out of the fucking van"

"Screw you!" the reply came, the voice barely audible over the sound of the rain as the three of them stood beneath it, surrounding the cab. Alice winced as the rear door suddenly slid wide open, the figure of Freddy stepping back to allow them entry and grimacing, Alice surged inside, leaning forward over the seats to open Dog's door, a grunt of pain escaping her as Bethany struck her in the side with the empty shotgun. The door suddenly flew open and as Alice leaned back, the furious figure of Bella surged into the cab, her features twisted into a mask of hatred.

"I give up!" Bethany raised her hands dropping the shotgun, "I surrend..."

Her words were cut off as Bella hammered a fist into her unprotected features, throwing her back so hard that the window behind shattered as her head struck it, the lips of the teacher moving soundlessly in a plea but the former soldier was already striking her again, once, twice, three times, before suddenly Dog was there, dragging her back, "For fuck sake Bella, you're killing her!" As the pair slid from the cab, the teacher tried to sit up, a hand fumbling with the lock on her door as she opened it, and then she fell heavily outside onto the rain soaked road, moaning in agony.

"Bethany!" Freddy took a step forwards but Alice turned, her head shaking as she met his gaze. "Dude, for your own good stay there!"

He nodded, hands raising before him and sat down upon the floor of the van, eyes closing his shoulders beginning to shake as he began to sob

Shaking her head, Alice scrambled back out of the van as Dog and Bella walked around the cab, one hand clasping to her side where the woman had struck her with the gun as she followed them to stand staring down at the woman on the ground.

"What are we going to do with her?" Alice asked, her question drawing the attention of Bethany as she glanced up at the trio that stood about her in the rain, her eyes already bruised and swollen, her nose bent at an angle, both her lips split and bleeding profusely, running down to the road.

"Pleathe don't kill me" her shoulders shook as she sobbed, her voice scratched and pained.

"Leave her" Bella shrugged, her voice cold.

"What?" Dog was incredulous, eyes wide as he met her gaze, "We can't just leave her here!"

"Why?" Bella asked, raising an eyebrow, "She has tried to leave us behind twice now...fuck her!"

"Alice!" Dog turned to look at the embalmer, his eyes beseeching, "Tell Bella we can't leave her!" For a moment, she stared back at Dog in silence, feeling the need to back him up but then she shook her head as she suddenly recalled the two men from back at the hospital, Nick and Peter, God that seemed to long ago now.

"Sorry Dog" she shrugged, her smile sad, "Some people deserve to be left behind"

He shook his head at her words, taking several steps away from the pair of them as he turned to stare out across the rainy moorland, a hand rising to scratch at his dreadlocked hair, then he turned and moved back to them, stepping behind Bethany as he held their gaze, "Fine, I'll make sure she can't hurt anyone

"Dog!" Bella shook her head, exchanging a glance with Alice, the pair of them watching as he withdrew the handcuffs that he had previously used upon the ghoul in the barn, and secured the hands of the female teacher behind her back. Grimacing, he took a step back, shrugging, "I am sorry, I know what she tried to do but we can't leave her...if we leave her then I stay too"

"For fuck sake" Bella grimaced, "Dog, you can't!"

He shrugged, smiling sadly, "Don't make me"

"I'm not joking" the former soldier grimaced.

"Neither am I" Dog stated, matching her anger with sad calm, "All I ask is that we take her back to the farm, give her a day or two to heal, then we drive her somewhere and leave her...but not here...not out in the open in this weather!"
Bella grimaced, "How about I deal with her"
"Deal with her?" Dog grimaced, eyes narrowing.
She shrugged, "Alice, get a shotgun from the cab"
"What?" the embalmer blinked, head shaking.
"You don't mean that" Dog shook his head as he held her gaze, "You aren't a murderer"
"And you aren't a priest anymore" she snapped angrily, her head shaking, "You cant save everybody no matter how hard you try!"
Alice felt her stomach knot as she saw the sudden pain register in Dog's eyes, her heart sinking as he gave a heavy sigh and turned to stare out across the moorland once more. Then with a sigh which seemed to shake his entire body, he turned back and bent, wincing as he helped Bethany to her feet, "I'll be sitting in the back with her"
Without another word he turned to walk around the front of the van, assisting the still sobbing woman and wincing, Alice met the gaze of Bella, seeing instantly that the woman was hurting as much as she had just hurt Dog with her words.

For a moment, the pair of them stood in the heavy rain in silence and then Bella sighed and turned to meet her gaze, forcing a sad smile, "It looks like you are up front with me, right?"
Alice nodded, sighing, "Can we go home now"
The bitter chuckle from Bella was raw and filled with pain, "Home? Where the fuck is that?"

Chapter Forty Five

"Thank you" the barely audible voice of the young man name Freddy dragged the attention of Victor as he sat on the floor in the back of the van, his back to the tool rack, and lifting his head he met the others gaze and then looked away.

He knew instinctively, even without looking that the young man had winced at his apparent ignorance and was now sat quietly in dread, worrying what the angry looking man with the beard and the dreadlocks was going to do next. Yet wasn't that the image that he had nurtured; a man that it was best to leave to himself, a grumpy and irritable loner to be widely avoided.

In the wake of his family's deaths in the fire and his eventual release from hospital, Victor had felt his place in the priesthood to be a mockery of how someone in his position should be. Whereas he had once put the members that made up his congregation first, putting their needs and desires above that of both himself and his family, he now saw sin at almost every turn; adultery, theft, addiction and lies, and the fact that his family had been taken from him while these had been left alive, had felt like a slap in the face from a God that he had dedicated his life to.

So, he had quit the priesthood ignoring the pleas of those higher in the church, resisting the urge to react with anger and violence when he had been told perhaps God was merely testing him. For nearly two years he had lived on the streets of London, and had been lost both mentally and physically, his broad frame having become near skeletal, his mental health at an all-time low, and then salvation had found him in the guise of an accident. He had been struck by a speeding car one night, two years to the day after his family's deaths, and had been left to die in the wet road. A passer-by had seen him, and called for the emergency services and he had been taken to the nearest hospital where, as chance would have it, the new hospital padre was a former friend of his from the priesthood who had recognised him. Over the course of the next year, Victor had moved in with his former friend, growing strong physically with a regime of exercise and a good diet, and mentally strong with the aid of therapy and his prescribed pills, yet he had kept his full beard and dreadlocks from his time on the street, enjoying the wide berth that strangers gave him. Just as he was using it to his advantage now.

In the front of the van, Alice and Bella began to talk, their voice's a low buzz against the heavy thrum of the rain upon the van in which they were travelling, and Victor leaned his head back against the tool rack and studied the silver-haired woman that was sitting behind the wheel. *"You can't save everybody no matter how hard you try!"* that was what she had said to him outside the van as they and Alice had stood in the rain around the bleeding and sobbing figure of the female teacher, her words cutting him deeply. She was right, he knew that, just as he knew that was part of the reason that her words had hurt him so much. Yet it was the second part of that reason which had left him feeling so out of sorts.

He liked her.

He liked that she seemed to like him.

Yet for the first time since he had begun to admit that there was something about the former soldier that he was attracted to, there was no guilt, no mental images of his deceased wife.

Just hurt that Bella had been so angry with him. Sighing heavily, he closed his eyes for a moment, giving himself over to the shake and rattle of the van as they drove through the moorland, then he opened them to study the woman that he had saved from Bella's fury as she lay on the floor in front of Freddy, her head resting upon his lap.

Wincing, he let his gaze drift over her bruised and bloodied features, letting out a shaky breath as he saw just how badly Bella had beaten the black-haired woman, and with just four punches. Yet he knew that Bella had been justified in her anger, after all, the female teacher had tried to abandon them back in the village, even leaving her friend Freddy behind, then gone on to assault Alice twice before she had been finally stopped. Turning his gaze away from her, he let it settle upon the brown-haired woman that was sat in the passenger seat of the van's cab, studying her for a moment as she laughed grimly at something that Bella had just said, a smile creasing his face. She was a good person, his favourite, after Bella of course, of this random bunch that he had found himself a part of, and he was glad that she had survived her night out on the wet moorland. It would be good to have her back with them at the farmhouse though the loss of Geri, the Scots woman, was going to cast a cloud over them. Another person lost.

He sighed, head shaking as he considered that Marcus had also been lost, chastising himself for not having given the young man much thought since Alice had relayed what had happened.

He had assumed that anyone who was going to change would have done so on that first day when everyone else had changed but with the delayed change from Marcus that was clearly incorrect. Yet why? What was different? Grimacing as he considered how Marcus and Moonshine had seemed fine one moment and then changed into ghouls, Victor considered the farmhouse and the people they had left there. Were any of those liable to become ghouls? Was Bella? Was Alice? Was he?

Feeling sick with dread as he suddenly pictured young Eric and Emily back at the farmhouse, he sat up straighter, his stomach knotting with dread as he pictured returning to the farm and finding that the youngsters had been violently killed by ghouls, surprising himself with how protective he felt about the brother and sister. "Hey what's that?" the concerned voice of Alice made him glance up, "I thought I saw something" "Where?" Bella grimaced, slowing the van and then stopping it, and clasping a hand to his side, Victor rose to his feet and moved to stand behind Alice's seat. Bella turned her head as he stood there and smiled awkwardly as he met her gaze, and he sighed, throwing her a weary smile, his pulse quickening as she gave a sudden blush.

"There!" the startled voice of Alice had them both snapping their attention forwards, Victor's grey eyes narrowing in curiosity as he stared through the windscreen down the long open road ahead, his brow furrowing as he spotted something moving amid the heavy rain and the drifting mist. "Ghouls" Bella grimaced, a finger rising to point ahead of her, a hand pointing down beside Alice's feet, "Pass me the shotguns, let's load them"

As the young woman handed her the first of the weapon's, Bella pushed two shells into the breech, Victor cursed, his eyes widening as the figure surged out from the mist, its body clad in a black and white tracksuit, its black features streaked with sweat and rain, "Holy fuck"

"Brandon?" the voice of Alice was thick with shock, and without even hesitating she opened her door and rushed out into the heavy rain.

"For fuck sake, Alice, be careful" Belle grimaced, throwing her own door open as she turned to pass Victor the loaded shotgun, "This is yours"

Nodding in thanks, he slid open the side door of the van and stepped down to the road, turning to throw Freddy a grim glance, clasping the shotgun with one hand as he pointed at the barely conscious figure of Bethany, "Watch her!"

Without waiting for an answer, he began to

stride forwards through the rain to where Alice now crouched beside the familiar figure of Brandon as the young man knelt in the rain, his chest heaving with the exertion of running, his features locked into a mask of utter terror. Grimacing, he stopped short of the young man, not wanting to unsettle him anymore than he was, noting that Bella had done the same thing. Letting out a shaky breath, Victor turned to meet her gaze, his stomach knotting as she saw the fear in her eyes, her voice thick with barely controlled emotion as she spoke, "Brandon, why aren't you at the farmhouse"

The young man sobbed at her words, his head shaking and beside him, Alice placed a hand upon his shoulder, and another beneath his chin, tilting his face up to hers as she nodded, "Are you hurt?" He shook his head, his eyes wide, and she nodded back at him, "That's good...can you tell me where Lauren is...your nurse...is she hurt?"

He sobbed, head shaking, "She lied to me"

Frowning, Victor turned to meet the gaze of Bella again, then took a step closer, "Ask him about the farm...is everyone OK, are the kids OK?"

"Did you hear that?" Alice asked the young man, her tone soft, soothing, "Is everyone OK? Why are you out here on your own?"

"Ghouls" his sobbed reply stole the breath from Victor's lungs, and for a moment, the bearded man felt his legs threaten to buckle, a deep unfathomable pain opening up inside him like the worst indigestion, stretching his heart.

His fears had been right.

He had left two more children to die.

Victor blinked as the hot tears stung his cheek, mingling with the ice cold touch of the rain and he turned his head, meeting the haunted gaze of Bella as she stood watching him, her face pale.

"What the fuck was that?" Alice rose to her feet suddenly, Brandon joining her, the pair moving quickly to stand in the gap between Victor and Bella as they stood staring off down the road.

He heard it then, a deep guttural snarl and moaning emanating from the swirling mist, his blood running cold as he realised its source.

"Ghouls" Brandon sobbed once more, his eyes turning to meet the gaze of Victor and grimacing, the former priest grasped him by the arm and began propelling him towards the van, aware of Bella and Alice running beside them, cursing.

In moments they were inside the rear of the van, Brandon wincing in dread as she saw Freddy and Bethany, until Victor manoeuvred him to sit down against the tool rack, "Stay here OK"

"Ghouls" Brandon repeated, turning to nod at a terrified looking Freddy, his fear gone, "Ghouls!" Grimacing, Victor moved back to stand behind the seat of Alice, watching as the two women locked their doors, the voice of Bella grim as she glanced into the rear, "With any luck they will walk straight past the van"

Time seemed to stand still as the trio stared out through the windscreen into the grey of the day, the mist and rain giving the moorland an almost ethereal atmosphere, then suddenly the ghouls were there, shambling into sight down the road towards the van, and Victor grimaced, his voice a grim whisper, "Don't move...don't speak...the ghouls are coming"

Chapter Forty Six

"Get out of my way!" Lauren's voice was fierce as she pointed a finger at Doctor Green, her head shaking as she stared at him as he stood before her in the heavy rain, "I need to find Brandon!" The silver haired man shook his head, hands raised before him as he held her gaze, his glasses as covered with rain as Lauren's, "This isn't safe!" "Listen to him, love!" Valerie urged from slightly behind her, and turning her head, the nurse met the gaze of the farmers wife, seeing the concern on her features as she continued, "This weather is awful...the track up is going to be all slush! You won't get the ambulance down there in this!" "So what?" Lauren threw her hands up in the air, her head shaking as she turned to study those that were standing about her; Jiyaa standing beside her, hands clasped to her face in concern, the large figure of the farmer beside his wife as the pair stood near the front door of their home, the brother and sister standing watching intently from the doorway, their feud momentarily forgotten, the girl holding the dog with the broken leg in her arms, a hand stroking its head. For a moment she let her gaze drift over them all and then she turned back to face Valerie, "Are you suggesting that I just leave him out there in this weather? He is severely autistic...he isn't allowed to roam around the hospital on his own let alone unfamiliar moorland in a storm with a pack of fucking ghouls chasing him!"

"No-one is saying just leave him out there" the deep voice of Robert stated, the farmer shaking his head as he took a step forwards, "But if you get stuck out there trying to save him what then? Who are we sending out to rescue you?"

Lauren grimaced, knowing he was right but also knowing that the blame for Brandon being lost on the moorland and at risk was hers to bear.

A shaky breath escaped her as she pictured the ghouls as she had last seen them snarling in excitement as they had given chase, nausea washing over her as she recalled the fear in the scream that Brandon had given before fleeing.

He must be so scared and confused by all this.

Was he still alive?

Had the young autistic man somehow managed to evade the horde of ghouls that they had seen chasing him through the rain and into the mist? Or was he now dead, torn to pieces by them?

She felt herself grow dizzy at the sudden thought, and she closed her eyes, tilting her head back so that the cold raindrops fell upon her features, sending chills coursing through her lean body.

Then with a heavy sigh, she nodded, turning to smile sadly at Jiyaa, and then the others, "I'm sorry OK...I am just worried about him...this is all my fault...I don't know what to do"

"Come on, lass" Robert nodded at her, "Come back inside the house and we can discuss what's to be done to get that lad back here safely"

"A cup of tea is what's needed" Valerie gave a nod, gesturing for her to come back into the house and smiling sadly Lauren nodded at her. "That sounds good"

Shoulders slumping, she took several steps towards the house, returning a smile at Jiyaa as the woman turned to her, gently squeezing one of Lauren's arms, "Come on, my friend"

The nurse nodded, watching as Valerie entered the house, her large husband hobbling in behind her, and then she turned, watching as Doctor Green caught up with them, the silver-haired physician wincing as he met her gaze, "I am sorry for stopping you getting in the ambulance, my dear, you understand my reasons?"

Lauren nodded, knowing that he was being sincere, "Yeah, you are a good man Doctor, I am really sorry"

"Oh?" he raised an eyebrow, chuckling softly as

she stopped walking and he turned to look back at her, "What for?"

Without another word, she spun on her heel on the muddy ground before the farmhouse, her arms pumping beside her sides as she sprinted for the now undefended ambulance, the gasps of shock from the doctor and Jiyaa loud behind her. She reached the vehicle in a matter of seconds, dragging open the drivers door before locking it behind her before leaning over to lock the passenger door too, her head shaking as the figures of Doctor Green and Jiyaa suddenly appeared before the ambulance, calling to her. Grimacing, she reached down for the keys that she had left in the vehicle after parking it there that morning after Dog and Bella had driven to the nearby village, sliding them into the ignition. With a rumble, the engine came to life, and deliberately avoiding the gaze of the kindly doctor and the gentle Jiyaa, Lauren put the ambulance in first gear and reached down to remove the handbrake only to freeze. She had been intending to drive forward and turn around in front of the farm but she knew that if she even attempted it one of the small group would try and get in front of the vehicle to stop her, and as much as she wanted to save Brandon she knew she wouldn't hurt a single one of these people. Grimacing, she pushed in the clutch, shifting the gear stick into reverse and then removed the hand brake, her left foot rising as she pushed down on the accelerator with her right, letting the vehicle gently roll backwards under control. For several metres everything was fine, Lauren using the wing mirrors to angle her drive back down the track, forcing herself to not think about the drop on the passenger side, and then she winced as the drivers side of the ambulance crunched, metal scraping as she failed to turn the wheel enough to avoid the rocks in the cliff face. She cursed as her wing mirror was knocked off, smashed from its position by a jagged rock that jutted out from the rise on her side of the vehicle, her stomach knotting in dread as she felt the ambulance tip towards the passenger side.

Heart in her mouth she braked hard, slamming the ambulance into first gear as she tried to move forwards once more, cursing aloud as the vehicle started to move and then stopped as if caught. Grimacing, she turned to stare back up the slope, realising that she had driven about a quarter of the way down it, then flicked on the headlights, and the windscreen wipers to clear her vision.

Halfway between the ambulance and the top of the rise, Doctor Green and Jiyaa were hurrying forwards, and as she watched the physician almost slipped in the wet mud, only barely righting himself before continuing onwards. They stopped short of the ambulance, their hands raising to shield their eyes from the bright light of the headlights, and sighing, Lauren switched them off and tried to open her door only to curse as she realised the rocky wall was stopping it from opening more than two inches. Gritting her teeth, the nurse shifted across the seat, over the gearstick and onto the passenger seat, her right hand opening the door wide. She cursed as she saw the drop to the moorland below just a foot away from her door, and carefully leaned out, a quick glance towards the back of the ambulance showing that the angle she was parked had left the vehicle on the edge of the drop with no way to walk past at all. "What have you done?" Doctor Green was suddenly beside the front of the ambulance on the passenger side, one hand gripping to the bonnet as if he feared falling over the drop. "I know, I know" Lauren stepped from the ambulance and closed the door, her head shaking as she met the gaze of the physician and the Indian woman, "I fucked up...I understand!" He nodded and winced, not pushing the issue when he quite easily could and would have been well within his rights. Instead, he gestured for her to move around the front of the ambulance, smiling sadly, "Come on, what's done is done" She winced, angry at herself, then turned to stare down past the ambulance as the sound of a vehicle came to them through the downpour, her brow furrowing as she saw a white van making its way up the muddy track towards them all, its headlights cutting through the mist, her voice thick with confusion, "Who the fuck is that?"

Chapter Forty Seven

It had taken what felt like an hour for all of the ghouls to make their way to the white van, though in truth it had been just a few minutes. Trapped within its metallic walls, the six occupants stayed as still and silent as they could, especially Alice and Bella, sat in plain sight as they were up in the front of the vehicle, faces downcast, and Victor stood in the shadows of the rear, watching his pair of friends in dread.

Like before, the ghouls seemed unable to focus upon stationary objects yet all it would take was one quick movement or loud sound, and the ghouls would tear the van apart to get to those hiding within, their strength far beyond human. So, they waited in silence, the two up front frozen like statues while Brandon sat sobbing quietly, hands over his face, and Victor and Freddy exchanged nervous glances while the black-haired Bethany now sat up beside the latter. Worried that the young man was going to give them away, Victor moved to drop into a crouch before Brandon, smiling as the autistic man glanced up and then the former priest placed a finger to his lips. For a moment, the young black man studied him without moving, then he gave a nod, a finger rising to his own lips in reply.

Smiling, Victor rose to his feet once more and then glanced forward as in the front, Alice gave a heavy sigh, her voice barely audible and she leaned to look in her wing mirror, "They've gone...the last one is about ten feet past the van"

"Thank fuck" Victor muttered, "Can we go?"

"Not yet" the voice of Bella was grim, "We need to let them get into the mist and then we can drive off...the farm is only a minute or two down this road...if they follow us now they will follow us back to the farmhouse"

Grimacing, Victor swallowed the sudden wave of dread that washed through him as he considered her words and the implications they carried.

The farmhouse.

Brandon had not yet told them anything about it, nor why he had been running through the rain pursued by ghouls but it didn't look good at all. Fighting a wave of grief that rose within him, Victor met the gaze of Bella and nodded, seeing on her face that she was thinking the same thing.

"Whath the fucking point" the bitter voice of Bethany sounded in the back of the van and cringing at how loud she had spoken, Victor spun to face her, a finger rising to his lips to hush her but she sneered at him, the blood beneath her broken nose and on her lips crusted and dried, "I couldn't give a fuck...everything's gone to shit...we are all fucked..."

"Bethany!" the young male teacher sat beside her winced in dread and she turned to fix him with a glare from her bruised eyes, her head shaking.

"Oh, fuck you, you vile little prick!"

He blinked, head shaking, "What...I thought..."

"Oh fuck off" she gave a bitter, pained chuckle

"Will you both shut the fuck up!" Bella turned to hiss at them through clenched teeth, "I am not fucking around...shut the fuck up now!"

"Fuck...you!" the voice of Bethany was loud, her feet turning to kick wildly at the back doors of the van, the sudden metallic din deafening.

"Bitch!" Bella snarled, and cursing, Victor moved to her side, desperately trying to restrain her.

"Get off me!" she screamed, her voice shrill as she struggled, "Freddy help me, I love you!"

"Leave her alone!" the young teacher was suddenly grasping at Victor, hands trying to drag him off the woman, clearly having forgotten her words to him just moments before, and cursing, Victor snapped his head back into the face of the other, throwing him back to the floor of the van.

"Oh my God!" the voice of Alice from the front was thick with terror, "Drive...fucking drive!"

Grimacing, Victor pushed himself away from the

black-haired woman and rose, watching as Freddy crawled to embrace her, his nose now bleeding just like hers had been minutes before. Grimacing, he studied the pair in silence and then raised his eyes to stare out through the dirty windows in the back doors of the white van, his blood running cold as he saw the horde of ghouls shambling quickly back towards the van, no doubt drawn by the noise the woman had made. "Fuck!" Bella turned the key in the ignition, the engine rumbling but refusing to fire just like it had done back on the street where they had found it, and then the van suddenly shook as something struck it hard from behind, one of the windows in the rear shattering with the impact. Instantly Brandon was screaming in terror, hands hugging to his knees and as Alice turned to try and calm him, there was another loud crash against the van, the vehicle suddenly beginning to rock as the ghouls began to jostle it, the sound of their snarls loud through the broken window. "Start you mother fu..." Bella's curse turned to a roar of triumph as the engine snarled into life, and the van was suddenly moving forwards, hurtling down the road through the heavy rain. Holding on to the back of Alice's chair, Victor stared out through the windows in the doors,

feeling sick with dread as she saw the ghouls
begin to follow them, several breaking into a run.
"Go on, floor it!" Victor grimaced, his eyes locked
to the ghouls as they slowly became dots in the
distance, as he addressed Bella, "Maybe we can
lose them in the mist!"
His words trailed off as the van suddenly began
to slow and grimacing, he turned to stare at her
as she stopped, "What's the matter?"
"We are here" her voice was thick with dread, a
hand gesturing out of the window beside her to
point at the side track which led off and upwards.
"Oh fuck" Victor turned away from her, staring
out through the rear windows as she began to
drive once more, steering the van onto the
winding muddy track that led up the farmhouse.
"What the fuck is going on there?" the voice of
Alice was confused, a grunt of surprise from Bella
following it, and sighing in dread, Victor turned
once more to the front, his eyes widening as he
saw the ambulance a quarter of the way down
the track but leaning to the side slightly, several
figures standing beyond the front of the vehicle.
"Oh my God" the words escaped him in a rush as
they pulled up behind the ambulance and parked,
tears stinging his grey eyes as he realised that it

was Lauren, Jiyaa and Doctor Green standing in the rain studying their approach in confusion. They were alive, which might mean that the children, Eric and Emily were alive as well. Even before Bella had stopped the van, he slid the side door open and leaned out, heedless of the drop below as he clung on to the van with one hand and raised the other in greeting, raw emotion coursing through him as he saw how happy they were to see him and the others.

For a moment, Lauren vanished inside the side of the ambulance but then the rear doors swung open and she jumped down, hurrying towards them as Bella parked the van, her eyes widening behind her glasses as she saw Alice in the vehicle. Without a word, the brown-haired embalmer opened her door and stepped out, the pair of them throwing their arms about each other as they hugged, and stepping down from the rear of the van, Victor watched as they stepped apart, the nurse shaking her head, "I thought you'd gone home…I don't understand"

"There was a problem" Alice's voice was grim, her head shaking, "Marcus, the porter we rescued at the hospital…he changed, he became a ghoul…"

Lauren paled, head shaking, "Geri?"

"Dead" Alice told her simply, "He killed her, he

nearly killed me…then this morning these two found me…I've been with them all day"

"She's lucky we found her" Bella stated coming around the front of the van, smiling grimly at the nurse, "If she'd been out there any longer…"

Lauren nodded at Bella, then reached out to squeeze one of Alice's arms once more as she smiled only for the expression changed to one of grief, head shaking as the former soldier pointed at the ambulance, "What happened here?"

"I have lost Brandon…we had an argument…he ran off, I was trying to reverse the ambulance out but I've got it stuck…"

"Hey" Victor called out to her, a hand gesturing into the van beside him, and as Lauren turned to look in his direction, he helped Brandon emerge from the vehicle, "Look who we ran in to!"

"Brandon!" Lauren clamped a shaking hand to her mouth as she took a step towards the young black man, her head shaking, "I am so sorry!"

"I am sorry I ran away" he intoned, staring down at the ground, "It won't happen again"

"Oh you" she stepped quickly towards him, dragging him into an embrace while he stood with his hands beside him, staring at Victor.

As she released him, she tilted her head, her eyes drifting down him, "Are you hurt…at all?"

"No" he shook his head, then blinked, "Are you my mum now, Lauren?"

She clamped her lips together, tears rolling down her features and Victor felt his throat tighten at the innocence of the young man, smiling sadly for a moment before meeting the gaze of the young nurse, "The children...Emily and Eric?"

"Both fine" she nodded, smiling as she took Brandon by the hand and stepped back towards the ambulance, "They will be pleased to see you!"

Victor nodded, smiling and then turned to stare down through the rain and mist towards the bottom of the track, the hairs rising on his neck as he heard the faint snarling suddenly rise up.

"We need to get to the farmhouse and lock up and hide!" he grimaced, gesturing for them all to start moving, "Come on, through the back of the ambulance and out the side, we need to go now!"

"What?" Lauren blinked, head shaking, and Bella grimaced, gently pulling on the nurse's arm.

"Ghouls, lot of ghouls, we found them chasing Brandon...and thanks to that bitch Bethany they have followed us back here!"

"Bethany?" she shook her head, "Who is she?"

"Just go!" Victor shook his head, "Alice, get them all safe and inside, I'll get these two from the back of the van...we can't leave them"

433

"Are you mad?" she shook her head, "Really?"

"Just go, please, get them and you to safety!" he forced a smile, nodding at her, "Please"

She hesitated for a moment, cast a glance at Bella then did as he had asked as the woman nodded.

"Dog!" as Alice and Lauren began to climb through the ambulance, helping Brandon, the silver haired woman stepped closer to him, her face incredulous, "You can't be fucking serious!"

"I told you, I cant leave people behind"

She grimaced, head shaking as she stared at him, and he winced, his gaze drifting past her to watch as the trio emerged from the ambulance and began to hurry towards the farmhouse, helped by Jiyaa and Doctor Green, then he gave a shrug.

"Look, go with them…I'll be along shortly!"

"You can't let them in the house!" she shook her head, "It puts the kids at risk!"

He turned his head at her words, nodding as he realised that she was right, her new argument finally winning him over to her point of view, and he gave a heavy sigh, "Fine, but I am locking them in the van for the night till this is all over!"

Turning his head to stare down the track, cursing in dread as he saw the first of the ghouls making their way up it, followed by its brethren, Victor stepped level with the open rear of the van, his brow furrowing as he found Freddy sitting there on his own, the set of handcuffs on the floor of the van beside his feet, the keys for it nearby. Cursing, Victor snapped a hand to his pocket, his stomach lurching as he realised that the keys were gone, no doubt having fallen from his pocket during his scuffle in the rear of the van, then he blinked in shock and confusion as the black-haired, blood stained figure of Bethany stepped into view from inside the van and struck him hard in the forehead with a large hammer. He grunted, legs giving way as he dropped to the wet mud, vaguely aware of Bella screaming in fury as she rushed forwards only to grunt and drop to the ground beside him, and the van. Blinking, fighting to stay conscious, Victor watched as two pairs of feet jumped down from the rear of the van and ran off towards the ambulance, splashing in the wet mud, then the excited murmur of snarls and grunts from the horde of approaching ghouls washed over him.

Chapter Forty Eight

"Go!" Alice charged on towards the farmhouse, one hand clasped to the hand of Jiyaa as they ran side by side, the Indian woman overjoyed to see her return, while Lauren ran on ahead, leading Brandon by the hand, Doctor Green puffing as he tried to keep pace with them all. As she turned to look back at him, he winced, nodding then raised his eyes to the dark sky overhead, and she did the same, concern touching almost instantly.

It was already overcast and gloomy because of the foul weather but the autumn night was approaching, reducing their visibility as it did so. She sighed in relief as they reached the top of the track, all five of them appearing to be winded by the run uphill, and she gestured towards the large farmhouse, "Go, keep running, Dog and Bella will be with us as soon as they can!"

In no time at all, they were at the front door of the property, Doctor Green hammering upon it while the others stood beneath the sloped porch, sheltering from the rain that had already soaked them all to the skin. Grimacing, Alice took a step back, staring at the top of the track, willing her two friends to hurry up, hope taking flight in her as she saw them approaching through the rain.

She glanced to the side as the front door suddenly opened wide, the square features of Robert the farmer staring out in shock as his gaze drifted from Brandon to her and then back again. Stepping back down the hallway, he gestured for them to come in, his head turning, "Val, the lad is back, and one of the ones who left is back too!" There was a murmur of confusion from his wife and he headed for the kitchen, his head shaking as he spoke once more, "I said the boy is back, Brandon, and that Alice girl is back too!"

Smiling, Alice watched as Doctor Green turned to the others, one hand gently guiding Brandon through the open door and into the house before he moved in behind him, turning back to face the three women only to gasp in dread as he stared past them, "Good Lord!"

"What?" she turned towards Dog and Bella as they loomed through the rain in her peripheral vision then cursed as she saw the hammer swinging towards her head, clasped tight in the hand of the black-haired Bethany, the woman screaming in raw hatred. Alice grunted as the blow missed her face and struck her hard upon the left shoulder, spinning her to the wet mud at their feet, and cursing and wincing in pain, she glanced up as the woman threw herself at a stunned Lauren, the hammer swinging wildly. "Bitch!" the nurse somehow managed to dodge the blows, her body weaving quickly, but then she staggered to the side as the young man Freddy stepped in and shoved her with his hands, pushing her back to land beside Alice. Instantly, Jiyaa was at her side, trying to help the two women stand, features etched with concern. "Inside!" Bethany screamed, pointing to the open doorway with her other hand, and as she pushed herself to her hands and knees, Alice felt sick with dread as she saw the long knife clasped in it. Without hesitating, Freddy spun and raced for the door, colliding heavily with the startled Doctor Green as the man stepped back towards the opening, shouting for Robert to come help. With a grunt of shock and pain, the silver-haired physician fell back to the floor, the male teacher falling atop him, and screeching in triumph, Bethany raced for the door, only to stagger off balance as Jiyaa grasped at her hammer hand, dragging her back. With a roar like a wounded beast, Bethany spun on the spot, her other hand thrusting hard against the chest of the Indian woman, and Alice screamed as she saw the point of the knife she had been holding seem to grow from the back of the raincoat Jiyaa was wearing. The combined screams of Alice and Lauren were loud over the heavy rain and behind the figure of Jiyaa, the features of Bethany were etched with raw delight as she sneered at them both over the shoulder of the woman that she had stabbed. Without warning, the knife point vanished, and Bethany thrust Jiyaa backwards to splash heavily down on the muddy ground, the arms and legs of the Indian woman appearing limp as she lay there staring up at the falling rain. Snarling once more, the female teacher backed inside the house, the door slamming shut behind her and roaring in hatred, Alice rushed at it, both of her fists hammering upon its surface, her voice a snarl, "I'll fucking kill you!"

"Alice"

She turned at the choking sob, her eyes meeting those of Lauren as the nurse knelt in a puddle beside Jiyaa, her head shaking, "She's dead!" Throat swollen with emotion, Alice held her gaze in silence, her body quaking as a wave of hatred and raw grief coursed through her, and she turned to the door once more, half crouching as she screamed as if she were possessed by a demon, the sound half-growl and inhuman.

"Alice" Lauren was suddenly beside her, hands grasping at her and she turned, grimacing as she saw the horde of ghouls emerging from the darkness of the early evening. For a moment, she stared at them in silence, then she let Lauren lead her by the hand, the pair of them running off into the rain, leaving the body of their friend behind.

Chapter Forty Nine

Cursing under her breath, Emily placed Lexie down upon the bed that she had been using since they had arrived at the farmhouse two days before, and stroked her head softly, earning several gentle licks from the injured dog, and she gave a smile, "Your mam will be back soon"

"Where are you going?" Eric looked up from where he was laying upon the other bed, casting aside the toy soldiers he had been playing with.

She paused before the bedroom door, turning back to meet his gaze as she opened it, "I am going to see what everyone is shouting about now...you wait here with Lexie"

He rolled his eyes, lazily picking up the toy soldiers once more, "Grown-ups are the worst"

She gave a weak smile, nodding at him, and then moved out onto the upper landing, cursing once more as she heard screams and shouts from downstairs, followed by the front door slamming. Almost at once another scream sounded, quieter than the others, and then Emily flinched in shock as a sudden pounding sounded from downstairs as if something was trying to smash the front door down, followed by more loud screaming. Instantly she knew that the ghouls were trying to gain entry, guilt washing through her as she recalled those that she and Eric had seen that morning. Had they found a way up the slope? Feeling sick, she moved along the landing and began to slowly descend the stairs, pausing as she reached the middle landing and stared down. She froze as she studied the scene below, her mouth opening in confusion, her head shaking slightly as she saw the familiar figure of Brandon standing in the hallway, one hand tapping repeatedly against the side of his head as he stared down the corridor and in confusion she followed his gaze. She felt the hairs rise upon the back of her neck as she saw the thin young man in the shirt and tie kneeling atop the struggling Doctor Green, one hand holding him down while the other punched down at him, repeatedly, and then she raised her eyes, watching in horror as a black haired woman in dungarees stepped towards the pair, a hammer in one hand and a bloody knife in the other, "Move, Freddy!" Feeling sick, Emily stood watching in disbelief as the woman stepped further into the light, the young girl feeling sick as she saw that the mouth and nose of the woman appeared to be covered in blood, both of her eyes appearing bruised. Muttering, the young man rose to his feet, and stepped back, and the woman cast a glance at him, "We have to kill these cunt's, then we can use the house as our own...its you and me Freddy, you want that don't you..."

He nodded, and she chuckled, stepping towards the fallen doctor, the hammer raising above him as he raised his hands, "Please...don't do this..."

"No!" Emily screamed, taking two quick steps down the stairs towards them, her head shaking as she pointed at the couple, "Leave him alone!"

"Shit!" the man named Freddy cursed as he glanced up at her, and the woman gave a snarl.

"Get her!"

"She's a kid!"

"Freddy!" the woman gave a scream of anger, then cursed herself as the large figure of Robert surged into the hallway, dwarfing the woman.

"Who the fucking Hell are you!"

With a scream like a banshee the woman turned, the hammer swinging for the big mans face but he turned it aside with burly forearm, then cursed as she thrust the knife into his stomach.

Emily screamed in concern as she moved down the stairs, gesturing frantically to Brandon to join her as he glanced her way, and sobbing he clambered quickly up the stairs and moved past her, his right hand grasping forward to hold her shoulder as she stood before him protectively, her courage making a mockery of her youth. With a roar like the wounded bear that he resembled, the knife still embedded deep in his stomach, Robert grasped the black-haired woman about the throat with both hands, lifting her easily from the floor to slam her back into the wall opposite, knocking several pictures from its surface to crash down to the floor, her legs kicking wildly. He grunted as she raised the hammer suddenly, smashing him in the forehead with it, and as he staggered back and dropped to his knees, the woman fell back heavily to the floor before him, crying out in pain. Instantly she rose, raising the hammer once more, only to scream in surprise and fear as the enraged figure of Valerie bust from the doorway, a large knife clasped in her hands, "Get the fuck out of my fucking house!"

The woman screamed again as the wife of the farmer stabbed at her, the blade taking her in the shoulder, and then Valerie raised the knife once more only to grunt in shock as the young man pushed at her from the side, sending her tripping up the hallway to land heavily upon her back. "Val!" Robert cried out in concern, heedless of the danger as the woman stepped forwards and

raised the hammer above him once again, only everyone to turn their faces towards the front door as it suddenly crashed open, almost torn from its hinges by the force of the impact on it. Emily screamed in terror as the horde of white-skinned naked ghouls surged through the entrance, grasping at the screaming figure of Valerie as she tried to rise, dragging her into their midst, their grunts of excitement loud. With a roar of anger and denial, Robert somehow made it to his feet, a large hand reaching down to drag the knife from his stomach, and with a roar he threw himself at the horde, stabbing and slashing, Doctor Green rising unsteadily to his hands and knees behind him; his nose bleeding and his glasses broken as he wrenched open the door to a walk-in cupboard and crawled inside. "Go!" the woman with the hammer screamed, pointing up the stairs towards where Emily stood with Brandon, "Go Freddy, get them!"
"The zombies..." the man managed to mumble, head shaking, but she pushed her way past him, insanity in her eyes as she charged up the stairs. Heart in her mouth, Emily hesitated a moment longer, stifling a sob as she saw the brave farmer in the distance finally overwhelmed by the grunting brutal mob of Neanderthals, his large

form vanishing amongst the heaving mass of white skinned bodies as they surged forwards. Then pushing Brandon ahead of her, she turned and raced back up the stairs in terror, the black-haired woman close behind her, hammer raised.

Chapter Fifty

"I didn't think they would pass" Bella crawled out from under the van that Victor had dragged her beneath shortly before the horde of ghouls had reached the van, the pair of them hiding in silence out of sight until it had finally appeared that all of the creatures had passed by. Forcing herself to her feet, leaning heavily upon the side of the van for support, she let Victor help her to stand, the pair of them standing face-to-face in the near darkness, each of them suffering bloody wounds from the unexpected attack by Bethany. "Are you OK?" Victor raised a hand to rest upon her right cheek, his bruised features filled with concern as he studied the face of the woman that he had grown incredibly close to in the past two days, his thumb gently gliding over the ugly bruise on her cheekbone, clearing the raindrops away, his head shaking, "This is my fault...I should have let you kill that bitch"

"No, this is her fault not yours" she shrugged, head shaking as she held his gaze, then she turned to stare up the slope past the ambulance towards the dark shape of the farmhouse, "Now we need to go and make that bitch suffer"

Victor nodded at her words, turning to take a step towards the rear of the ambulance, fully intending to climb through only to pause as he heard the door of the van open behind him, and he turned, watching as Bella reached in and then rose with a shotgun in each hand, "Here" Reaching out to take it from her, he glanced down as their hands touched, his fingers overlapping hers and for the longest time they stayed frozen in place, the heavy rain falling upon them as they stood in the near darkness. Sighing heavily, he raised his gaze to meet hers, something unspoken passing between them and without a word of warning, the former soldier stepped close to him, her lips gently brushing against his own before she stepped back, a look of shock upon her features, "Dog...listen...I..." He nodded, his throat tight with emotion, "In case we don't make it through this...I want you to know that...you matter...to me"

"Ditto" she replied, then they both turned as faint screaming sounded at the farmhouse, Victor grimacing as he took a step towards the rear of the ambulance, and Bella shook her head, "No, I've had an idea...you see if you can get it up the slope and I'll follow in the van, in case we need to abandon this place, we can fit everyone in the ambulance and the van and drive out of here!"

For a fraction of a second, Victor held her gaze, nodding slowly and then he winked and turned, climbing through the ambulance and out the side, while Bella shut the rear doors tight behind him. Sliding the side door shut, he wrenched open the passenger door, placed his shotgun upon the seat and climbed inside, scooting behind the wheel, sighing in relief as he found that Lauren had left the keys in the ignition after reversing downhill. Starting the vehicle, he put it in first gear, and put his foot down on the accelerator, simultaneously taking the handbrake off then cringed as he felt the ambulance rock slightly, swaying over to the passenger side and the steep slope beyond. "Fuck!" he shouted, his fingers flicking on the headlights and the windscreen wipers, his eyes staring up in the direction of the farmhouse, nausea washing through him as he imagined his friends and the children facing off against the ghouls and the insane Bethany, for some reason the latter scaring him slightly more. These were inhuman beast, once human but now acting on their base impulse...kill and feed. Bethany knew what she was doing was wrong. It was a choice. All of this was happening because of him and his refusal to leave people behind no matter what Bella had told him. If he had left her behind after she had tried to steal the ambulance then she wouldn't have been in the vehicle to alert the ghouls once they had walked past the vehicle. With a roar of anger, he let the vehicle roll back slightly, turned the wheel as if he was going to drive sideways into the rocky wall and floored the accelerator again, cursing as the ambulance lurched forward and sideways, scraping against the wall with a metallic screech, the vehicle rocking once more and he grimaced, one balled fist leaving the wheel to strike the dashboard. "Come on you mother fucker!"

There was a loud metallic clang as the ambulance came free of whatever had been impeding its movement, and the vehicle surged forwards, tilting wildly, and grimacing, Victor straightened the wheel, steering it up the dirt track, a quick glance in the passenger side mirror showing that Bella was right behind him in the white van that they had taken from the village, her lights on. The ambulance bumped as he reached the top of the slope and he drove up before the farmhouse, his heart skipping a beat as he saw the crowd of ghouls all fighting to get in through the front door of the building. Those at the rear of the group turned in his direction as they saw his approach flinching as the headlights shone upon them, many raising hands before their eyes, and grimacing, Victor floored the accelerator. He drove into those clustered in the doorway at speed, the impact scattering them before him, the ambulance lurching as several went under the wheels. Grimacing, Victor drove on, slowing as he neared the barns and then turned the vehicle in a circle on the area between the farmhouse and the drop to the valley below, watching as Bella parked her van directly in front of the front door, then turned his gaze to the ghouls that were lying about the area, dazed and injured from his collision with them, several trying to rise already. Grim faced, he opened the door beside him, clasping the shotgun as he climbed out and kicked the door shut, then stepped around the front of the vehicle, watching as Bella exited the passenger side of the white van she had been driving and shoved her shotgun into the mouth of a rising ghoul, the blast opening the back of its head. Stone faced, Victor stepped through the rain towards another of them, pressing the end of his shotgun against the soft spot over its heart as it struggled to rise, and fired, dropping it limp to the wet mud. He glanced up as Bella fired her second barrel into the chest of another, and reloaded, watching as he turned his remaining barrel upon another ghoul, and moved to join her, gratefully accepting the shells that she passed him. As he emptied the spent cartridges and began to reload, she glanced about, "I say we clean these ones up and then drive the vehicles round the back, see if we can get people out of the upper windows onto the roofs"

Victor nodded, taking a step towards another of the ghouls then paused as he saw a figure lying upon its back several feet from them, previously unnoticed by the pair, and heart in his mouth he moved to stare down at it, a guttural curse of anger escaping him as he recognised their face.

"Dog?" Bella took a step towards him, "Who...?"

"Jiyaa" he shook his head, his throat tight, "She's been stabbed...she's dead"

"Bethany" Bella snarled, and Victor felt his heart sink as he nodded, realising that this was partly his doing for allowing her to escape, his head dropping for a moment as he stared down into the blank eyes of the poor woman, then glanced up once more as he heard Bella snarl again as she stepped towards a nearby ghoul as it tried to rise and pushed her shotgun in through its snarling mouth, "Kill them...kill them all!"

Chapter Fifty One

"Fuck!" Lauren flinched as a sudden gunshot rang out in the darkness, and cursing, she almost fell from the large wooden pergola that she and Alice had climbed at the back of the farmhouse, her fingers only just managing to grasp back to the wet wooden structure. Eyes wide, she turned to look at Alice, the woman just below her, flinching as the gun fired again, "Gunshots!"

"Dog and Bella?" Alice raised an eyebrow.

"I hope so" Lauren nodded back at her friend, feeling blessed once more that the woman that she had felt closest to in the group had returned to them, Lauren began to climb once more, guilt touching her as her thoughts drifted to poor Jiyaa, her other friend. If only she had learned before that morning that the woman had spoken English, she might have gotten to know her better, maybe the last two days might not have been so lonely for Jiyaa. In the chaotic moments following Jiyaa's brutal murder by the black-haired woman, Lauren and Alice had fled around the rear of the farmhouse, feeling sick with dread as screams had sounded from within the large building. Out of their minds with worry and anger, they had reached the back door only to find it locked, and had been forced to hide in the shadows of the doorway as several ghouls had come into sight, over spilling from the huge crowd at the front. As the ghoul stragglers had departed, Alice had pointed to the pergola that stood at the rear of the building against the wall then leaned closer, whispering that they should climb it and get in through the upper windows. Sighing heavily once more as she pictured the way that they had been forced to leave Jiyaa lying upon her back in the rain, Lauren raised a hand from the pergola to wipe the raindrops from her glasses, then dragged herself up to sit upon the cross beams atop that had formed a large grid, reaching down to haul Alice up to sit beside her. For the briefest of moments, they sat there, staring down at the back of the farmyard below them, Alice grasping at Laurens left arm as a couple more of the ghouls suddenly shambled beneath them and off into the rainy darkness once more. Then slowly, they rose up, hands reaching out against the back wall of the farmhouse to steady themselves, their shoulders level with the large windows on the upper floor. They both turned, exchanging glances as more gunshots sounded from the front of the house, then turned as screams sounded from inside the room whose window they were standing before.

"Emily!" Lauren grimaced, grasping at the wet windowsill as she stared into the bedroom, her stomach lurching as she saw the young Asian girl rush inside the room with Brandon, her charge stepping over to the opposite wall while Emily slammed the bedroom door and leaned upon it. She staggered back as something or someone struck the door hard, the handle turning and beside Lauren, Alice let loose a roar of anger as the black-haired woman appeared in the doorway, the young man standing behind her. Within the room, the young boy Eric gave a scream of terror, and Emily backed towards him and Brandon, her arms spreading out wide beside her as if she were trying to keep them both safe behind her and Lauren felt her heart swell with emotion at the young girls bravery. "Bethany, you mother fucking bitch!" Alice swung a fist up, crashing it on the window, and Lauren tensed, fearing they were about to get showered in glass only for the pane to wobble in the frame. Yet within the room, all five of the occupants saw them, the bruised and swollen features of the black-haired woman twisting in shock and anger as she stared back at them, one hand clasping to the hammer she had attacked them with earlier, the knife that she had killed Jiyaa with gone.

With a snarl, the woman turned her gaze back on the teenage girl, and she stepped towards her, the hammer raised above her head ready to strike. Outside in the rain Lauren and Alice cried out in dread only for the Bella's dog to throw itself from the bed, its yelp of pain as it landed on its bad front leg loud even through the window but despite its agony, it rushed forwards, sinking its teeth into the left ankle of the psychotic woman, sending her off balance into the wall beside the door. With a snarl she raised the hammer once more, clearly intending to strike the dog then cursed as Emily rushed forwards and grasped at the hammer with both her hands, and with a cry of defiance, Eric threw himself from the bed to wrap his arms about her other leg, the three of them crashing down to the floor. Instantly the young man was beside the pile of bodies, desperately trying to drag the children away from his companion, only to stagger away cursing as the dog turned upon him, snarling, while Brandon stood against the wall, the palm of one hand flat against it while his other patted himself upon the side of his head, his features twisted in grief. Turning her gaze upon him, Lauren began to hammer upon the window, calling out to him, Alice stepping precariously past her on the wooden cross beams as she shouted obscenities at the black-haired woman. As if in a daze, Brandon turned his face towards them, eyes widening as he saw Lauren standing at the window, and he took several steps towards her, then winced and covered his face as the young man kicked out at the dog, knocking it back to lay whining on its side, then stepped in to drag a screaming Eric from the legs of his friend. "Brandon!" Lauren called out once more, her eyes drifting to watch as Emily now fought desperately with the black-haired woman for possession of the hammer while the man held a struggling Eric in his arms, one hand clasped tight over the boys mouth, then turned back to her charge, "Open the window, quickly!"

As if in a dream, Brandon slowly walked across the room, wincing each time someone shouted, his hands reaching out for the window clasp. Beside Lauren, Alice cried out in concern and the nurse turned her gaze, her stomach sinking as she saw the black-haired woman rise to her knees, one hand pinning Emily to the ground by her throat while the other raised the hammer high then seemed to notice the danger, her shrill voice loud as Brandon opened the window, "Freddy, don't let them in!"

With a curse, he released the boy and rushed towards the window, only to falter and slow as Alice heaved herself up and into the room, her right fist hammering hard into the man's face. As he staggered back, crying out in pain, the black-haired woman gave a snarl of anger and began to bring the hammer down towards the teenage girl beneath her only to scream in agony as Eric rushed at her from behind and grasped her hair, dragging her roughly backwards and off. "You fucking little cunt!" she gave a roar of hatred, twisting her hair free as she rolled to her knees then grunted in shock as Alice rushed in and kneed her hard in the face, rocking her back to collide with the wall. With a grunt, she toppled forwards, righted herself and rose with surprising speed, straight into a punch from Lauren, the nurse stepping in quickly, her right fist snaking out to crack the woman in the face. Crying out, she fell back against the wall, her right hand sweeping out before her with the hammer, desperately trying to keep the two furious women away, "Freddy help me!"

"Leave her alone!" the voice of the young man suddenly shouted, a sob from behind making both women take a step back from their foe and turn, each of them cursing in concern as they

found the young black man in the grip of Freddy as he stood behind him, an arm wrapped about the neck of the terrified Brandon, the other hand grasped tightly to his black and white tracksuit. "Let him go!" Lauren screamed at the man, taking a step forward, Alice moving with her only for them both to pause as the black-haired woman stepped alongside Freddy and pointed the hammer at Brandon's face, her free hand rising to point at the two women as she snarled angrily. "Stay back…I fucking swear to God, I'll kill him!" "Let him go!" Lauren repeated her words, head shaking as she stared in hatred at the couple, her heart breaking as Brandon gave a sob of terror. Taking a step forwards, Alice grimaced, her eyes locked to those of the woman with the hammer, her voice barely more than a whisper, "I am going to kill you…I promise"
"Fuck off cunt!" came the reply, the woman reaching back to open the door to the landing beyond then turned back towards them, "You…all of you…out of the room and downstairs!"
"Fuck off!" Emily pushed herself to her feet, moving to embrace her brother, "The ghouls are there! They killed Val, Robert and Doctor Green!" As Lauren and Alice glanced at the girl, seeing the dread on her face, grief coursing through them at

her words, the black-haired woman gave a bitter snarl, "I don't fucking care...down the stairs!" "What are you hoping to do?" Lauren shook her head suddenly, the madness of it all washing over her, "What are you getting out of this!" "The house...safety...food...weapons" came the sneered reply, the blood-stained features of the woman twisted in grim amusement, "I've never been good with sharing...so you need to go!" "You don't need to do this!" Lauren shook her head, fists forming at her sides, "Listen to me..." "Out!" the black-haired woman shouted at her, mouth twisting, "Out or I kill the retard!" "Don't call me that!" Brandon suddenly shouted, his features suddenly filled with indignation and rage, twisting in the grip of the physically smaller Freddy, pushing the man back out of the open door, "Don't call me that don't call me that!" "Fuck!" Bethany spun towards the black young man, hammer raising only to curse and stagger back as Alice and Lauren struck her at the same time, the trio crashing back through the open door into the stunned Freddy, driving him back down the landing. Fighting frantically, they bounced off a wall then careened into another, all three women shouting and cursing as they fought. Alice cried out in pain and shock as

Bethany swept an elbow around, catching her in the cheek, then snapped her own right fist hard into the woman's face, a punch from Lauren following close behind, and screaming, the black-haired woman pushed herself away from them, the friends crashing to the floor beside the railings that supported the upper floor banister. As Bethany staggered back away from them down the landing, she struck Freddy as he tried to back away from her and he spun sideways, the upper banister stopping him at the waist and then he went over, his legs kicking up high towards the ceiling as if he were doing a backflip. He screamed as he fell, and lying atop Alice, Lauren turned her head, staring through the railings as the man landed atop the horde of ghouls huddled on the floor of the corridor, fighting among themselves as they shovelled bloody gobbets of meat into their open mouths, the stomach of the nurse twisting as she realised they were consuming someone she had known. The ghouls erupted in a storm of excitement as the man landed in their midst, his screams of raw terror turning to agonised cries of pain as they began to grasp and pull at him, snarling at each other in their eagerness to claim the fresh meal. In seconds, he was gone from sight, dragged beneath the maelstrom of bodies but his screams remained, loud as they echoed around the stairs. With a scream borne of utter madness, Bethany suddenly lunged at the pair as they lay on the floor, hammer raised, and cursing, Lauren rolled to the side and tried to rise, grunting in pain as the hammer came down hard on her left forearm. "Bitch!" Alice kicked out with one of her boots into the black-haired woman's right kneecap, the sickening snap loud as Bethany's leg bent to the side in a manner that nature had never intended. Howling in pain, she fell back, bracing herself against the banister, the hammer swinging weakly before her in an attempt to keep Alice and Lauren away from her as they rose quickly. "Keep back!" she shook her head, sobbing in pain as she tried to edge along the banister towards the other end of the landing, perhaps hoping to hide in one of the other bedrooms, but Alice and Lauren moved with her, both their faces grim. They all turned as the stairs creaked behind and below them, Lauren feeling sick as she saw several of the ghouls moving onto the lower stairs, their heads turning to look up at the three women above, beige eyes wide as if surprised. They had only stayed downstairs where the food was, their limited intellect having not considered searching the house for more, until they had begun making noise above them on the landing. Snapping her face back towards them, Bethany suddenly dropped the hammer, her hands rising beside her head as she forced a sickly smile and nodded, "You win...I surrender...I give up!"

"Like you did in the van you mean?" the voice of Alice was thick with hatred, her words a growl.

"What?" the black-haired woman blinked, her head shaking, "I am giving up...please...you win!"

"Too fucking late...you killed Jiyaa!" Lauren shook her head, and as if rehearsed, both she and Alice rushed forwards, pushing the woman back down the staircase, a scream of terror escaping her as she tumbled head over feet before finally stopping halfway up. Taking the hand of Alice in her own, Lauren stepped back to the wall behind them, her eyes locked to the bruised face of Bethany as she raised her head to look at them, then screamed in terror and pain as the ghouls that had been climbing the stairs reached her. With an excited snarl, one of them grasped at her right arm, bending it back behind her, twisting and jerking it wildly as he grunted and without warning the limb came loose, blood spraying up the staircase walls, coating the gleeful ghoul.

The scream of Bethany was agonised, her body all but invisible beneath the white-skinned ghouls as they began to tear the clothing from her, powerful fingers thrusting into the meat beneath, and then her head was yanked back by the hair as one of them began to eat her face. Lauren and Alice stayed long enough to see her die, her remaining arm going limp in the grasp of a ghoul as it took a bite from her bare bicep, tissue and skin stretching as it tore its mouth away, chewing contentedly as it moaned around the meat in its mouth, and then they slipped away, back towards the bedroom where Emily and Eric stood waiting for them in silence.

Chapter Fifty Two

"What are we going to do?" Emily gasped in dread as the two women entered the bedroom, and closed the door behind them, and Alice raised a finger to her lips to silence the girl.

"We have to keep quiet" her voice was a whisper as she stepped closer to the girl and her younger brother, while Lauren hurried over to crouch beside Brandon as she sat with his legs crossed, a hand gently stroking Lexie as the dog lay beside him, its head resting upon his left knee, "There are ghouls on the stairs!"

"Is she dead?" Eric asked, "You know, the bitch!" Emily snapped her head down towards her younger brother at his language but chose not to reprimand him, no doubt realising that it was a fitting description, even from a six-year-old. Alice flinched as something heaved out on the landing, and gritting her teeth, she stepped back to the door, her ear pressing against it, eyes closing as she listened to what lay beyond. Lauren stepped from the side of Brandon to move back alongside her, the face of the nurse twisting into a frown as she met her gaze, "Bad?"

"It's not good" Alice forced a smile, her head shaking, a hand rising to point at the door, "They are coming up the rest of the stairs!"

"We need to barricade the door!" the nurse stated, taking a step towards it, her hands pressing against its surface as if she intended to hold it back while the others gathered furniture. "We can't" Alice shook her head, gesturing towards the closed door with her head, "They will hear it...our best bet is to get back out the window onto the pergola and close the curtains behind us...hopefully they won't see us there!" "What?" Emily glanced between them, her voice hushed like theirs, "Where are we going?" "Out of the window" Alice turned to her, "There is a wooden pergola and some beams across the top, we can hide there...trust me, it's safe" "No" the teenage girl shook her head, "We'll fall" "Emily!" Eric moved to her side, head shaking as he stared up at her, "We can't stay here, we'll get eaten by the ghouls!" Cringing at the simple horrific truth of his words, Alice nodded, a hand reaching out to gently rest upon the right shoulder of the girl, "He's right" "Shit!" Emily shook her head, wincing and Alice stepped back to lean against the door, forcing a grim smile as she stared back at the young girl. "You need to go with Lauren" she whispered, nodding as she spoke, "I need you to look after Lexie and your brother, can you do that for me?"

"What?" Lauren turned to look at her, eyes wide behind her glasses, "What about you?"

"I'm coming but I will come out last!"

"Alice" the nurse shook her head, only to fall silent as her friend sent her a determined look. "You need to go first, help Brandon out there, then Eric and Emily with Lexie...then I'll come"

Another loud creak sounded somewhere beyond the door, the grunt of one of the ghouls sounding close behind it and as Emily clapped a hand over her mouth, Alice stepped away from the door to crouch beside Brandon, scooping the injured Lexie up into her arms and then nodding towards the open window, "Go on, quickly now!"

Casting her a look of concern, Lauren clambered back onto the windowsill and then stepped down onto the pergola, turning to reach back for Eric as the young boy followed her, completely unafraid. Shaking her head as she looked through the window beside her, watching as Eric moved to sit down on one of the cross beams, legs dangling as if he were just sat at the park, Alice turned her head, watching as Brandon began to climb through the window to join the boy and Lauren. Frowning, the black young man sat beside Eric, his legs out before him, resting over the next cross beam, and Alice nodded at Emily as the girl stepped up to the window, "Go on, you can do it" Emily paused, about to argue with her when something heavy bumped against the bedroom door, and it was all Alice could do to not cry out in shock and dread. Backing to the window, she turned, watching the door intently as she whispered to Emily, "You have to go now, they are right outside!"

It was all the encouragement that Emily needed, the teenage girl swinging her legs up high as she clambered up onto the windowsill, taking the hand of Lauren then paused, "You are coming?" Alice nodded, watching as the girl moved to sit down on the pergola cross beams, and then she lifted Lexie up and through the window, passing her to Lauren, "Here you go"

"Get out of there now!" the nurse insisted, and nodding, Alice pulled herself up onto the edge of the windowsill, then froze in terror, her heart skipping a beat as the door handle turned a fraction of an inch then something struck the door hard, jostling it in its frame. Sat upon the window, heart in her mouth, Alice pictured the door crashing open and the horde of white-skinned ghouls surging inside to find her upon the windowsill, their grunts of excitement loud as they tore her to bloody pieces and ate them. Just like they had done with Bethany and Freddy. Just like they had done earlier with Valerie, Robert and the good-natured Doctor Green.

"Alice!" the harsh whisper of Lauren was loud in her ear as the nurse grasped at her, and forcing herself to focus, Alice climbed through the window, back out into the heavy rain as she lowered herself onto the pergola, then cursed and reached quickly back through the window, her hands dragging the heavy curtains shut before she closed the window tight behind her. Almost at once there was a crashing sound from back inside the bedroom, and cringing, Alice dropped to crouch upon the pergola, her back resting against the wall of the farmhouse, her breathing ragged as she listened to the grunts of the ghouls as they charged inside the bedroom. Beside her, Lauren sat with her legs dangling, the border collie clasped in her arms, while Emily, Brandon and Eric sat close by, their faces grim as they stared back at window they had just left, all five of them soaked to the skin by the heavy rain. Turning her head, Alice glanced at Lauren as the young nurse sat beside her on the top of the pergola, the border collie clutched in her arms.

Reaching out, Alice gently stroked the dog's ears, earning herself a lick in return and then she raised her eyes to meet the gaze of Lauren, a faint smile creasing her features as the nurse nodded at her, her voice a whisper, "I'm glad you're back" "Yeah, me too" Alice nodded, reaching out to put an arm about the shoulder of the nurse, tilting her head to the side as she rested her head against that the younger woman as Lauren leaned her way, her eyes closing as she sighed. She winced as Lexie suddenly began to bark and snarl, and snapped her eyes open to watch as Lauren fought to control the animal as it leaned forwards, staring down through the cross beams of the pergola roof and Alice followed its gaze grimacing as she saw two ghouls standing directly beneath the pergola, staring up at them. "Fuck" the whisper of Emily had Alice turning to meet the gaze of the young girl, her stomach knotting as she saw the girl raise her legs to rest them before her like Brandon had, her rain-soaked features twisted in undeniable terror. "It's OK" Alice whispered, removing her arm from Lauren's shoulder as she sat forwards, nodding at the girl, "They can't reach us!" Wincing, the teenage girl nodded, and Alice turned her gaze back upon the pair of ghouls.

As she did so, the larger of the two gave a grunt, one hand reaching up as if it intended to climb a post of the wooden frame but then snarled, grunting once more, louder this time, and Alice felt the hairs rise on her neck as even more ghouls began to appear through the heavy rain. Grunting in excitement, their faces turning towards the five and the dog huddled atop the large wooden pergola, hands reaching for them, their presence sending Lexie into a new barking frenzy and it was all Lauren could do to hold her. Alice cursed as the weight of the ghouls pushed against the wooden supports as they clustered about, grunting and snarling in excitement and the pergola seemed to shift slightly, drawing a scream of terror from Brandon and the children. Behind them, the bedroom window seemed to shake in its frame and turning, Alice stared back in terror, watching as the curtains were torn away to reveal a horde of white cracked faces staring back at them, their beige eyes wide. "Go!" Alice shouted as she saw one of them lean forward to stare out at them, grunting angrily as its face struck the window, "Move now!" Grimacing, Lauren rose to her knees, clasping the barking dog in her arms as she moved across the wooden grid roof of the pergola to where the

children and Brandon were seated, Alice
following suit then turning back to the window.
It shattered as a ghoul swung a fist into it, the
glass falling through the roof of the pergola, and
snarling in excitement as it saw them, the white-
skinned creature clambered through the window
frame and out onto the wooden cross beams.
It grunted as it took a mis step, one leg slipping
through one of the open sections and it staggered
off balance to fall upon the horde waiting below.
Yet more were in its place almost at once,
clambering out onto the roof of the pergola,
hands reaching towards where Alice, Lauren,
Brendan and the children waited, Lexie barking
at them as if daring them to come any closer.
In that moment, Alice knew that it was over.
There was no escape.
They were trapped both above and below by the
ghouls and there was nothing but pain ahead.
Her heart broke then as she turned her head,
seeing the fear upon the face of Emily as she
hugged her younger brother to her, shielding his
face from what was to come, her other hand
clasping to the right hand of a sobbing Brandon,
and then Alice turned her gaze to meet that of
Lauren, nodding as she sighed heavily, "We tried"
The nurse nodded, somehow managing to give

her a weak smile, "We did our best"

Alice suddenly winced, cringing in shock as the harsh blare of an ambulance siren sounded in the night, her head turning to watch as bright lights cut through the rain and the darkness around the edge of the building, the roar of an engine loud. "Dog!" Alice almost sobbed as she cried out in elation, watching as the ambulance and the white van that they had taken from the village roared into view. Gathered in a group around the base of the pergola, the ghouls snarled in sudden pain as the headlights off first one and then another vehicle shone towards the base of the wooden structure, the fluorescent blue lights swirling around atop the ambulance sending the bestial creatures clasping hands to cover their eyes.

As the lead vehicle surged closer, Alice suddenly cried out in dread, thinking that her friend had steered too close to the pergola and had doomed them all but then the speeding vehicle struck the cluster group of ghouls hard, throwing them back from the wooden structure. Instantly the white van pulled up next to the pergola, crashing into those that the ambulance had missed, several going under the wheels, and leaning over the edge Alice saw the face of Bella stare up at her from the drivers window, voice loud through the crack in her window, "Get on the roof...hold on!"

"You heard her!" Alice turned, addressing the others with her, "Come on, let's do this!"

Gritting her teeth, she turned to watch as Lauren stepped to the edge of the pergola and swung her legs over, stepping onto the roof and moving to sit down in its middle. Heart hammering in her chest, Alice turned to Brandon, "You next hun"

He flinched, head shaking but then Eric was nodding at him, "Come on dude, its easy look"

Without another word, the young boy stepped from the pergola onto the roof of the white van, and turned to gesture to Brandon, "Come on, you can do it, your my best friend!"

As if he were a different, more confident person, Brandon rose and stepped from the pergola to the roof of the van, sitting beside the boy, his legs crossing as he smiled sheepishly, and Alice reached for Emily, "Come on, its our turn"

"What if we fall?"

"Then we get up and run" Alice sent her a grim smile, then cursed as she glimpsed a hand of a ghoul reaching for the girl, those remaining on the roof of the pergola having reached them while they had been distracted, "Look out!"

As Emily ducked the reaching hand, Alice

stepped towards her, snatched her hand and then turned to the edge of the pergola, "Jump!" Cringing as the snarl of the approaching ghouls sounded right behind her, they both leaped forwards through the dark and the rain, landing upon the roof of the van, Alice crying out in dread as her boots slipped beneath her and she fell, slipping for the edge, only to stop sliding as Brandon grasped at her reaching hands, the strength of the gentle young man staggering. For a moment, she hung there, her legs kicking wildly, half-expecting to be dragged from the van by the ghouls below and half-expecting to be attacked from those above, but then she was hauled back onto the roof to lay on her back. Grimacing, staring up into the rain that was falling onto her face, she reached down with a hand, pounding the roof several times with a fist. Instantly the van began to move, barely at a crawl but enough to put some distance between them and the pergola, and turning her head, Alice watched the ghouls atop it snarling, their primitive forms backlit by the bedroom behind. Forcing herself to sit up, Alice moved alongside her companions, watching as the ambulance suddenly fell silent, the blue lights fading as it began to reverse from where it had stopped, turning itself around to pull up on the passenger side of the white van, the cabs level with each other. Peering over the edge of the van, Alice watched as the passenger window of both vehicles began to unwind and then Bella began to crawl from one vehicle to the other, before reaching back and retrieving her shotgun her vehicle, a hand rising as she passed it up, a grim smile on her features, "We are going to try and make as much noise as possible and lead the ghouls away from here...you guys stay safe"

"You'll need the gun!" Alice shook her head.

"No, Dog has his" Bella nodded up at her, "The keys are in the van, when you think it is safe, get everyone in the van, block the entrance again"

Alice nodded, suddenly struck with concern for her two friends, "Be careful, I already thought we'd lost you once, I thought Bethany..."

Bella grimaced, "She tried...where is she?"

"Dead" Alice stated, "She's deader than disco"

Bella didn't even try to hide the satisfaction on her face, "Did you make her pay for Jiyaa?"

Alice nodded, smiling grimly, then turned her head as the ghouls atop the pergola started to drop down from it, others climbing through the window and doing the same, "You better get out of here while you can...please...be careful"

Bella threw her a wink, "You too!"
And then they began to drive away, the
ambulance moving at no more than five miles per
hour, the sirens and lights once more resuming,
and shaking her head, Alice, Lauren, Brandon and
the children watched as the ghouls began to
follow along behind it, grunting and snarling.
Like a fluorescent Pied Piper of Hamlin leading
some giant albino rats away to God knows where.

Chapter Fifty Three

Victor opened his eyes to the cold sunlight that was coming through the paper-thin space between the bedroom curtains, blinking several times as he lay beneath the thick duvet and layers of blankets, studying the dust motes as they danced lazily in the air. The house about him was cold and quiet, and he sighed heavily. The generator had clearly gone off in the night. They would have to go out and get some fuel for it today, as well as getting wood for the fireplace. But that was hours away. Turning his face back towards the window he laid for what felt like an eternity, studying the thin strip of light once more, trying to work out what time it might be, then he turned his head as Bella moved beside him, muttering in her sleep, her face screwing up as she rolled against him, her face upon his chest. Releasing a shaky breath, he put a protective arm about her, his fingers tracing patterns upon her back as they lay pressed together, their bodies warm beneath the duvet and closing his eyes, he cast his mind back to the night two days before. Once they had cleared all of the ghouls that they could see away from the front of the farmhouse they had jumped in their respective vehicles and driven around the rear of the property to find the others from their group crouched atop the pergola, completely surround by snarling ghouls. As he had driven at the lower group, he had glanced up, his eyes desperately seeking sight of Emily and Eric, realising as he spotted them that there were people missing from their number. Grim faced he had crashed through the horde, crushing many, throwing others back to the ground, and then sat watching in his mirrors as Bella drove up beside the pergola, letting their friends clamber atop her van before driving off. Grimacing, he had watched Alice nearly fall then manage to get back atop the van, and he had driven alongside them, allowing Bella to clamber in beside him in the front of the ambulance, and together they had driven away from the farm. Back around the front of the farm they had gone, going in several circles before the house, the lights flashing and the sirens blaring and he had cursed as the ghouls had poured from the open front door of the farmhouse like fat white maggots bursting from an infected wound, their snarls and grunts loud as they had tried to encircle the ambulance, drawn by the clamour. Then, when he was certain there were no more, Victor had driven off down the track, just fast enough to allow the ghouls to keep up with them.

For nearly an hour they had driven about the moorland, the windscreen wipers darting furiously back and forth, and without giving it conscious thought, Bella had slid along the seat to sit as close to him as she could, his left hand moving to rest upon her right leg, her hands holding to it. And so, they had driven in silence, bonded in grief, and perhaps something more. Finally, once they had put ten miles between them and the farm they had turned back for home...their new home, Victor putting his foot down on the accelerator, and leaving the by now large horde of ghouls far behind them in the rain. They had reached the farmhouse by ten PM, parking the ambulance behind the van which was now blocking the track once more, and squeezed past it to discover their friends safely barricaded inside the building, and Doctor Green still alive, the physician having managed to crawl inside a cupboard where he had hidden while the ghouls had devoured Valerie and Robert just feet away. They had sat as a group in the large living room for nearly an hour upon their return, talking quietly about those that they had lost, and their plans for the next day and the days following, and then wearily, they had headed for bedrooms. Doctor Green had elected to stay downstairs with a shotgun, his prior aversion to them gone in the wake of what he had experienced, and while Lauren had found a room for her and Brandon to occupy, Victor and Bella had found a different bedroom for Emily and Eric, the pair sitting with the children until they had finally fallen to sleep, Lexie curled up on the foot of the girls bed. Finally, they had made their way to another of the bedrooms, Victor about to leave Bella until she had taken his hand and asked him to stay. And so, he had, the pair closing the door behind them, silently undressing each other before climbing into the double bed, their union passionate but silent, their eyes locked together. They had awoken earlier the next day, once more repeating the night before then while Bella had gone to check on the children, Victor had headed down to the kitchen to make them a drink, shaking his head as Lauren and Alice had turned to smile knowingly at him from the large table. "Shut up before you start" he had smiled, moving to sit with the pair while the kettle had boiled. When Bella had reappeared, they had spent the day together, carrying out more repairs to the front door and securing the building as best as they could, before gathering with the group to bury the remains of Robert, Valerie and Jiyaa out

the back of the farmhouse, Victor giving a small
Christian service for the couple but unsure what
to do for the Sikh woman, the group resorting to
speaking about their brief memories with her.
The rest of the day had past in a blur of activity,
before they had retired to the bedroom again.
"Dog?" he blinked, glancing down as beside him
in the bed Bella came slowly awake, stifling a
yawn as she looked at him, "What time is it?"
He shrugged, smiling, "I have no idea, you OK?"
"Yeah" she nodded, smirking slightly, "You?"
Victor grinned, the pair rolling to face each other,
his right hand rising to brush some hair from her
face, "Yeah, for the first time in ages I think I am"
"Oh you think you are?" she sent him a look of
mock offence, her head shaking, "How rude"
"I know right" he chuckled then laughed aloud as
she pushed him onto his back and rolled astride
him, "And what do you think you are doing?"
Her smile was mischievous, "Convincing you"

"I feel sorry for Brandon" the voice of Emily
dragged Lauren's attention away from where she
had been leaning against the doorframe, staring
off across the moorland before the farmhouse,
her eyes resting upon the teenage girl that was

sitting several feet away with a book on a chair, the border collie Lexie asleep down near her feet.

"What's that?" Lauren smiled, following the girl's gesture as she pointed with a hand, a smile creasing the nurse's face as she saw Brandon and Eric sitting side by side on a couple of old tyres, the young black man holding his favourite book in his hands while the six year old read it to him.

"Best friends" Lauren smiled, glancing back at Emily, a serious expression creeping into her features as she nodded at the girl, "Thank you"

"What for?" Emily turned her nose up, frowning.

"For helping Brandon the night before last"

The girl pulled a face, acting confused, "Did I?"

For a moment, Lauren held her gaze in silence and then she nodded, "You know you did, more than once...just like you did with Eric"

"Ugh" she rolled her eyes, "I have to protect that little shit, he's my brother, I don't have a choice"

Again, Lauren studied the girl intently and then she shook her head, "You don't have to act tough all the time...its ok to like people"

"Who is acting?" Emily raised an eyebrow and the nurse chuckled, her head shaking at her.

"Hey, I was a girl once, I know how it is...adults don't know anything and everyone wants to ruin your life right?"

To her surprise Emily closed the book upon her lap and nodded, "You totally get it"

Lauren chuckled, "Of course I get it, I'm still technically a teenager myself"

"Shut up"

"I am" Lauren nodded, grinning, "I'm nineteen"

"Oh" the grunt off surprise from Emily had been genuine, then a smirk appeared on her face as she gave a shrug, "I thought you were way older"

"Thanks a lot" Lauren grinned, head shaking.

"Your welcome" Emily replied, unable to stop the smile she was hiding from showing in her eyes.

Not wanting to ruin the moment, Lauren turned back away and removed her glasses, cleaning them upon her clothes before placing them back on her face and turning to glance back out over the moorland, her brow suddenly furrowing.

They had survived the mass attack by the ghouls. Somehow, their luck had held out once more, just as it had during their escape from the hospital. She frowned then, trying to work out how long ago that had been, a grunt of surprise escaping her as she realised that it was now Friday, and that it had all happened since Monday.

Why did it seem so much longer than that?

She winced as she recalled all those that had been lost in such a short amount of time, her head shaking as she pictured their faces, old Mary back at the hospital, Robert and Valerie whose home they had now taken possession off, the arrogant Marcus, the brave and dependable Geri, the unfortunate Jennifer and poor sweet Jiyaa, a cold place opening up inside Lauren as she realised that only she, Brandon and Alice remained of those who had been in their initial group back at the hospital before they had been rescued by Dog and Bella in the ambulance.

A faint smile turned the corner of her mouth up as she pictured Alice, her head shaking as she considered how many times they had saved each other in the past five days, and all the pain and grief they had been through together, sudden realisation striking her in that moment just how important the woman's friendship was to her.

"Lauren?"

The nurse turned to watch as Emily sat studying her, the young girl's lips pressed together as if she were reconsidering speaking, "What is it?"

Emily held her gaze in silence for almost a minute, her young features screwing up for a second then she leaned forwards in a secretive manner, "Dog and Bella"

"What about them?" Lauren raised an eyebrow.

The girl groaned, head shaking, and then fixed her with a look of disgust, "Are they doing *it?*" Lauren was unable to stop the peal of genuine laughter that coursed through her body as embarrassment flushed through her, her head shaking as tears of amusement came to her eyes, and as the teenage girl began to laugh along with her, the nurse realised that it was the first time she had laughed so honestly for almost a week. God it felt so good.

"This feels somewhat unfair"
Alice turned from where she had been standing staring down at the grave of Jiyaa, a finger rising to wipe a tear from her eye as she met the gaze of Doctor Green as he walked over towards her, an expression of infinite sadness upon his features. She stayed silent, watching as he moved to stand before the graves of Robert and Valerie, his head shaking as he turned to meet her gaze, a hand gesturing back towards the farmhouse, "This is...was...their home. They opened their door to us all, a group of strangers in need, and they paid the ultimate price. It seems wrong that we stand here and enjoy their home while they lie there" She winced at his words, realising that he was right, her gaze drifting to the grave of Jiyaa once

more before she glanced back to the doctor as he began to speak once more, his voice breaking, "I hid like a coward...whilst they died...I could hear it from inside the cupboard...but I did nothing" "What could you have done?" Alice asked simply, her head shaking, "Emily told me what happened, she said that Robert charged at the ghouls and got overpowered...no offence but he was a big man...if they managed to overpower him then..." She let her sentence trail off unfinished and the doctor nodded, one hand rising to remove his glasses while the other rubbed at his tired eyes, his shoulders sagging as he sighed heavily and replaced them, "I understand and appreciate your words my dear...but I feel that I should have done something...it just feels wrong that they and Jiyaa should all be...dead...I am so much older" Alice stayed silent, unsure what to say in the face of his guilt and self-loathing. She knew without question that he was wrong, just as she knew no matter what she said he would feel no better. Sighing heavily, his head shaking, Doctor Green turned his eyes skyward for a moment, studying the grey clouds, and then he met her gaze once more, forcing a smile, "I am going to put the kettle on, would you like a cup of coffee?"

She nodded, "Please"

Smiling sadly, he began to turn away only to stop as she placed a hand upon his arm, "You matter"

He nodded, his eyes welling up with tears behind his glasses, and he gently patted her hand upon his arm, "Thank you"

With that he was gone, back towards the house, and releasing a shaky breath, Alice turned away from the grave of Jiyaa and began to make her way around the end of the farmhouse towards the front where the white van blocked the track. She turned her head as she reached it, studying the figures of Lauren and Emily as they sat near the front door of the farmhouse talking, Eric and Brandon sitting further long, and as the nurse raised a hand at her, Alice felt her cheeks redden. Waving back, she turned away and moved to stand near the front of the van, staring out across the moorland, the clear weather allowing her a good view of the surrounding land for miles.

For several minutes, she stared intently at every stretch of moorland that she could see, eyes straining for a sign of white bodies moving, tensing herself to give the call that would send everyone charging back inside the farmhouse. Yet there was no movement upon the moorland save for sheep, and smiling in relief, she turned her face towards the track, her thoughts drifting to Dog and Bella, hoping that they returned from their mission out in the ambulance unharmed. Frowning, she considered their task, wishing that she had gone with them to scout out the other farms and lone houses upon the moors, searching for food, fuel, weapons and other survivors, the latter now tempered with caution following the ill-fated rescue of both Bethany and Freddy.

She grimaced as anger flared within her for the woman that was nearly two days dead, her head shaking as she pictured the woman's behaviour, the words of Doctor Green suddenly returned to her. He had said that Robert and Valerie had given their everything to help strangers in their time of need and he had been right. Yet Bethany had gone in the other direction, showing a casual willingness to abandon everyone in pursuit of her own survival, just like the two men; Nick and Pete, had done previously at Thames hospital.

Was that how people would be now?

One or the other, acting either good or bad?

Samaritans and psychos.

She chuckled softly to herself, "That can be the name of my autobiography"

Alice turned at the sound of an engine, her heart in her mouth for a second until she saw the ambulance driving back up the track towards them, the familiar figure of Dog smiling as he raised a hand in greeting while Bella drove. They were together, and she was happy for them. A sign of hope in a world which seemed hopeless. Smiling, she turned to cast a glance back at Lauren as the nurse sat in the autumn sunshine, then began to squeeze past the van as she made her way towards the ambulance and her friends. Maybe there was hope for all of them after all.

About the Authors

Kelvin V.A Allison

Born in Portsmouth, England in 1973, Kelvin V.A Allison has somehow found his way to the hill strewn paradise that is County Durham, where he lives a life of calm and insanity in equal measure in the village home that he shares with his fiancée, three children and a neurotic dog. An author of 32 novels, including the ten book World of Sorrow series, he is also an avid board gamer, and a lifetime fan of fruit filled sugared pastries. He would prefer it if you didn't judge him.

Lisa Hutchinson

Much younger than her co-author, Lisa Hutchinson, a born and bred native of the rolling hills and endless countryside of County Durham, enjoys the quiet life in the small village of her birth where she resides along with her son, and has put her past-experience as a carer along with her love for horror movies and her vast knowledge of crime and serial killers, into co-creating this, her second novel.

By Kelvin V.A Allison

PHINEAS LUCK SERIES
Highgate
Desmotarian

THE BLIGHTED
Kraken
Ascentia

WORLD OF SORROW SERIES
Demons
Wonderland
Angelous
Rebirth
Cursed
Hell Diver
The Returned
Downfall

HOPE CHRONICLES
Hope & Glory
False Hope

STAND ALONE NOVELS
Skin Shifters
Thorns
Renascentia
Pariah
The Trouble with Rabbits Fluid
Bad Seed
Shuft
Ubasute
Witch Rock; Ubasute 2
Ghost Line
Pandemonium
Juggernaut
Unfinished Tales

By Kelvin V.A Allison and Lisa Hutchinson
12

Printed in Great Britain
by Amazon